the TEA SHOPPE MYSTERIES

4 Mysterious Deaths Steep
in Coastal Maine

DARLENE FRANKLIN, CYNTHIA HICKEY,
LINDA BATEN JOHNSON, TERESA IVES LILLY

BARBOUR
PUBLISHING

Petit Fours to Die For ©2021 by Teresa Ives Lilly
Buns to Die For ©2021 by Darlene Franklin
Scones to Die For ©2021 by Cynthia Hickey
Crumpets to Die For ©2021 by Linda Baten Johnson

Print ISBN 978-1-64352-752-9

eBook Editions:
Adobe Digital Edition (.epub) 978-1-64352-754-3
Kindle and MobiPocket Edition (.prc) 978-1-64352-753-6

All scripture quotations are taken from the King James Version of the Bible.

This book is a work of fiction. Names, characters, places, and incidents are either products of the author's imagination or used fictitiously. Any similarity to actual people, organizations, and/or events is purely coincidental.

Published by Barbour Publishing, Inc., 1810 Barbour Drive, Uhrichsville, Ohio 44683, www.barbourbooks.com

Our mission is to inspire the world with the life-changing message of the Bible.

Member of the
Evangelical Christian
Publishers Association

Printed in Canada.

PETIT FOURS TO DIE FOR

TERESA IVES LILLY

CHAPTER 1

I tied the pink-, green-, and yellow-striped apron around my waist, covering my blue jeans and the solid pink polo shirt that was part of my uniform. The apron made me appear a bit old-fashioned, but that's how I needed to look if I was going to make this thing work. Taking over the daily running of my grandmother's tea shoppe, Tea by the Sea, was the last thing I ever expected to do with my life, but I sincerely hoped it would turn out to be the best thing.

None of the many jobs I had in the past suited me at all. Plus, my boyfriend of two years told me he was moving across country, and I wasn't invited to go along with him. That was the moment I realized there was only one thing to do. I moved to Maine and went to work in Gran's tea shoppe.

Until a few weeks ago, I wasn't ready. I thought life in the big city of San Antonio was where I was supposed to be. But, hey! After all the failed jobs and the final straw, a failed relationship, even I understood the writing on the wall. I was meant to be a small-town girl, and you can't get much smaller than Sea Side, Maine.

Gran always knew that about me, and she'd been waiting patiently. At first, she tried to get her own daughters to help take over the tea shoppe, but they weren't really small-town girls. When I finally called and asked if I could come to Sea Side, she chuckled over the line and said, "It's about time. I've been waiting for you to come help me run this place for years."

So, it was settled. I packed what little I owned, shipped it to Maine, hopped on the next flight to the airport nearest Sea Side, and took a bus to the middle of town. Of course not having a car, even in a small town, proved to be a bit of a problem, especially as winter began to set in.

Just thinking about how cold my toes would be every day before I reached the tea shoppe, which was only a few blocks away from the small apartment I'd rented, made me imagine ways to convince Gran how much we needed a company vehicle, one I could use to drive back and forth to work.

At this point, I'd been working at the shop for a full two weeks. At first I was just going over the books, learning how to do the ordering and taking care of payroll. However, Gran wanted me to spend the third week mingling with the customers. No, she didn't make me a waitress, but she wanted the regulars to meet me and get to know me better. Gran wanted everyone to be comfortable with the change if she ever completely turned over the reins to me.

Gran was a hoot from the moment I arrived. She talked incessantly about writing a cookbook and perfecting English tea. I got the feeling that, even though she was in her seventies, something about one of our customers, Sir Geoffrey, had caused her sudden interest in English tea.

But that was none of my business! Believe me, I wasn't about to start trying to play Cupid. I couldn't even keep my own relationship together, and it was just too bad. Jason was handsome, muscular, and a lawyer to boot. He was everything I thought I wanted in a man. There was only one problem: he just didn't love me.

"I guess the apron looks fine." I took it off and put it in my purse. Then I tugged on my boots. They were perfect for San Antonio. Chic, the newest fashion in cowboy boots. Here in this little coastal town, I knew I was going to have to exchange them for a pair of warm, fur-lined snow boots. I wished I'd already done that, because it had begun snowing the previous night. The thermometer outside my window told me it was going to be a very cold day.

I slumped my shoulders. It was all part of my problem. I was never in the right place at the right time. Gran said not to worry. "You're in the perfect place at the perfect time, now that you're here." I wasn't sure there was such a thing as perfection.

As I walked along the freshly shoveled sidewalk in front of the stores from my apartment complex to the corner of Main and Fifth Street, I turned my head to the left and shivered. The ocean, or *sea* as Gran and most of the old-timers called it, was silent and the bay frozen. It was so majestic, but rather frightening at the same time, to see such power standing still. The morning's snowfall blanketed the town beautifully. If I weren't already freezing, I would have stayed outside the shop just to breathe in the clean, frigid air. This was Monday though, and the week was just beginning.

The bell jangled over the front door of the tea shoppe as I pushed it open. Gran was standing behind the counter, drinking a cup of coffee and leaning over the newspaper, pencil in hand. She was crazy about doing crosswords and didn't even look up when I entered.

"Gran, what are you doing drinking coffee? This is a tea shoppe. What if your customers see you?"

A grin spread across her face. "Georgina, everyone drinks coffee in the morning." She generally spoke to me in a tone that made me feel more like a child than an adult. "You're late, by the way. You need to get used to being here before we open at seven."

I rushed across the shop, slipped off my coat, and hung it on a hook in the hallway behind the kitchen door. I could feel my toes, but just barely. As I suspected, they were frozen. When I joined Gran at the front, she looked down at my feet and shook her head. "You're going to have to get some *real* boots."

"These are real boots." I knew what she was talking about, but arguing with her was always fun.

Gran's arms were akimbo, her hands pressed into her hips. "Young lady! You may be old enough to take over my tea shoppe, but I think I could still put you over my knee. You haven't been here during winter for a long time, and you don't know what you need. I'll make a list. Later today, you run over to the sporting goods store and get some winter boots, gloves, a better coat, a hat, and a scarf."

The image that came to mind wasn't pleasant. "I'll look like an overdressed snowman."

"Yep, but you'll be warm. Besides, you'll not only be making the baskets for the Victorian Christmas Festival this year, but you'll be selling them at the event. The festival is held outside on Friday night, Saturday, and Sunday. Believe me, you'll need to be bundled up."

I stared at her, my mouth gaping. "You've got to be kidding!" I imagined my toes turning into ice cubes as I stood outside all day.

"I am not kidding. I'm going to be busy working on my cookbook. This is all part of taking over the shop. I've stood outside for the last, oh, I don't know, twenty years during the Victorian Christmas Festival. I'm ready to give up that job."

I brushed away what might have been a small crumb from the counter, although we'd left the place sparkling clean the night before. "All right, I'd be happy to stand outside and freeze this year. And, for your information, I had already planned to buy some boots after work today."

She pretended to frown at me, but her eyes were twinkling. "It's too early in the morning for your sass." Gran grabbed her mug and headed back to the kitchen. "I'm leaving things in your hands today. You do remember we need to have the sample tray ready by eleven? The mayor's secretary is picking it up and taking it to him at city hall. I just hope he likes something we offer. It would do wonders for us to be able to cater his political rally."

I smiled. Even if she talked about wanting to get away from the tea shoppe, Gran couldn't help herself from doing what it took to keep it going. She'd been running it for what seemed like forever.

"Not to worry. I plan to send him a tray with three different petit fours, a bun, a scone, and a crumpet. He's sure to like something, if not everything. Remember, I've lived in a big city where there were endless choices. There's nothing he could get catered in that could taste better than your heavenly creations."

Gran smirked. "Go on with you now. Flattery won't get you on my good side. Just make the customers happy, keep the shop running smoothly, and I'll be content." She chuckled and walked away.

By eight the shop was beginning to fill with patrons. Even though Gran and I thought tea was for lunch, many customers couldn't wait that long for our treats. My favorite was our petit fours. We served the usual flavors, except during holidays, when Gran always came up with something extra special. For this winter season, we were serving peppermint chocolate petit fours. They were truly to die for.

The mayor's sample plate was sitting on the counter. I added the peppermint petit fours, which I'd actually helped Gran make on Friday. Our baker usually made most of the sweets in the shop, but Gran liked to make some of the seasonal specialties. We both knew these would be a favorite during December, so we'd made ten dozen and froze them. I had to wait for the final crumpet the cook was working on before I could put the plastic lid on and seal it.

The room had scattered wooden tables with mismatched wooden

chairs set at each one. Everything was painted green, pink, or yellow. Bright colors to bring joy into people's lives, Gran always said. A small Christmas tree was on each table. That was the extent of decorating Gran would allow in the tea shoppe. She didn't want to detract from the actual tea shoppe ambience.

The ladies from the local church were sitting at the corner table. I called them the Bible Study Ladies. They came to the shop every Monday and discussed whatever book of the Bible they were studying. They were sweet ladies, like four southern belles. In fact, when I thought about it, I realized they all had southern accents. I made a mental note to find out where they were originally from.

A few college students, cramming for an exam, sat in another corner. A businessman, obviously in no hurry to get back to work, sat sipping a cup of Earl Grey. A mother and daughter, wearing long dresses and Victorian hats, sat at another table having their own private tea party. All in all, a good crowd for a Monday morning.

The bell jangled again. I looked up. A well-built, dark-haired man with a deep scowl entered and stomped up to the counter, his face almost buried in his parka.

"Are you sending the mayor samples today?" His voice boomed across the shop.

I frowned. What business was it of his? I looked around for Gran, wondering if orders were private.

"You don't have to answer. I can see it on your face." He glanced around. "Is this the order then?" He pointed at the sample tray. I couldn't help but nod.

"Grrr." A bear-like growl escaped his lips. "The mayor knew I was planning to have Tea by the Sea cater my political campaign party. He got the jump on me though. Now I'll have to search for something else."

So, this was Don Johnson, the mayor's opponent in the upcoming mayoral race. I stared at him openly. He wasn't handsome, but he had a stubborn chin. I liked him. I'd met the mayor a week ago, when he came in and ordered the tray. Gran talked about him as if he were God's gift to the town, but I didn't see it. To me, the current mayor seemed arrogant. Don Johnson was angry now, but he didn't appear to have the same aura as the mayor.

Just then, the cook called me from the back. The crumpets were ready. I placed a paper towel over the other treats on the sample tray and turned away. "Excuse me for a minute."

Mr. Johnson shook his shaggy head back and forth and huffed. "Doesn't matter now. I can't serve the same thing as the mayor. Guess I'd better search the internet to find something for my rally."

I barely heard the last words because I'd stepped into the kitchen. The cook had the crumpets lined up on a tray. I slipped one onto a napkin and carried it back to the front. It had only taken a minute or so, but Don Johnson was gone when I returned.

I placed the crumpet onto the tray and put a plastic lid over the samples, then grabbed a few pieces of scotch tape and secured the four sides. If the mayor's secretary decided to sample the goods before she got them to him, I wanted to make it a little more difficult for her.

Now all I had to do was wait for her to show up.

The Bible Study Ladies were waving, trying to get my attention. I wiped my hands on my striped apron and hurried over to their table.

"Morning, ladies. Is there anything I can do for you? Your waitress should be right over."

Savannah, the youngest of the group, probably in her early fifties, grabbed my hand. "My dear, we are so glad to see you," she drawled. "We wanted to tell you. We just know you are the answer to your Gran's prayers."

"Gran prays?" I gasped then slapped my hand over my mouth. Of course Gran prayed. She attended church on a weekly basis, but I always thought her relationship with God was, well, private.

"Your grandmother has been telling us for years about how she wanted you to come and take over the shop. We've lifted her request up to the Lord many times, and here you are, a true answer to prayer."

The four of them nodded in unison.

I didn't feel like the answer to anyone's prayers.

Charlotte cleared her throat. She was the oldest of them. I guesstimated she was at least seventy-eight, perhaps older. My eyes met hers. She winked. "Now, we just need to continue praying for you to find a husband."

Chapter 2

I slipped away from the Bible Study Ladies as quickly as I could that day. They were a sweet group of women and meant well, but the whole praying for me to find Mr. Right wasn't something I wanted to discuss with them. Unbeknownst to me until I arrived in town, Gran had been reading my letters out loud to all the regular customers for the last few years, so everyone knew about my unsuccessful jobs and failed relationship.

For the first week I worked at the shop, anyone who'd ever heard one of the letters had offered me their sympathy, and several mentioned their single sons, brothers, or cousins as possible dates for me. The Bible Study Ladies were the worst. They always made a display of patting my hand and telling me how the Lord had someone just perfect for me. After these two weeks, it was pretty obvious. They'd decided to personally take over the job of finding Mr. Right for me.

When I reached the counter, the bell over the front door jangled. I wondered if after a few months I would even notice the sound anymore.

I looked up. It was Phyllis Gates, the mayor's secretary. She was a petite woman who always seemed to be bustling around. I guessed she was about forty-two, with gray and white beginning to take over what was once mousy brown hair.

This morning she looked rather disheveled and even more rushed than usual. Her faux fur coat gaped open.

"Good morning, Phyllis. I've got the samples for the mayor right here." I pointed at the covered tray.

She eyed it critically and sniffed. "Hmm. Personally, I thought the mayor should do something a bit fancier. I suggested a full high noon tea, but would he take my advice?"

I stared at her, not sure if I was supposed to answer or not. Based on her rampage, I didn't think so.

"No! Of course not, he doesn't E-V-E-R"—she spelled it out—"take my advice. To him I'm just someone who should be seen at my desk, typing and filing, but never heard." She actually stomped her foot to emphasize her statement.

Gran insisted I sympathize with the customers, so I reached a hand across the counter and patted hers the way the Bible Study Ladies did mine. She instantly pulled back as if I'd stung her.

"Mayor Dalton is meeting with his pro tem, Robert Casey, today. I need to get back to the office. Should I just take the tray, or is there a bag to put it in?"

"I think the tray will protect them. I've taped the sides, which should help." I lifted the tray, stepped from behind the counter, and handed it to her. I couldn't think of anything else to say except, "Have a nice day."

She glared at me for a second then swirled around and scampered out of the shop. I thought my boots were inappropriate, but her thin, high-heeled boots were ridiculous. I was wondering how the mayor dealt with her scurrying around the office all day, heels clicking on the floor, when Gran's voice startled me.

"She reminds me of a hamster on one of those wheels." Gran came out of the kitchen and stood beside me. "She just runs around, doing everything she can think of for the mayor, and he doesn't care a jot."

"I feel sorry for her," I answered, remembering the touch of sadness I'd noticed in her eyes.

"Don't. She wouldn't have it any other way. She might complain about her job and the mayor, but she loves everything she does. I'm not sure she'd know what to do if the mayor ever did notice or commend her for anything. She likes to make everyone feel sorry for her."

"Still, that can't be a very pleasant way to work. She says he never takes her advice, but I'm guessing mayors don't ask their secretaries for advice, as a general rule."

A smile crossed Gran's face. "That's exactly what I mean. She complains about things he doesn't take her suggestions about, but generally they're things she's not in charge of."

"Why does he keep her?" I picked up a petit four from the tray the cook had set out on the counter earlier and plopped it into my mouth.

"She's the best secretary in town. Her job is to type, file, and run errands for him, and she does all those to a *T*."

"What's a pro tem?" I murmured, swallowing the delicious treat.

"Oh, you must mean Robert Casey. He's the pro tem. Basically that means he's the one who would take over if Mayor Dalton couldn't fulfill his duties for any reason."

"Wouldn't that be like a vice mayor?"

"No, he's not paid for the position and doesn't work for the mayor or the town. But if the mayor got sick or died, he would fill in until a new mayor could be elected."

I was intrigued. I'm not a very politically minded person, so this was all new to me.

Gran continued. "The man lives in perpetual hope that the mayor will get good and sick so he can step in and 'clean things up,' or so he likes to tell everyone. We thought he'd run for mayor this upcoming election, but he surprised us all. He may end up being the pro tem again, because no one else has ever mentioned wanting the position."

Gran stepped back and looked around the shop. She jammed her hands onto her hips. "Speaking of jobs, aren't you supposed to be working on those baskets for the Victorian Christmas Festival? The festival starts Friday night. That only gives you four days to get them made. The petit fours won't actually be put in the baskets until right before the festival begins, but you need to decorate the baskets with silk poinsettias and Christmas bows."

I followed her to the kitchen. In one far corner, away from the ovens, was a long table set up as a workbench. A hot glue gun and about ten glue sticks lay on the table, but nothing else.

"The baskets are in the storage room. The silk flowers and ribbon are in that box on the floor." She pointed to a large white box.

"All right, Gran. I won't let you down. How many baskets should I make?"

I assumed she'd say something like fifteen or twenty. To my surprise, she called over her shoulder before leaving the kitchen, "One hundred."

I felt my jaw drop. I picked up the glue gun and pushed the glue sticks around a bit. Ten glue sticks were never going to be enough if I had to make one hundred baskets, and four days would never be long enough for me to get them all done.

I turned and shouted, "Gran, you've got to be kidding!" The kitchen was silent. She'd slipped away.

Lord, maybe I need to rethink the whole idea of taking over the tea shoppe.

I considered finding her and turning down the job, but I knew in my heart I wasn't going to. Sea Side, Maine, had already started to steal my heart, and I didn't plan to leave. Staying meant taking over

Tea by the Sea, which meant making one hundred petit four baskets, so I set down the glue gun and went looking for the baskets.

I found the boxes filled with baskets, grabbed about ten, and placed them on the worktable. Then I opened the box of silk poinsettias and snatched a roll of gold ribbon. With a sigh, I sat down and started creating. I thought about the trays of petit fours in the freezer and knew there weren't enough for our daily customers, our special orders, the Victorian Christmas Festival, and the mayor's party. I'd enjoyed helping to make the petit fours last week, but I hoped Gran planned on having our baker make the rest we needed.

The feeling of inadequacy flooded me, and I wondered if I was really going to be able to step in and take over the tea shoppe.

When I was only a few minutes into making the baskets, my phone rang. It was Gran calling from her home. "I'm feeling a little under the weather. Guess I've caught the cold going around. I think I'll stay home for a few days and let you handle everything. There's no need to worry about me. I've earned a week's rest."

I was surprised because Gran had seemed fine earlier. I wasn't sure I believed she was sick, but she was right. She'd earned a few days' rest.

I suggested some hot soup and lots of rest, then hung up my cell and turned to face the job in front of me. There was nothing I could do but take things one step at a time. This morning, decorating baskets was the main thing to accomplish.

As I worked, I actually found the process soothing. Several hours later, my shoulders started to ache, so I stood up and stretched then meandered out to the front to see how things were going. A few customers were scattered throughout the shop. They all seemed content with their tea and treats. Our waitress was on break, and the baker had gone home for the day.

A man was sitting at the front counter, sipping a cup of tea and eating a scone, with his London Fog coat slung over the counter. I'd met him a few times since moving to town. He was the new pastor at the local church. He'd taken over the pulpit about six months before I got to town. When I first met him, I was surprised to hear he was a pastor. He seemed so young. Gran informed me he was actually thirty-two and single.

I watched him for a few seconds. He was definitely not my definition of a pastor. If I had to describe him, I'd say something more like tall, dark, and handsome. He stood about six feet two, had dark brown hair, and was really good-looking, with a clean-shaven face and steel-blue eyes.

Suddenly he looked up and met my glance. I turned away quickly, hoping he didn't think I was checking him out. I moved to the front of the shop and stared out the picture window. The street in front of the shop was clear, and I could see the snow-covered coast. That was a sight I loved and could never grow tired of.

After a few minutes, I walked back to the counter and slipped behind it.

"Hello, Pastor. I noticed you're a regular here." I spoke in a friendly tone, hoping it would dissuade him from thinking I'd been staring at him earlier.

He smiled.

As I suspected, perfectly white, even teeth.

"Yep. Best tea around." He held up his cup. "I'm partial to tea, having spent a few years in England after high school, and your Gran's scones are the best. I love her petit fours as well."

I nodded in agreement then felt tongue-tied. I wasn't much for talking to men, much less a pastor. Luckily, he filled the void.

"I'm glad you're here, Georgina. May I call you Georgina?" He tilted his head slightly.

"Yes."

"I'm not sure if you know it, but I'm overseeing the Victorian Christmas Festival this year, since it's being held to raise money for the church." He took a bite of his scone and a sip of his tea.

I rolled my eyes. *No wonder Gran put me in charge. She's trying to play matchmaker.*

"I see." I reached up and smoothed my hair, wondering if it was a mess, as usual. "I just got started on the petit four baskets today. Would you like to see one, Pastor?"

He swallowed his tea while nodding. "When I'm not in church, everyone calls me Mathew."

"Are you sure?" I pulled on my ear, something I tended to do when I was feeling shy. It was embarrassing, so I dropped my hand to my side.

"Yes, even your grandmother does. I believe it makes it easier to communicate with my members. At church, everyone reverts to calling me Pastor, or sometimes Pastor Mathew."

Slightly more convinced, I said, "Okay, Mathew, follow me." I turned and began to lead him toward the kitchen. Suddenly, the tea shoppe door flew open, the bell clanging from the force. Billy Deck, our delivery boy who works part-time after school running errands and taking small orders to customers, rushed in the door, his eyes moving back and forth until they lit on me. He sped across the room and stopped in front of me. His nose was red from the cold. I couldn't imagine why he seemed in such a tizzy.

"Heard the news yet?" he blurted, an urgency in his loud voice.

"News? What news?" I asked, wondering what could be so important he felt he needed to come into the tea shoppe in such a wild flurry.

I was just about to pull him into the kitchen, away from the startled customers, when he shouted, "The mayor's dead! I heard the police talking about it, and they say it's murder!"

CHAPTER 3

Needless to say, I was stunned, especially since I'd just sent the mayor the sample tray earlier in the day. I bent over, grasped his arm, and pulled Billy toward the counter, shushing him.

"Slow down." I shook his shoulders gently. "Tell me what you're talking about."

"Mayor Dalton is dead. I saw the ambulance at city hall, and I heard a few of the police officers talking about it. They said it had to be murder 'cause it wasn't suicide."

"What? Are you telling the truth, Billy?"

The boy nodded.

"Are you sure you heard them say 'murder'?"

Billy didn't answer. He looked a bit pale.

I was holding him by the shirt. "Is there anything else you can tell us, Billy?" My voice was insistent.

Mathew moved forward and pried my fingers off Billy's shirt. "I think we can let the boy go now. I'm sure he's given us all the information he can. Isn't that right, Billy?"

The boy's head bobbed up and down.

Mathew walked him to the front door, speaking softly. I assumed he was advising the child to keep this story quiet, but I knew Billy. That wasn't going to happen.

After watching Billy tear away on his bike, Mathew came back to the counter, his face a bit ashen.

"Do you think Billy is telling the truth?" My eyes met Mathew's.

Mathew nodded. "Doesn't seem to be any reason for him to make this up."

I wrinkled my brow. "Did you know the mayor very well?"

"No, but he did go to the church. This is a terrible thing to happen, especially at Christmastime." I heard the sincerity in his voice.

Yes, this is terrible, especially because Gran was hoping the mayor would let us cater his big campaign party! I didn't say that out loud, but I couldn't help from thinking it and then wondering how I could be so callous. Hoping the guilt didn't show, I faced Mathew.

"I. . .I don't even know what to say. I haven't lived here long enough to get to know the mayor, but I'm sure if he was voted into office, he was well-loved."

I noticed a strange look on the pastor's face. He stood up and slipped his coat on. "I'm going back to the office. I'm sure someone from the mayor's family will be contacting me pretty soon, and I need to be available."

I shivered at the thought. This perfectly lovely man was going to be the one who had to help plan and carry out the funeral for Sea Side's beloved mayor. Rather a gruesome task to have to take on and, like Mathew said, especially at Christmas.

My eyes swept the shop, and I realized that all the customers had heard Billy's announcement. Several had risen and were making their way out the front door, each of them sporting a grin like the cat who caught the canary. I imagined they were eager to start spreading the news of the mayor's death. Small towns were known for their intricate gossip chains.

Mathew sluggishly moved toward the front door, but just as he reached for the handle, he had to step back to allow the door to swing open again. This time an older gentleman, wearing a severely outdated double-breasted overcoat, came in. Mathew didn't leave. Instead, he hurried back to stand beside me. I wasn't sure why, but I got the sense he was there to give me moral support.

I saw the man's eyes sweep the room, and then he came toward us. I looked up at Mathew. "Who is he?" I asked him quietly.

The gentleman must've heard me, because he spurted out, "I'm Detective Rawls."

"Hello, Rawls," Mathew said, his voice even, not quite friendly.

"Hello. Is Mrs. Holland here?" The man spoke in a dull, monotone voice.

"No, I'm her granddaughter. Is there something you need? I'm in charge."

The man huffed, obviously not pleased by my answer. "Mayor Dalton died a few hours ago." His words were blunt, and his eyes seemed to bore through me with a cold glare as if I weren't even there.

"We just heard," Mathew spoke before I could. He reached out and took my hand in his, giving it a gentle squeeze. I felt comforted by the action.

The detective eyed Mathew. "How did you hear, Pastor?"

I was surprised the detective knew Mathew. I wondered if he attended Mathew's church as well.

"A young delivery boy named Billy Deck told us about it. You know how these kids are. They know about everything before anyone else." Mathew tried to joke, but the detective just grunted and cocked his head.

"Hmm." He pulled a notepad from his coat pocket and wrote something in it. I assumed it was Billy Deck's name.

"And did this"—he looked at the notepad again—"Billy Deck happen to tell you how the mayor died?" His voice dripped with sarcasm.

"Murder!" I blurted out. I wanted to slap my hand over my mouth but didn't move a muscle.

The detective's head turned, and he seemed to actually acknowledge me. I couldn't help but gulp. Somehow, his stare made me feel as if I was the person he'd decided had murdered the mayor.

"Indeed, murder. In fact, we're pretty sure it was poison, since there was no blood or trauma to his head." He took a step toward me.

My eyes were locked with his. "Goodness, that's terrible." I could feel my hand slip to my throat. "Do you have any idea. . . ?" Suddenly a thought formed in my mind. *Why did the detective come to the tea shoppe right after finding out the mayor was dead, unless. . .*

"You don't think that I? That we. . ." My hands started to tremble, and I felt a bit faint. I could feel the blood drain from my face. Mathew must have noticed, because he stepped even closer and put an arm around me just as I started to faint. He helped me to one of the chairs at a table and sat me on it.

"Put your head down for a minute. You look like you might pass out."

I spread my knees and bent over, my head falling gently between them. If the situation wasn't so serious, I might have burst out laughing. First good-looking man I'd spoken to in a long time, and here I was, hanging my head upside down in front of him.

I heard a few chairs scraping as our remaining customers rose and quickly left the shop. I kept my head down for a few moments, then sat up straight when I felt better.

First, I looked at Mathew. He wore a sympathetic smile on his face. Then I turned so I could see the detective. He wore an accusatory look.

"Can we go on?" Rawls asked.

I nodded.

"Very well." Rawls had his pencil poised. "Please tell me what was on the tray you sent to the mayor's office this morning."

As I rattled off the contents of the sample tray, my mind was feverishly thinking of the ingredients in each one. Flour, sugar, butter, vanilla, peppermint, milk, pecans. . . Was the mayor allergic to nuts?

"According to our sources, the mayor only ate one thing today before he keeled over and died. A petit four that came from this tea shoppe." He didn't exactly accuse anyone, but I could tell by the look on his face that he was doing more than simply reporting occurrences.

My mouth opened and closed, but I made no sound. This tended to happen to me whenever I was flustered. Realizing I must look like a codfish caused me to clamp my lips together and sit up even straighter. I did some deep breathing through my nose, then met the detective's eyes once more.

"Exactly what are you trying to say, Detective Rawls? That the petit fours were poisoned? I can assure you, that is impossible. Gran and I made them together, and I packaged them this morning. In fact, I ate one myself. As you can see, I'm alive and well." I stood up, straight and stiff, one hand jammed against my hip, a sinking feeling tugging at me.

"Detective Rawls, is there any proof the petit fours were poisoned?" Mathew asked. "Did he eat anything else on the tray? Are you going to test everything on the tray?"

"We will, yes, but we're pretty sure it was the petit four, since that seems to be all that was missing from the tray."

"And who told you the mayor didn't eat anything else today?" I asked. "His wife? She wouldn't know what he did once he left the house."

"No, his wife died over five years ago. But if you must know, it was his secretary."

I threw my hands up to express my frustration then quickly lowered them. "Oh! I see. His secretary knows if he ate breakfast? Or grabbed a donut on the way to work? Or, well, I could give a million scenarios of what else he could've eaten today."

I saw a change on the detective's face. After meeting Phyllis Gates, I could only imagine the man had been persuaded to believe whatever she told him. She was a force to be reckoned with, but I could tell I'd made a dent in her statement by the way he started jotting in his notebook again.

"We doubt he stopped to get anything on his way to work because, according to his secretary, the mayor was on a diet and was only having a light lunch and dinner each day. In the past, he always ate breakfast at a local diner. They confirmed he didn't come in for breakfast today. The secretary told us that although she was out of the office part of the day, when she got back, he was dead. And now I've confirmed that only one of the petit fours on the tray was missing."

After a few more of what Rawls called "preliminary questions," the detective left the shop. I think Mathew and I had been holding our breath, because as soon as the door closed behind the detective, we both let out heavy sighs.

I was still feeling rather stunned knowing that I, or at least the tea shoppe, might be accused of murder, when I felt a hand on my arm.

I tilted my head and stared at Mathew's hand. He was offering me comfort, but I felt numb.

"Can you believe that?" I whispered, not really meaning for anyone to hear. Mathew heard me, though, because he hadn't left my side.

"No. The whole thing seems impossible. Murder just doesn't happen in this town."

I spun around to face him. "What do you mean? Do you think I, we, the shop, had something to do with this murder? I don't believe he was murdered at all. I'm sure they'll find out it was really a heart attack or something." My jaw was tense, and my teeth clenched. My words sounded brave but unconvincing. I was simply voicing what I wanted to be the truth.

Mathew lowered his hand to mine. "Hey, I don't know what happened, but I'm sure neither you, nor Tea by the Sea, had anything to do with Mayor Dalton's death. The only thing we can do now is wait until the police have proof."

"Do you think they'll do an autopsy?" My words were clipped and terse. I'd never spoken to anyone about things like murder and autopsies before.

Mathew shrugged. "Don't see how they can prove he was poisoned without doing one. It may take a few days for them to get the results. Until then, you shouldn't worry about anything. Of course this town loves a good story to gossip about, so who knows what you'll hear? I say, carry on as usual, but don't allow anyone to get you into a conversation about the mayor, his death, or poison." He smiled, and even though I was worried about this situation, I found his smile absolutely charming.

I tried to relax my shoulders but had a feeling it would take a day at the spa to work out the tightness in them. I felt a giggle forming as I thought about how much tension being accused of murder could cause.

"And he suspects you of murder?" Gran's voice screeched so loudly I had to pull my cell phone away from my ear. I could tell she really was sick, because her voice sounded a little raspy. "Why didn't you call me right away? I could've set that man straight." She sneezed.

"Gran, it all happened so fast, and Mathew was still here when Detective Rawls started questioning me. He didn't actually accuse me, but he did say they think one of the petit fours I sent the mayor to sample had poison in it. We won't know anything for sure until they do an autopsy and check the other petit fours on the sample tray. I'm sure it will all turn out to be a big mistake."

Gran was quiet then said, "Georgina, you haven't lived in a small town very long. You have no idea how much damage even untruthful gossip can do. If the story gets around that he was poisoned by our food, it could put us out of business."

"Gran, Tea by the Sea has been around as long as I can remember. I'm sure it's weathered gossip before. Mathew. . . I mean, Pastor Mathew assures me we have nothing to worry about." I wasn't comfortable calling the pastor by his first name in general conversation. It wasn't the way I'd been brought up, but even Gran had referred to him as Mathew several times. We spoke a few more minutes, but I could tell the stress wasn't good for her. She was coughing, and her voice sounded scratchy. I ended the call.

I didn't want to talk to any customers about the mayor's death, so I closed up the shop, making sure to turn off all the lights and lock the front door. I doubted in a town this small anyone would try to break in. Plus, everyone knew we didn't keep any cash in the register overnight. However, the idea niggled at the back of my mind that maybe, just maybe, if the mayor had really been poisoned eating one of our petit fours, then someone had gotten in and put poison in it.

How would someone know exactly which petit fours I would put on the sample tray? I wondered. We'd sold many of the petit fours from that batch during the day, and no one else had complained about negative effects. Unless there was a crazy person running around town putting poison in random food, then someone must have poisoned the petit four after I placed it on the tray.

It had stopped snowing, so I decided to put off boot shopping for at least one more day. As I strolled toward my apartment, watching small flakes blowing in the wind, I kept running different scenarios over in my mind. When I reached my door, not one proved to provide any possible way the one specific petit four could have been poisoned before I set it on the tray.

I pushed open the apartment door and entered. The room was rather stark, with only a couch, coffee table, and small kitchen table. I'd been in town a short time, and major furniture shopping was not at the top of my to-do list. I didn't really like the apartment. Since I'd decided to stay in Sea Side, I hoped I might find a small house, so I didn't want to waste any money on furniture I might have to replace.

I tossed my coat on a chair, grabbed a can of soda from the fridge, slouched down on the couch, and turned on the television. I desperately needed the distraction from my thoughts. After channel surfing for fifteen minutes and realizing there was nothing interesting on, I finally put down the remote and headed for a shower.

As the warm water soothed my aching shoulders, a despairing thought suddenly flashed through my mind. What if the detective decided to close the tea shoppe? That really could destroy the business.

CHAPTER 4

I glanced at the calendar hanging on the kitchen wall in the tea shoppe the next morning. It was Tuesday. I wanted to finish making the baskets today so I'd be prepared for the upcoming Victorian Christmas Festival, which started on Friday night. If there was any chance the shop would be closed by the police, we couldn't afford to miss out on the advertisement from the festival. Plus, the church needed the funds we would raise selling off these baskets.

I glanced around the shop. I hadn't been here long, but I already loved everything about the business. Even though Gran was planning eventually to pass the reins to me, she would be devastated if we had to close, especially under suspicious circumstances. She'd owned the tea shoppe in Sea Side for as long as I could remember.

Our baker had been at the shop since early in the morning, preparing for the day. When the trays of treats were ready, I opened the front door. Within a few minutes, customers started to fill the shop. At first I was surprised at the increased number of people but quickly realized morbid curiosity was bringing them in. Although most of the customers were willing to risk a cup of tea and one of our Christmas cranberry scones, no one ordered a single petit four. The number of customers pouring in gave me hope that none of them really suspected the mayor was poisoned by me or anyone at the tea shoppe, at least not on purpose.

As soon as our waitress showed up for the day, I removed myself from the front. No customers outwardly questioned me, but all the sideways glances were enough to make me feel uncomfortable. I decided to stay behind the scenes for the day.

I moved toward the table where all the supplies for the baskets were and sighed. I knew, with some good effort, it wasn't going to take as long as I first imagined, but it wasn't going to be my favorite activity. I sat down, picked up some ribbon and the glue gun, and began creating.

A few hours later, the back door opened again, and a brisk breeze chilled the room. Mathew stepped through the doorway. When my eyes met his, I couldn't help but catch my breath. He was very good-looking. I wondered why he wasn't already married. I was sure that by now the Bible Study Ladies would have matched him up with a nice, quiet woman in the congregation.

Mathew shook off a few snowflakes that had settled on his broad shoulders.

I pulled my thoughts together. "Why are you using the back door?" I asked in a rather sharp tone.

"Hello, Georgina." He emphasized the pleasantry, which made me feel a bit ashamed of my abrupt words. "I thought I'd come by and help with the baskets." He strolled across the room and stopped at the end of the table. "That is, if you need help." His eyes moved around the room where baskets were piled up. "Looks like you've got it well in hand."

My cheeks felt warm. "I've been at it all morning, so I'm actually almost done, but I appreciate the offer."

He moved toward the front room, slipped the door open an inch, and peeked out. With a wag of his head, he closed it and returned to the table. "As I suspected. You've got most of the gossips in town out there."

My mouth opened, and I stared at him in disbelief. I was aware his statement was true, but it wasn't something I expected to hear from a pastor.

"I know that doesn't sound very nice, but the truth is the truth. I do my best from the pulpit to curb the tongues in this town, but the fact is, gossip is our church's biggest problem."

My shoulders sagged. If that was true, then the shop's reputation was at risk, especially if the autopsy proved the mayor was poisoned, and if they found the poison was in the petit four he ate.

"Pas—Mathew, can I get you a cup of tea?" I stood up and walked toward the door to the front room.

"Yes, that would be nice."

I pushed open the door and walked toward the teacups. Several of the customers' heads lifted, and their eyes locked on me. I hadn't felt so awkward since my disastrous singing debut in the sixth-grade school play. I turned my head and kept my eyes staring straight ahead of me. I reached the counter where we kept teacups and pots of hot tea, filled a cup, and quickly made my way back into the kitchen. When the door closed behind me, I couldn't help but let out a breath.

"Curiosity killed the cat," I joked, immediately wishing I could take back the statement. "I mean. . ." I looked at Mathew, hoping he could see the regret I felt.

"Don't worry, Georgina. That's what I was talking about." He had slipped his coat off. "This town is full of people who are too curious for their own good. They look for things to talk about and things to construe. Just be yourself, and they won't have any fuel to add to their fires."

"I hope so." I handed him the saucer with the full teacup on it, then sat down across from where he had already pulled up a chair for himself. I grabbed the scissors and began working on a basket.

Mathew took a sip of the tea and gave an appreciative sigh. "That hits the spot."

I'd grown up in a house where men drank coffee, so I wasn't used to seeing a man enjoy tea. I suppose, I somehow thought it would make him look, well, weak. In Mathew's case, however, that wasn't true. He was a fine specimen of a man, and holding a Blue Willow teacup in his hand, drinking green tea, didn't oppose that image.

Mathew set down the cup. "Georgina, after seeing the crowd out front, I think there's something we should do."

I lifted my head. "What's that?" I glanced at the baskets I'd been working on for hours and wondered if he wanted me to make even more.

"I think we should look into the mayor's death ourselves."

I dropped my scissors, and they clattered on the table. "What?"

"It's going to take several days for the autopsy report. If the mayor was poisoned, the detective will start his own investigation. All of that will take time and will interfere with your business and the Victorian Christmas Festival."

I groaned. Everything he said was true, even though I didn't want to believe it.

"If we looked into it now, perhaps we could solve the whole case before the festival." Mathew clapped his hands and rubbed them together, as if playing sleuth was something appealing.

"And what if he actually was poisoned by the petit four? You realize it would definitely destroy the tea shoppe's reputation, right?"

"We'll start off with that as the assumption."

I was surprised. "So you believe the mayor was poisoned by the petit four?"

"For now, we will just assume that's the case. If we can prove anything different, then that's great. But if not, then we need to prove that neither you nor anyone at the tea shoppe poisoned the mayor. You say you didn't put the poison in it, and it seems impossible that it was a random act, so we need to figure out exactly who had the opportunity to poison the petit four."

"And the motive!" I added emphatically.

"Yes, and the motive."

I'm sure I looked skeptical, but there was something about his suggestion that made sense. At least we would be proactive, instead of sitting around worrying and waiting for the autopsy results.

"I'm in. Where do we start?" I bubbled. I noticed that his eyes lit up when I said that.

"Hmm, well, we will assume the poison was put in the petit four after you put it on the tray. Tell me who had access to it."

Before I spoke, I grabbed a notebook from the table and flipped it open to a clean page. On the top, I wrote, "Suspects."

"I put the petit four on the tray, and no one in the shop went near it. I think we can forget about our waitress or baker or any delivery people. In fact, I can only think of two people who had access to it. The mayor's secretary, Phyllis Gates, and the mayor's opponent, Don Johnson."

I explained Don Johnson's strange behavior and how Phyllis Gates was definitely unhappy with the mayor. Both of them had motive, and both of them had time to poison the petit four.

"However, Mr. Johnson wasn't sure I had a tray made. I think he actually came by to put in an order for his political rally, but when he got here, he realized the mayor had already hired us. I doubt he was walking around with poison in his pocket just in case he had the opportunity to kill the mayor."

Mathew nodded. "I agree, but there is a slight chance there, so we still need to look into him a bit more. What about Phyllis?"

"She took the tray from here to his office. I did have it taped so she couldn't sample any herself, but I don't know if she gave it to the mayor with the tape still on. She had enough time to poison the petit four, but again, was she just carrying around poison? Does she even know anything about poison? The mayor may not take her advice, but without him in office, she will probably lose her job, so it doesn't make sense for her to have killed him."

I could see my two-sided arguments, for and against both suspects, were frustrating to Mathew. He stood up and began to pace back and forth in front of the table. He stopped behind me and read the notes over my shoulder.

"This is all good information, but it's not enough. We need to follow up on Don Johnson and Phyllis Gates and find out if anyone else had the opportunity or motive to poison the petit four. The sooner we get started on this, the better. Can you sneak away from the shop?"

I stood and wiped my hands on my apron then slipped it off. I'd just finished the last basket, and I knew the waitress could handle all the customers. I turned to Mathew and said, "Sure, where should we start?"

A grin spread across his face. "Where else, but the scene of the crime? The mayor's office." Mathew picked up his coat, did an about-face, and marched out of the kitchen. I flung down the apron, grabbed my coat, and scuttled after him.

The mayor's office wasn't far from the tea shoppe, so we walked. Actually, Mathew walked, and I jogged to keep up with his long strides. He carried my notebook and several times reread what I'd written. I wondered why a pastor seemed so interested in murder.

"Um, Mathew, are you an undercover detective?" I asked in a

joking tone. He stopped and turned around to face me. I saw red creep up his neck.

"I do love to read mysteries, but I assure you, I didn't offer to help you in order to act out the part of a cheap novel. I'm genuinely concerned about the tea shoppe and the effect this could have on the festival. The church gets its support from the festival. I also don't want anyone in my congregation falsely accused of murder."

As he spoke, he took my hands in his.

I stared at his hand for a few seconds, blinked, then turned back toward the mayor's office. We both began to walk again.

"What's our plan?" I asked, my voice beginning to shake with anxiety. I wasn't sure going to the mayor's office was the right thing to do.

"I think if we just look around a bit, talk to everyone in the office, we can start to get an idea of exactly who saw the mayor that day and who had the opportunity to poison the petit fours."

I nodded my head reluctantly. Since I had no better idea, I would just do what Mathew thought was best.

CHAPTER 5

Sea Side City Hall was a fairly new building. It was not as pretty as some of the businesses in the historical downtown area, but it was decorated for Christmas with lights and a large silver wreath. The Christmas lights were turned off during the day. The front door of the building wasn't taped off, so we assumed the police had only closed off the mayor's office. I entered the building and stomped the slush off my feet, noting how quiet it was. Word of the mayor's death had obviously spread. Either everyone in the offices was out, or they were observing silence out of respect.

We walked down the hall, stopping long enough to admire the Christmas tree. Then we made our way into the mayor's outer office and stopped outside the door that led into his private office. The door was crisscrossed with strips of yellow tape. Mathew moved closer to the door.

I slipped up beside him. "We can't go in there," I whispered, biting my bottom lip.

"Of course not. I want to solve this, but not break the law."

I giggled. "Well, most sleuths in books I've read break all the rules and enter rooms they aren't supposed to."

Mathew just smiled.

Before we could do anything else, I heard a strange sound and turned to see an elderly woman pushing a rolling mop bucket into the outer office. Her hair was gray, and she was slightly stooped. I moved to the side as she passed, but Mathew stepped out, blocking her way.

"Hello!" He spoke in a friendly tone. The woman looked up at him. I could see she was surprised.

"Hello." Her voice crackled. "What are you two doing here? Didn't you hear the mayor's dead?"

I was stunned at her tone of voice. Her words were so blunt.

"Yes, we're aware of his death. We're just trying to find out a bit of information." Mathew eased into the conversation. "I'm Pastor Heinz." He gave her what I thought was an award-winning smile, at least as good as any I'd ever seen on television. "What's your name?"

She looked up at him, her eyes wide. "I'm Helen Cranz." I noticed she held herself very stiff.

"We were wondering who might have visited the mayor yesterday." He stepped closer to her and tilted his head slightly, giving the impression of total interest.

The woman's stance seemed to relax, which made me wonder why she had seemed so defensive at first.

"Hmm, now just a minute. Let me think. I was running late yesterday. Luckily I live close by." She glanced up at Mathew, who nodded in understanding. "Well, first person I saw was his snooty secretary. She had a tray of some sort in her arms, and she carried it into his office. Usually, she comes back out here, sits at that desk"—she pointed at the secretary's desk—"and spends the rest of the day scaring the heebie-jeebies out of anyone who wants to see the mayor. But yesterday, when she came out of his office, she left the building right off. I figured His Majesty—that's what I always call the mayor, because he thinks he's royalty, the way he struts around the town acting like he has the power to build or destroy anything he wants—was sending her to pick up his dry cleaning."

I could see Helen was almost winded from her words, her chest heaving up and down. Something about her story was getting her all wound up.

"What made you think that?" I asked.

"Oh, he usually has her pick up the dry cleaning the same day every week, and believe me, she doesn't like that job. She might act like working for the man is all sorts of wonderful, but there's many a time I heard her talking to herself and saying how much she hated him for making her be his little errand girl. Come to think of it, she was acting a bit strange that day, sort of sneaky. Kept looking behind her as she left the building."

I was getting nervous about being there, so I tried to hurry her on. "And was there anyone else that you know of who came to visit him yesterday?"

"Sure, that other man, you know the one who gets to take over if the mayor gets sick or dies?" Her eyes were closed tightly. She seemed to be searching for the correct word.

"Pro tem, Robert Casey," Mathew offered.

Helen clapped her hands together and pointed at Mathew. "Yup, that's the one. He comes by a few times each week, always begging the mayor to let him do something in the office, but His Majesty never does. I happened to be nearby and heard him talking to himself, pretending to have a conversation with the mayor."

My ears pricked up. "What did he say?"

She harrumphed. "Something like, 'You'll get really sick, and then maybe I can do some good in this office.' "

I wondered if Helen Cranz ever did anything except hover by the mayor's office, since she knew so much about his day. She also seemed to enjoy sharing what she overheard.

"Then His Majesty's son arrived. He waited until the mayor came back to the office—I guess from the bathroom or somewhere. They had a pretty loud argument, but I couldn't make head nor tails of what it was about."

I looked at Mathew. He had his hand covering his mouth, and I assumed he was holding in laughter. It was almost comical listening to the woman tell us about the mayor's movements that day.

Just then, we heard the sound of high heels clicking on the floor. Helen stopped speaking, grabbed the mop handle, and pushed the wheeled mop bucket away from us. I had a few more questions for her, but I couldn't very well run down the hall and accost her.

My thoughts were interrupted by a high-pitched voice that caused me to turn around. Phyllis Gates was standing behind us, arms crossed. "What are you doing here?" she asked, her eyes staring straight at me.

"I, we. . . We were just stopping by to. . ." I didn't finish my sentence, because I wasn't sure what to say. I wasn't about to explain that we were trying to figure out whether she poisoned the mayor.

"And, what were you doing speaking to that woman?" She pointed at the retreating back of the cleaning lady. "She's a busybody and a snoop. She's always hovering around the mayor's office."

I decided to skip explanations and try to get some information. "Helen told us that Robert Casey, the pro tem, stopped by the office yesterday. Did you see him?"

"Not yesterday. The man's a nuisance, always bothering the mayor. You know, whining about being given some kind of responsibility. The mayor would never give him anything to do."

"But are you sure he wasn't here yesterday?"

"He had an appointment, but I didn't see him. As I told the police, I wasn't in the office the whole day. I delivered the tray of samples from the tea shoppe, then left the office to pick up the mayor's dry cleaning, and then I—" She stood up straight.

Mathew moved forward. "Yes, was there something else?"

She shook her head then took a breath and said, "I had a

hair appointment. I wasn't supposed to do personal things on the mayor's time, but it was the only opening they had for the next few weeks. I knew the mayor wasn't going to be in the office until later in the day, so once I delivered the sample tray, I rushed over to the beauty shop. I returned later in the day and found the mayor dead! So I can't assure you the man never came to the office." She brushed past me but suddenly stopped and swung back around.

"Why are you asking so many questions anyways?" She squinted at us.

Neither Mathew nor I answered.

"You're playing detective?" She glared at me, snorted, and threw her hands up in the air. "Oh great, now we can all relax. The tea shoppe girl is on the case." She whipped back around and stalked away.

I could feel my cheeks heat in embarrassment. I looked up at Mathew. The crinkles around his eyes were proof he was laughing behind his hand again. A smile spread across my face.

"She's really something." I shook my head in amazement.

"Yes, quite a power to be reckoned with. But you do realize she just admitted she had the opportunity to poison the petit four before she left the office for the day."

My jaw dropped at the thought, and I watched as she disappeared. I gulped. "I wouldn't put it past her, and she was the one who found him." I glanced around the room and wondered why she had come to the mayor's office, which she knew was taped off. She was now working out of a different office.

Just then we heard the mop bucket wheels again. Helen Cranz had reappeared.

"She gone?" Her voice wavered.

Mathew nodded.

Helen wheeled the mop into the secretary's office, left it by the door, and moved closer to the mayor's office. She peeked into the room, her heavyset body causing the caution tape to sway. I moved closer to her and let my eyes sweep the office. Nothing seemed unusual or out of place. The desk was covered in file folders.

I pulled back. "He must've been working on a lot of projects."

I wasn't sure what sound I heard, but it definitely came from Helen. She turned around suddenly and said, "I left my glasses somewhere in his office the other day while I was cleaning, before he keeled over. I can't hardly see without them. Do you think anyone would mind if I just slipped in and got them?" She didn't wait for a reply. Before Mathew or I could even blink, she swiped down the yellow caution tape and pounded into the room.

She walked straight to his desk and pushed a few file folders around. When she looked up and noticed Mathew and I both staring at her, she gave a crooked smile. "You all just keep a lookout for me. I won't be but a minute." She pushed things around a bit more, and one or two folders actually fell into the trash can beside the desk.

I whispered, as loud as I thought I could get away with, "What are you doing? You can't just move things around."

She straightened. "I'm not."

"Well, you pushed a few things off the desk."

"Nothing important. Most everything on the desk is junk mail that came in the day he died. He didn't have time to sort through it all, but my glasses aren't here." She stomped across the room and stepped over the threshold into the room we were in.

I noticed Mathew hadn't said a word to her. He seemed to be frozen in place. She turned back and eyed the office again.

"Think I should clear off his desk and take out the office trash?"

"No!" Mathew finally found his voice, and mine added to the harsh tone. Helen flinched and took a step backward.

"I don't think we should disturb anything else," Mathew said. "The police aren't going to be very happy when they find out you moved things already."

Helen's head whipped around, and she faced him. "Why do the police have to know anything? I didn't do any harm. I was just looking for my glasses."

I sighed in consternation, not sure what to say or do. On television mysteries, the sleuths usually broke into the crime scene and touched things, but this wasn't a TV show. This was real life. I glanced at Mathew.

"Do we have to say anything? If questions arise, we can always tell them about this little visit." I was trying to plead with Mathew, using my eyelashes, but I think it probably looked like I was batting my eyes in a ridiculous manner. I saw a smile cross his face, and once again he looked like he was trying to hold back laughter.

"I suppose we can forget about it, unless it becomes important. I'm sure the police have already searched the office and photographed everything. Maybe they won't even need to come back here. But from now on I think this office should stay locked so no one else can 'harmlessly' slip into it."

"Don't see why. I'm the only one who would probably want to go in, and I've already done it. My glasses aren't there, so that's that!" Helen swirled around, grabbed the mop handle, and once again pushed the bucket out of the office and down the hall.

I must have been holding my breath, because I finally took in a large gulp of air. "I'm sure glad this part of our mystery solving is over. I'm shaking."

Mathew's face immediately showed concern, and he took my

hand. "I'm sorry! I should've thought this through. I probably shouldn't have brought you here."

I pulled my hand away and glared at him. "What do you think I am, some fragile rose? I wanted to come with you."

"Yes, but you just said you were shaking. I should've known visiting the place where the mayor died would upset you."

I tapped my forehead with my hand. "I'm not upset about that. I'm just a little shaken up by the way Helen just traipsed into the office and started moving things around. I mean, we could get in trouble for tampering with the evidence."

Mathew moved closer, placed his hand under my chin, tilted my head up, and met my eyes. "We didn't do anything. You have nothing to worry about. Since we've all decided not to mention it, everything will be okay."

I could actually feel the warmth of his fingertips spreading from my chin up my cheek. It was lovely.

"Are you ready to go talk to Robert Casey?"

I nodded slowly, my eyes still staring into his.

Mathew lowered his hand, turned toward the door, and began to walk. I started to follow him, but something made me turn back around for a moment and glance into the office one more time.

"I wonder if the police had this locked or not. Maybe someone else unlocked the office." My voice sounded far away as I tried to comprehend what was bothering me.

"I can call the station later and mention we found the office unlocked," Mathew answered as I broke my reverie and joined him at the door. "I'm not very happy about Helen moving things, but we can at least make sure no one else does."

We walked out of the office, down the hall, and pushed open the front door. Somehow, the icy air that met us gave me a refreshing jolt. We began to stroll down the sidewalk. We passed the apartments next to city hall.

"Those apartments are pretty old," I stated, noticing the peeling paint, moldy roof, and various broken windows.

"Yes, the Sunset Apartments are slowly deteriorating. I think that was one of the projects the mayor was working on. He wanted to tear them down, expand city hall, and add a covered parking lot."

"Well, the apartments need to go, but what about the residents?"

"The mayor had plans to relocate them all. From what I've heard, there was no opposition to the project."

I thought it sounded like a good idea. Sea Side was such a quaint town, and an eyesore like the old Sunset Apartments didn't seem to fit in.

"Before we go see Robert Casey, why don't we get something to eat? It's been a while since coffee. We can discuss the festival, get our minds off all of this," Mathew suggested.

I agreed and even let him take my hand and tuck it into the crook of his arm as we continued walking. It seemed funny, but for some reason, I no longer felt cold.

CHAPTER 6

Mathew asked where I wanted to eat. Nothing came to mind, so I suggested Tea by the Sea. "We make lovely sandwiches in the shop."

He didn't look convinced but seemed content to agree. We were still near the Sunset Apartments when I noticed Helen Cranz stepping out the front door of city hall. This time she had no mop, just an old gray coat she was quickly buttoning. She wore the same shoes she'd had on earlier. They didn't look like they provided much warmth.

"That woman needs some boots. Her feet must get cold walking in the snow. I've learned that already."

Mathew glanced over at her and added, "She said she lived nearby. I hope that's true."

I pulled a small notebook and pen out of my coat pocket and wrote, "Helen Cranz needs boots!" I thought maybe I'd buy a pair for her when I got some for myself.

The tea shoppe was busy, which was a good sign. The air was filled with the pleasant fragrance of cranberry scones. Mathew and I entered from the back into the kitchen, grabbed a plate full of tea sandwiches and a couple of scones for dessert, then headed out front to find a seat. I noticed the Bible Study Ladies at their table too late to avoid them. I was a bit surprised, because this wasn't their regular day.

Before I could sit down, I saw Savannah waving her hand at me and almost shouting, "Yoo-hoo." I had the feeling that if I didn't stop at their table, they would make an even bigger scene.

"Why don't you sit over there?" I pointed at the table farthest from the Bible Study Ladies and pressed my hand on Mathew's arm to push him in the direction away from the group. "I'll join you in just a minute."

He gave a conspiratorial wink. "I'm glad it's you that has to deal with them and not me." He laughed and actually skipped once, then walked toward the table I'd indicated.

I covered my mouth to keep from bursting out in glee and made my way to their table. I saw four sets of eyes light up when I stopped.

"Hello, ladies. What brings you to the tea shoppe today?"

Savannah fanned her hand up and down. "Oh, we wanted to see what would happen next."

I tilted my head and blinked. I felt confused. "What would happen next? What do you mean?"

Maybelle, a spritely woman in her sixties, answered, "My cousin works at the police department, and he hears a lot of things. Now, I know he's not supposed to share them outside of the office, but, well. . .I am his cousin."

I blinked again, wondering what she was trying to tell me.

"He called me about an hour ago and told me that the detective working on the mayor's case just got the results from the autopsy. I called the girls, and we headed over here." She reached out and patted my hand. "You can count on us for support, dear. We know you had nothing to do with it."

My mouth opened, but no words came out. All I could assume from what I'd heard was that the autopsy had determined, somehow, that the mayor was poisoned by the petit four. I frowned and wondered what that would mean to Gran and the shop. When I looked at the four faces again, they were all nodding, sympathy in their eyes.

Without another word, I spun around, rushed across the room, and bounded into the chair across from Mathew. My actions startled him. He looked up at me. "What's wrong?"

I opened my lips to speak but stopped when I heard the bell over the front door jingle. I slowly turned my head to face the person I dreaded seeing the most. Detective Rawls was standing in the doorway, swatting at the snowflakes on his shoulder and scanning the room. When his eyes met mine, I saw a frown come on his face, and he began to plod toward me.

Mathew reached under the table and took my hand in his. I wasn't sure it would help, but I didn't pull away. It crossed my mind to wonder if he treated all his congregants like this, or if he felt something more for me.

"There you are, Miss Quin." Detective Rawls's voice boomed across the room. I actually felt myself shrink back as he approached.

"Yes, Detective?" I couldn't keep my lips from trembling, and my voice sounded strained.

"I'm sorry to tell you that we have to close down the tea shoppe for a few days. The autopsy has come in, and the mayor was definitely poisoned by your petit four. I'll need to have my team come in and search the entire building, take fingerprints, and. . ."

I stood up while he was speaking and let go of Mathew's hand. "That's fine, Detective, but could you keep your voice down? I hate to have you upset our customers." My eyes swept the room, and I realized it was too late. Everyone was watching the scene.

My shoulders slumped. I started to walk from table to table and quietly ask the customers to come back another day. Each of them left quickly, except the Bible Study Ladies. They assured me several times they wanted to stay for moral support, but Mathew finally marched over and had a word with them, after which they got up as a group and swept out of the shop without even a wave goodbye.

I wondered what he said to them, but there was no time even to consider it. The detective had followed them out to invite his team to come in and begin their job.

I could feel tears in my eyes, burning. I pressed them closed for a moment.

Mathew whispered in my ear, "We should get all the baskets out before they tape off the whole shop. The detective may not allow us to have them for the festival if this investigation takes several days."

I felt my chest tighten with anger. I couldn't believe his main concern was for the festival, but I agreed to help take the baskets out the back door. I'm not sure if that was considered tampering with evidence, but I felt the tea shoppe would need the positive advertisement the baskets would bring to hopefully overcome some of the negativity an investigation would cause.

We strolled quickly to the kitchen, opened the back door, and began hauling the baskets out to his truck. The ground was frozen, and we had to be careful not to slip. We were each able to carry about five baskets at a time, so both of us had to take ten trips, but we worked quickly and quietly.

Once all the baskets were loaded and we were back in the kitchen trying to get warm, Mathew suggested we go somewhere else for lunch. I was feeling exhausted and worried. I needed to tell Gran what was going on. Mathew must have noticed my hesitation.

"Perhaps we should reschedule. We can do some more investigating tomorrow?"

I felt a wave of relief. Mathew was a pleasant man, and in other circumstances I would have enjoyed spending the day with him. But the events of the day had overwhelmed me, and I just wanted to go home and climb into bed.

"You do want to continue our sleuthing?" Mathew asked.

"Yes, of course. I want to find out who did this. I'm just tired now."

Mathew took my hand and squeezed it. "I understand. It's been a long day. I'll take the baskets to my office at the church. I'll be there if you need me. I need to spend some time preparing for the mayor's funeral."

I felt a bit guilty. Here this man who was needed by a grieving family had been spending the day helping me instead.

Just then the investigation team entered the kitchen. Mathew and I slipped out the back door. He got into his truck and drove away. I slowly made my way back to my apartment. The other businesses along Main Street were decorated with lights and wreaths. The general Christmas aura gave me a sense of peace, even though I was worried about the tea shoppe. I knew the phone call to Gran would be difficult, but it had to be done.

When I was settled at my kitchen table later that evening, eating a ham sandwich, I pressed Gran's number on my phone and took a deep breath.

Chapter 7

As I'd feared, Gran was very upset. In her own words, "Nothing like this has ever happened to the tea shoppe before."

I wanted to choke on the guilt I felt; however, I knew it wasn't my fault. I hadn't poisoned that petit four, but after her reaction, I was even more determined to help find the true culprit. After an hour of trying to soothe Gran, I hung up the phone and spent some time in prayer, asking the Lord to help find the murderer, and quickly.

The rest of the evening, I tried to relax. On a sheet of paper, I wrote out as much information as I could think of about who may have had access to the petit four. By the time I was ready for bed though, I was no closer to solving the mystery than before. The list of suspects so far was Phyllis Gates, Robert Casey, Don Johnson, and the mayor's son. I wasn't sure what his name was, but I thought someone had mentioned him once in the tea shoppe. The name Sawyer came to mind, so I jotted it on the paper with a question mark.

I tried to imagine why any of them would want to kill the mayor, but I knew very little about them and even less about the mayor himself.

When I finally crawled into bed, I pulled my blanket up to my neck and fell into a deep sleep right away.

I awoke on Wednesday not sure what to do for the day, since I wasn't going into the shop. Detective Rawls had informed me he would have us shut down at least a day or two. I sat up, swung my legs over the side of the bed, and yawned. Just then my cell phone rang. I reached out and answered it.

"Good morning, Miss Quin."

A smile spread across my face when I heard Mathew's soothing voice, but I immediately clamped my lips together. I had to remind myself, he was a pastor, not my boyfriend. *Was he even a friend?* We had only agreed to be partners in crime solving.

"Good morning, Pastor."

"Hello, Georgina. Remember, you can call me Mathew. I hope I'm not calling too early. I wanted to let you know the mayor's funeral is to be held on Friday morning. His secretary seems to be the one in charge and has made all the arrangements. Right now, there isn't much I can do since I haven't been able to contact his son. So, if you want to continue investigating, today would work. We could visit Robert Casey, the mayor's pro tem."

I had originally planned to do some decorating today. My eyes scanned my apartment. It was nearly Christmas, and I didn't even have a tree yet. My box of ornaments was sitting against a wall waiting, but there was little point in trying to enjoy the holidays with the mayor's death and the accusation of murder hanging over the tea shoppe.

"Sure, that's a great idea. But somewhere along the way I have to buy a pair of winter boots." I rubbed my hands up and down my arms. I was cold. The apartment didn't have a very good heating system.

I could hear Mathew laugh. "Sounds like a plan. There's a winter apparel shop in town. We could stop there after we visit Robert Casey."

When we ended the conversation, I finally felt motivated to

get out of bed. I searched my wardrobe for the warmest pants and sweater I owned. I wasn't used to Maine's damp, cold weather, and I was going to have to make some adjustments to my clothes. When I was finally clad in a slouchy gray turtleneck sweater, thick sweat pants, and a coat, I was able to face the outdoors.

Mathew offered to pick me up since I didn't own a car, so I was waiting outside when he drove up to the building in his Ford truck. When he stopped in front of my apartment, he slid across the seat and pushed the passenger door open. There was a running board for me to step on. With my hands grasping the door, I was able to pull myself onto the front seat.

"Thanks for picking me up," I gushed. Then I felt my face turn red. I couldn't believe I was acting like a high school girl every time the man was around. If Mathew noticed, he didn't react.

"It's probably easier for us sleuths to stick together." He tossed his head back, laughing at his own words. I enjoyed the way his skin crinkled around his eyes when he laughed.

"Sorry about the truck," he said. "It's great when moving things for the church but not so great for passengers." He patted the seat, which I had to admit was not very comfortable. The floor was littered with miscellaneous tools.

"Not a problem. Remember, I grew up in Texas. Everyone there owns a truck."

"Okay then." Mathew revved the motor and pulled the truck out into traffic.

We didn't have to drive very far, but I kept my eyes peeled out the window as we drove down the different streets. I couldn't get my fill of seeing the lovely architecture of the unique homes. Each house was a bit different, and sidewalks ran in front of them all. A few pine trees were sprinkled up and down the street but also many barren trees waiting for their new buds to appear. I couldn't wait to see them all bloom in the spring.

Thinking of trees, my lack of a pine came to mind. "I need to get a Christmas tree."

Mathew turned and gave me a grin. "There's a great tree farm farther outside Sea Side. It's where everyone gets Christmas trees."

I was glad to hear that. Since I was so new to town, I didn't even know where to begin looking.

When we finally stopped in front of a lovely blue Victorian house on Cove Street, I sighed.

"What's wrong?" Mathew asked. He turned the engine off and slipped out of his seat belt.

I shook my head. "Nothing. It's just the apartment I live in isn't even close to what I want. A house like this would be ideal. I've been too busy training at the tea shoppe to start looking around, and now with this murder hanging over me, I can't even think about moving."

"When it comes time, I'd love to help you. I'm also looking for a house, but taking over the church has kept me busy this year. I'm lucky I grew up a few miles away from Sea Side, so it wasn't too much change for me, but I'm still working on getting completely settled."

We got out of the truck and walked side by side up to the lovely wraparound porch, and Mathew knocked on the front door. We waited a few minutes. I was glad to see the door finally being opened, but it only moved an inch. Through the crack, I could see a tall, lanky man. His eyes were swollen, and his clothing looked unkempt.

"Yes?" He blinked several times as if the light hurt his eyes.

"Robert Casey?" Mathew asked.

"Yes." The man looked beyond us, befuddled.

"I'm Pastor Mathew, and this is Georgina Quin. We'd like to talk to you."

Robert didn't answer. He stepped back and allowed us to push open the door. We hesitated, but when he didn't invite us in, we went ahead and stepped into the front hall. Robert drifted into the living room and dropped lethargically onto the couch.

Mathew and I looked at each other. I could see the questions in his eyes and knew he saw the same questions in mine. The room was festively decorated, but the mood in the room felt dull and heavy. I sat on a wingback chair, facing Robert. Mathew tried to get comfortable on a straight chair. The man didn't even ask what we wanted. He just sat with his head slumped down.

Mathew cleared his throat. "Robert. . . Um, may I call you Robert?"

Robert nodded.

"Georgina and her grandmother own Tea by the Sea."

Robert lifted his head. His eyes opened wide. He stuck a shaky hand out and pointed at me. "You. . .you. . . You're the one who killed the mayor."

I felt like I'd been slapped across the face. I shook my head and opened my mouth to deny the charge.

Mathew interrupted. "Now, Robert. Let's not throw accusations around. The police are looking into the mayor's death, but no one has accused Georgina or the tea shoppe."

Robert looked up at Mathew. "Why are you here? Are you here to give me comfort, or are you blaming me for the mayor's death?"

I sat up straighter, uncomfortable with his question. He was right to be suspicious. We didn't actually think he was the murderer, for sure, but we were here to consider it.

Robert spoke rapidly. "Why would you think that? Why would I want to murder the mayor? Without him, I'm nothing."

With a hand on my hip and a sarcastic tone, I tossed out, "I thought if something happened to the mayor, you as pro tem would take his place."

He turned to me, and I watched his countenance shrink. Then he actually began to cry. Through his sobs, he said, "That's not what I want. I can't be mayor, even if only until a new one is picked. I love being pro tem. It gives me a bit of prestige in the community, but the idea of actually having to take over for the mayor, well. . .I just can't do it."

"I was told you were always hoping the mayor would get sick so you could clean things up," I pressed but immediately regretted the words. It was obvious this wasn't true.

The man leaned his head into his hands and moaned. "That was just a bunch of bluster to make me look good. I didn't like him as a person, but I wouldn't even know where to begin taking over for him. He was gifted at his job. I mean, just the apartment project he was working on would be way too much for me to handle, even if I could get my hands on the files."

Robert started gulping. For a moment I thought he might pass out. Mathew rushed over to him and patted his shoulders until he quit crying. Then Mathew handed him a card with the name of his church on it and told him they'd love to have him join the congregation. "We have grief support groups in the church as well. I think the mayor's secretary is quite efficient and will be able to guide you into filling in for the mayor until the next one can be appointed. The city needs you."

Robert looked up, a smile of gratitude on his face. He thanked Mathew and wiped his eyes, but he didn't stand up to follow us to the door. He ran a shaky hand through his hair and allowed his head to drop down again.

We slipped out the front door and made our way to the truck. We didn't speak until we were driving away from Robert's house.

"That wasn't very pleasant." Mathew broke the silence.

I felt a tear slip down my cheek. My voice trembled. "I feel so sorry for him. I expected to meet a happy man, ready to step in and take over city hall, but I believe he's truly distraught." I swiped at my tears. I was angry at myself for the way I'd snapped at the man.

"I agree. At least until we find some other evidence, we should consider him innocent. It would be pretty hard to act as disturbed as he was. I'll have our grief team visit him. He needs some kind of intervention."

I nodded. I was afraid if I tried to say anything, I would break down. We still needed to speak to the mayor's son and Don Johnson because, from what we knew, they were the only other people who had seen the mayor that day. After visiting with Robert Casey, however, I wasn't sure I wanted to follow up with the others.

"Why don't we go get you those boots and grab a cup of coffee?" Mathew offered. I noticed he didn't mention tea.

"All right, but we need to talk to Don Johnson and the mayor's son. The funeral is Friday morning, and the festival begins on Friday night, which is only two days from now. There won't be much time for investigating once that all begins. I haven't even seen the festival site. Maybe we should skip coffee and stop by the park."

Mathew agreed. He cricked his neck and glanced at the sky. "I'm sure it's going to start snowing in a day or so. We'd better hurry on all accounts. Sawyer Dalton, the mayor's son, lives out in the country. So does Don Johnson. We don't want to get stuck on some of those back roads in a snowstorm. Why don't we try to see them both tomorrow?"

I blinked. I still wasn't used to the heavy snows in Maine, but I wrung my hands, worried, now that Mathew had broached the possibility of getting stuck on the roads in the country. I didn't answer his question.

He must have noticed my reaction, because he once more patted my hand. "Don't worry, Georgina. I've lived in Maine my whole life. I can handle the snow. I only mentioned it because I don't want to miss the festival. If we got stuck in the country, there would be plenty of people to take us in for a day or so, but then we'd have to forfeit the festival. I'm going to be praying nothing like that happens. By the way, the tree farm is out by Don Johnson's home as well. We could get your tree tomorrow."

His words sounded cheerful, so I sat back, my right hand grasping the door handle as I tried to relax. Since I knew little about snow, I was going to put myself in Mathew's hands, and he was putting us both in God's hands. That was all that was necessary.

CHAPTER 8

Mathew steered down Main Street and drove by the tea shoppe. I could see several people peeking in the front window. *What do they think they can see? It's not like there's a dead body in there or anything.*

A police car was still parked nearby, but the officers must have been in the shop with the detective. I felt tears pressing the back of my eyelids. The move to Maine had filled me with such hope for a new future. Now, with this murder hanging over the shop, I wasn't sure how it would affect my life. When it was proven that we didn't poison the petit four, would the town forgive and forget, or would the damage have been done?

Mathew interrupted my thoughts. "Do you want to stop and talk to the detective? See if they've made any progress?"

I shook my head. "No, he makes me nervous." I found myself clasping my hands at the thought of the man. "I'd rather wait until we've been proven innocent in this whole thing."

"Good idea. Well, let's get you those winter boots. I'm not taking you to cut down a Christmas tree wearing those flimsy things." Mathew pointed at my not-very-warm boots.

I nodded, almost wishing I could ask him just to take me home, but I did need better boots, especially if we were going out to the tree farm the next day.

The Hunter's Boutique was filled with Sea Side memorabilia and a variety of winter clothing. I assumed they replaced the coats, boots, and gloves with bathing suits and beach towels in the summer. Since I knew little to nothing about winter boots, I allowed the salesgirl to show me what she thought I needed. I cringed at the look of most of them but finally settled on a pair that was practical and useful but still had some style. I was happy with the fringe of fur around the top.

After deciding on a pair for myself, I glanced around to find some for Helen Cranz. I doubted she would want the same style, so I bought her a useful pair that would fit pretty much any woman's foot.

I could see a glint of laughter in Mathew's eye when I held up my bag and announced I was all finished.

"Got what you needed?" he asked.

"Yep. Now my toes will be warm. I got a pair for Helen too."

Mathew's eyebrows lifted. "Being a Good Samaritan?"

"I felt kind of sorry for her." I shrugged my shoulders. "Helen Cranz doesn't come across as a very pleasant person, but I thought she seemed sad."

"Hmm. I thought she seemed angry, but the boots are a lovely gesture." Mathew held the door for me, and we strolled out of the store.

With bag in hand, I climbed up into the truck.

"Still have the energy to go to the festival site?" Mathew asked before heading into traffic.

"Sure," I answered. I tilted my head and observed the man's profile. He was very handsome.

Mathew drove us to the festival site, a local park just outside town. Several people were already setting up their booths. The city workers were stringing lights in the trees, and the big Christmas tree was set up in the center of the area.

Mathew frowned at the tree. "The festival usually starts on Friday night. At about eight, we have the tree lighting. The mayor is the one who usually flips the switch, so I don't know what will happen this year. Robert Casey should fill in for him, but I'm not sure he'll be in any condition to do it."

My shoulders sagged. This was just another letdown. I'd been looking forward to experiencing the entire festival the way Gran always described it in her letters, but now we didn't know for sure if the festival would even go on as planned. So far, my life in Sea Side was not turning out as I'd hoped.

Mathew showed me the spot where our booth would be set up. It was a great location, the point where three sidewalks met. Almost everyone who visited the festival would pass our booth at some time or other.

"I've been to festivals in Texas before, but how do you think Gran will want me to handle this one?"

Mathew pretended to stand behind a counter. He lifted an imaginary basket and said, "Here is a basket filled with goodies from Tea by the Sea. Help us support the local community church by purchasing one." He cocked his eyebrow and gave an adorable smirk. I was sure if he was the one selling the baskets, every single woman in town would purchase one.

"Hmm. I can give it a try, but I'm afraid I won't make the same impact on women as you do."

Mathew stepped closer to me. "But you will on the men."

We stood facing one another. I wondered if he was feeling the same attraction for me as I was for him.

I told myself to get my head out of the clouds. This man was the pastor of a church, way out of my league. I broke the mood by stepping back and pretending to take the basket from his hand. "Gran's not going to help this year. That leaves it all up to me."

Mathew shook his head. "You have nothing to worry about. The ladies from the church who frequent the tea shoppe told me they would be taking turns helping you at the festival."

I opened my eyes wide at the thought. "The Bible Study Ladies?"

Mathew laughed. "Is that what you call them?"

"Yes. I tend to nickname our customers." I tucked my head and turned away.

"It's difficult to tell them apart most of the time. I often think of them as numbers. You know, lady number one, lady number two. . . ." It was Mathew's turn to look embarrassed.

I felt a little relieved.

"They take a bit of getting used to, but believe me, they'll be helpful at the festival. They'll sell every basket, even if they have to force people to purchase them. You know they have that southern charm, and they really do mean well." His jaw softened into a handsome grin.

I snickered. "I'm sure they do. If they weren't always talking about finding me a husband, I wouldn't have a problem with them." When I finished speaking, I slapped my hand over my mouth and peeked at the pastor. I hoped he didn't think I was hinting at anything.

He winked at me, causing heat to rise on my cheeks.

Mathew, I'd discovered, was almost a mind reader. He smiled. "Don't worry, Georgina. The ladies have been traipsing every single woman in town by me ever since I moved to Sea Side. I can totally sympathize with you. Maybe if you and I spend more time together, they'll ease up on both of us. They'll think we're courting."

I thought that sounded like a great idea, but his comment made me wonder. *Is he interested in spending time with me, or is he just using me as a way to keep the Bible Study Ladies' matchmaking at bay? If so, how long will we keep up the charade?* I had no problem spending time with this handsome man.

Throwing caution to the wind, I said, "I'm game if you are." I tried to act nonchalant, but my heart was pounding just a little bit faster.

He took my hand in his. "Good, I'm glad that's settled. At least we'll have some relief from their matchmaking during the holidays. Now, it's been a long day. Let me take you home."

I nodded.

Mathew continued to hold my hand, and we walked back to the truck, both rather quiet. I wondered what he was thinking. I knew what was on my mind, and it wasn't murder.

"Have you found the culprit yet?" Gran's voice yelled over the phone. I pulled my cell away from my ear.

"Not yet, Gran. Mathew and I talked to Robert Casey. We don't think he had anything to do with the mayor's death. Tomorrow we'll talk to Don Johnson and Sawyer Dalton." I sat down on my couch and felt my body finally relax. *Tomorrow I will also have a Christmas tree, which will definitely help the ambiance of the apartment.*

"And what about that sassy secretary? She's the one who had the most access to the petit fours."

I rested my head back, trying to imagine Phyllis poisoning the mayor. It made no sense. She complained about him, but I had no doubt she loved working for him. The worse he treated her, the more she probably enjoyed it, because she could complain publicly and get attention and sympathy.

"I don't know, Gran. I'm not going to consider her high on the list right now. We'll see how Don Johnson and Sawyer respond tomorrow."

Gran didn't sound convinced. "Georgina, have you tried on the dress yet?"

I squirmed on the couch, trying to get more comfortable. "Yes, but are you sure I have to wear it?"

"Yes! It's a Victorian Christmas Festival. All the vendors dress in Victorian clothes. There will be carolers strolling through the park, horse-drawn carriage rides, and the local theater puts on small snippets from different Dickens plays. Everyone will expect you to dress the part as well."

I blew out my breath in frustration. The dress hung on the doorway between my living room and bedroom. It was truly lovely with its rose floral pattern, but I wasn't too sure I'd be able to maneuver in it.

"All right, Gran. I'll wear the dress, and I'll sell every one of those baskets. You just rest and recover."

"I hope so, Missy!" Gran said with obvious humor.

For a moment, I wondered just how sick Gran really was.

"Do you need me to stop by? I could bring you some soup or something."

Gran coughed and moaned a little. "No. I'm fine. I just need to keep resting. I should be fine in a day or so."

We said our goodbyes, and I turned on the television and found a mystery movie to watch. Throughout the entire hour and a half, I laughed at how the characters broke so many laws while investigating the murder. I knew it wasn't very realistic, but it reminded me that Mathew and I needed to be careful not to break any laws while we were sleuthing. The movie made me think of something else. *In asking questions, we might be putting ourselves in danger.* We were looking for a murderer, after all.

Following the show, I spent some time in prayer then slipped between the cold sheets on my bed, gave a little shiver, and fell asleep almost instantly.

Thursday morning I stumbled through the apartment, waiting for my coffee to perk. I peeked out the window and was glad to see it wasn't snowing. The sun was shining, which gave me hope we wouldn't end up stuck somewhere out on a country road.

Mathew had agreed to pick me up again, so I hurried around the apartment, gathering my things. I slipped on my new boots, admiring them and enjoying the warmth they offered. I wasn't sure when I'd be able to deliver the boots to Helen Cranz, but I assumed it would be sometime this weekend.

When it was time for Mathew to arrive, I opened my apartment door and stepped out into the hallway. When I turned around to lock the door, I saw an envelope taped to the knob. Curious, I grabbed it, tore the envelope open, and read the short note.

I dropped the paper and stepped away in fear. I turned my head from side to side, searching the area, wondering if whoever left the message was nearby.

After assuring myself there was no one around, I reached down and retrieved the note. My hand was trembling, but I folded the paper carefully, tucked it in my purse, and ran down the hallway and into the parking lot. Mathew was in his truck waiting for me, so I rushed over, glad to see he had the door opened. I jumped into the passenger seat and slammed the door behind me.

Mathew turned, his eyes searching my face. "What's wrong?"

I pulled the note out of my purse and handed it to him. He read it and scowled. Without saying a word, he put the truck into DRIVE and pulled out of the parking lot.

"We are taking this note to Detective Rawls," he announced.

I frowned. "But then he'll know we're looking into the murder. What if they discover papers have been moved in the mayor's office? He might blame us." I knew I was rambling out of fear.

Mathew didn't reach out to comfort me, and he didn't offer any words to ease my thoughts. He was intent on driving straight to the police station, and as we got closer, I grew more and more nervous.

"Are you sure this is the thing to do? I mean, this note could just be a joke."

Mathew steered into a parking spot, cut the engine, and faced me. "Georgina, this note is serious. Even though it doesn't actually threaten you, it's scary to think someone would put this on your apartment door." His lips were pressed together in a thin line. He turned the note toward me, and I reread it:

Mind your own business.
Stop snooping or else!

Mathew opened the truck door and got out. I reluctantly opened the door on my side and slid out. For a moment I considered running back home or to Gran's, but I found myself trudging behind him into the station.

We took the note to the front desk and asked for Detective Rawls, but they told us he wasn't in the office, so Mathew handed the note to the desk clerk and insisted the man make sure that Detective Rawls got it as soon as possible. He emphasized that it could be a note from the mayor's killer.

Once he was convinced the man would do the job, he turned and stomped out of the station. I scurried behind and allowed him to help me up into the truck.

When Mathew was behind the steering wheel again, I

murmured, "What should we do now?"

Mathew turned the engine on but didn't shift into gear.

"Probably just go home and keep out of things, but I'm even more determined now to find the murderer. Should we go ahead and drive to Don Johnson's house?"

I nodded at him mutely, surprised. I couldn't believe he wanted to continue sleuthing. I was sure after the way he'd responded to the note that he would have insisted we give up the hunt. I settled back on the seat. I thought, *If he can do it, so can I.* I wasn't going to allow someone to intimidate me.

The driveway leading to Don Johnson's cabin was a rugged dirt road that ran about a quarter mile through some lovely wooded areas. I was speechless as we crested a hill and his house came into view. It was amazing—a gigantic log cabin built in a small valley, surrounded by hills covered in trees. It was obvious he either came from wealth or made a lot of money somehow.

I turned and glanced at Mathew. "Why would anyone who lives in a place like this want to be a mayor? He obviously has plenty of money."

Mathew shrugged. "Maybe power? From the little I've heard about him, he and the mayor go way back to high school. They competed in everything, including love."

I knew what that was like. I'd competed against a girl in my high school in many things and had lost my boyfriend to her in the end. I didn't think I'd enjoy living in the same town as my rival, but I knew I wouldn't kill her if I did.

Before we could reach the door, Don came strolling down a path that led from behind the cabin. He had on a red and black jacket and carried an ax over his shoulder. This time he didn't look angry, but I could remember the dark glitter in his eyes the day he'd stomped into the tea shoppe.

"Pastor? What are you doing here?" He cocked his head, looking first at Mathew and then at me. He didn't seem to recognize me.

"Don, this is Georgina Quin. She's taking over Tea by the Sea from her grandmother."

I watched his aura change. He set down the ax and crossed his arms over his chest. His eyes bore into mine. "What do you want?"

His attitude change caused Mathew to slide a step closer to me, but he focused on Don. "We're talking to everyone who saw the mayor on the day he died."

The man stepped back as if he'd been slapped.

"Why? Why are you talking to everyone? You aren't the police. Why did you come to see me? Are you accusing me of something?" His voice quavered.

Mathew moved toward him and laid his hand on the man's shoulder. "Don, we just want to prove that Georgina didn't poison the petit fours. Do you think you can talk to us about that day?"

Don's shoulders drooped. He sighed and turned. "Come in and have a cup of coffee." He marched up the front steps, crossed the porch, and opened the door. Mathew grabbed my hand and pulled me along.

"But, but. . .what if he's the murderer?" I tried to whisper, but I'm sure my words echoed through the entire valley.

Don's eyes met mine for a split second, and then he disappeared inside.

Mathew didn't stop moving, so I allowed myself to be dragged along.

"Hope you like caramel macchiato." Don handed me a large mug filled with steaming liquid. I looked at the dark coffee, my mind on poison. Even if he was the murderer, he probably wouldn't want to have to deal with dead bodies, I thought, so I took a sip and nodded.

Don sat on a wooden rocking chair. Mathew and I were on the couch across from him.

"Now, what do you want to know?" Don took a sip of his coffee.

"Well, we know that you stopped by the tea shoppe that morning and saw the tray I prepared for the mayor."

He sat up straight. "What do you think? I brought poison with me and tampered with the tray you made?"

"No, I don't think that's what you did. We're just trying to figure out where everyone was during the day. We heard you stopped by the mayor's office later on."

Don picked up his mug of coffee and took another long sip, then placed it down on the mahogany table again. "I did stop by. I was angry. Dalton found out I was going to order refreshments from Tea by the Sea for my campaign party, and he purposely put in his order first. After I saw your sample tray, I wanted to confront him. Sure, I went storming into his office. We had an argument, but I can assure you, when I left the office, the mayor was alive. He hadn't even eaten any of the samples yet. The box had a lid on it, and I never touched it."

Mathew dipped his head up and down as Don spoke. I could tell Mathew believed everything the man said. I did too.

"But now that the mayor's dead, you won't have any competition. You'll win the race hands down," I said, just to double-check his reaction.

A frown furrowed his brow, and he shook his head. "That's the problem. I honestly don't care about being the mayor. It was the competition I lived for. Dalton and I have been competing since high school. For every time he won and I lost, there was another time when I won and he lost. Without him to compete against, my life will be out of balance. I'll probably withdraw from the race."

I was stunned. *Doesn't anyone in this town actually want to be mayor?*

Mathew scooted forward on the couch. "Don, don't make any rash decisions. The town will need a new mayor."

Don stared at Mathew, questions in his eyes. "What about Robert Casey? He'll take over for the next few months anyway. The town can just vote him in." He crossed his arms.

I leaned forward, elbows on my knees. "We talked to Robert Casey yesterday. From what he told us, we aren't sure he can fill in for the mayor now. He's pretty torn up about Dalton's death." I looked at Mathew, wondering if I'd spoken out of turn. He nodded, so I went on. "Robert only liked the pro tem position because of how it made him look in the public eye. He doesn't want to be mayor, nor does he have the ability, it seems. The city is going to need someone qualified."

By the way Don tilted his head, I could see I'd made him think.

Mathew stood, so I did the same. "Thank you for speaking with us, Don. We have some other stops to make before it starts snowing, so if you'll excuse us?" Mathew placed his hand on my elbow and began to press me toward the front door.

I wasn't sure we should leave the man alone, but I knew we still needed to see Sawyer Dalton and get a Christmas tree, so I allowed him to lead me out onto the porch. Don stood and followed us.

"Thanks for the coffee." I smiled.

He nodded then turned to Mathew. "Pastor, I want to do the right thing. I'll be praying about it, but would you put in a word with the Man Upstairs for me?"

Mathew shook Don's hand, promising to pray, then walked by my side to the truck.

Once we were in the truck and settled, Mathew turned out of the driveway onto the main road. After some time, he spoke. "I'm beginning to wonder if there's anyone in this town who really would want to murder the mayor. So far, our top three suspects have all been put into precarious positions by the mayor's death. His secretary may be out of a job, his pro tem forced into a job he doesn't want, and his biggest rival may have to become mayor, even though he never cared about the job in the first place."

I sighed and stared out the window. We were on our way to see the mayor's son, Sawyer. At this point, he was our last suspect. By process of elimination, if we believed Don Johnson, Robert Casey, and Phyllis Gates were all innocent, then we had to assume Sawyer Dalton was the culprit.

"Do you think we should tell someone where we're going?"

Mathew didn't answer right away. After a minute he asked, "Do you want to skip our visit to Sawyer?"

"Um, have you ever met him before?"

"No. He doesn't attend church, well at least, not mine. However, he has been the subject of plenty of gossip."

I pressed my fingers against my eyelids. "I guess we should go on. I mean, the sleuths in the books never give up." I tried to laugh, but it sounded like a frog croak.

Mathew winked at me. "Come along, Watson!" he cried. "The game is afoot!"

I giggled. "Oh, so you think you're the great Sherlock Holmes? I'm just your trusty sidekick?"

He sat up straighter, stuck his chest out, and murmured, "Indubitably."

CHAPTER 9

Sawyer Dalton lived five miles farther out of town. His home, if you could call it that, was a rather run-down travel trailer set on a small lot. On both sides of his unkempt land were lovely farms, and I wondered how they felt about this eyesore. I was really surprised by the sight of his place. Because he was the mayor's son, I expected him to live in a fancy house, but that wasn't the case.

Mathew pulled up beside the trailer, his truck rocking from side to side as it dipped into deep ruts that made maneuvering the driveway almost impossible. I leaned forward, peered at the forlorn trailer, and felt a heavy sense of sadness.

"No one should live in a place like this." I barely whispered the words.

Mathew shook his head. "Can't really afford anything else. His father always paid his way in life. After they had a falling out, Sawyer apparently had trouble holding a job."

I noticed a curtain flutter from inside. Someone was definitely home. We clambered out of the truck and walked slowly to the door. There was no sidewalk, only frozen, uneven ground. I was glad the snow from several days earlier had melted, or we could have easily twisted an ankle stepping in the wrong place.

Mathew knocked on the door. We waited, but no one answered.

"I saw the curtains move. Someone is in there!" I whispered urgently.

Mathew knocked harder, and we finally heard footsteps. A voice yelled out, "Okay, okay, hold on."

A few seconds later, the door was flung open by a very

angry-looking young man. He was short, blond, and dressed in a greasy white T-shirt. From the odor, we could tell he'd recently had a few drinks.

"What d'you want?" His words screeched out belligerently, and he glared at us. He was rather bleary-eyed, but he also looked as if he were ready to pounce violently on someone.

A frightened whimper slipped from between my lips. Mathew stepped in front of me, which allowed me to move back and take a deep, calming breath.

"Mr. Dalton, um, Sawyer, do you mind if we ask you a few questions?" Mathew used a steady tone.

"About what?" Sawyer shot back.

"Your father's death," Mathew answered bluntly. I was shocked. Mathew was usually so pleasant. I didn't say anything. Mathew was more equipped at dealing with people like Sawyer than I was.

Mathew's directness must have impacted the man, because Sawyer pulled back as if he'd been slapped and shouted, "My father was murdered. Someone poisoned him. What kind of questions could you have for me?" He lifted a hand to his forehead and swayed on his feet.

Mathew reached out and laid a steadying hand on Sawyer's shoulder. At that, the man seemed to sag. He moved to the side, and we were able to slip into the trailer without any hindrance.

Once inside, I scanned the room. There weren't many places to sit, and the couch looked too dirty to touch. I caught Mathew's eye, but he put his hand on my elbow and steered me straight to the couch. We both sat, rather gingerly. I clasped my hands in my lap, afraid to touch anything.

Sawyer dropped onto a chair by the kitchen table. "So, what's this all about?"

I opened my mouth to speak but found Mathew's steadying hand on my arm. I assumed he wanted me to allow him to do the talking. On quick reflection, I decided this was best. I had little experience in dealing with people who'd had a death in the family.

"Sawyer, the police have been looking into Tea by the Sea and are keeping the shop closed. Obviously, that's not good for business, so Georgina and I have been speaking with everyone who saw your father that day. Trying to make a timeline of sorts. We hope to help the detective or at least prove that no one at the tea shoppe had anything to do with your father's death."

Sawyer lifted his head and met Mathew's eyes.

"The detective told me Dad was poisoned by something from the tea shoppe. I'm not sure why he hasn't arrested anyone yet." He turned and glared at me.

I swallowed, and my mouth felt dry. I knew I hadn't poisoned the petit four, but seeing the look in Sawyer's eyes, I realized he believed I killed his father.

I squeezed my hands together to keep from fidgeting. I wanted to appear confident. "Sawyer, I didn't have any reason to poison your father. I've never even met him."

Sawyer stood abruptly and ran his hand through his hair. "Then who did it? Who else had access to your pastries? When I saw him at the office, he hadn't eaten anything from the tray. It was sitting on his desk. He actually asked me if I wanted to try the samples, but I was angry with him, so I left the office."

"What were you angry about?" Mathew inserted.

"That he was running for mayor again. I'd just found out, and I hate to say, we argued about it. I said some pretty mean things to him. But when I left the office, he was alive."

Mathew leaned forward. "Why didn't you want him to run again?"

Sawyer swiped at his eyes, which had begun to brim with tears. He swung his arm around as if showing us something.

"Do you see this place? This isn't my home, but I couldn't stand the house my father bought once he became mayor. It's just a house for show, not family. Before he was mayor, we used to go fishing together, hunting—you know, the things fathers and sons do together. He promised me he wasn't going to run again, that things would go back to the way they were before, but I guess he decided he just loved the limelight too much." Sawyer plopped himself onto the chair again, his head down on the table.

The room grew silent, except for an occasional hiccup from Sawyer as he tried to regain control. Mathew stood, walked over, and placed his hand on the young man's back. "Sawyer, tomorrow is the funeral, and I know that will be difficult. I'll be there for you. I'd like to pray with you right now." He sat on the chair across from Sawyer. "Would that be okay?"

Sawyer lifted his head and nodded.

I took this as a cue, so I let myself out and walked to the truck. After I opened the truck door, I took a few gulps of the cool air. The trailer had been so hot and humid inside. Once I felt a bit refreshed, I grabbed the inside door handle, stepped onto the running board, and lifted myself into the truck. I flipped open our suspect notebook and jotted down my thoughts.

As I waited for Mathew to join me, I reviewed what I'd just learned from Sawyer. I found myself feeling even more confused.

Sawyer was obviously overwhelmed with grief. I could see how upsetting it was for him to find out that his father was going to run for office again instead of spending time with him, but he seemed more hurt than angry. I didn't believe Sawyer killed his father. If Mathew agreed with me, we were back to square one. Robert

Casey, Don Johnson, and Sawyer Dalton were all innocent, of that I was sure.

After about twenty minutes, I saw the trailer door open. Mathew stepped out onto the wobbly front stoop. Sawyer was standing inside the doorway. He no longer looked angry, but his shoulders were slumped over. The two men shook hands, and then Mathew began to walk toward the truck. Sawyer remained in the open doorway for a minute then disappeared into the trailer.

When Mathew joined me, he didn't open the conversation, so I just stayed quiet. He started the truck then backed away from the gloomy-looking trailer and began to drive. We went at least five miles before he spoke.

"Sawyer is very sad at the loss of his father, not only because he died, but because of the unfulfilled dreams of having his relationship with his father healed." Mathew sighed. "I'm not sure what he'll do now. His father probably left him a lot of money, which won't help that poor young man at all."

"I feel so sorry for him," I choked out. I could feel the pressure of unshed tears on the back of my eyes.

Mathew turned his head and smiled. "Pray for him. That's the best thing you can do. I'm hoping I can talk with him more and encourage him to go to college. He needs some new goals."

I was amazed at Mathew's words. He was right, of course. However, I would never have considered that. I assumed Sawyer was a sad, lost case, but Mathew was able to see a bright future for the young man. I wondered if having a deep relationship with God, the way Mathew did, gave him this outlook. If so, I needed to spend more time with God.

"Now, what about that Christmas tree?" Mathew seemed to have shaken off the sorrowful mood. "It's time to get you into the holiday spirit." His infectious laughter filled the truck cab.

I glanced out the side window at the clouds. The sky didn't look too ominous, so I no longer worried about being snowbound. "If you feel up to it. But I'll understand if you don't. I'm sure your conversation with Sawyer wasn't an easy one."

"No, it wasn't, but I think I convinced him to think about moving closer to town and attending church. I'll encourage college soon enough. What he needs now is community and support." Mathew stopped at a stop sign then continued driving.

"That's true. When I first moved to Sea Side, I felt so alone, but becoming part of the tea shoppe community has helped."

"Same with me. The church and the locals in town have welcomed me with open arms. I feel like I'm truly home. So I'm game for a trip to get a Christmas tree. I think the cool air and the smell of pine are just what we both need."

I couldn't help but agree, so Mathew turned at the next corner and headed toward the Christmas tree farm. I opened my purse, pulled out a small hairbrush I carried with me, and ran it through my hair. After being in Sawyer's trailer, I knew I'd want to give it a good shampoo in the evening. For the time being, I just wanted to enjoy the rest of the day, selecting a Christmas tree with a handsome man by my side.

CHAPTER 10

Having never been to a Christmas tree farm in the north before, I was stunned by the site. The rows of lovely fir trees, many with freshly fallen snow still lingering and glittering on the branches, were beautiful.

"I hate to cut one down," I stated, as Mathew pulled an ax from the back of the truck.

"Yes, I know what you mean, but they are careful here to preserve the beauty. The only trees that can be cut are marked with a red ribbon. If you look closely, that's like every third tree. It thins the area around the younger trees and allows them room to grow. Plus, for every tree that's cut down, they plant two more here. The owners are also part of a group that plants trees in other states, where the trees have been wiped out either by fire or by companies who strip the land."

I was impressed to know this, so I began happily searching for the right tree. There were many bigger ones I would have loved to bring home, but they weren't right for my small apartment.

"As soon as this murder investigation is over and we prove that Tea by the Sea had nothing to do with it, I want to get serious about finding a house to rent at a reasonable rate until I can afford to buy one. I've always loved the idea of setting up a Christmas tree in a room with a large front picture window so anyone walking or driving by can share in the pleasure of seeing it as well."

Mathew cocked his head and beamed. "That's exactly how I feel. One of my favorite memories as a child was running home in the evenings around Christmastime, seeing all the lit trees in the front windows. Nowadays people keep their curtains drawn tight. I want my house to be a place where my congregants feel welcomed. Right now I need to focus on becoming a good leader for the church, but once I get married, I'll be searching for that type of home as well."

I tried to concentrate on looking at trees, but after his words, images of Mathew and me together in a lovely Victorian house, welcoming guests to share our Christmas tree, kept flashing through my mind along with a question. *Lord, is there any chance Mathew is the one for me? Am I the one for him?*

"So, what do you think. Does that sound good to you?" Mathew's words drew me from my reverie. I stared at him blankly. I wasn't sure what he'd said.

He waved his hand in front of my face. "Hello, hello. . .anyone home? Georgina, I just asked if you'd like me to help you set up your tree once we get it to your place."

I gulped. "Yes, that sounds great. But you have the funeral tomorrow. I don't want to keep you out too late."

He glanced at his watch. A smirk crossed his face. "I think I can handle staying out till about seven and still get up in the morning."

I felt rather foolish then. His earlier comments had me so flustered, I wasn't sure what I was saying. I clamped my lips closed, turned, and really began to search for the perfect tree. Within a few minutes, I found just the right one. I stepped back and allowed Mathew to wield the ax. Before long, we were carrying a five-foot-tall tree between us to his truck.

After placing it in the truck bed, we walked to the checkout area to pay. The woman behind the counter barely glanced at me, but she locked her eyes on Mathew. "Hello, Pastor," she purred. "If I'd known you needed a tree, I would have happily brought you one."

Mathew glanced up. I thought I saw him pull back slightly. He spoke in a careful tone. "Hello, Miss Margaret."

A trill of laughter escaped her lips. "Please, I've asked you to call me Maggie. Everyone else does. I was speaking to Miss Savannah, and she mentioned you could use someone to clean your apartment. I'd love to help you out."

Mathew cleared his throat. "She must have me confused with someone else. I do my own cleaning."

Margaret didn't flinch at his words but finally acknowledged my existence with a curt nod.

Mathew held out the money. She snatched the bill from his hand, turned in a huff, and stomped to the other end of the counter to put it in the cash register.

I pressed my lips together to hold in my laughter but kept my eyes averted from Mathew. I could see a blush on his neck, and I didn't want to cause him any further embarrassment. This was obviously the work of the Bible Study Ladies' matchmaking.

Once Margaret handed some change back to Mathew, he did an about-face and made a beeline for the door. I jumped in surprise and rushed out after him. We both scrambled into the truck. Before Mathew put the key in the ignition, he turned to face me, his mouth in a crooked grin.

"Well, that was embarrassing."

I covered my mouth but couldn't refrain from giggling.

"Okay, that's enough of that!" Mathew gave me a stern look, but I could see the laughter dancing in his eyes. "I'm taking you home to set up this tree." He pushed the key in, started the truck, and began to drive.

I didn't say anything more. I knew he wasn't angry with me, but

I'm sure he felt uncomfortable after being put on the spot by Miss Margaret.

When we arrived at my apartment, Mathew backed into a space where we could get the tree straight from the truck into the apartment. He unstrapped it, and together we lifted the fir over the side of the truck and carried it through the walkway to my apartment door.

I was a little afraid of finding another threatening letter, but there wasn't anything on the door. With a sigh of relief, I got out my keys and opened the door. Mathew was able to carry the tree the last few feet and leaned it up against the small wall between the fireplace and the sliding glass door that led out onto my minuscule porch.

Mathew turned and scanned the apartment but didn't speak.

I laughed out loud. "It's not very nice, is it?"

He shrugged. "I was trying to find something to say, but believe me, it's no better than mine. Hopefully the tree and a few decorations will brighten the place."

"What about you? Do you have a tree?"

He nodded. "Yes, one smaller than yours. I'm not home very often, so I didn't do much decorating." He moved across the room and glanced out the window. I saw his brow furrow.

"Detective Rawls is walking up the sidewalk."

I rushed over to the window to look out. The detective was headed toward my apartment.

When we heard knocking on the door, I felt frozen in one spot, so Mathew strode across the room and opened the door.

Detective Rawls stepped into the apartment. "Miss Quin, I want to know what this letter means." He held up the note I'd found on my apartment door earlier.

The thought of running to my bedroom, slamming the door, and throwing myself on the bed crossed my mind, but I just stood still, staring at the man.

"Um, it's a threat," I stated.

"Yes, but why would anyone send you such a letter? What have you been doing?"

I gulped and opened my mouth to respond.

He moved forward. "Don't even waste your breath. You've been questioning all the suspects." He swung his head around and faced Mathew. "And you've been right alongside her, Pastor. Why would you both take such a risk? Don't you realize someone murdered the mayor? Now that same someone isn't happy with you sticking your noses where they don't belong!"

I slunk down onto my couch, and Mathew joined me. He took my hand in his.

"Detective Rawls, we were concerned about the tea shoppe, so we thought if we. . ." I faltered, and he held up his hand.

"I don't even want to hear it. You two need to stay away from anyone related to this case. My officers and I are handling it, and we don't need two amateurs getting in the way." He walked over and threw the letter in my lap. "This is only a copy of the letter. I kept the original. I want you to keep this as a reminder to stay out of it. Do I make myself clear?"

Both our heads nodded up and down, but neither of us spoke.

"I'm leaving one of my men outside the apartment on patrol. He won't disturb you, but we have to make sure everyone stays safe," He stomped to the door, "Though I don't know why we bother when you obviously aren't concerned about that yourself." He grabbed the handle and opened the door. Without a backward glance, he disappeared.

Several moments passed before either of us spoke, but finally Mathew stood up and said, "Should I stop by and get you tomorrow to set up the booth for the festival?"

"That would be nice, if you don't mind." I felt relieved he hadn't said something about Detective Rawls. I was pretty sure we were both done sleuthing. I did wonder if, after the festival, I'd even see Mathew outside of church again.

"I'll load the baskets into the truck and stop by to get you about one o'clock. We should be able to set everything up before the festival starts at five." He moved to the door then turned back to face me. "Georgina, I'm sorry I dragged you into this sleuthing business. I never thought about how dangerous it could be."

I gazed up at him. "Don't feel that way. I wanted to find the culprit as much as you did. Remember, it's my tea shoppe that's on the line, and my reputation." I grabbed his hand and gave it a squeeze.

Mathew leaned forward and placed a kiss on my forehead. It was soothing.

I tilted my head up, and we locked eyes.

"I don't want you to get hurt, Georgina." He pulled my head against his chest, and we stood together for several minutes.

I stepped back. "I'm glad we're done with the sleuthing. I thought we would find the murderer so easily, but now I'm afraid. I'm sort of glad there's a patrol car out there." I paused, then my thoughts brightened. "I'll be glad to get focused on the festival and leave the mayor's death to the police."

"All right, Watson, no more detective work," Mathew joked. I was standing beside him, and he reached over and ran a finger along my cheek then left the apartment.

When I closed the door, I leaned my head back and took a deep breath. I was glad to be done with the investigating. Remembering his soft caress, I decided I'd like to invite Mathew over for dinner one night before Christmas.

CHAPTER 11

It was strange to lounge around in the morning. The detective still hadn't allowed us to open the tea shoppe, so there was nothing for me to do early in the day since I'd sworn off sleuthing.

Knowing I was going to be wearing a Victorian Dress at the festival, I took time to find some warm leggings to wear under it. I could always take off a layer or two if I somehow ended up feeling too hot. I put on some thick socks and slipped on my new boots. I was very pleased with the way they fit and how toasty I knew they would keep my toes.

Once I poured a cup of coffee, I sat down to enjoy it, but my cell phone rang. I saw Gran's name flash across my screen.

With hesitation, knowing I couldn't keep any secrets from her, I answered. "Hello, Gran."

An hour later, after she'd dragged every bit of information out of me, including the news about the threatening letter, Gran finally let me go, but only after I promised on my life never again to stick my nose into police business.

I set down my phone and leaned back. My eyes scanned the room. I was happy with my Christmas tree. I had decorated after Mathew left the night before, using red and green lights and my old-fashioned ornaments, which made me feel very nostalgic. The white feathered angel with its lighted halo smiled down at me.

My phone rang again. This time there was no name, just the word "Unknown." Normally I would ignore it, but I picked it up and swiped. "Hello?"

For a few seconds, it was silent, then I heard some heavy breathing.

"Who is this?" I asked.

"Mind your own business!" a deep voice moaned.

I raised my voice. "Who is this?"

Whoever it was hung up, but I yelled into the phone three more times, "Who is this?" My hand was trembling when I finally set down the phone. I didn't know what to do, if I should call Detective Rawls or run out to the patrol car, or nothing. I decided to wait until Mathew picked me up and ask him what he thought.

I hoisted myself into the passenger seat of Mathew's truck. He grinned at my Victorian getup. The tea shoppe baskets were in the back seat and in the truck bed. Gran told me our baker would be dropping off the treats to put in the baskets. She'd been baking at her own home since the shop closed. We'd have to spend the first hour filling all the baskets while the Bible Study Ladies set up and decorated the booth.

On our way to the festival grounds, I tried to inform Mathew as casually as possible about the phone call. It didn't work.

"What!" he yelled, stomping on the brake. "When did this happen?"

I chewed on my lower lip. "Earlier this morning."

"Why didn't you call me, or the police?"

I pulled back farther from him. "I wasn't sure what to do. I wanted to discuss it with you first." My voice was barely a whisper, and my lips trembled. Mathew must have noticed, because he seemed to calm down. He took a deep breath then said, "We need to call Detective Rawls."

I nodded. "Can we do it from the festival?"

"Yes." Mathew started driving again.

"I'm sorry," I said, and turned to look out the window. The scenery of Maine always helped to calm me.

"Georgina, you haven't done anything wrong. I'm sorry for yelling." He reached across the seat and placed his hand on mine. "I was scared. This is actually all my fault. I should never have suggested we start this investigation, and all it's gotten you is threats. We basically interviewed a handful of innocent people."

I pushed a strand of loose hair off my cheek. "No one seems to have had any reason to want the mayor dead."

"Especially right now, with the Sunset Apartments deal needing to be completed."

"Once the town votes on a new mayor, can't he or she finish the project?"

Mathew shrugged. "Maybe. If Mayor Dalton left good records, the project can probably be pushed through. Without them, though, a new mayor might not see it as a priority and may not work on it right away."

I frowned. Something niggled my mind but passed before I could capture it. "By the look of the mayor's desk, it will be hard for anyone to figure out anything very quickly. It was a real mess. Maybe Helen Cranz was right. She should do some straightening in there."

"I'm sure once the murder is solved, she'll get the chance." Mathew steered into the parking lot and stopped the truck. Luckily, we wouldn't have to carry the baskets far. Our booth was only about twenty yards from the parking lot.

"Okay, I'll start unloading, but you need to call Detective Rawls. Tell him everything you remember." Mathew jumped out of the driver's seat. I pulled out my cell phone, stared at it for a few seconds, then started pushing numbers.

"Now, aren't these just lovely baskets?" Savannah drawled. "You did a splendid job, Georgina."

I lifted another basket onto the booth counter and placed a scone in it. Gran and I decided until the investigation proved Tea by the Sea innocent, we probably shouldn't fill the baskets with petit fours.

I was still smarting from the tongue-lashing I'd received from Detective Rawls. He hadn't been too happy I'd waited so long to tell him about the phone call.

Trying to get my mind off it, I kept busy. It was almost time for the festival to begin. As promised, the Bible Study Ladies were all there helping. They were each dressed to the nines in Victorian dresses that put mine to shame. They'd also created a very nice booth.

At first our conversation was all about the festival and the baskets. However, after they noticed Mathew talking to me privately, they began giving me knowing looks and sideways glances.

Once he finished unloading the truck, Mathew lingered at the booth while I told him about Detective Rawls's reaction. Obviously the man was furious with me for not calling earlier, but in the end, he assured me he'd have a patrol car keeping watch on my apartment for a few more days—which made Mathew happy.

The festival began right at five. Everyone had decorated their booths in festive Christmas decor. The ladies had hung poinsettia teacups across the top of our booth along with a hand-painted sign with the shop name on it. The counter was covered in an old-fashioned Christmas tablecloth, and the ladies had made red and green aprons for all of us to wear. I was sure Gran would approve of everything.

Once people started mulling around the festival, our booth was an instant success.

After an hour, my face felt frozen in place from smiling so much while handing out baskets. Mathew walked around visiting with many of his congregants at other booths, but he stopped by ours around half past six.

"I'm doing a run for burgers and fries. Several of the other people running booths were too busy to stop for dinner, so I agreed to run out and bring something back. Jot down what you want on your burger, and I'll get it."

I did as he asked then turned back to the booth and picked up a basket to hand to the next customer. When I glanced up, I was surprised to see Robert Casey, the mayor's pro tem, standing beside the booth.

"Hello," I bubbled out, immediately regretting it. I was glad to see him out of his house, but the last thing he needed was undue attention.

"Hello, Georgina." He looked uncomfortable.

"I'm glad to see you." I lowered my voice. "Are you going to preside over the tree lighting tonight?"

He nodded, his hands stuffed in the pockets of his gray down coat. "I may not be able to do everything required of a mayor, but I think I can push a button to light a tree." He laughed nervously.

"That's great. When is the tree lighting?" I glanced across the walkway. The big Christmas tree was set up in the center of the festival area.

"Eight."

I could tell by his curt answer our conversation was over. I lifted a basket and handed it to him. He eyed it and was about to turn it down, but I pushed it into his hands. "It's on the house." I hoped he didn't suspect me of putting poison in the scones.

He took the basket, gave a wan smile, and strolled away. I couldn't help but think it was going to take every ounce of his bravery to stand in front of all the people tonight and light the tree. I bowed my head and said a little prayer for his courage.

I could see Mathew delivering bagged food to several other booths. However, he wasn't staying long at any of them. In fact, I thought it looked more like he was just tossing them onto the booths and jogging by. I could feel a tingle run through my system. His odd behavior was a sure sign something was amiss.

When he reached our booth with the last bag, he handed it to me but stepped behind the booth and pulled me to the side.

"I saw something," he whispered.

I was reaching into the bag but stopped. "What do you mean?"

"I was driving by city hall, and I saw a light on in the mayor's office. I thought it was strange, so I stopped in front of the building. As soon as I did, the light went off, but I stayed there for a few minutes trying to decide if I should go in or not."

I waited for him to go on. When he hesitated, I pressed, "And? What happened?"

"Phyllis Gates came out the front door a few minutes later. She stood on the front steps, looking around, and then started walking away. She had a long red folder in her hand."

"Hmm. The mayor had several red folders on his desk. I wonder what's in the one she took."

We looked at one another, and the glow of curiosity in Mathew's eyes made me step back.

"Mathew, did you call Detective Rawls?"

He looked away for a moment then shook his head. "Not yet. I was so intrigued. All I could think about was getting here and telling you. But I'll call him right now."

Mathew stepped to the back of the booth and pulled out his cell phone. I moved closer to the front, pulled the burger out of the bag, unwrapped it, and took a bite. In general, fast food was not my favorite, but I was so hungry, it hit the spot.

The crowd around the booths was thinning as most people were walking toward the big Christmas tree. Everyone was getting ready for the tree lighting. I was trying to see through the crowd.

Maybelle slipped up beside me.

"Georgina, you go on over to the tree lighting. I'll keep a watch on the booth."

I blinked at her, placed a hand over my mouth, and mumbled through a bite of burger, "Are you sure?"

"Of course. I've lived here a long time. I've seen that tree lit plenty of times, but this is your first Christmas in Sea Side. You should get to see everything."

I was grateful for her kindness. It would be nice to have Mathew join me, I thought, but when I glanced over, I saw him deep in his conversation with the detective. After I stuffed the last morsel of burger into my mouth and wiped my hands on my apron, I headed toward the growing crowd.

Just as I was getting ready to slip into the circle and stand beside Savannah, I noticed Sawyer Dalton hovering near some bushes that blocked the view of the parking lot. I was glad to see him out and about, but something in the way his eyes kept shifting over the crowd made me curious. He seemed to be waiting for someone.

I stepped back, turned, and began to walk toward him. Then I heard a familiar sound, the clicking of Phyllis Gates's heels. I moved closer to a tree, pulled at my overwide Victorian skirt, and hid behind the trunk. I felt silly, but after what Mathew had told me about Phyllis coming from the mayor's office, I thought it was strange to see her meeting Sawyer. Since they were both still potential suspects, I decided it was best to observe them from a safe distance.

When Phyllis reached Sawyer's side, they started to converse. I turned my head toward the Tea by the Sea booth and was glad when my eyes met Mathew's. He'd finished his phone call and was looking for me.

I waved my hand frantically until he started walking toward me. When I pointed at Phyllis and Sawyer, Mathew's eyes opened wide. He gave a quick nod of understanding and casually strolled toward me. I knew he didn't want to move too quickly and attract attention, but I felt like it was the longest thirty seconds of my life. When he finally stood beside me, I scooted over so he could hide behind the tree as well. I was sure my dress was sticking out the other side, but there was nothing I could do about it.

"What do you think they're up to?" I whispered.

"Don't know," Mathew answered, and peeked his head out for a second. "Hmm, this is bad. Phyllis just gave the folder to Sawyer."

I couldn't help myself. I had to see. I peeked from the other side of the tree. Sure enough, the red folder was now under Sawyer's arm.

"What should we do?" I asked.

"Detective Rawls told me he was going to send out a patrol car to pick up Phyllis. I think one of us needs to stay with her, and the other with Sawyer."

I nodded. "You take Phyllis. I'll take Sawyer."

Before Mathew could answer, I moved away from the tree and began to stroll on the sidewalk in their direction. Sawyer and Phyllis had completed their conversation and were walking in different directions. Sawyer was headed straight toward me.

Without a second thought, I put my head down, took a few steps, and allowed myself to crash into the man. I fell back from the impact, and he lifted his arms to catch me, the red folder flitting to the ground.

Chapter 12

"Georgina?" Sawyer pulled me to a standing position.

"Yes, oh, I'm sooo sorry to bump into you." My eyes lowered to the folder, which lay open on the ground. I bent over to help him retrieve the papers and picked up a stapled copy with the words Last Will and Testament printed across the top.

When I stood with it in my hand, I saw Mathew farther down the sidewalk. He had a firm grasp on Phyllis's arm. He was steering her toward us.

"What is the meaning of this?" Phyllis was trying to pull away from Mathew, but he wouldn't release her.

I held up the will. "What's this? Something from the mayor's office?" My voice dripped with accusation.

Phyllis pulled back as if she'd been slapped.

Sawyer lunged forward and tried to grab the paper. "That's mine. It's none of your business."

Mathew blocked him. "It is when Phyllis stole it from the mayor's office. Everything in that office is evidence. I've already called Detective Rawls."

Phyllis screeched and turned to Sawyer. "See, I told you it was a bad idea. I didn't want to get involved!"

"Shut up!" Sawyer reached for the papers. I held them back.

"I'm not going to jail for you." Phyllis continued screaming. Sawyer stopped reaching and stood with his hands balled into fists.

Mathew tried to calm Phyllis down. I turned to Sawyer. "So, you did kill your father after all?"

Sawyer's mouth opened and closed. "No. I loved my father." His face had gone pale.

"Then why did you have Phyllis steal this file for you?" I waved it in front of his face.

Sawyer clamped his lips together. Seeing that I wasn't going to back down, he sputtered, "It's the only copy of my father's will, and the police won't let me into the office to get it. We can't finalize anything without this will. My father didn't keep a copy at home or with the lawyer. He felt his office was the only safe place in this town. I asked Phyllis to get it because she's the only one who knew where he kept it. She didn't touch anything else in the office, right?" He looked at her, and she nodded.

I sighed, and Mathew released his grip. I held the will up to the light so I could read the first few lines. It was definitely Mayor Dalton's will.

"I think that sounds plausible," Mathew answered, but his eyes were on mine. "We can leave it up to Detective Rawls. He's looking for Phyllis right now."

Phyllis actually hissed at him. "I can't believe you, Pastor. Why don't you and Nancy Drew stay out of my business? I didn't think giving this poor man his father's will was wrong."

Mathew tilted his head. "I'm sure you thought you were doing what's best, and you can explain that to the detective. We didn't want to get you in trouble, but remember, Georgina's tea shoppe is still shut down. The longer it takes for the police to discover who the murderer is, the worse things could be for her business."

With a hand on her hip, Phyllis asked, "How did you know I had the folder?" She was looking at me, but Mathew answered.

"I saw you coming out of city hall carrying a file. I felt it looked suspicious," he explained.

Phyllis straightened up and pulled at the bottom of her coat. In a rude tone, she said, "I'm sure *you* thought *you* were doing the right thing. But now the suspicion of the mayor's death will be focused on Sawyer or me, and the true culprit has even more time to get away."

I had to agree with Phyllis, but Mathew had already started the wheels in motion when he called Detective Rawls.

I faced Mathew and placed my hand on his arm. "Is there anything we can do?"

He shook his head. "Phyllis and Sawyer will have to explain things to Rawls. We did what seemed necessary." I could see the regret in his eyes.

Just then, a police car pulled into the parking lot nearby. The door opened, and Detective Rawls unfolded from the front seat. Mathew stepped away from me and moved closer to Sawyer. In a forced whisper, he encouraged the young man, "Just face this thing head on, Sawyer. That's the best way to handle it."

Sawyer's shoulders drooped. "Yes, Pastor." He turned and made his way toward Rawls. Phyllis swung her head back and forth as if looking for an escape, then gave me one last long glare and scurried to catch up with Sawyer.

"They'd never turn themselves in if they were the murderers." My voice trembled from all the excitement. "I think they would've run."

"I only hope Detective Rawls isn't too upset with them and believes their story," Mathew added.

I shivered, and Mathew put an arm around me and pulled me close to his chest.

"Are you cold?"

"No, but I think the whole episode with Phyllis and Sawyer frightened me. I'll be fine in a few minutes." It was true, but I still turned my head and laid it on Mathew's chest for several seconds.

In the distance, we heard Robert Casey's voice booming over the sound system, doing the countdown. At zero, the area was flooded with sparkling lights from the Christmas tree. It was breathtaking even from where we were standing.

There was a long moment of awed silence throughout the entire park, which was finally interrupted by Robert Casey's voice. "This tree lighting is in honor of our beloved and missed Mayor Dalton. I'm sure he would want this festival to be the best one ever, so please continue to enjoy yourselves."

This was followed by a round of applause, and then the crowd began to meander away from the tree. Mathew and I walked back to the Tea by the Sea booth. There was nothing more for either of us to say. I picked up a basket and handed it to the next customer with a forced smile on my face.

Mathew slipped away, and I didn't see him again until it was time for him to take me home. Even then, the ride was silent.

"Georgina, all you were supposed to do was sell baskets and help save the tea shoppe's reputation, not get more involved in this murder." Gran's voice raged through the phone, which was sitting on my lap set to speaker. I was resting on my couch in a sweatshirt and a pair of fluffy pajama pants, staring at the powder-puff-looking house slippers on my feet.

After the festival, Mathew had brought me straight home. I took a quick shower and slipped into my favorite lounging clothes. I even indulged in a cup of hot cocoa with marshmallows in an attempt to warm myself all the way through. I knew Gran would want to know how well we did selling the baskets, but I knew I also had to tell her about the incident with Phyllis and Sawyer before someone else did. That set her off on a twenty-minute rampage.

By the time she allowed me to hang up, I was utterly exhausted. I turned off the Christmas tree lights, trudged to my bedroom, and flung myself onto the bed. After a quick prayer, with the promise of a more in-depth one in the morning, I was soon in a dreamless sleep.

Gentle flakes were falling from the sky when Mathew picked me up the next day. I didn't think it would accumulate, but it would mean a cold festival day. At the last minute, I grabbed the bag with the boots I'd bought for Helen Cranz. Perhaps I'd try to take them to her sometime during the day.

We hadn't heard anything from Detective Rawls after he took Sawyer and Phyllis away the previous night. Knowing the man's stoic attitude, we probably never would. I only hoped he hadn't arrested either of them.

Mathew dropped me off near the booth then went to park his truck. I was looking forward to a pleasant day and planned to avoid thinking about the mayor's murder and suspects for the whole day. The Bible Study Ladies were already at the booth. When I slipped behind the counter, Charlotte handed me a cup of steaming coffee, and Florence tied the Victorian apron around my waist.

"I like my coffee black, but I put some of that caramel stuff you young people like in it." Charlotte guffawed.

"Charlotte, it's pretty cold out today. Are you sure you should be here?" I didn't think she was bundled up very well for a seventy-eight-year-old woman. In fact, it probably wasn't good for any of the Bible Study Ladies.

Charlotte waved a hand as if swooshing away a fly. "Don't you worry about me. I've lived here for the past twenty years. I'm used to the cold. You, on the other hand, are looking blue around the lips. Are you going to be warm enough to hand out baskets all day?"

I shivered and took a long sip of the hot coffee. "I'll be okay." I tried to sound convincing, but my cheeks were saying otherwise. At least my toes were warm. Gran's suggestion for new boots had been a great idea, even if I'd had the same idea on the same day. I looked at the brown bag beneath the counter. Helen Cranz needed boots, and I didn't want to wait any longer to give them to her.

"Good morning, Georgina." The words interrupted my thoughts. I lifted my head and met Don Johnson's eyes. He gave a huge grin. "Yep, it's me."

"Don, how good to see you." I smiled. "Stop by for some of our delicious scones?"

He eyed the baskets. "My preference is your petit fours." He actually had the gall to chuckle.

"Um, we thought, well, with the mayor's death, we thought it best to put the petit fours on the back burner for now. Perhaps bring them back for Valentine's Day."

He leaned closer to look over the baskets. "Probably a wise call." He straightened and looked at me. "So, I've decided to go ahead and run for mayor after all. Even if there isn't another candidate, I still have to win fair and square. Do you think Tea by the Sea will be able to cater a campaign event?"

I was surprised by his request but wasn't about to pass up what was sure to be a large order for the shop. "I'm sure we can do that. Why don't you let us know how many people you expect, and we can write up a proposal."

He shook my hand. "I want to tell you, I appreciate how you and Pastor visited me the other day. It helped me get a new perspective on the situation."

I grinned. "I'm just glad to see you smiling."

After a few more pleasantries, Don strolled away. I watched as he disappeared in the crowd.

It seemed that everyone was getting over the mayor's death and moving on with their lives. I still couldn't see Sawyer, Don Johnson, or Robert Casey as the murderer, nor could I imagine Phyllis going to such extremes. However, Sawyer may have wanted his inheritance early, Robert Casey was getting to act as mayor, which, although he'd denied it before, could still have been something to make him want to kill the mayor for, and Don Johnson was going to become the next mayor without any competition.

I rubbed my temples, wondering if this murder would ever be solved. Since beginning our investigation, Mathew and I had decided all of our suspects were innocent, but I just reminded myself of how at least three of them could still be guilty.

Mathew appeared suddenly, interrupting my thoughts.

"Sold many baskets today?"

"It's been slow so far, but last night we sold almost half the baskets. I'm wondering if I'll need to make a few more before this thing is over. I'll call Gran later and ask if she has any more supplies."

"I think the ladies can handle the morning crowd. Would you like to stroll through the festival grounds with me? You didn't get to see much last night." He put his hand lightly on my shoulder. I could feel a warmth spread through me.

"Sure, that would be nice." After a word to Charlotte, I stepped out from behind the booth and placed my hand in the crook of his arm. We began walking. Almost every business in Sea Side was represented. Many were giving out small incentive gifts or flyers. Only a few were selling their merchandise, but overall, I could see our baskets were probably the best.

"I called Detective Rawls this morning. He wasn't happy to hear from me, but he did tell me he didn't arrest Phyllis or Sawyer. Nothing else in the mayor's office had been disturbed, so for now he believes they were just after the will."

I sat down on a bench and looked up at Mathew. "I'm surprised Sawyer was worried about it. I'm sure he gets everything."

Mathew shook his head. "I'm not too sure about that. The mayor was pretty upset Sawyer wouldn't live with him and behave like a good citizen. He may have cut Sawyer out of the will. If that's the case, then Sawyer won't have any say over Dalton's estate."

I glanced at my gloved hand and picked a few pieces of fluff off my fingers. "I hope he didn't cut his son out of the will. Sawyer really loved his dad. He said he just wanted his father to behave like a father, but if Sawyer thought he was still the beneficiary of the will, he may have decided to kill his father."

Mathew lowered his head. "I hope not."

Several flakes landed on my gloves. It was getting a bit colder out, which reminded me I wanted to take the new boots to Helen Cranz, so Mathew escorted me back to the booth.

"Want me to drive you to Helen's?" Mathew took my hand in his.

"Yes, I'd like that. I don't know where she lives though."

"I'll look it up." Mathew pulled out his cell phone and pressed a few buttons. "She lives in the Sunset Apartments."

I wasn't surprised. She'd told us she lived close to city hall. I wondered how the apartment project would affect her. From what I'd heard, the mayor had offered new housing to everyone so Helen would benefit from that, I thought.

CHAPTER 13

As we were about to pass city hall, I put my hand on Mathew's arm. "Stop. There's Don Johnson. He's going into city hall."

Mathew cocked his head. "That's strange, what does he need in there?"

"Maybe we'd better see what he's doing."

Mathew pulled the truck to a stop in front of the building. "I'll let you out here and go park, but wait just inside the door for me."

I slid out of the front seat and began to walk toward city hall. I hoped the front door was unlocked. I was actually surprised when it opened. I pushed with one hand, because before hopping out of the truck I had, without realizing it, grabbed the bag with the boots.

The sack crinkled in my hand as I stepped inside. I saw Don down the hallway, heading in the direction of the mayor's office. Ignoring Mathew's instructions, I began following him at a distance.

When I reached the mayor's office, I saw the door was ajar, so I slowed down and glanced inside. No one was in the outer office, but through the other door that led into the mayor's office, I could see a figure bent over near the desk.

Could Don Johnson be going through the mayor's papers?

I moved closer, trying to make sense of what I was seeing. When the person straightened, I gasped.

"Helen! What are you doing?" I was actually dumbfounded to find her in the office, and not Don. I scanned the room, wondering if he was in the office as well, but aside from Helen, the room was empty.

She straightened, pulling something out of the garbage can.

Her eyes locked with mine, but there was no smile on her face.

"What are you doing here?" she growled, which surprised me. The last time I saw her she wasn't exactly nice, but she didn't seem angry.

I held up the bag with a smile. "I bought you some boots. I wanted to stop by your place, but I saw Don Johnson come into the building, and well, I followed him."

She placed a hand on her hip. "He isn't here."

As my eyes adjusted to the dark office, I realized Helen was holding something. My legs began to tremble.

"I was coming to see you at your home," I murmured. My eyes froze on the red folder in her hand.

A bitter laugh bubbled from her lips as she held up the folder. Across the top, in bold black lettering, it read, SUNSET APARTMENT DEMOLITION PLAN. "My home! My home! Did you know the mayor wanted to destroy my home?" She shook the folder.

My mouth dropped open at the sound of her spiteful words.

"I'm sorry." My words sounded flat and untrue.

"But I couldn't let him do that, now could I? Not my home!"

I wasn't sure what she was trying to tell me. She was obviously very upset.

"I heard the mayor was going to find homes for all the residents of the apartments. I'm sure it would've been a nice upgrade."

"How can anyone find a home for someone who doesn't want to move? I grew up in those apartments. I didn't want to move, but they said I would have to. But now without a mayor, without these plans, they'll forget all about it. Only His Majesty wanted to tear down my home. No one else cared."

Helen took a step toward me. I wasn't sure why, but her movement frightened me.

"Why did you have to stick your nose into my business?" Her voice trembled with raw emotion.

"Your business? I haven't. . ." My voice faded as I suddenly realized what she was talking about. Helen was the one who'd called me on the phone, the one who'd sent the letter, and the one who'd killed the mayor. My investigating was definitely getting into her business.

I took another step backward, but her eyes were locked on me.

"I see you understand me now." She looked down at the desk, picked up a letter opener, and held it in her hand.

I gulped. "Helen, I'm sure you didn't mean to kill the mayor. It was an accident."

She chuckled. "Poison? Not many people have accidents with poison. Oh, I thought about using this letter opener, but I'd just finished washing the floors in here and didn't want to get any blood on them." She glanced around the room. "After his son left, I tried to talk to His Majesty about my home. I explained how much it meant to me, but the sot just laughed at me. He dared to tell me my home wasn't worth a wooden nickel. So I went home and got my bottle of herbicide. It's very poisonous. I waited for him to go to the men's room, then I slipped into his office. I'd overheard the secretary tell him the samples from the tea shoppe were on his desk, so I opened the sample tray and stuffed the poison in the bottom of one of those little cakes. I stayed near the office and waited. I wasn't sure if he'd eat that one first, but as luck would have it, when he returned from the men's room, he opened the tray and tossed the thing into his mouth. I had the satisfaction of watching him die, begging me to get him help."

My stomach turned. For a moment, I thought I was going to throw up, but I took a few gasps of air. I needed to get out of the office and away from Helen. If I could slip out of the room, I could run for help, but she kept moving closer with the letter opener, poised to strike.

For a moment, I was paralyzed with fear. I had no weapon, and she looked crazed. I moved slowly, not wanting to alarm her. I was just barely able to slip out of the mayor's private office before she caught onto what I was doing and rushed straight to the door of the outer office before I could reach it.

"Poor little tea shoppe girl. Everyone believes you were the one who poisoned the mayor. Once I kill you, I'll tell everyone you admitted it. I'll say I had to kill you in self-defense because I figured out how you murdered him. All I have to do is hide the poison in the tea shoppe pantry. I'll make sure to press your fingers on it after I wipe my fingerprints off." She kept hooting with laughter as if what she was saying was a funny joke.

"Now, just stand still, Missy, and I'll be real quick about it." She lifted the letter opener once more and lunged at me. The only thing I could think to do was throw the bag with the boots in it at her. The bag hit her in the face. She let go of the letter opener, but she lunged at me, knocked me to the ground, and got on top of me.

I squirmed under her weight, but with a strength I would never have guessed she had, she grabbed my hair and pulled my head back. I saw her reaching behind, feeling for the letter opener. I was trying to get out from under her, and I kept praying, *Lord Jesus, help!* My heart was pleading, although I was too frightened to speak out loud. She had the advantage over me, and I wasn't able to get up.

I squeezed my eyes shut, expecting to feel the letter opener slide into my heart or slice my neck. Instead, I felt the heavy weight of Helen's body lifted off of me. I opened my eyes in surprise and saw Mathew holding Helen in a tight grip.

"Are you all right, Georgina?" Mathew's voice was grim.

"I—I think so."

Mathew had already kicked the letter opener farther away. "Get up and call Detective Rawls."

I stood up, stumbled across the room, and sat on a chair against the wall. I began to press the numbers on my cell. My entire body was shaking, and I couldn't keep tears from slipping down my cheeks. I quickly informed the detective of the situation then put down the phone.

I wanted Mathew to comfort me, but he remained standing across the room holding the outraged Helen.

I noticed Mathew's lips moving and realized he was praying, which brought back the reality that God had answered my prayer. By sending Mathew into the office at just the right time, God saved me from what could have been my death.

"What's going on in here?" I turned at Don Johnson's voice.

I pointed across the room. "She. . .she tried to kill me."

The man's eyes opened wide.

"She killed the mayor," I gasped.

Don stepped farther into the room. "Need any help, Pastor?"

Mathew shook his head.

Although the room seemed to be spinning, I looked at Don and asked, "What were you doing here?" The words came out in a tremble. "I followed you in and found her. . ."

"I wanted to walk through the whole building, spend some time praying about whether God wanted me to become the mayor or not. Even though I said I was going to run, I wanted to assure myself it was what God wanted. I was passing by here again when I heard your voices."

I slunk further down as I felt the fear leave my body, replaced with exhaustion. I felt as if I could just lay down my head and sleep.

Within minutes, the room was filled with police officers, and Detective Rawls was barking orders. One officer was trying to get my statement, but my teeth were chattering so hard, I wasn't able to speak clearly. Rawls called out, "Leave her alone, Daniels. We can get her statement later. Can't you see she's in shock?"

I was grateful, but when I turned to thank him, his lips were thin and stern, which meant I had a lot of explaining to do.

When two officers got Helen Cranz onto her feet, balanced between them, she wobbled slightly but then turned and faced me. I could feel the hate emanating from her. It was hard to feel pity for her at this point, knowing she'd murdered a man and would have murdered me too if she could have, but I knew I needed to forgive her.

I walked across the room, picked up the bag with the boots, and moved back to stand in front of her. "Helen, I'm sorry the mayor was going to tear down your house, and I forgive you for trying to kill me." I handed the bag to the officer who'd handcuffed her. Then I turned and walked out of the room.

Mathew wasn't far behind. He took my arm and supported me all the way out to the parking lot. Once more he drove me home. I didn't try to talk. The events of the day had been too overwhelming. I just needed sleep.

When Mathew pulled up to my apartment, he slid out of the truck, jogged around the front, opened the passenger door, and helped me down.

"Want me to walk you in?" His eyes searched my face.

"No. I'll be fine." My words were curt, although I didn't mean to be rude.

Mathew pulled me close for a moment, pressed a small kiss

on the top of my head, and whispered, "Thank God you're okay, Georgina."

I mumbled something incoherent and shuffled away from him. All I wanted was the warmth and comfort of my bed.

On the following Monday, I tied the green-, pink-, and yellow-striped apron on over my yellow polo and blue jeans. I slipped my feet into my new warm boots, shrugged into my cozy thermal coat, grabbed my purse, and headed out the door.

I rushed down Main Street, wanting to get to the tea shoppe as early as possible. Detective Rawls had his men take down the Temporarily Closed signs, and he had called me on Sunday to say the shop could reopen on Monday.

The Sunday paper's article had cleared up any question about whether the mayor had been poisoned by anyone or anything from Tea by the Sea, giving explicit details about Helen Cranz's part in the murder and her attempt on my life. Needless to say, I expected a fairly large Monday morning crowd, even if they came just to satisfy their curiosity.

Our baker had to quit by the end of the month and had handed in her notice, so now I was going to have to do more of the baking and a lot of the sandwich making.

I opened the front door, thrilling at the sound of the bell jangling overhead. I would never take that sound for granted again. Gran was already in the shop, leaning over a cookbook and sipping on her mug of coffee, as if the murder had never happened.

I hung up my coat, poured myself a cup of tea, and joined Gran at the counter. She leaned closer to me and whispered in my ear, "Thank you, love, for saving the shop."

I scanned the room, feeling a real warmth and fondness for the place.

"Nothing Sherlock Holmes and his trusty sidekick Watson wouldn't have done."

Just then the front door opened, the bell jangled, and I glanced up as Mathew walked in.

Gran snickered. "Speaking of. . ."

I slapped her arm lightly. "Gran!"

She laughed, grabbed her mug, and headed into the kitchen giving me one last wink.

Mathew moved across the room and sat on the stool across from me. "Good morning, Georgina. Are you happy to have the shop open again?"

I poured a cup of Earl Grey and pushed it across the counter to him. "Of course, but I'll miss the excitement of sleuthing."

Mathew reached over and covered my hand with his. "Well, I can't offer any more detective work, but there are many fun and exciting things to do in this town. I'd love to be the one to share them with you."

Our eyes met, and I felt a blush creep up my neck. I'd wondered if Mathew would even want to see me again once the murder was solved. I had my answer.

"That sounds really nice."

He stood and smiled at me. "I've enjoyed sleuthing with you and can't imagine ever wanting to play detective with anyone else. Promise to always be my sidekick."

I stared into his eyes. They weren't laughing. He was serious.

"Always," I whispered.

With a gentle hand, he reached out and touched my face. "You know, Georgina. I believe I may be falling in love with you. Do you think, perhaps, you are falling in love with me?" His words were spoken quietly, so only I heard.

I lifted my head with a smile and sighed as I leaned into his arms. "Indubitably!"

Mathew held me for a moment. I finally stepped back and searched his face.

His eyes never left my eyes until he leaned forward and pressed his lips on mine.

The sound of Gran's cackles caused us to pull apart, but Mathew kept his hand on mine.

Gran came out of the kitchen, walked over, and patted my shoulder. "Well, that's one good thing that's come out of all this." She nodded at Mathew, who gave her a sideways grin and a wink. "But let's just hope we don't ever have another murder here at Tea by the Sea."

In unison, Mathew and I both said, "Amen!"

Teresa Ives Lilly's ninth-grade teacher inspired her writing by allowing her to take a twelfth-grade creative writing course during the summer, which stirred within her a passion for writing. Nevertheless, until her salvation in 1986 when she discovered the genre of Christian romance, Teresa hadn't written anything for publication. Since that time, however, she has gone on to write over twenty-five novellas and novels, including two published by Barbour Books. Teresa lives in San Antonio, Texas, where she and her husband are close to their three grown children and one grandson. Teresa believes God let her be born "at such a time as this" to be able to write and share her stories of faith. Her book *Orphan Train Bride* was a bestseller for two weeks on Amazon.

Buns to Die For

Darlene Franklin

DEDICATION

To my beloved mother, Anita Bremner Gardner, who loved
the Lord with all her heart and taught me to do the same.
I caught my love of a good story and fascination with all
fictional sleuths from her. I learned all about coastal Maine
from the twenty-eight years she spent in East Boothbay.

CHAPTER 1

Sir Geoffrey Guilfoyle winked at me before he bit into one of the hot cross buns I baked that morning. His ring, with his family crest, sparkled in the light as if to emphasize the gesture.

I nearly swooned, foolishness for a woman three-quarters of a century old. Even if Sir Geoffrey was bona fide English nobility—and handsome to boot.

I probably should explain myself. I'm Evie Holland, owner of Tea by the Sea in the town of Sea Side, on the beautiful Maine coast. I've lived here all my life and wouldn't move to Britain even if Sir Geoffrey asked me.

At the time, the tea shoppe was still in my name, although I'd handed daily operations to my granddaughter, Georgina Quin. She has a good head on her shoulders. Look at the way she handled the murder of the mayor last Christmas.

Between Georgina and our permanent waitress, Diane Little, we kept things running smoothly. Diane played an important role in our success. Why, she can charm a lobsterman into ordering a cucumber sandwich.

With Georgina's help, I'd been able to devote myself to adding a "proper British tea" to our tasty combinations of sandwiches and muffins. Sir Geoffrey's patronage inspired me to research original recipes, and he'd become my official taste tester.

The traditional British hot cross bun was the glue holding our March and April menu together, and I wanted to get it right.

Georgina was more concerned about the cost. The ingredients in the recipe I used cost more than the alternatives. We'd devised a plate that added "all the trimmings" for a dollar more. People thought they were getting a bargain.

"It looks genuine." Sir Geoffrey's face didn't move a muscle. "Nicely plump, evenly glazed."

I hoped he noticed that I had formed the cross on the bun out of flour and water instead of drizzling white icing across the top.

If he sounded like a food critic, it's because he'd been judging baking contests ever since he was a boy, attending local fairs with his mother. I often wondered how he kept his perfect physique, given his penchant for our pastries. My pleasantly round figure testifies to my fondness for my own product.

He cut into the bun, one of those proper gentlemen who wouldn't eat with his bare hands. He held the plate at eye level and studied the texture of the bread. "The leavening is even."

I'd learned not to hurry him. He liked to put on a show. Anything I said would slow down his examination. Only one thing ever distracted him from the task at hand.

And here it came. Marshfield, Sir Geoffrey's bulldog, raced through the door left open by our delivery person. Before I could snatch the tray out of the dog's way, he gulped down a bun in one bite.

I groaned.

Marshfield was as fond of our pastries as his owner. The problem is, several baking staples make dogs sick. In the case of hot cross buns, raisins can be deadly.

Sir Geoffrey always took his dog's side. "You don't begrudge Marshfield a taste, do you?"

I tolerated it, up to a point. "It doesn't matter what I think. If the health department finds that dog in here, eating our food, they could shut us down."

"You worry too much." Sir Geoffrey rubbed the dog's head.

"For someone who loves his dog, you have a funny way of showing it. Raisins can be toxic to dogs. He'll probably get sick. Is that what you want?"

"Nonsense. I don't believe it." He patted Marshfield's head again. "Now sit down like a good boy so the bad lady will stop scolding you."

The dog settled at Sir Geoffrey's feet, his expression shouting, *Who, me?*

The dog didn't fool me, but I didn't say anything more. Time would prove my point. When the inevitable happened, I would offer my help.

"Let's finish before Marshfield decides he wants seconds." Sir Geoffrey plopped the bite into his mouth and chewed. After he swallowed, a smile leapt to his face. "Now that is a proper hot cross bun."

I grinned. I couldn't help it. Sir Geoffrey's approval was as good as a Paul Hollywood handshake, the closest I would get to *The Great British Baking Show* here in Sea Side, Maine.

Georgina held up the design for our spring menu with NOW THAT'S A PROPER HOT CROSS BUN! written across it. "May I quote you, sir?"

"With my pleasure." Sir Geoffrey liked the attention. "Americans don't bake with sultanas very often. Why did you use them?"

"I used Paul Hollywood's recipe." I didn't admit that I had just found out what sultanas are, golden raisins made from small white grapes.

He grunted. "These taste like you've sat in his master class."

An ugly gurgling sound interrupted our conversation, and a second later an unpleasant stench spread across the room. The raisins had created havoc on Marshfield's system more quickly than I would have expected.

Sir Geoffrey rushed to his dog's side. The bulldog was as pugnacious with me as his heavy jowls threatened, but Geoffrey treated him like a much beloved son. My scolds of "Naughty dog! You know you can't eat table food!" interrupted murmurs of "Poor dog, those raisins will get you every time. Maybe we should ask Miss Evie to bake pet-friendly treats from now on."

"I can't make a proper hot cross bun without raisins." I couldn't help it—the words gushed out.

Sir Geoffrey's head whipped around, and he glared at me. "Then you should keep them where my dog can't reach them."

"I refuse to change my menu because of a dog. You know I make pet-friendly treats, but it's up to you to control your animal."

Marshfield came into the shop only because Sir Geoffrey insisted. I hoped that after today he would recognize the wisdom of keeping his pooch at home.

He huffed. "I'd best get Marshfield home and get him cleaned up before my company arrives tonight. Send me the bill."

"That's not necessary," Georgina said immediately.

She should have agreed. I know the customer is always right, but in this case, I doubted it. I always worried that the health department would show up around the same time the dog was having one of his episodes. But as the heir apparent, Georgina earned the right to make her own decisions. I wouldn't question her in front of our customers.

My best option was to speed Sir Geoffrey out the door. "Let me get your—" I stopped myself before I said "cookies." To Geoffrey they would always be—"'biscuits' you ordered for your guests tonight."

He checked out the contents—gingersnaps, lemon-thyme thins, chocolate macadamia crunch. "They smell tantalizing. I'll have trouble leaving them alone until tonight."

Knowing Sir Geoffrey the way I did, I had expected him to say that. "Here's some extras to tide you over. Just keep them away from Marshfield. Chocolate is even worse for dogs than raisins."

At the mention of his name, Marshfield looked up at me hopefully. He really was a sweetie, and I was a softie. I went to the tin where I kept specially baked dog treats. Sir Geoffrey wasn't our only doggone customer.

"Package the chocolate separately next time." Sir Geoffrey was more upset than usual about my scolding Marshfield. Maybe he was secretly worried about the family reunion. The dog had scarfed up the dog treat and come back for more. I handed him another one. "No more. I'm sorry you got sick. If you had asked politely, I would have given you something delicious, made especially for you."

He drooled as if he understood me.

I counted out six of the dog biscuits for Sir Geoffrey. "These are on the house, since Marshfield got sick."

We did want to keep him in our good graces.

He nodded, but his attention was focused on the box of cookies. "These are all so very British."

"I gave it my best effort." I was pleased he'd noticed.

"I'm sure they're delightful. But I would also like to enjoy American 'cookies' as well. How about three dozen of those—what do you call them—chocolate chunk cookies? And something with peanut butter."

"Chocolate is bad for dogs," I reminded him.

Georgina caught my eye. I could read her thoughts. *Why are you turning away business?* She baked the cookies. I mostly experimented with new recipes.

"We'll get right on it." She made a note on her order pad. "I bet you'll be glad to see your family again."

Sir Geoffrey's smile faltered, and my antenna went up.

"It's just my sister-in-law, Daisy, and her son. They called last night to say they were flying in."

I thought I understood. The way he told the story, they hadn't parted on the best of terms when he'd chosen to make his home in America.

Georgina raised her hand in a Girl Scout salute. "I promise, we'll make the best American cookies you've ever eaten, sweet delicacies to linger on your tongue and not in your gut."

He laughed. "I have yet to see a biscuit that will soften Daisy's demeanor." Once Marshfield had recovered, Sir Geoffrey grasped his walking stick in his right hand and called the dog to heel before heading out the door.

"I'm surprised he asked for chocolate chunk and peanut butter." Georgina watched him walk to his car. "Brits usually complain they're too sweet."

"Maybe he's developed a sweet tooth." We'd know soon enough, when his family arrived. If I timed my visit well, I might get to meet them. It would take quite a woman to make Sir Geoffrey tremble. Daisy seemed an unlikely name for a harridan.

Perhaps Sir Geoffrey felt guilty for leaving his family behind. I'd often wondered why a man with a respected, comfortable life in England would come to our small coastal town. I'd finally decided he had wanted to see the New World like his ancestors before him, hundreds of years ago.

Georgina had our driver deliver the cookies that evening, but the next morning I decided to take him a gift box. Fridays were Sir Geoffrey's regular days to go fishing with his neighbor Roland Whitaker, a professional fisherman by trade and a good friend. I often went to Geoffrey's house while they were out to drop off something sweet to enjoy when they returned. This time I'd also packed a bag with Marshfield's favorite treats as an apology.

It takes twenty minutes to drive from Tea by the Sea to Sir Geoffrey's house, even though it's only three miles away across the inlet between the two buildings. But since I need the land to get from here to there, it's easily an eight-mile trip.

My watch had just passed seven when I stopped. I saw no sign of Sir Geoffrey's car. Perhaps they had all gone fishing or out to breakfast, saving our baked goods for later. I knocked on the door just in case someone was there.

Marshfield answered my summons with a loud bark. Strange. Sir Geoffrey never went anywhere without his dog.

Not that Sir Geoffrey's habits were any of my business.

I rapped on the door, and it swung open. "Hello? Is anybody home?" An unpleasant smell assaulted my nostrils, different from the pungent ocean air that invades our homes with the fog. Marshfield greeted me warmly, and silence reigned through the rest of the house.

I decided I'd look through the house to see if everything was okay. No one responded to my hails. Through open doorways I spotted suitcases in both guest bedrooms. Apparently the company had arrived, but I saw no evidence of their presence in the house at the moment.

The unpleasant smell grew stronger as I approached the kitchen, reminding me of the butcher shop where I'd gone to do my shopping as a young wife. I knew what that smell meant, but I didn't want to acknowledge it. Maybe it was just an accident and everyone had gone to the hospital. I built up my hopes as I walked into the kitchen.

Sir Geoffrey lay face up, spread-eagled in a pool of blood, a surprised look on his face. A six-foot long fishing lance protruded from his chest, right around where his heart would be.

Chapter 2

Marshfield had followed me into the kitchen. He snarled when I approached Sir Geoffrey's body after depositing my box of goodies in the pantry—out of Marshfield's reach. To be safe, I attached his leash to his collar and roped it around the door handle.

After that, I called the police. The sergeant told me the detective was unavailable but to please stay at the house until he arrived, with a warning not to touch anything. My toes curled at the thought, but I agreed.

Next, I called Georgina to let her know what had happened.

"Not you too." Her voice was sharp. After all, it hadn't been all that long since she got involved in solving a mystery. "Could it be a natural death?"

The hole in Sir Geoffrey's chest left no doubt. "No." Grief over my friend's death hit me, and I struggled to pay attention to my granddaughter.

"How long has he been dead? Can you guess?"

Long enough for the blood to stop pumping. Although it still looked fairly fresh. "The blood has started to coagulate, so it's been some time. But Marshfield doesn't seem to be hungry, so I'm guessing it happened after he woke up this morning and maybe, what, fifteen or thirty minutes before I arrived?"

"Which would make it—"

"Between six and seven o'clock," I said.

"Mathew and I are coming over there," Georgina said. "You shouldn't be alone."

The police wouldn't be pleased to have more people in the

house, tramping over the evidence, so I declined her offer. After we disconnected, I decided to do a little snooping. I wouldn't touch anything of course, but I would take pictures if I found anything interesting.

Marshfield whined when I walked past him. I put my hand on his leash, and his stubby tail thumped the floor. I sighed. I couldn't take him for a walk, as much as we both would enjoy it. I compromised by chaining him to the dog post in the front yard.

Marshfield pulled unhappily at his chain. He must have known his master was gone. Animals understand death in a more immediate, practical way than we do. He would miss his friend. Was there more? Did he feel fear because of whatever had happened?

Those useful "5 W" questions ran through my brain. Half of the answers could be answered fairly easily. Like, when did he die? As I said to Georgina, my best guess was between six and seven this morning. After six, because that's when Sir Geoffrey normally fed Marshfield and took him for a walk. Before seven, because I arrived shortly after that.

The answer to "what happened" seemed equally obvious, unless he was already dead when someone pushed the fishing lance through his chest. But that didn't make sense. I suppose someone could have shot him about the same time. If there was a bullet, the coroner would find it.

Where? Where I found him. I could barely imagine a different answer, and there was way too much blood for him to have been dragged to the kitchen from somewhere else without leaving a trail.

But as to who, or why, I didn't have a clue. A few locals thought Sir Geoffrey's British ways made him snobbish. His pantry shelves, filled with everything needed for an afternoon tea, from leaves to teapots to cozies, testified to his continuing love for all things British.

But if snobbery was the basis for murder, Sir Geoffrey wouldn't be the only target. Why, they might even come after me because of my efforts to serve a proper British tea. Fortunately for me, most people liked the idea, and that made my business successful.

If somebody hated Geoffrey for that, did they feel the same way about me and my shop? I dismissed the possibility before I spooked at every customer complaint.

A package of British shortbread cookies, Bremner Biscuits, was on a pantry shelf, perhaps a gift from his guests. He had encouraged me to serve the biscuits at the tea shoppe. I had considered it a victory when Sir Geoffrey abandoned buying expensive cookies from his homeland after he discovered I could make them for him fresh. The catch phrase "The best of British baking as approved by Sir Geoffrey Guilfoyle" became a major selling point for my goods.

Tires crunched on the driveway. *The police.* I hurried to let them in.

Instead of the police, Roland Whitaker, Sir Geoffrey's best friend and closest neighbor, was walking to the house with two strangers, presumably Sir Geoffrey's sister-in-law and nephew. Why had they left the house without Sir Geoffrey so very early in the morning?

I stood at the door where they could see me, and wondered what I should say to them. A suspicious thought crossed my mind. Did they already know?

They were full of good humor. I hated to spoil their day.

Roland noticed me first. "Hello, Evie, did you bring us some of your wonderful treats?"

"I. . . Um, I'm afraid I have some bad news for you."

"Evie?" the woman chirped. "Oh, you must be the lady who bakes those delightful biscuits. My brother-in-law told me all about you."

"And you must be Daisy Guilfoyle, Sir Geoffrey's sister-in-law." She was waspishly thin and had the same nose-in-the-air accent, but her smile was warm.

"And this is my son, Freddy Guilfoyle," Daisy said.

"Call me Freddy," he said.

I half expected her to trot out all the titles associated with that name, but she didn't. Perhaps he didn't have any. He was a little bit younger than I'd expected, no more than ten years older than my Georgina, maybe less. Sir Geoffrey's nephew, yes, but born somewhat later in life.

"What is that awful smell?" When Freddy scrunched his nose, he reminded me very much of his uncle. The same Roman nose and eagle-eyed stare underneath the same pronounced brow. The features that made Sir Geoffrey appear distinguished served to make his nephew look petty and ill-natured.

I wondered if Freddy was now Sir Freddy. His own father had died years ago.

"Perhaps you're smelling the ocean. Geoff said it could be quite brackish," Daisy said.

Roland brushed past me and headed for the kitchen.

"Don't go in there."

My warning came too late, but at least he stopped at the door.

"It smells more of the hunt than of the sea, Mother." Freddy remained unaware of Roland's discovery.

Roland turned around, his face ashen. "Stay back. It's Geoff." He stared daggers at me. "You should have told us."

I didn't bother apologizing.

They almost trampled me and Roland in their rush to the kitchen. At least Daisy had the good sense to stop at the entrance. Freddy barged right in.

"Don't touch anything. The police are on their way."

Freddy's hands were already on the fishing spear. He tugged on it, then thought better of it. He bent and put his hand over Geoffrey's mouth.

"He's dead," I said. No one could have survived that kind of attack. But Freddy must have had a stronger stomach than I did. I couldn't bring myself to check his breath.

Daisy inched into the kitchen. I had to take charge before they trampled everything.

"Step away from your uncle's body, Freddy. The detective will be upset that you touched the spear."

"We can't just leave him like that!" Freddy said.

"I'm sure the police will do their job." Daisy eased her son away. She too stooped down but had the good sense not to touch the body. "Rest in peace, Geoffrey."

When she straightened up, she gave me an appraising look. "Are these local police any good?"

Roland sputtered, but her query didn't surprise me. Sir Geoffrey had asked the same question of me when Georgina got involved with the mayor's murder last year.

I gave her the answer I'd given him. "They're good at their jobs, but it takes time to get from here to there in coastal Maine. It's only two hundred miles from New Hampshire to Canada as the crow flies, but if you drive along every bend and curve of the land, it's more like two thousand." I paused. "My impression is that England's coastline is less convoluted."

Daisy nodded, and Freddy clasped his hands together. "Thank you for staying with my uncle, Ms., um, Holland. But you can leave since we are here now."

I wasn't ready to do that. The sergeant had told me to stay put.

Besides, my gut instinct told me that one of these three people was probably responsible for Sir Geoffrey's death. What if they started removing clues?

"The detective is expecting me. It's best if I stay."

I thought it strange that he asked me to leave but didn't seem to mind Roland's continued presence.

Roland scowled. "She won't leave the three of us here alone. She thinks one of us did it."

Every hair-sprayed-hard strand on Daisy's head bristled at Roland's statement. "Well, I never!"

Freddy grinned at me slyly. "Perhaps we are thinking the same thing about you. I suggest we wait in the living room, away from—this." He gestured to his uncle's body. "Did you say you brought more biscuits?" he asked hopefully.

Fair enough. "Perhaps we should save them for later. We wouldn't want to contaminate the scene any more than we already have."

Roland and I took our seats in the front room. Daisy went in search of the facilities, and Freddy excused himself to go out to their rental car. He returned with an open bag of chips. He popped one into his mouth. When he saw my frown, he shut his mouth and swallowed. "I'm sorry. When I'm nervous, I munch."

Daisy sobbed quietly into a tissue. Roland rose and left the room and returned a few moments later, checking the hallways and side doors. "I don't see Marshfield anywhere. Where is he?" he asked.

"He's outside. Didn't you see him when you came to the door?"

Roland shook his head. "Quiet."

Everyone stopped talking. He opened the door a crack. People in Sea Side said Roland can hear fish jumping in the water from a mile away.

As always, the crash of waves over the rocks and raucous calls of seagulls filled the air. I listened in vain for Marshfield's small snuffling sounds. Perhaps he was asleep.

Surprise lit Roland's face. "At least we don't have to wait much longer for the police. There's a car coming down the road. Hopefully it's them."

The patrol car arrived in the yard a couple of minutes later. Daisy and I both headed for the front door. She stopped me. "I'm the lady of the house. I should open the door."

I grabbed the knob seconds before she did. "But he's expecting me." I opened the door. The detective stood over Marshfield, who lay on the ground as still as death.

Chapter 3

The detective noticed me as soon as I opened the door. He said a few words to his sergeant before approaching me. Up close, I could see the detective was Tom Bennett, newly hired after the last murder. I'd wondered whom they would send.

"What's wrong with Marshfield?" I felt responsible because I had left him outside. I owed it to Sir Geoffrey to take care of his dog. "Is he—dead?"

Tom shook his head. "No, but he's weak. Like he was poisoned or sumpin'—"

Daisy came out on the porch. "I'm Daisy Guilfoyle, Sir Geoffrey's sister-in-law. You're here about his death, aren't you?"

She probably wondered why we were wasting time on a dog.

Tom nodded. "Don't worry about the dog. We'll get him the help he needs."

"And get his stomach contents analyzed," I said. "In case it's connected."

We went back into the house and joined Roland and Freddy, who had taken advantage of my absence to return to the kitchen.

"Mahnin', Mistah Whitakah." Tom's gaze swept every detail of Roland's attire, as if assessing where he'd been and exactly what he'd been doing all morning. "And you ah?" He turned his attention to Freddy.

Before Freddy could say anything, Roland burst out with, "He's the doggone fool who touched the spear when we found Geoffrey like this."

Freddy glared at him. "I am Lord Frederick Guilfoyle, Baron

of Durrow," he said to no one in particular. He smiled as if the title pleased him.

Sir Geoffrey had never introduced himself with all the tags, although he didn't complain when we used them.

Tom ignored the introduction to concentrate on the body. Without breaking his concentration, he said, "I've worked with the Mounties from up north a time or two. They say their law is similar to British law. They would frown on touching things at the crime scene."

After writing in his notebook, he looked directly at Freddy. "You have done your uncle a great disservice by disturbing the crime scene."

"I didn't want to leave him like that," Freddy said.

Another car approached. "That's probably the coroner." Tom tucked his notebook in his shirt pocket. "All right, everyone, return to the living room. My sergeant will sit with you until we're ready to question you."

Freddy sputtered, where his uncle would have held his head high, perhaps answered with a cutting comment. I missed Sir Geoffrey intensely in that moment.

I let the men go ahead of me—to guide them in case they got "lost." Of course Roland knew the house, but he might want to wander off.

Tom placed a hand on my shoulder before I left the kitchen. "I'm sorry to ask you to stay as well, but since you discovered the body. . ."

Yes, I understood. Wasn't the person who discovered the body automatically a suspect? I shuddered at the thought. At the first hint of suspicion, I would call my lawyer.

During tense times, I like to feed people. I decided to ask for permission. "I left breakfast treats in the pantry when I arrived this morning. Do you mind if I bring them out for everyone?"

He chewed on it for a moment. "Since you brought them with you, they're not technically a part of the murder scene." He walked into the pantry and came out with an open box. He was frowning. "How many items were here?"

"A baker's dozen—thirteen. Six hot cross buns, two scones, and five donuts."

He shook his head. "There's only eleven now."

"Let me see."

He set the box on the table. Two of the hot cross buns were missing. I could see the sugary imprint of where they'd been. "I guess someone discovered the box and helped themselves," the detective said.

I wished it was that simple, but an ugly thought occurred to me. "Tell me, did the dog vomit anything?"

Tom looked at me curiously. "I doubt there was much left in his stomach."

"Tell the vet that he probably ingested several raisins." I explained how the raisins had made Marshfield sick at the tea shoppe yesterday. "I would guess someone fed two buns to the dog. That was downright cruel if they knew how sick the raisins would make him."

He closed the box and set it back in the pantry. "I'll hold on to the box for now." He peered at me. "We'll need everyone's fingerprints. My sergeant will get them when he finishes with the dog."

I hated to think of the many things we had touched, one way or another, that morning. And of course we'd all been there before. That reminded me of something. "Our delivery person also cleans here once a week. She did a special cleaning yesterday, in preparation for the arrival of Sir Geoffrey's family. Any prints should be relatively new."

"A detailed cleaning, then."

"Oh yes. Sir Geoffrey wouldn't be—wouldn't have been—satisfied. . ." I broke down. "I can't believe he's dead."

Tom gave me a moment to regain my composure before he asked how to contact our delivery driver.

"Phoebe Oberlin." I looked up her number on my cell and showed it to him while he made a note.

Apparently the age of electronics hadn't taken over the need for handwritten notes. He tucked the notebook away. "You may join the others. Only—don't mention the buns or the cleaning yesterday."

I wouldn't talk about it with Roland or either of the Guilfoyles. I just might talk things over with Georgina when I got home. She would probably insist that I call in her fiancé, Mathew, the pastor of our church. Like it or not, our tea shoppe was once again embroiled in a murder.

How should we handle it? Last year's mystery had given our little shop a certain amount of notoriety and increased business. Two murders, on the other hand, could seem like bad luck.

Oh, for the freedom to make a phone call. To go home! I hoped Georgina's experience helped her understand the situation.

"Why did he keep you so long?" Freddy demanded when I returned to the living room. "What were you talking about?"

Roland took a long look at me. "You won't get her to spill secrets." He laughed. "Some eateries are known as gossip central. And you can generally get the pulse of Sea Side at the Tea by the Sea." He put a finger to the side of his nose. "But no one is better at keeping secrets than Evie here. I've told her some of my secrets that she's never repeated to anyone else." He paused for effect. "And that was thirty-five years ago."

My mind went blank for a minute. Thirty-five years ago, the tea shoppe was a new business that took every ounce of my time and mind and energy. Roland was a teenager working on his first job on a fishing boat, the career path he'd eventually followed. At the end of the day, he would stop by and ask for any leftover donuts for half price. I gave him what I could. I didn't have a son of my own, just two daughters.

And he had a helpless crush on Georgina's mother. She didn't give him the time of day. She'd already met her future husband. The memory brought a smile to my face. "I think things worked out for the best, don't you?"

He winked, and his smile grew wider. "See what I mean? Even now she doesn't reveal my secrets." He grew serious. "With all sincerity, I say, I wouldn't be the man I am today without Evie Holland."

I was touched. "Those were rough times for both of us," I told him. "Made me feel good to think at least one teenager wanted to hear my wisdom. My daughter was out searching for her own way."

"This sounds like Sea Side's version of *The Young and the Restless*," Freddy drawled. "What's next, a May-December affair?"

I snapped around but managed to control my tongue. I had no reason to defend myself against bad manners.

Roland laughed it off. "May-December? You think I was interested in Evie?" At least he wasn't offended. "No, I was interested in her daughter, who wanted nothing to do with me. It's a good thing too, or else I never would have married my Maggie."

"Freddy can't object to May-December romances," Daisy said comfortably. "I was fifteen years younger than his father."

Daisy's words reminded me of something Sir Geoffrey had told me, but I couldn't chase it down. Maybe it would come back to me later.

Freddy shrugged. "Enough about old times, Mother. I want to know what the detective said to Ms. Holland."

Someone knocked on the door. I jumped up to answer it before Daisy could. Two technicians stood there. They'd come from the only lab in a ten-mile radius that performed forensics when needed. I recognized them but couldn't remember their names.

"Mrs. Guilfoyle?" the young man around Georgina's age asked.

"That's Mrs. Holland, from Tea by the Sea." His companion was a middle-aged woman of Vietnamese descent. "She found the body." She turned to me. "Where is Detective Bennett?"

"Down the hallway, in the kitchen." I pointed the way.

They carried forensics kits with them. I shuddered, glad I didn't have to dig into the muck of death.

Freddy followed them but was turned back.

No one said anything for a few minutes. Roland stood by the window, watching what was going on outside. When another car approached, he announced, "The vet's here to look at the dog."

I joined Roland at the window. Marshfield had been Sir Geoffrey's pride and joy. I drew a sigh of relief when he wobbled to his feet to greet the newcomer. I recognized the vet, Dr. Stetson. He loaded Marshfield into the back of his van before speaking with the officer for several minutes.

"Bet you're wishing you could eavesdrop on their conversation," Roland said.

"Am I that obvious?" I was a little embarrassed.

"It has to be related to Sir Geoffrey's death."

The police officer backed away from the van, and Dr. Stetson took off. Then the officer grabbed a small black bag from the back of the patrol car and headed toward us.

Fingerprint time, I'd guess.

Once again I opened the door.

He apologized for how late it was getting. "You must be eager to go home."

Not really. If I was at home, I'd be worrying about Sir Geoffrey and wondering what was happening. At least this way I had a chance to help.

CHAPTER 4

The sergeant took our prints, ignoring Daisy's protests.

"Be quiet, Mother." Freddy proffered his fingers willingly. "We want Uncle Geoffrey's murderer to be brought to justice."

If he was the murderer, he was doing a good job of playing innocent.

Tom called me in right after they took my fingerprints. I was a little nervous, but he only asked me a few routine questions about my arrival. What had I touched and observed, that kind of thing. Then he dismissed me. "I'm sure your tea shoppe needs you. I'll be in touch if we have any more questions."

I was almost disappointed that he didn't tell me to stay in town. It was as if he didn't think me capable of murder.

Well, I didn't think I could murder anyone. But they say everyone is capable of murder if pushed hard enough. Not many things get me angry nowadays though. Irritated? Frequently, almost every time Sir Geoffrey brought Marshfield to the tea shoppe. Hostile anger? No.

Tom instructed me to leave by the back door—so I couldn't report to the others, I supposed. I sat behind the wheel of my car, feeling the weight of the morning's events. Georgina needed me at the tea shoppe, but first I wanted to check on Marshfield.

Fortunately, Dr. Stetson's clinic was on the way back to the tea shoppe, more or less.

"Evie, this is an unexpected surprise." Anne Stetson, the vet's wife, worked as his receptionist and assistant. Her face grew somber. "I heard about Sir Geoffrey. What a terrible thing to happen."

I plopped into a chair.

"My goodness, you're shaking." She disappeared into a side room and reappeared with a cup of coffee and some crackers. "This should perk you up. I could offer you something sweet, but. . ."

I shook my head. The crispy, salty cracker did help settle the acid I didn't realize had been building in my stomach.

Once Anne was satisfied I was better, she asked, "What brought you here, Evie? Are you ready to adopt another dog? We have three young pups at present."

"Not yet." I shook my head. "I was worried about Marshfield, Sir Geoffrey's dog."

"That poor thing's in mourning. His master died—and dogs can tell."

I nodded. I knew exactly what she meant. "But what upset his stomach?"

Her expression told me what I wanted to know.

"He ate the raisins in my hot cross buns." I made it a statement.

"He ate several." A smile replaced the frown on her face. "The good news is he should make a full recovery. My husband was able to pump out all the stomach contents that were left."

She glanced at me. "You do know that raisins are poisonous to dogs, don't you?"

I stamped down my annoyance at the question. I already felt guilty enough for Marshfield's illness. I started to tell her someone else had given the dog the buns on purpose. But the detective had told me to keep my mouth shut.

Instead, I simply said, "I know." I sighed. "And I had certainly warned Sir Geoffrey plenty of times." I left my comments at that. "I'm so glad to hear he'll make a full recovery."

"We're lucky we got to him in time," Anne said. "If the affected dog isn't treated within the first ninety minutes, poisoning can be fatal."

Ninety minutes. My mind started reeling. "And the dog got here, when?"

"About nine fifteen."

That means he must have eaten the buns around eight. Either Roland, Daisy, or Freddy must have fed the buns to the dog. No one else was in the house.

And it seemed logical that the dog poisoner was also the murderer.

Anne's voice interrupted my thoughts. "Marshfield should be well enough to leave in a couple of days. Only, do you know who's going to take him in?"

My nose wrinkled while I thought about it. "I have no idea. Someone as thoughtful as Sir Geoffrey may have included provisions in his will."

She made a snuffling sound that suggested she was about to make a request of me, a request I wouldn't welcome. I swallowed past my frustration. "What is it?"

"They may not finish the probate for several weeks. I'd hate to see Marshfield stuffed in a kennel for that long."

I put all my mental energy into discouraging her from making the request she was about to voice. "I expect Daisy and Freddy— that's Sir Geoffrey's nephew, who inherited his title—will be here until after probate is completed."

Anne shook her head. "But Marshfield doesn't know them. He knows you. He trusts you. You're his friend who brings him tasty treats."

It was inevitable. "The tea shoppe is a dangerous place for a dog," I reminded her.

"I'm sure you'll figure something out." She smiled brightly, taking my agreement for granted. "So that's settled, then. I'll let you know as soon as we can release Marshfield."

Georgina would have something to say about it. Speaking of my granddaughter, I decided to head home before any more time passed. I wasn't in charge of daily operations at the tea shoppe anymore, but I'd missed the entire breakfast service—an innovation Georgina had introduced—and by now they were involved in lunch prep.

A dented white car followed me when I left the clinic. When I looked in the rearview mirror, I thought I spotted the sergeant who was working with Tom Bennett. Had the detective sent someone to keep an eye on me? And why was that?

Was I under suspicion? A tremor passed through my body. I told myself not to be silly. I hadn't done anything wrong.

The person who discovered the body fell under suspicion. Mystery Fiction 101, right after, "Look at the spouse first."

Since Sir Geoffrey had no spouse, that left me, the one who discovered the body, with a big target on my back.

The white car didn't stay on my tail. Perhaps we were just headed to the same place—the tea shoppe. Except, why would he go there? What connection did he suspect between us and Sir Geoffrey's murder?

While I was debating the question, the sergeant passed me right before we made the final turn to my road and raced ahead of me, exceeding the speed limit in the process.

I puzzled over his behavior until I arrived at the tea shoppe about ten minutes later. The white car was in the parking lot.

Was Georgina in trouble? I hurried to the shop.

I could hear Georgina from the entrance. She ran her words

together, and her tone was nearly a shout. Compared to her, the sergeant was practically whispering.

Georgina stood a few feet away from him. "I told you nothing happened. Gran did nothing wrong."

I stayed outside the door where I could listen without being seen.

"How do you explain the accounts I heard, then?" The pages of a notebook riffled. The sergeant consulted his notes. "This is the second time this week Sir Geoffrey's dog got sick from eating something your grandmother baked."

I could imagine Georgina's eyes bulging. "But that was just an accident!"

"An accident Sir Geoffrey blamed Mrs. Holland for. His exact words were, 'Maybe we should ask Miss Evie to bake pet-friendly treats.'"

Too bad Mathew wasn't there. He would have helped Georgina calm down. It was time for me to make my presence known. I rattled the doorknob and walked in.

"Mrs. Holland." The officer acted as though he'd been expecting me. "I thought you would be here when I arrived, since you left before I did."

"I went to check on Marshfield—that's the dog you're accusing me of poisoning. He's recovering nicely, thank God." The sergeant's badge read E. JENNER. Ethan? No, Enos. I pulled the name from my memory.

I had checked on Marshfield out of genuine concern, but in the present circumstances it probably made me look guilty. I couldn't admit that I felt responsible for his illness. I'd be making Enos's argument for him.

Instead, I redirected the conversation by blurting what I had just learned about the dog. "Marshfield will be my guest for the time being, at least until the will is read."

I was certain Sir Geoffrey had made arrangements for his dog, not because he'd told me, but because he was that kind of person.

Enos shook his head as if it didn't matter. "Since you knew the dog was allergic to these"—he consulted his notes—"sultanas, why did you put them where he could reach them this morning?"

My irritation stepped up, and I reminded myself not to get agitated in the same way Georgina had. "I didn't. I put them on the top shelf of the pantry, where that little bulldog couldn't reach. The box was sealed, but of course a determined dog could take care of that."

He wrote everything down. "When was that?"

"As soon as I entered the house. About 7:15 this morning."

Enos frowned at his notes. "The box was found at 8:32 this morning, on the countertop in the pantry, open, with two of the buns missing. How do you explain that?"

Suddenly I felt like laughing. I was old enough to be his grandma, and he was playing one of my own tricks on me. I relaxed. I'd have batted my eyelashes if they were long enough. "I would guess that the murderer fed them to the dog, wouldn't you? I know you checked out fingerprints. Check out who else's fingerprints are on the box." I couldn't resist a final sentence. "Except for Detective Bennett's, of course. I doubt you suspect him."

Enos looked at me for a few long seconds. "As a matter of fact, we have. And there were only two sets of fingerprints on the box. Yours and Bennett's."

I managed to keep my composure—just barely. Of course it was too easy. "They could have worn gloves."

"That's one possibility." Enos nodded. "But often we find the most obvious solution is the correct one."

Georgina had had enough. "You're as good as accusing my grandmother of harming that dratted dog, and maybe Sir Geoffrey as well. I'm calling a lawyer."

Enos cocked his head. "I'm following the line of evidence, ma'am."

Keep your temper, Evie, I reminded myself. "Sergeant, I'm not going to answer any more questions unless I have a lawyer present."

"That's your right." He made a few notes in his notebook and tucked it back in his belt. I wished I had Supergirl's vision so I could read what he'd written about me. "I was about finished anyhow." He snapped his hat on his head.

"You might want to drive the speed limit on the way back," I called after him as he left the tea shoppe. "It would be too bad if you were caught speeding."

"What was that about?" Georgina asked.

"How long was Enos here before I arrived?"

"Five minutes, thereabouts."

I explained about seeing him on the road. "What did he say before I arrived?"

Georgina shuffled her feet. "He was asking me if you'd had any arguments with Sir Geoffrey. I just said you'd asked him to leave his dog at home. That was before I knew someone had fed the poor thing more of the hot cross buns." She hugged me. "Oh Gran, surely he doesn't think you killed Sir Geoffrey?"

"Of course not." But beneath my reassuring words, I knew something was wrong.

CHAPTER 5

Our server popped her head in the door at that moment. "We have people ready to order lunch."

Georgina looked at me, distraught. "We're not done talking about this. Please promise to stay nearby until we've had a chance to talk things over with Mathew."

"Mm-hmm," I grunted noncommittally. Mathew had helped Georgina when she came under suspicion of murder last Christmas, and they had fallen in love. A month ago they had become engaged, and my granddaughter was still dewy-eyed.

But I was used to acting on my own, and I didn't know how long I could stay. That depended on the phone call I had to make. I wanted to get my lawyer's advice before I spoke with the police again.

I dialed the number for Paul Tuttle and Associates. To date, his associate consisted of his daughter, Meg.

Wait a minute. Meg was now Mrs. Jenner, married to Enos the police officer. I closed my eyes in frustration. The Tuttles were Sea Side's only lawyers.

I told myself not to worry. They must have dealt with this issue before, about her office representing someone her husband had arrested. I usually worked with her father, in any case. He would steer me to someone else if necessary.

In addition to my own problem, I also wanted to ask about the dog. I had to make sure Paul knew Sir Geoffrey was dead, although I suspected by now everyone in Sea Side, maybe even in the entire county, had heard the news. But maybe not. For the most part, the people of Maine respect the privacy of the famous literati and artists who make their home in our state.

Besides, Sir Geoffrey was most definitely *not* "from" Sea Side. He technically wasn't even an American. A person has to be born to a local family to claim he or she is from the town. Even Georgina, who was born when her parents were in college, is from "away."

I felt a sting of sympathy for Sir Geoffrey. He never really belonged to Sea Side, although we loved having him. But he'd been gone from England so long he didn't belong there either. Meeting Daisy and Freddy had made me aware of how very American he had become during his stay in our small town.

Stop daydreaming, Evie. The police wouldn't speculate on how Sir Geoffrey felt about his adopted home. Even if they did, it wouldn't be for the same reasons. I dialed my lawyer.

A minute later I was speaking with Paul. "I'm sure you know that Sir Geoffrey Guilfoyle died this morning. Murdered, in fact, from all appearances."

A faint chuckle whispered down the line. "I know. You found the body."

"That's part of the reason I called." I plunged ahead. "Enos Jenner was just here—"

"My son-in-law?"

"Yes. He pretty much accused me of poisoning Marshfield—Sir Geoffrey's dog, you know—on purpose. I want a lawyer with me the next time I speak with the police." I paused. "Is there a conflict of interest, since he's your son-in-law?"

"I have no problem representing you in the matter." I could hear the smile in his voice. "But, Evie, is the poisoning of the dog connected with Sir Geoffrey's murder?"

"It may be." I started to explain but decided to wait until we met face-to-face.

"That might be a different matter. I haven't handled many murder cases." He hummed to himself. "Come to my office right after lunch, by one o'clock, and don't talk with anyone about the dog." His voice was stern enough to scare me.

"Yes, sir." I had one more thing to ask him. "My other question is also about the dog—"

"Save it." He hung up abruptly.

He was right. I just thought he might like to look up the answer before I arrived.

I checked the clock. Georgina would be busy cooking lunch. I thought about offering my help. Business would be brisk today.

But people would ask questions, and I wasn't willing to talk about what had happened. A wearied grief had settled on me. I wanted nothing more than to rest in my recliner until I left for Paul's office.

Georgina came upstairs about half an hour later with Mathew in tow. She brought my favorite lunch, a cranberry-turkey salad sandwich on oatmeal bread, with a broccoli salad and an indulgent orange muffin. "I figured you must be hungry."

I hadn't planned on eating, but when I bit into the sandwich, I discovered I was ravenous. To my surprise, Georgina stayed with me while I ate.

"I prepared cold-plate specials for our lunch service. If they need me for something, they know where to find me." She gave me a fierce hug. "Are you all right, Gran? That must have been a shock, discovering the body."

I expected her words to trigger tremors, but I remained calm. "I'm much better, after that wonderful lunch. You take good care of me." I patted her hand. "I'll be leaving in a few minutes to see my lawyer."

"Your lawyer?" Mathew joined the conversation. "Is it that serious?"

I didn't want to worry them. "Anne Stetson asked if we would take care of Marshfield until we learn if Sir Geoffrey made arrangements for his care." I shrugged. "I guess no one's come forward to take him off their hands."

Mathew chuckled.

Georgina's reaction held no humor. "Oh Gran, no! How can we bake with him around?"

I squirmed. "We'll figure it out. I'm sure he can learn how to behave, with the right teacher. He's a pretty smart dog." I hoped. I glanced at the clock. "Paul wants me there at one. I'd better get going."

I hugged my granddaughter. "After that lunch, I'm ready to take on the world."

She rose to her feet. "Let us come with you."

I shook my head. "You have to keep the shop open. And Mathew, I know you need to get everything settled before you leave for that pastor's conference after our services this weekend." They would protest if I explained I wanted to protect her from the sordid mess. She'd felt the same way about me during her scuffle a few months ago.

I arrived at the Tuttle Law Office with one minute to spare, and Paul saw me in his office right away. "Thank you for coming so promptly. I planned on calling this afternoon, but you called me first."

My insides churned at his words.

"I'm in charge of Sir Geoffrey's American estate. I'm glad his family is in town."

I nodded. "They were staying at Sir Geoffrey's house. I don't know where they are now." I paused for a moment. "You said you were going to call me?"

Paul's expression grew serious. "Ah, yes. Sir Geoffrey made some rather—unusual—provisions in his will. I told him he should warn you, but he said he would let it be a surprise when the time came." A faint smile played around his lips. "I think he expected to outlive you."

The odds were I would have outlived Sir Geoffrey in any case, because women live longer than men. Even so, he was physically fit for a man of our years and not in any imminent danger of death.

In the end, it hadn't taken much to end his life. Only a six-foot fishing spear.

I swallowed the gulp in my throat. "He promised me his recipes."

"He did, did he?" Paul smiled. "I expect they're in his desk."

That didn't do me any good. I couldn't just waltz in and grab something, even something as innocent as recipes, without the permission of the new owner.

"You should see the expression on your face. I'm teasing you." Paul's grin gave way to a chuckle. "Not to worry. You see, *you're* the new owner of Sir Geoffrey's house and everything in it. He considered you a good friend, and he trusted your judgment in handling his affairs."

I must have misunderstood him. "Are you saying I'm his executor?"

"That duty falls to me. I repeat: you're his heir. He left you his house, his dog, his money, everything he had invested in America. There's a lawyer in England handling his other affairs. I have contacted her to let her know of Sir Geoffrey's death."

"I can't believe it."

"Believe it." He nodded. "He specifically directed you to—let me read it exactly as he worded it." He ran his finger down the will in front of him. "'Tell her to keep my dog in healthy teas and cakes and use the money to enjoy herself.'" He looked up at me. "I suggested he set up a fund to take care of the dog, but he insisted that all his funds be left to your discretion. He trusted you with his dearest companion."

My thoughts tumbled around like a spinning dryer, too fast for me to catch more than a glimpse of any one thing.

He was saying something about making arrangements with the bank when I blurted out, "Now they'll have even more reason to suspect me."

"But you just now learned the provisions of the will." He grew serious. "Or else you're an even better actress than I thought."

I shook my head. "Here I was, coming to you today, hoping you could tell me who Sir Geoffrey wanted to take care of his dog. I promised the vet I would look after him until we found out." Was it possible they knew Sir Geoffrey's intentions?

Paul must have sensed my uneasiness about the project. "Among the provisions of the will, Sir Geoffrey had plans developed to build a kennel next to Tea by the Sea, which he has already paid for. He knew the dog would need a place to roam freely when you're working."

Bless Sir Geoffrey.

"I'll have the contractors contact you to set up a schedule as soon as possible."

"Thank you."

"Tell me about your conversation with Enos."

At least Paul didn't call him "my son-in-law" in this context.

I gave it to him, verbatim.

"No other fingerprints." He stroked his chin. "Someone must have worn gloves." He wrote on his pad. "Did any of them leave the group?"

"We all did, at one time or another." I closed my eyes to recapture the scene. Nothing remarkable. "No one was gone for more than a couple of minutes."

Paul tapped his notepad. "We'll check out the possibilities."

His eyes focused inward as if he was drawing the house and calculating routes and timing. He blinked. "I'm assuming none of them has any disability that would prevent them from moving around at normal speed."

"Not that I noticed. But we didn't walk about much. Of course we both know Roland. He might move better on the open sea, but he's as fit as a fiddle, as they say."

"The Guilfoyles will probably want to see me about Sir Geoffrey's estate. We can compare our observations."

In all the detective shows I have watched, no one worries about a suspect's disabilities unless there is some indication of it at the crime scene. Didn't they mostly concern themselves with forensic details like how tall the killer must be, whether or not they are right-handed or left-handed, that sort of thing? That made me think. "Do you think they'd be able to calculate the height of the killer from the angle of the spear?"

Paul blinked. "Probably. But only if he was killed while both he and his killer were standing."

I thought some more. "Maybe forensics can figure out the killer's height from the length of the spear and the angle of the wound."

Paul smiled faintly. "We need to do some detective work ourselves, in case forensics doesn't give us any help. Tell me more about your argument with Geoffrey over the dog at the tea shoppe."

The incident at Tea by the Sea felt like a dozen days ago. Just the day before, Sir Geoffrey had complained I'd had hot cross buns within reach of Marshfield. As I repeated the conversation, I realized how petty I sounded. "We'd had the discussion many times before. Sir Geoffrey left the dog outside yesterday, but Marshfield came in when someone opened the door." The memory stirred up the same irritation. "I'm sorry, Paul, but it's unreasonable for anyone to operate a bakery without chocolate and raisins and other foods harmful to animals. Sir Geoffrey should have left Marshfield in the car."

Paul raised his eyebrows. "Or Sir Geoffrey should have trained his dog better, like service dogs. I agree with you, but you should avoid stating your opinion so openly for the time being." He shrugged. "It makes you sound angry and spiteful."

I crimped my lips shut.

"I know you are speaking as a responsible business owner who likes the dog. Or at least Sir Geoffrey thought well of you, and how you felt about Marshfield. Enough to trust him to your care."

I thought of Odie, my faithful canine companion until his death five years ago. Sir Geoffrey and I used to take Odie and Marshfield on walks together, and Sir Geoffrey was a friend when poor Odie died. I felt partly responsible for Marshfield's misbehavior. Because I gave him dog-friendly treats on our walks, he decided anything from my hand must be fair game.

"What's on your mind?"

I looked up. "Every person who steps into the tea shoppe over the next few days will want a piece of me."

Paul tapped his pen on his blotter. "Do you want my advice?"

"That's what I'm paying you for." I opened my hands. "But I can't afford to go away on a trip, even if Enos will let me."

He leaned forward. "Far from it. I suggest you stay right at the tea shoppe where you belong. Let people see you. Tell them how much Sir Geoffrey liked your hot cross buns. Let it slip, without telling the story, that Marshfield loved them too. Make it humorous."

He grew serious. "I know you'd rather go home and hide, but you have it in you to act like nothing's troubling you. You might even throw a welcome party for Marshfield when he goes home with you. When people see the two of you are in fact good friends, they won't suspect you of holding a grudge."

It was an excellent suggestion, even if all I wanted was a chance to mourn my friend in private. But I'd always intended the tea shoppe to be a place for our community to support each other. It was my turn to depend on them. There was no room for a stiff upper lip in my profession.

"I'll let you know when I bring Marshfield home."

"If Enos wants to see you again, call me straightaway. In the meantime, don't worry. You above all people know that your neighbors will make up their minds for themselves. They'll judge you on all the decades of your life, and not on the past couple of days."

I relaxed and stood. "Thank you. I feel much better than when I came in."

"I'll add my psychiatrist's bill to my legal fees," he said with a smile.

CHAPTER 6

The more I thought about what my lawyer said, the more I realized he was right. I not only wanted to remind people of who I was, but maybe I could also learn more about the others, Roland especially. I knew Roland, sure, but we hadn't remained close. That long ago summer was years in the past—a lifetime ago—Georgina's lifetime.

I spent time in the tea shoppe that afternoon and told our guests that soon we would have a new mascot. The contractors showed up the very next day, even though it was a weekend. I loved their plans for the kennel and gave them an immediate go-ahead. They promised to finish the kennel by the end of the week.

By Monday Marshfield had recovered enough to leave the vet. When Anne called, she asked, "Have you learned who will be taking care of Marshfield?"

I debated with myself. Loose lips sink ships and all that, but our vet keeps his patients' confidentiality as seriously as any people doctors. I decided to tell her some of the details I hadn't told the folks at the tea shoppe.

"Um, yes. It's me."

She laughed. "I wondered if that was the case. Sir Geoffrey asked my husband's opinion about it a while back. He gave you a glowing recommendation."

"Please don't tell anyone. They'll guess soon enough."

"I won't."

"I'll come by for him tomorrow morning." I wanted one last night of uninterrupted sleep. I wasn't sure how Marshfield would respond to the change in scenery, or if I could teach control inside our shop. Odie had been perfectly behaved, but I had trained him as a puppy. Marshfield was a different matter.

I worked with Georgina Tuesday on the early morning shift before I went to the vet's office. She was lonely with Mathew out of town for the week. The sea traffic alone makes it worth our while to open the shop at five in the spring. We fixed coffee to serve with the previous day's leftovers while we continued baking for the day.

Two of our regulars, a pair of fishermen, called "Short" and "Long" both because of their given names and because of their natures, came in before dawn. They asked for day-old doughnuts and filled their thermoses with our best blend of coffee.

Jacob Short said, "We'd best get to our boat before the patrol wants to take a look."

"Ayuh," Caleb Long said.

"Why? What's going on?" Their words set an alarm bell off in my head.

"Word has it that they're pumping the boats to figure out who's selling contaminated fish for pet food," Short said.

"Beware," Long said. "For Marshfield."

Of course they knew about the dog.

I thought about their warning when I went to the store on the way to pick up Marshfield. I hadn't bought dog food in years. A gap appeared on the shelves where the Sealife pet food normally stood. In fact, I saw that the creator of Sealife, Leah Packer, was in the process of removing the product from the shelves. As a local brand featuring the best of Maine seafood, Sealife was a favorite of many locals for their pets. Sad as I was to see the problem, I wouldn't take a chance with Marshfield. I reached for a package of food that contained no fish parts. "What's up with the Sealife products?"

Leah swept her eyes over the items in my shopping basket.

Collar, new tags, leash, bowls, and a big bag of food. "Oh, have you adopted another puppy?"

"Something like that." If she didn't make the connection with Sir Geoffrey's death, I wouldn't tell her. "I used to give my old dog Sealife all the time. Has the company had to go out of business?"

"Not yet, but we've hit a rough patch." She packed another bag into the disposal cart. "Although the police say they're close to arresting the person responsible for the damage." She lowered her voice. "I would avoid any dog food with shellfish in it for now. They don't know how far the problem has spread."

When I got to the vet's office, Marshfield's foot thumped in time to his wagging tail. He placed his right front paw on my knee and barked.

My heart melted. "It's like he's asking me where Sir Geoffrey is. He must be lonely." I bent over and rubbed his head, tugging at his ears the way I had seen my friend do so many times. He accepted the caress, then moved away from me and barked again.

Anne and I looked at each other. I brought my face closer to the dog's. "Your master's gone, and you can't go with him." Oh, if only circumstances were better and I had something of Sir Geoffrey's that I could give to Marshfield for a familiar scent to reassure him.

I decided to see my lawyer again. I wanted to ask when I could get into Neptune Cottage, Sir Geoffrey's house. Since we had decided talking on the phone might not be wise, I drove straight to his office.

Paul was able to see me right away, "I have a few minutes. What's up?"

I explained that I wanted to get something of Sir Geoffrey's to cheer up the dog.

"Wait until tomorrow. I have an appointment with the Guilfoyles this afternoon, when I will inform them about your inheritance. I'll tell them you have full access to the house."

"Good. I'll go over in the morning."

"I'll tell them to expect you."

I asked him if he had heard anything about the Sealife pet food recall, but he hadn't. After we left the office, we stopped for a walk along a deserted stretch of rocks. Marshfield chased about, barking at seagulls overhead and chasing the spray of the ocean waves hitting on the rocks. I wondered if he remembered doing the same with Odie.

As the older dog, Odie had taught Marshfield how to taunt the seagulls and how to make a game of escaping the sea waves. Sir Geoffrey and I spent hours watching them, becoming good friends in the process.

After Odie died, it hurt too much to go on the walks anymore, although Sir Geoffrey invited me. Now I had lost both of them.

Eventually Marshfield grew tired and sat beside me, whimpering as he put his head in my lap. "I miss them too," I told him. Perhaps I should adopt a puppy as a companion for my new dog. I wasn't sure I could give two dogs the time and attention they craved, but they could keep each other company.

That decision could wait. Until Marshfield had switched his allegiance to me, he needed to know he was my number one dog.

He sniffed around my car, perhaps smelling the bread I baked daily. I gave him one of my pet-friendly treats and made a note to bake more. Lots more. I wanted him to learn that if he was patient, he would get one of these delicious-and-good-for-him treats. I aimed to discourage him from jumping on the nearest tray of cookies and crumpets.

Back at the tea shoppe, I attached the new leash to his collar. He strained toward the front entrance, but I kept him on a short leash and led him around to the back entrance, where we climbed the stairs to my apartment. I set out a bowl with water and a second one with his dry food. He sniffed and looked daggers at me. Why was I giving him such ordinary, bland food when I made such delicious treats?

"Suit yourself." He wouldn't starve anytime soon. He'd come around when he was hungry. Because Georgina and I had settled on our spring menu, I didn't have to try any new recipes for a few weeks. By then Marshfield's behavior would have improved. If not, the kennel would be there.

I fixed myself a simple lunch. Although Marshfield begged, I didn't feed him anything. Nobody wants a dog bothering them while they eat.

I heard footsteps coming up the outside stairs. Marshfield raised his head and growled. I put the leash on him and walked to the door.

Daisy and Freddy Guilfoyle waited on the other side. Their smiles disappeared when Marshfield barked at them. Daisy's face folded into a frown.

"It's okay," I told the dog. "They won't hurt you." Not while I was there. With one hand holding tight to the leash, I opened the door to my unexpected guests. "I didn't know you knew where I lived."

"We asked around at the tea shoppe," Freddy said.

They came in, and Freddy walked around the room as if I was under inspection.

My apartment is a converted attic. My bedroom is in one corner, where I can look over the ocean. I have windows on every outer wall, including the alcoves under the eaves.

After our daughters left home, my husband and I stayed in our house. But after his death, I didn't want to rattle around the empty house. An apartment with a room overlooking the ocean sounded ideal, and I had the space remodeled. Not everyone would be comfortable with such tight spaces, but I love it.

Neither Guilfoyle spoke, and I wondered about the reason for their visit. "Can I get you something?" No need to bring up the hot cross buns. "I have some maple nut scones, combining New World flavors with an English treat. Fresh coffee, to boot, or I can brew tea."

Daisy sat down primly on my loveseat. "That won't be necessary. This isn't a social call."

Well, la-di-da, although it didn't surprise me. I settled in my armchair, and Freddy sat next to his mother. He spoke first. "We saw Dr. Stetson today. He told us about Uncle Geoff's arrangements for the dog."

Marshfield snuffled as if he knew he was the topic of conversation. I fed him a doggy biscuit to keep him satisfied. "It came as a total shock to me. I had no idea."

Daisy sniffed as if she didn't believe it. "That seems unnatural. Geoff was so protective of his dog."

"I've had experience." I left it at that. I didn't need to justify myself to her.

Freddy laughed outright. "Then why did you get so upset when Marshfield ate the hot cross bun? Dogs do things like that all the time."

"Do you intend to punish him every time he sneaks something from your pantry?" Daisy persisted. "I understand you do a lot of baking."

"That won't be a problem. I'll train him to behave himself, sans physical punishment. When necessary, we'll have a kennel."

I patted Marshfield's head, and he groaned with pleasure. "We're friends, aren't we?"

He laid his head on my feet on cue.

"We should have brought the dog food with us," Daisy said.

I opened my mouth to remind them I had keys to the house but decided against mentioning it.

Freddy chuckled. "Remember, Mother, Mrs. Holland can come and go as she pleases."

Both of them looked at me as if daring me to disagree.

"I appreciate the offer. But since you mention it. . ." A better opportunity was unlikely to appear. "I would like to take an inventory of the house as soon as possible."

All traces of good humor fled Daisy's face. "Isn't there a law against profiting from the death of the victim?"

Marshfield barked. I crossed the room and opened the door.

CHAPTER 7

When they didn't move, Marshfield barked again. I hushed him. I didn't want rumors floating around downstairs about an argument with the Guilfoyles.

"Very well. If you insist, I'll take my leave." Daisy stood. "I came with an olive branch. I thought you might be interested in this." She handed me a small padded envelope marked PET FOOD RESEARCH. "Geoff mentioned in passing that he was close to revealing the fishermen involved in the tainted pet food. I suspect this flash drive holds that information, although I haven't looked at it."

I reached out but then pulled back. "As much as I want to see it, the police should have it."

"Oh, I've already given it to them. But I made two copies. One for us, and one for you." She paused. "My brother-in-law obviously thought highly of you. He'd want you to know about this so you can take better care of his dog."

Those unexpected words put her past rudeness out of mind. Almost.

At the door, she said, "I doubt we'll ever be close, but Geoff trusted you. I decided to take a risk."

Freddy followed. "Thanks for the visit." His handshake was as limp as an eel's. It was like grasping a flopping fish.

They went down the stairs as quietly as they had arrived.

As much as I wanted to dive into the report, Marshfield needed some exercise. I decided to go for my usual walk that took me down Sea Side's main street. Let people see that Marshfield and I were on excellent terms, that he was healthy, and that I intended him no harm. I packed a small bag of dog treats to give to Marshfield along the way. The snacks served a double purpose—training him and advertising the product to my neighbors.

I started making dog biscuits for Odie years ago. I have a file full of pet-friendly recipes and created a few of my own. If there was a reality show where people had to create treats for their dogs on special occasions, I would sign up.

People stopped us when we set foot in the parking lot. News spread ahead of us till somebody came out of nearly every house to say hello. The half mile to the town park took twice as long as usual, but I didn't mind. Once I walked through the iron fence, I let Marshfield off the leash. Later I would take him for a nice walk along the beach. For right now, we'd be satisfied with open air and space to run.

"It's good to see Marshfield about again." For the second time that day, I'd run into Leah Packer. This time she was with her spaniel.

The dogs greeted each other in the usual fashion

Leah seemed more relaxed than when I'd seen her at the store. "Have you received good news about the dog food investigation?" I blurted the question without thinking.

A startled look passed across her face. "Not exactly. The police have indicated we should be able to restart production in time for the summer season."

Ah. That was highly suggestive. "Do you have any idea who they suspect?"

She looked at me sideways. "I didn't take you for a gossip."

"I'm not." I sat back, indignant, and fiddled with Marshfield's leash. "But I can't shake the feeling that the pet food contamination and Sir Geoffrey's murder are connected somehow." I wished I'd taken the time to look at the computer files Daisy had given me before having this conversation.

"Of course." Leah spoke under her breath. She put a hand to her face. "Is it too awful for me to say I hope they are connected somehow? I hope we don't have both a poisoner and a murderer in our midst. I hope they're one and the same."

The temperature in the air dropped about ten degrees with that statement, and I missed my sweater.

"We've bought from the same locals for years. Whitaker, Black, Cabot." She shook her head. "I hate to think one of our locals sold us bad food." Her face creased into a frown.

"What's the matter?"

"I just remembered the last time I saw Sir Geoffrey." Her voice had raised in timbre. "It was at the grocery store. I was stocking the shelves." She looked me, fear in her eyes. "Sir Geoffrey and Roland were having an argument."

My breath caught in my throat. "Do you remember what they were saying?"

Tears shone in her eyes. "I heard quite a bit. They couldn't see me from where they were standing."

I waited, hoping she could tell me more.

"Sir Geoffrey said—I'm sure of it—'Stop doing what you're doing, or I'll have to go to the police.'" Her eyes held fright. "I should probably tell them what I heard."

She must know that Roland had discovered the body along with the Guilfoyle family and me.

"It's probably nothing," I assured her. "The last time I saw Roland and Sir Geoffrey, they were on good terms." But then I thought about the flash drive at my house. I needed to look at it as soon as possible.

Marshfield trotted over in search of a snack. I offered one to Leah's dog as well.

When he scarfed it up, Leah asked, "Would you be interested in selling those wholesale? Perhaps it's time we added new products to our line." Her smile started to slip. "If we're still in business, that is."

The invitation pleased me. Timidity had kept me from asking before. "I would be honored. Let me know how you wish to proceed, okay?"

We said goodbye. I put Marshfield back on the leash and headed away from the center of town to avoid running into people. I was tired, my mind preoccupied by what I had learned from Leah.

Once we were back at the apartment, Marshfield headed straight for his rug, curled up, and fell asleep. If I was smart, I would do the same thing. But I was determined to at least look at what was on the flash drive from Sir Geoffrey. I plugged the drive into the slot on my computer.

When I tried to open the file, my computer asked for a password. Aggravating. Daisy must have encountered the same problem. Or maybe not. Maybe Sir Geoffrey had it set up to retain the password in the memory of his computer.

I didn't want to call her about it. Instead, I lay down for an hour. Maybe I would have a solution when I awoke.

The password eluded me that day, and I went to bed without finding the key. I decided that the next day I would ask for Georgina's help.

Frantic knocking at my door woke me early the next morning. The sun was already shining, and I had overslept. I stumbled out of bed as Georgina walked in, talking a mile a minute. "Mr. Tuttle called. He said you haven't answered your phone, and he wanted to warn you that the police are on their way. He said to refuse to speak to them until he arrives. Oh Gran!"

I hugged her, because that was what I always did, but inside I trembled.

Georgina took a long look at me. "Get dressed while I go get you something to eat. I don't want you facing them on an empty stomach. You can eat a proper breakfast later."

I couldn't argue with her. She brought back a pineapple muffin, one of my favorites. I added a bit of heart-healthy butter and a teaspoon of orange marmalade and ate it while drinking coffee. I told myself God was still in control and Paul Tuttle was a fine lawyer.

I debated about getting Georgina involved. I wanted to protect my granddaughter. What grandmother wouldn't? But the truth was I needed her. "I don't have much time. But I could use your help."

"Anything." That was my girl, jumping in ahead of danger.

"There's a flash drive in my computer. It may have information relevant to Sir Geoffrey's murder, but I can't figure out a way in. Please play with it while I'm gone—see what you can do."

Without another word, she walked over to the computer, reached for the drive, and tucked it into her pocket seconds before the police knocked at the door.

The detective, Tom, stood on the small landing with Enos in his shadow. My phone beeped as I let them in. Relief rushed through me at the signal from my lawyer. The appearance of both officers together worried me, and the hour of the day was unsettling.

Perhaps they had worked the night through. They both looked ragged.

"Good morning." I spoke through the screen door without opening it.

"May we come in?" Tom pulled at the door, taking my acceptance for granted.

I lingered on the hook while I debated what to do next. "You can come in, but I won't answer any questions until my lawyer gets here."

Enos entered first with an apologetic smile. Marshfield ambled toward him and received a loving pat. Perhaps he remembered the officer's kindness on the day of Sir Geoffrey's death.

"I heard you inherited the dog," Tom said.

My mouth opened, but I caught myself before I answered the question. "Let me feed him. He must be hungry." I busied myself with adding fresh water to one bowl and pouring my second-favorite brand of doggie kibble in the other, since Sealife wasn't available.

I wondered how long the police would wait patiently. As I put away the food, Tom asked, "Is your lawyer on his way?" He looked at me pointedly. "We can always continue this discussion at the station."

Paul knocked on the door before I had to answer. I smiled in apology at the two officers, opened the door, and went outside. "They're threatening to take me to the station."

I got the words out before Enos opened the door. He looked at me then at his father-in-law.

"Nonsense." Paul gently pushed Enos back inside and closed the screen door after him, leaving us on the landing. "Ms. Holland wants a moment's privacy with her lawyer. That is her right."

"If she feels the need for an attorney—" Enos paused. "Of course that's her right."

The fresh pot of coffee I had started finished brewing. Pouring everyone a cup gave me another two minutes of reprieve. I handed out the mugs, placed a plate of muffins on the table, and sat down next to Paul, across from the police.

"Now I'm ready to talk."

Paul began shaking his head.

"At the discretion of my attorney."

His lips lifted at one corner.

"You watch too many cop shows," Tom drawled. "We just have a few questions."

Enos began the questioning. "Tell us about the dog."

Paul gave a small nod.

"Yes, he's mine." I knew better than to offer more information. Let them ask the questions.

"We can see that, Ms. Holland," Enos said quietly. "Please tell us, step-by-step, how he became yours."

Hmm, was this a variation of the good cop, bad cop routine?

"It's very simple," Paul said. "She inherited the dog under the terms of Sir Geoffrey's will."

A barebones answer. Silently I thanked him for the guidance.

"When were you made aware of your inheritance?" Tom took up the line of questioning.

"Last Friday."

"And yet you agreed to take care of the dog before you spoke with your lawyer."

I wasn't sure where he got that information, and I fought to suppress a squirm.

"Why did you take home a dog you called"—Tom glanced at his notebook—"'a danger to himself and the tea shoppe'?"

"All Marshfield needs is a firm hand to teach him what's acceptable behavior. I'd have a hard time turning away an injured fox, let alone this sweet fellow."

The dog bounded to my side at the mention of his name, and I petted his head and slipped him a treat.

"Was it your belief that Sir Geoffrey was an inadequate pet owner?"

"He loved Marshfield. But he didn't teach the dog the difference between home and public behavior, and that was a problem for me." I realized my voice had become louder.

Tom smiled, and Paul shook his head.

I had put my foot in my mouth in spite of my best intentions.

CHAPTER 8

I brought the volume under control and kept my mouth shut after that thoughtless remark, restricting myself to sentences of two or three words when "Yes" or "No" wouldn't suffice by itself.

After an hour, Paul spoke up. "Gentlemen, you have bothered my client long enough. Go about your business of finding the person who left Marshfield without a master and Mrs. Holland without a friend."

I could read the look in Tom's eyes. He thought he'd found that person. But he satisfied himself with saying, "Please don't leave town for the time being."

I didn't have any plans to travel, but the familiar warning stirred up a desire to take a sudden trip to Boston. Or Perhaps Prince Edward Island, if I could get away after the tourist season started around Memorial Day. I might just plan a trip as a way of saying, "So there."

Marshfield was squirming, so I put him on his leash and took him out the door with Paul. After the dog relieved himself at the nearest tree, Paul said, "Do you mind taking a ride out to my house? We can walk along the shore without fear of seeing anyone, and Marshfield can have a good run."

Marshfield agreed to join us in the car when I bribed him with a treat, and we headed for Tuttle's Point. Paul lives in one of the more remote spots in Sea Side. He says he likes to escape his clients from time to time.

Paul didn't say much as we drove. When we pulled up in his driveway, I took a deep breath of the ocean air redolent with pine.

"I'm so glad my grandparents chose to build out here," he said. "Let's walk and talk."

Out here I could let Marshfield run free. So far he had come readily when I called. I don't know if he liked me that much, or if he expected goodies every time he obeyed. Rewarding him for good behavior gave better value than punishing bad behavior. It worked with my other dogs, and Marshfield had already improved.

"Tom doesn't appear to understand dogs very well. Anyone who saw Marshfield with you could tell he thinks you're his new best friend. If he'd seen you harming Sir Geoffrey or if you had poisoned him, he wouldn't take to you so readily."

My laugh came out half chuckle, half sputter. "I'm sorry I let Tom get to me."

"You're right. It wasn't wise, but he's doing what we pay him for." A small smile tugged at Paul's mouth. "I have to remind myself I'm glad he's good at his job. Even if he has his eyes on the wrong people every now and then."

"I used to agree with you." I grimaced. "Before I was the one under suspicion."

We walked a few feet farther. Marshfield came upon a flock of seagulls and chased after them. I called him back twice, the second time more sharply than the first.

The look on Marshfield's face said, *Oh Mom, do I have to?* but he returned. I sat on a large rock and put my arms around his neck. I fed him a treat and said, "That's a good dog."

"You've never asked me if I murdered Sir Geoffrey," I said to Paul after a moment of silence.

He sat on another rock and turned his ice-blue eyes on me. "Today we are relaxing. And don't worry, I'm not charging for this walk."

I must have looked relieved, because he smiled. "But tomorrow I want you to come to my office, and we'll go over every second of what has happened so I can check and double-check the record. I'll charge it to the estate."

"Would that be considered a conflict of interest?" I rubbed Marshfield's ears. "I mean, if they did decide I was the murderer, I couldn't inherit his estate."

"We'll answer that question in the unlikely event they arrest you."

I squirmed. The very thought made me nauseated.

He chuckled at my discomfort. "Don't worry. If they had enough to arrest you, they would have done it this morning. They didn't even ask you to come in for questioning."

Maybe to him that was nothing to worry about. "They were going to take me in for questioning if you hadn't arrived when you did."

"It's upsetting for ordinary citizens. But look at it as part of the process of finding the murderer." He looked at me sharply. "You did the right thing, waiting for me to arrive."

Marshfield barked, as if adding his agreement to Paul's instruction, before chasing after the sea waves. A cool morning breeze blew in from the ocean, and I shivered.

"There is something I should probably tell you about now," I said.

Paul waited for me to explain further.

"Daisy Guilfoyle brought me a flash drive." I explained about recent events—the Guilfoyles' visit and what I'd learned from the owner of Sealife. "Daisy said she also gave a copy to the police. So far I haven't been able to open it. Password protected and all that."

Paul's eyes twinkled. "Sir Geoffrey always did consider himself a sleuth. Since you have no idea what's on the drive, and since it belongs to you as owner of the house, you're free to investigate it if you wish."

Immense relief swept over me.

"But be careful. Don't try to do it on your own. If you do learn something, talk with me about it before you do anything more. Besides"—he flopped his hand over—"an investigation into Sealife isn't necessarily a motive for murder."

Maybe not, but it was a suggestion. Sealife bought from a handful of local fishermen—the suspect pool was small. Sir Geoffrey had looked into the situation, and he had argued with Roland. It wasn't enough to convict a mosquito of a bite, but it deserved a deeper look.

I really needed to get into that drive.

After an hour, Marshfield settled down at our feet as if to say he was done. Or maybe he wanted a companion. I stood up. "I'm ready to leave."

Paul rose to his feet. I let the dog run free again. He stopped every few feet to mark rocks where the sea had washed away any other dog's scent. I greeted the sight of the car with a sigh of relief. Paul drove me to his office, and I drove home.

Back at the tea shoppe, I checked in with Georgina. Busy at the register, she saw me come in. The shake of her head informed me she hadn't been able to access the drive yet.

Clearing my desk might also clear my head. I had a stack of items needing to be filed: new recipes, the vet's information about Marshfield, and the papers Paul had given me about my inheritance.

As I filed the recipes, I felt another pang for my lost friend. Never again could we claim, "Approved by Sir Geoffrey Guilfoyle," about any of our items. In fact, in honor of his passing, we should run a special of all his favorite dishes. I made a note to discuss the idea with Georgina

I glanced through Marshfield's medical records to check for any recurring problems. The most interesting thing I found was his pedigree, which began with his registration name and a brief physical description, and then listed five generations on both the sire's and dam's side. My dog was six and a half, which made him about fifty years old in human years.

I glanced at Marshfield, who had curled up on my couch where the sunshine reached him through the window. "You come from a distinguished family, Marshfield. And both your parents won awards for obedience, so I expect you'll learn proper behavior inside the tea shoppe soon enough."

I almost passed over his registration as lacking interest, then took a second look. The ten-digit number and letter sequence looked like a computer-generated password. Was it possible? Why not try? I turned on my computer and entered the registration number when asked for the password for the flash drive. It opened immediately.

I held my breath then slowly released it and started reading.

The first several pages included a datebook of Sir Geoffrey's fishing trips with Roland, as well as notes on how to spearfish and the pros and cons of different fishing spears. He had a folder with several pictures with fish, including his first "spear," about thirteen years ago, shortly after his arrival in Sea Side.

A journal-type entry was attached to the image. He felt like he had turned back time. Like his ancestors, he had to catch with his bare hands or with a net or spear.

He wrote articulately about the sport of spearfishing and of his friendship with Roland. I would have enjoyed reading it if Sir Geoffrey hadn't been murdered.

Of course, if he were still alive, I wouldn't be reading it.

The mood of the writing had shifted about six months ago, when Roland speared a floundering crab. Since Sir Geoffrey wasn't an expert on crabs, he believed Roland's reassurances that the crab was good eating for dogs. Roland planned on including it in his sale to Sealife, along with his usual catch of fish.

Bingo. Sir Geoffrey knew for certain Roland was selling to the pet food company. From then on, he kept meticulous records of what they caught on which days. He made note of several days when the catch included dead fish.

Four months later, the first dog died from food poisoning. Sir Geoffrey learned about it from Dr. Stetson, who recommended he stay clear of Sealife until they figured out the problem.

After a second dog died, Sir Geoffrey looked into the problem. What caused the contamination, and how did it enter the food supply? The more he researched the situation, the more Roland's activities gave him pause.

Then, just a couple of days before his death, he wrote that he had scheduled an appointment to speak to Roland about his suspicions.

Sir Geoffrey wrote no more entries after that. I didn't know if he had spoken to Roland or not. I was glad Daisy had turned the file over to the police. My impression was that Sir Geoffrey had seen Roland catch fish that might have been contaminated. Period. Suggestive, but nothing concrete.

I couldn't help but hope I would find a substitute for my name to pencil in for the murderer. I had always liked Roland, but since I knew I wasn't the murderer. . . Anyone, if pushed far enough. . . Was Roland that person? I had to find out. Sighing, I placed the flash drive back in the bag I received it in. To my surprise, I noticed two more drives tucked down in the bottom.

Daisy had only mentioned the one flash drive, and I wondered if she knew about the others. In any case, they belonged to me. To my relief, the second drive opened with the same password as the first. Safety wardens have it right. Using the same password for multiple accounts makes it open season for anyone intent on unlocking any personal secrets.

The second drive contained images of older photos. The first files held images of two young boys. Sir Geoffrey and his brother? As they grew, he began to take on his adult appearance. Before long Daisy and then a very young Freddy appeared in the pictures.

Twenty-five years ago, the brother stopped appearing in the pictures, and I speculated about the brother's premature death. Not too much later, pictures of Tea by the Sea, me, and my dishes, made an appearance. The images reminded me of happier times, and I felt a pang of grief.

The final file on the drive held the most interest. Sir Geoffrey kept a record of his dealings with everyone in Sea Side. I increased the print size to make it easier to read and scanned it, looking for anyone who might have had a motive for killing Sir Geoffrey.

CHAPTER 9

I read through half the file that afternoon. The sections where he reasoned through his decision to leave his America estate, including Marshfield, to me, interested me the most.

When it was time to take Marshfield for another walk, I decided to leave the rest until the morning. My mind was tired, and I might miss a vital clue.

The next day, Daisy called me before I opened the computer. "The funeral home has asked me to get clothes for Geoff. I've picked out a few things, but I wanted to have your permission."

I thought better of saying, "That's not necessary," before the words left my lips. Instead, I said, "I'll be right over." I decided to take Marshfield with me.

On the way over, I thought about giving some of the furnishings to Sir Geoffrey's family. He might have left it lock, stock, and barrel to me, but that didn't mean I had to keep it. I stopped by Paul's office to ask his advice. The fifteen-minute wait was a small price to pay for my unscheduled consult, although Marshfield wasn't happy being left in the car.

"That's generous of you." He paused. "Especially since they're the obvious suspects, apart from you and Roland."

I shivered. I'd been trying to overlook that part. "Do you think it's safe for me to go?"

He didn't automatically dismiss the thought. I didn't know whether to relax or to up the tension.

"If they are innocent, they might be scared of you, the potential murderer. But they invited you, which suggests they're comfortable around you. And if either one of them is the murderer—why would they harm the person the police are focusing on?" He shrugged. "I see no reason why you shouldn't go. Arrange with Georgina to call you in half an hour or so. You can say you're expecting a call, in case they have any ideas."

He had gone back and forth so many times, I let go of a small laugh. "When the light is yellow, proceed with caution."

"Exactly. Also, you should get someone to catalog everything in the house. Not by yourself, because police might interpret that as an attempt to get rid of evidence. But you do want to protect against theft."

He riffled through his drawer and pulled out a thin manila file. "I'll ask my secretary to make a copy for you. It's the inventory Sir Geoffrey had drawn up of his most valuable possessions."

I walked out of the office in deep thought. Marshfield renewed his barking when I opened the car door, and I fed him a treat to reward him for his patience. Paul's advice echoed in my thoughts. The police couldn't object. They'd released the crime scene the day of the murder so the Guilfoyles could stay there. As the new owner, I could come and go as I pleased. The proof of that lay in the bundle of keys Paul had given me.

I made arrangements with Georgina to call me in forty-five minutes, and then I drove to Neptune's Cottage. Sir Geoffrey had named the house that because he said the King of the Sea must enjoy the view of the crashing waves conquering the coast.

I wiped a tear away from my eyes. A bit fanciful, perhaps, but it was those touches that made me care for the man. Yes, I could admit it now. I loved him, as a dear friend.

Emotions bubbled up within me. When the tears flooded my eyes, I looked for a spot where I could pull over without drawing attention to myself. I was in the vicinity of the Sea Side Chapel. I couldn't think of a better place to have a quiet cry and talk with God. It was a favorite stopping place of tourists and residents alike, unlikely to be crowded on this May day before summer tourism hit.

Sea Side Chapel is available for the entire community, visitors, and the summer residents. Pastors, priests, and rabbis from our several places of worship rotate through the chapel on different days of the week. I don't go there often, and I didn't know whom I might encounter today. Hopefully no one. I didn't want to explain the tears.

Tissue packs, as well as pocket New Testaments, candles, and gospel tracts, sat on a table in the foyer. A sign indicated that the items were provided for free. It was clean and inviting as always. I picked up a couple of votive candles to light in the windows around my home in memory of Sir Geoffrey.

Marshfield padded through the chapel quietly, as if he understood the sanctity of the place. When I sat down, he climbed on the bench beside me and laid his head on my lap. As I cried, he licked my hand, and I felt as though we were mourning Sir Geoffrey together, his dog and me.

When my tears came to an end, I added a prayer for God to guide me as I searched for the truth regarding his death. I owed that much to my friend.

I tarried long enough in the chapel to have messages waiting for me from both Daisy and Georgina. I assured Daisy that I would arrive shortly and asked Georgina to wait another forty-five minutes before calling. I arrived at Neptune's Cottage a little over five minutes later.

I gave Marshfield a treat before we got out of the car. I wondered how he would respond to his former lodgings. He dashed ahead, ready to charge into the house. When Freddy answered my knock, the dog skidded to a stop. I could almost hear him thinking, *Who are you?*

"You brought the dog?" Freddy asked. He held his left arm at an awkward angle as he twisted the doorknob, and I wondered if he had injured himself somehow.

"I thought he might like to visit."

The dog dashed ahead of me, his toenails clattering across the floor. He went down the hallway, popping in one doorway after another. When he reached the kitchen at the other end, he started whimpering. He sniffed around the area where Sir Geoffrey had fallen before lying on the exact spot, as if his whines and warmth could bring him back.

Freddy frowned.

Daisy came into the kitchen. "That's disgusting." When she tried to pull the dog away from the spot, he growled at her.

Was Marshfield reflecting an earlier bad encounter with Daisy? Or did he simply want to be left in peace? If only he could tell us who had taken his friend.

"Mum, he's mourning for Uncle Geoff. Leave him alone. It's not like there's any blood for him to lick up."

Now, that was disgusting. The cleaning crew I had hired had done a good job of cleaning the kitchen and removing the smell.

"He's better off staying in here while you show me the outfit you've chosen for Sir Geoffrey's burial."

The sight of his best suit—a dark blue of the finest wool, with a pinstriped shirt—threatened to bring tears to my eyes again. But the sight of the medals that Daisy had added changed the tears into an incredulous chuckle. When I looked more closely, I wanted to cry again.

"He was awarded that medal during the battle in the Falklands," Freddy said. "That's what my father told me. Uncle Geoff never talked about it much."

"He served aboard the same ship as Prince Andrew," Daisy added. "He refused to talk about the war, but he loved to talk about the jokes he and his fellow shipmates played on the prince."

The England Sir Geoffrey talked about was full of county fairs and Scotland holidays, not of hobnobbing with royalty and the British Navy in a time of war. I suspected that, like many before him, he came to America to escape some of the memories of his past. I doubted he would welcome these reminders of his service.

Daisy must have sensed my hesitation. "Please humor us in this. There are so many more things back home that should be buried with him, that cannot be because of the circumstances." She paused. "We would have preferred to take him home for burial, but the police insisted he stay here in case they need his body again."

"Won't do them much good after he's embalmed," Freddy said.

"When do you plan on holding the service?" I asked.

"The funeral home suggested we wait until his pastor returned from some conference he's attending this week. Not very thoughtful of him, taking off like that."

I started to defend my soon-to-be grandson-in law, but another thought crowded it out. Surely they would have a closed casket funeral. Nobody wanted to think about the gaping hole where the spear had gone through him. "It's a pity no one will get to see those medals for bravery."

Daisy looked puzzled for a moment, and then she nodded in understanding. "He'd probably prefer it that way. Geoff was never one to brag."

Freddy shook his head. "I would show them. Of course I was

never in the service. I didn't feel the need to go fight someone else's war in the Middle East."

It had never felt like someone else's war to me, not after the attacks on 9/11, but I know people who feel that way. From my perspective, we fought the communists for forty-odd years one way or another before the Berlin Wall fell. The war on terror could easily take as long. It has already been almost twenty years, after all.

But 9/11 happened in America. The Brits might support us and share our rage, but it's not their war.

Daisy smiled at him indulgently. "Don't let my son fool you. When he was taking his A levels, he was eager to rush off and fight instead of going to university. He picked up all that 'it's not my war' nonsense at uni, but the truth is—"

"Mother!" Freddy said sharply.

"—he was rejected for a physical impairment."

The little she said had Freddy fuming. I was curious, of course. Sir Geoffrey had often referred to his nephew as a "poor specimen." Was it connected?

After Daisy let that tidbit slip, her lips pinched shut and she didn't elaborate further. Perhaps all those pictures on the flash drive would provide a clue—if I was that curious about someone else's afflictions.

That's the problem with playing detective. It means sticking your nose into everyone else's business. You learn all sorts of ugly things about people. Generally, I want to believe the best of people I meet.

I didn't like the idea of Sir Geoffrey being bedecked with all those medals. Suppose at some future date someone exhumed the body? They would think, from all the medals on his chest, that the military was of great importance to him. The man I'd known never wanted to talk about war.

But when he had made his funeral arrangements with the local funeral parlor, he hadn't specified anything about his appearance, except requesting burial rather than cremation. I couldn't deny his relatives this small comfort.

Georgina called when I was in the middle of making arrangements to come back. I apologized to Daisy and said I must leave but would be back sometime the next day.

The prospect of a return visit didn't please Daisy. I decided not to remind her she was my guest.

Something felt off in Neptune's Cottage, and it was more than the absence of its former owner.

CHAPTER 10

By the time I climbed the steps to my apartment, I was ready for a long, hot bath. No more investigating for me for the day. I hurt from the inside out, as if the realization of what a friend I'd lost in Sir Geoffrey had drained my power pump.

But before I could run the bathwater, someone knocked at my door. Georgina entered, bearing two trays in her hands.

"You really don't need to feed me."

"Who says I'm doing this for you? I want to learn the latest news." Her grin wasn't quite full throttle. "I do need to speak to you, but it's about something else."

We swapped our war stories of the day, something we often did. I was surprised to see it was nearly three o'clock. We were having an afternoon tea in the truest sense of the word.

Business had burgeoned since Sir Geoffrey's death, and the most popular item of all was the infamous hot cross bun that had sickened Marshfield. "Our customers are asking when they can see the dog again. He was as much a fixture at the shop as Sir Geoffrey."

"Give us a few more days. I want to be sure he's ready to resist temptation."

We both chuckled, then Georgina grew serious. "Gran, people want to see you."

I started to protest, but she continued. "And not just because the police have questioned you."

I very much doubted that.

"Of course there have been some good-natured quips, but most people are concerned about you. You've got a lot of friends here.

The Bible study ladies ask about you every time they come in." She referred to a group of women from our church who had helped her with the Christmas festival.

"Even the early morning fishermen want to see your smiling face. They ask after you every day."

Her words took a second to register. "Including Roland Whitaker, I suppose."

"Of course." Georgina reacted a moment later. "Oh. Should I not tell him anything?"

"As long as you haven't told anyone about the flash drive from Sir Geoffrey." I looked at her pointedly.

She looked a little guilty, as if she had accidentally mentioned it. Her ability to put people at ease and get them to talk made her good at her job.

She shook her head. "I haven't said a word. However, people observed Daisy Guilfoyle drop something off, and everybody's curious. There's talk of everything from jewelry to a secret love affair to a list of Marshfield's requirements for care. I just listen and nod and say it's interesting, that's all."

I relaxed a tad, but to a guilty person, the fact I had secret communications from Sir Geoffrey might pose a threat. My second-floor apartment, long my refuge, began to feel like an open target.

Georgina didn't seem to notice my worry. "As soon as you feel able, I need you back. It's not the same without you popping in to scold us or to give me advice."

I didn't state the obvious: that someday, far too soon, she would have to handle the tea shoppe on her own.

I didn't have to say it. Her look said it all. We hugged tight.

After we finished eating, she headed to her home half a mile down the road. The food and friendly visit had perked me up, and the reminder about Roland made me anxious to find out what else I could.

I opened the second flash drive and debated about whether to continue reading Sir Geoffrey's journal first or look at the pictures. Pictures, I decided. I might discover something I wanted to ask Daisy and Freddy—should I say "Sir Fred" now? It felt natural with his uncle. With him it would be awkward. But they wouldn't stay in America indefinitely.

Sir Geoffrey must have had volumes of family photos, or perhaps digitized 8mm film and saved images from them—several pictures had that feel of jerky movements. He included the briefest of notes: dates, places, names, but no indication of the action.

He had picked out key events. His brother's first birthday. Geoffrey's first year at public school. A boarding school, of course. I couldn't imagine sending my children away at such a young age, but the system had worked for centuries, and who was I to question it?

I especially enjoyed the image from the first time he presented a trophy to a fellow student. He was about thirteen, I'd guess. In spite of his gangly body and pimpled face, he already carried an air of authority.

Nearly every picture included a bulldog of some sort. Marshfield's ancestors? No wonder he brought the dog with him to the tea shoppe. A dog had walked across the stage with him at his graduation.

His college pictures revealed the first glimpse of the Sir Geoffrey I had known. He included several pictures of his navy unit. Prince Andrew appeared in several of them. I knew someone who knew royalty. I was practically rubbing elbows with the British royal family.

He had one portrait of a young woman with Farrah Fawcettlike long, curly locks. The brief note, "My Elaine, August 3, 1954–June 24, 1978," spoke volumes about a broken heart.

Pictures dwindled until young Freddy came along. Sir Geoffrey doted on his nephew, as if Freddy were the child he'd never had.

The cascade of pictures stopped abruptly when Freddy was about ten. No pictures of his parents either. Perhaps his father had died by then.

The last picture, dated twenty-five years ago, showed a tomb-stone. "John Archer Guilfoyle, March 16, 1948–October 23, 1995." The caption read simply, "Why?"

Sometime in 1995, something happened that put a strain on the Guilfoyle family and ultimately drove Sir Geoffrey to America. At least that was the impression I received from him.

I wanted to find out more, but the only ones who knew the truth might want to hide it. Some of his service buddies had kept in touch. If necessary, perhaps I could speak with one of them.

I tucked the possibility away but decided to start with the best research tool available. By 1995 we were well into the computer age, and the death of British nobility, even a minor one like the brother of a lesser-known peer, was newsworthy. I typed the name and dates into the computer.

Within seconds I had a list of more than ten thousand articles. I had made the search parameters too large. I started over again, inputting "John Archer Guilfoyle, death" and the date on the tomb-stone. The headlines on the shortened list told an immediate, grip-ping story, using words like *tragic accident, car accident*, and *neglect*.

The *London Times* ran a series of articles about the accident. I started with their accounts.

The first article, published on the day of John's death, gave an obituary-like statement of dates and survivors.

After that, the articles became the stuff of tabloids. Suspicion turned to proof that John's ten-year-old son, Freddy, had been driving. The police decided to investigate the matter fully.

A final article appeared several months later, and the results were inconclusive. In essence, John had brought about his death by letting young Freddy drive. The paper made a point of the danger of letting a child drive. A small footnote mentioned the "child's condition" might have contributed to the accident.

What condition was that? Look as much as I could, I didn't find another reference.

Sir Geoffrey's relationship with his family went cold after the accident. I would look at the tabloids later. They might have more juicy tidbits, but then again, were they reliable?

I shut down the computer and took Marshfield for a walk. We got no farther than the next house down the road when my neighbor Carol hollered hello. She didn't mind Marshfield roaming her yard.

"It's good to see you out and about, Evie. It's not like you to keep yourself holed up."

I smiled and nodded.

"You must have heard the news. They just announced it on the radio."

The news? "Has there been an arrest?" Now, why did I say that? Just because it was on my mind didn't mean that was the only news in town.

"Not the one you might expect." She paused for emphasis. "They caught the person responsible for poisoning Sealife's dog food."

"Who was it?" My heart raced.

"Roland Whitaker—Sir Geoffrey's friend."

Surely she wasn't implying. . . "What does that have to do with it?"

"One murdered, the other arrested. It looks suspicious. Partners in crime, perhaps?"

Partners in crime? I couldn't believe anyone would suggest Sir Geoffrey had participated in Roland's scheme. "That's impossible."

"What? Do you know something?"

I did, but I didn't want the news to spread throughout Lincoln County. "Sir Geoffrey would never do anything like that."

But something had happened with his family. Perhaps there was a dark side to him that he kept hidden from me.

Every block or two, someone stopped me to tell me the news and to ask after Marshfield. A few doors closed as I walked by, but the friendly chats outnumbered the cold shoulders. Perhaps the burden of suspicion had passed from me.

I didn't get the full story about Roland's arrest until the pre-dawn fishermen came into the tea shoppe the next morning as usual. Caleb Long started them off. "It happened right when we all got to our boats, yestiday mahnin'."

My antenna went on alert. Marshfield—I had brought him downstairs after feeding him breakfast and stuffing my pockets full of treats—barked, as if agreeing with their pronouncement.

Jacob Short put in his two cents. "Seems they set up a trap for him the morning of Sir Geoffrey's murder. They had to test the food first though. It was tainted all right."

The morning of the murder? "Do you happen to know what time of day that was?" I asked him. I held my breath waiting for the answer.

"I saw Roland meeting with a feller about six thirty, and after that he slipped away."

If Roland had been meeting with agents posing as sellers at six-thirty on the morning of Sir Geoffrey's death, there's no way he could have been the murderer.

He must have met up with Daisy and Freddy right after that. Who was covering for whom?

CHAPTER 11

When I lay down that night, I wasted a few minutes wondering if the police would return their attention to me since the investigation had pegged Roland for a different crime.

I decided I shouldn't take on tomorrow's worries. In police time, the days since they had questioned me stretched out like a month. I took comfort in the fact I was still footloose.

I slept soundly while my mind worked on the logistics. A pair of questions arose when I woke up. What if the police had delayed talking with me again in order to get a warrant for my arrest? And was British nobility immune to arrest in America, or did that privilege extend to diplomats only?

I would ask my lawyer the next time I saw him. I wanted Sir Geoffrey's murderer brought to justice—but more than that, I felt a need to know the person's identity. No laws would impede that investigation.

I contacted Mabel, the housecleaner who helped with deep cleaning at the tea shoppe, and asked for her help in sorting through Sir Geoffrey's things. We would start with his office. I didn't want any important papers to slip away while I was looking at clothes and artwork.

Daisy would have to wait for me to go through her brother-in-law's belongings. I couldn't delay too long though. Daisy wouldn't enjoy being suspected of pilfering any more than I would.

The more time passed, the more possessive I felt toward Sir Geoffrey's things. For whatever reason, he wanted me to have them. I wouldn't keep all of them, of course. But I would go through them piece by piece, choosing for me and Georgina. He'd brought several items from England that would make perfect decorations for the tea shoppe.

I decided against warning Daisy of my arrival. Surprise was my friend in this case.

Before Mabel came by, I tended to tea shoppe business. A list of Sir Geoffrey's favorite treats would be featured on our menu for the next six weeks. I also jotted down some ideas for menus to center around the treats and left it for Georgina, suggesting we discuss it in the evening.

Next I made a point of stopping in the tea shoppe to say hello to our guests, with Marshfield by my side. I kept him on a tight leash to make sure he didn't lunge at someone's table. His behavior had already improved. I had always suspected it had more to do with his owner's handling than it did the dog.

"It's good to see you," Beverly Potter, one of our regulars, said. "I've been worried about you. First Sir Geoffrey was killed, and now they've arrested Roland. Take care of yourself."

I relaxed in her hug, glad that someone was concerned for my safety. Tears tickled my eyes, and I couldn't hold them back. I dug out my tissues.

Her face collapsed into concern. "Sir Geoffrey's death has hit you hard, hasn't it?"

I coughed. "It's been a trying few days."

I went to the kitchen and made Georgina aware of my destination. She wasn't happy with me. "Gran, are you sure that's safe? If you find something, will they try to hurt you?"

I refused to admit that her worries echoed my own. I wanted to protect my granddaughter from life's realities. She probably felt the same way about me. I saw her as young and inexperienced. She saw me as old and fragile. Ah, the bonds of family love.

"Mabel will be with me. I'll call you when I arrive. If I haven't called back within an hour, give me a call. It's going to take time to go through his stuff, and I have to do it while they're still there, in case items start walking off."

Her mouth formed an O.

"I'm almost more concerned about theft than whether or not they murdered him."

Her expression said, *Come on, Gran.*

"Think about it. The closest the police have come to making an arrest was questioning me." I managed a chuckle. "You know as well as I do that the tea shoppe is the first place to hear town news."

Georgina's face held on to some disbelief because I hadn't convinced her. Because either Daisy or Freddy, or both together, were our only remaining suspects in Sir Geoffrey's murder.

"A stranger did it?" My granddaughter looked daggers at me. "You, with all your TV watching, know how unlikely that is. Maybe in New York, but not here in Sea Side. Anyone who's a stranger stands out a mile."

I ran through the possibilities. Had Daisy and Freddy made themselves known in the town? Everyone knew about them of course, but how many could identify them by sight? Was it remotely possible that a third Englishman was hiding in town somewhere, pretending to be one of the Guilfoyles?

Possible, but unlikely. Georgina was right. Mabel and I had better be cautious while we were at the house.

When Mabel arrived at my apartment a few minutes later, I invited her to come in for a cup of tea and a muffin. I offered her lemon blueberry, her favorite.

"You shouldn't feed me. I don't expect you to give away your livelihood." Mabel licked the lemony sugar from her fingers.

I shook my head. "You're my guest." I leaned forward to invite a confidence. "Perhaps I want to ask something of you."

"It's yours." Her eyes twinkled. "For twelve dollars an hour, and I don't do windows."

I sat back and laughed. "I wish it was something as simple as windows. But no, it's about how we go about our work at Neptune Cottage."

She raised her eyebrows. "We've worked together before. It shouldn't be a problem."

"Which is why I know I can trust your discretion. I don't know if you realize that Daisy and Freddy are the only suspects left standing in Sir Geoffrey's murder."

She lifted her eyes from the teacup and stared at me. "Aside from you? I guess you're right." She hesitated. "Are you having second thoughts about going over there?"

"No-o." I dragged out the word. "I need your help to catalog Sir Geoffrey's belongings, check our list against the inventory Paul Tuttle gave me, and see if anything is missing."

Mabel stirred sugar into her teacup. "But if I know you, you also plan to look for any clues to the murder."

"Yes." How much should I say? "I'm looking specifically for any information about an old accident that caused Geoffrey's brother's death, and also about a disability his nephew supposedly has. I don't know exactly what it is, but I think it could be important."

Mabel nodded. "I may be able to work disabilities into the conversation. My brother is in a wheelchair."

My mind stampeded briefly. She couldn't say, "My brother is disabled, and by the way, what's your problem?"

"Don't worry." She must have sensed my hesitation. "If I can work it naturally into the conversation, I will."

"Yes well, that brings me to my request. A condition, really. We must stay together. I don't want either one of us alone with either of the Guilfoyles."

Her conspiratorial grin diminished. "You're serious about this." She shook her head. "Of course you are. I'll stick to you like fog on a spring morning."

As long as her caution didn't drift out to sea.

We stopped by the tea shoppe for a couple of cold plates for lunch before heading to Neptune Cottage. Since I hadn't left Marshfield alone since I brought him home, he came along with us.

Marshfield raced across the tea shoppe parking lot ahead of me, straining at his leash and barking at a few cars as they pulled in. I scolded him. "Bad dog. If you're going to be the tea shoppe's mascot, you must play friendly with our guests."

He barked as if he had received a compliment and sniffed the air for a treat. Instead, I waited until we got into the car and he settled down peacefully. He gulped his reward down in one crunch. Once we reached the open road, I rolled down the window a couple of inches. He stuck his nose in the streaming air and howled at the world.

The scenic route added about five minutes to our drive time, but it was worth it. Nothing refreshes my spirits like salt air and sunshine, and Sir Geoffrey had chosen the spot for his home well.

When we passed the final turn, Marshfield must have sensed where we were headed. He whined and tucked his head beneath his front leg.

I reached back and rubbed my hand over the top of his head and gave him another treat. "It's okay. We'll face it together, shall we?"

The presence of the rental car suggested the Guilfoyles were in. Mabel and I got out of the car, I let Marshfield out, and we climbed the stairs to the porch. I took out my key, knocked on the door, and waited a couple of seconds before entering.

Marshfield didn't want to go in, not one bit. He hugged my side as if we were glued together, and refused to look up from the floor. I understood the sentiment. I was a poor substitute for his best friend.

Daisy came to the door, Freddy close behind. Both were dressed to go out.

"I'm sorry, Mrs. Holland. This isn't a good time." The angry expression on her face gave truth to her words. "You should have called ahead."

"That's all right. I have the *master* keys here for anything that's locked." Just sliding in the word to remind them I was the owner, after all.

Daisy frowned. "I want to be here when you go through Geoff's estate."

"You're welcome to stay." I stuck my tongue in my cheek, hoping at least one of them would stay behind.

They pushed past us and walked to their car.

I went inside ahead of Mabel and let Marshfield off his leash.

Mabel took her time coming in the door. "They're arguing about who should stay."

"We'll see who wins."

"Three, two, one." Mabel counted.

Freddy walked in.

"I'm glad you could join us, Freddy."

He headed for his room and returned with a camera. "Mother suggested I take a video of you at work." He tapped the lens. "Who knows what secrets are hidden in this house?"

I felt Mabel's eyes turn in my direction, but she spoke to Freddy. "What a wonderful idea. That way we'll have a record when we go through your rooms as well." She took out her phone.

"Shall we get started?"

CHAPTER 12

I decided to speak up before Mabel or Freddy took over completely. "We'll start in Sir Geoffrey's study. Freddy, why don't you grab a couple of chairs from the kitchen while Mabel and I bring in boxes from the car."

I hadn't expected to bring much home with me today but had come prepared. I was glad I had brought file boxes. Someone must have rifled through his desk. Sir Geoffrey never left his papers scattered all over the desktop like that. I could only hope he had kept his most important papers locked away safely.

I shuffled through the items on top of the desk. To my relief it appeared to be mostly mail. I saw no evidence that any of the envelopes had been opened. The envelopes, flyers, and other items on the desk had a certain order to them, seven or eight piles—the number of mail delivery days since Sir Geoffrey's death? That sounded about right.

I found the library file catalog on Sir Geoffrey's computer and printed out the list before handing it to Mabel. "Please check the books while I go through the desk." Mabel is twenty years younger than me, so I didn't feel guilty about asking her to climb on a step stool.

I tackled the mail first. Nothing unusual. I kept the personal mail to take home and put the bills in a separate bag to take to Paul.

I was aware of Freddy following my every move, so I didn't react when I ran across an envelope from someone named L. Sussex in Durrow, England. I considered myself lucky that it hadn't been opened.

I wanted to go through Sir Geoffrey's file cabinets before I turned on his computer. I had wondered if locating the correct key would be a problem, but Sir Geoffrey had the cabinets well marked, each label corresponding to a key on my key ring.

I looked through the file drawers one folder at a time. I made a brief note of the contents of each and tried to imagine what could be missing. One by one, I slipped them into the box I was taking home. After about an hour, the first box was full.

After about an hour and a half, I found the file I knew must be there. With newspaper clippings, court documents, and doctor's findings stacked in plastic sleeves, it wasn't as thick as I had expected. I didn't open it on the desk, not with Freddy watching our every move. Instead, I placed it in the second box and closed it. One more box should do it.

I poured myself a cup of tea from the thermos I had prepared for the morning and offered Mabel a cup. We ate our lunches. I gave Marshfield a treat for being so well behaved. He had spent the morning curled on the rug in front of the fireplace. He scrambled to his feet as if expecting to leave. I hugged his neck. "A little bit longer. That's a good boy."

"How much longer do you think it will be?" I startled when I heard Daisy's voice from the doorway. "I'm supposed to have a hair appointment at two."

"No one's keeping you here." I finished my tea. "We'll be gone as soon as I finish going through the desk."

"I guess I can wait." She noticed a couple of photo albums Mabel had laid out. "I wondered where these had gotten to!" She grabbed the first one and held it close to her chest. "Surely you don't object if we take these. They're old family photos. Geoff didn't tell me he was taking them."

I felt a bit like Scrooge because I couldn't agree to her request. Sir Geoffrey left them to me for a reason. "I want to look at them before I make a decision." Even then, I might decide to keep them.

"Well, I never." She stomped to the middle of the room and sat in a chair next to Freddy.

I felt cruel, which made me uncomfortable. Resolutely, I added the albums to the last box and decided to cut our losses. "That's it for now. We'll be going."

Mabel waved the list in her hands. "Let me take that box," she said, pointing to the first one I'd packed.

I appreciated it, because it was heavier than the others. I picked up another box.

"Let me take this one for you." Freddy grabbed the third box, the one with the picture albums.

"Freddy," Daisy warned. He shrugged her off.

When Freddy reached for the door handle, the box slid out of his hands, and he slipped and fell. An ornate ring tumbled out of his shirt pocket.

Marshfield jumped off his rug and barked, snarling in Freddy's face, daring him to move. The situation had taken a frightening turn. I pulled the dog back sharply and punched in 911. I knew that ring well: the original Durrow family crest, which Sir Geoffrey wore with great pride. When the dispatcher answered, I reported a theft at Neptune's Cottage.

Marshfield pulled against my grip. I wondered what was troubling him, Freddy's fall, the sight of the ring, or a different memory?

The ring had unsettled me, but I'd worry about that later. I bent over him, asking, "Are you all right?"

"I think so."

Mabel stared at the ring. "You must be the murderer." She blurted out the words.

The scene froze for a long second.

Mabel found her voice again. "I mean, that's Sir Geoffrey's ring. He said it would never leave his finger—until he was dead."

I warred inside. We had no business accusing anyone of murder, especially not as defenseless as we were.

Freddy protested, "This is all a dreadful misunderstanding." He rose to a sitting position but stayed on the floor. Daisy stared off into space, as if she were deaf and dumb to everything that had just happened.

He picked up the ring and tossed it on the table. "I should never have touched it. But it's mine by rights. I'm the Baron of Durrow."

He sounded like someone who had achieved a lifelong dream, only to find that it was hollow inside.

"You should have waited." I didn't need to say any more. His posture showed deep regret for his actions.

For taking the ring—or for murder? I didn't know.

In the distance, sirens approached in response to my 911 call. I didn't know if it was the police or an ambulance from the Sea Side Infirmary for Sailing Folk.

Daisy's eyes widened in disbelief when she heard the sirens, but Mabel, who had retreated into a corner after her accusation, brightened. "The police can sort it out."

I had almost begun to believe Freddy's protests about his innocence—of murder—until I saw the panic in his eyes.

The sirens grew louder.

"Freddy didn't kill Geoff." Daisy marched to her son's side. "I did."

A police car pulled up beside an ambulance. Tom and Enos came to the door. The detective's eyes measured me.

I stood tall, reminding myself I had every right to be in the house. "Come in. We've had an incident."

I didn't say anything else. I was more confused about the murder than ever. Nothing added up.

Mabel had no doubts. She pointed to Daisy. "She killed Sir Geoffrey. She just confessed to us."

Tom raised his eyebrows. "Is that so?"

Daisy drew herself to her full height, full of British starch and backbone. "Yes. I killed my brother-in-law."

I felt the detective's gaze drilling into me, as if asking me what role I played in this affair. Mabel preened herself as if she had solved the murder.

Even as they led Daisy away in handcuffs, I wasn't convinced. We had a confession, but did we have the murderer?

CHAPTER 13

Freddy followed the police in his rental car. A hollow feeling filled my chest as I bent over to pick up the files that scattered across the floor when Freddy dropped the box. The pages of carefully kept documents scattered across the floor made me sick. How could I ever get them back in order again, since I didn't know what was in the files in the first place? I wouldn't attempt to do it here.

Had he dropped the files on purpose to keep us from finding something? No, that didn't make any sense. We could still see everything; it just wasn't in order. Time would fix that problem.

With the departure of the Guilfoyles, Marshfield had grown calmer. But he was more than ready to leave, and so was I.

"Let's just dump everything in the box," I said to Mabel. "I'll sort it out at home."

"I don't believe Daisy did it." Mabel handed me the first photo album. I checked it, worried that the fall might have ripped the delicate pages. But the thick album cover seemed to have protected the pictures within.

"Me neither." I placed the cover on the top and hugged the box to my chest. "I'm hoping to find clues in here." We left the house, and I set the box in my trunk. "Why I think it's up to me, I don't know, but. . .I feel like I owe it to Sir Geoffrey."

"Besides, you're nosy." Mabel grinned at me. "That's okay. So am I."

We bumped elbows in agreement. "As long as the Guilfoyles are out of the house, do you mind continuing with the inventory?" I asked her. "I need to take Marshfield for a walk and check in at the tea shoppe."

"Sure. I'll come back with my van."

I felt the need to remind her. "And if the Guilfoyles return before you're done, lock up and leave. I don't want you with them here alone."

She shuddered. "You have my word."

Mabel took care of the other two boxes. I tried to help, but Marshfield hugged my legs, making it hard for me to balance.

Mabel opened the back door and invited Marshfield inside. He promptly jumped in and settled down.

"It's like he was born to it." I climbed in the front seat and buckled myself in. As we headed down the road, Mabel said, "The dog seems to have taken to you as his new owner."

"You think so?"

"He seems to see you as his protector. Or maybe he thinks he's protecting you."

"Maybe we're just helping each other out." I found I was enjoying Marshfield's company immensely. I'd forgotten how much I appreciated a dog's simple companionship. Sir Geoffrey knew me better than I knew myself and had given me the gift I needed the most.

After we unloaded the boxes, I drove Marshfield a short distance from the tea shoppe, where the houses weren't so close together. "I'm sorry, fella, we'll have to keep our walk short today."

Marshfield barked in protest but ran after a squawking seagull.

We spent fifteen minutes on the Point. I checked in at the tea shoppe to face the crowd. If the news had spread about Daisy, I needed to do some damage control.

When I walked in, my neighbor Carol spotted me. She pointed to me and started clapping. Soon applause echoed around the dining room.

Georgina hugged me close. "Congratulations, Gran. I'm passing the hat of family sleuth on to you."

I hugged her back.

"Mind if I ask you a few questions?" Norman Dexter, our local beat reporter, asked.

"Not yet." I laughed it off, but this wasn't the time to talk about it.

"Speech!" several voices called at once.

The noise was agitating Marshfield. He barked and tugged at his leash. Grateful for the excuse, I said, "I'm sorry, but the dog has had a trying morning. Let me get him settled, and I'll be back down."

I knew I had to say something. While I took Marshfield upstairs, I worked on formulating a speech in my mind. If I kept at it much longer, I'd get as good as the presidential press secretary in saying an abundance of nothing.

"I appreciate your vote of confidence. I'm sure you understand that the police don't want me to say much. But to answer your most burning question, yes, Daisy Guilfoyle said she killed Sir Geoffrey. And yes, the police took her away in handcuffs along with the traditional warning. And that's all I'm going to say."

People shouted questions as I left the dining room. Once we closed the kitchen door behind us, Georgina said, "You made a very carefully worded statement back there."

"Get me a salad and bring it upstairs. These walls have ears."

She joined me upstairs a couple of minutes later. "You weren't supposed to put yourself in danger."

"I didn't. We weren't." I stopped. "You can't repeat any of this."

"I won't. But nothing's to stop Mabel."

She would talk, I knew, and our stories might differ.

"Okay. You didn't say, 'Daisy murdered Sir Geoffrey.' You said,

'Daisy *said* she killed him.'"

"Semantics." I tried to shrug it off.

She arched her eyebrows at me. "You're the one who taught me their importance. What happened?"

I told her the sequence. How Daisy had sat in the library with us as we finished going through Sir Geoffrey's things, how Freddy offered to help us take the boxes out to the car but fell, dropping the box and Sir Geoffrey's ring on the floor. Mabel's accusation and Daisy's immediate rebuttal.

"It all feels a little too convenient," I said.

"Do you think Freddy killed him, then?" Georgina asked.

I shrugged. "I don't know. I'm hoping there's information in these files about the condition or accident or whatever it is that gives him problems."

Georgina sighed as she turned to go. "Why can't you let the police sort it out from here?"

I furrowed my eyebrows. "I just can't let it go. Sir Geoffrey was my friend." I shot my zinger right before the door closed behind her. "Kind of like you let the police sort it out when the mayor was killed."

I heard her grumbling all the way down the stairs.

After church the next day, I made a pot of tea and settled in the living room to go through the boxes. I set aside the first one I'd packed to look at later. After a moment's consideration, I placed the box that had spilled across the floor next to the first one.

I hoped that the clippings about the trial following that long ago accident would satisfy the itch that was bothering my conscience, I had to remove the source of the irritation and be satisfied in my own mind about what had happened to cause Sir Geoffrey to be estranged from his family. Before I added the third box to the others, I removed the file in question.

The file held more clippings than I had expected. Sir Geoffrey had followed the story in six different papers, with one-off clippings from several more. They were sorted by date, with the latest at the front. That piece was dated ten years ago. One of those "What really happened back then?" type of articles, a true crime drama that had happened to someone I knew personally.

The articles brought the story to life. I had read some of them online, but seeing them this way, laid out in order, gave me a different perspective. When I saw the pictures of the handsome young Freddy Guilfoyle in his public school uniform, with his hair just turning from white blond to brown, he was clearly the pride and joy of both his parents and his uncle.

When the articles hinted Freddy had been a reckless mischief-maker, I asked myself, *What ten-year-old isn't?* I had two fairly mild-mannered daughters, but I'd had three brothers and watched my friends' sons grow up. Ten years old seemed about the right age to fall from a tree or a roof or to go to overnight camp for the first time.

Or drive a car on a deserted stretch of road. Plenty of parents let their young children take a turn behind the wheel, although I don't think it's wise.

Whoever was driving that day, a tragedy occurred. The articles guessed about the nature of Freddy's condition. Was that a factor? Or was it his parents' fault for letting him drive?

I went back to the earliest documents and read them through, paying close attention to the variations in accounts. I didn't learn anything new. The overview had made me sad for the young Freddy.

He had gone from the prized scion of a proud house to a public spectacle.

I didn't know how well Daisy and Sir Geoffrey had coped with the changing situation. Did they join the public in blaming Freddy for his father's death? About the time Freddy finished uni, Sir Geoffrey emigrated to America and dropped out of the boy's life.

Not the kind of behavior I had come to expect from my friend. Oh, I knew the arguments. The boy had become a man, ready to be on his own. Perhaps Sir Geoffrey felt he was giving Freddy what he wanted, the run of the family estate.

But not all university graduates are ready to face life alone.

I considered the situation from Sir Geoffrey's point of view. The boy was now a man, with his mother alive and involved in his life. My friend had spent the past dozen years helping to raise his brother's son. He had a right to seek his own dreams.

But everything I'd seen in my searches revealed Sir Geoffrey's love for his nephew. They might have grown apart, but I didn't sense animosity toward Freddy. His sister-in-law, perhaps. But not Freddy.

I continued sifting through the pages, mostly pictures. Young Freddy looked horrific after the accident. If he already had physical problems, surely the accident made things worse.

The biggest surprise came at the end of the file. Sir Geoffrey had kept medical reports from Freddy's birth on. Jackpot!

The accident that killed Freddy's father wasn't his first. As an infant, he'd been involved in an accident that had mangled his left arm and left it considerably weakened and almost useless.

Chapter 14

The file on the accident contained a police report. I read everything several times over before I understood what had happened.

In the early morning hours after a New Year's Eve party, the Guilfoyles' chauffeur had side-swiped the parking attendant's booth. The police suspected he was legally drunk, but he wasn't tested, and they didn't know for certain. The man protested his innocence, but he was dismissed on the spot.

No one realized anything was amiss until they arrived home and changed Freddy for bed. His left arm was bent at an alarming angle, and he screamed when they touched it. They walked back out into the freezing night air, which shook off what remained of the alcohol fog. The side of the car that held the infant seat was dented in a couple of inches, enough to crush the baby's fragile bones.

One of them called for an ambulance. Sometime after that, John called his brother.

"Didn't Freddy cry?" Sir Geoffrey had asked.

Yes, of course, but they thought it was colic. He cried a lot.

For a number of nightmarish days, they thought Freddy might lose his arm. The doctors had managed to save it and provided the parents with detailed instructions on how to exercise the limb. His physical development slowed down, his ability to crawl and walk was delayed, but not for unnaturally long. When Freddy left for school, a professional physical therapist took over. But the therapist's notes left no doubt that Freddy would never gain full use of his arm again.

I thought about Freddy and what, if anything, would make a

person notice his disability. I had never seen him in short sleeves. And I assumed he was right-handed, so I thought nothing of his not using his nondominant left hand. I replayed his dropping the box in my mind. The box had fallen to his left—as if that arm wasn't able to support its weight.

The next file I opened contained articles and documents about the second accident, the one that killed Freddy's father. Buried in the fine print of the police report was a very interesting note. The Guilfoyles' car had a manual transmission—which would require the use of both hands to drive. And in England the gearshift is to the left of the driver. . . .

Freddy had no business driving a car like that. No wonder he felt guilty for his father's death.

I put down the papers and shook my head over those silly young parents. My heart broke for the innocent child whose life was changed forever, for the young boy encouraged to try something he wasn't equipped to handle, for the guilt that must have consumed everyone concerned.

The last physical therapy test in the file indicated Freddy had 20 percent use of his left arm. He wasn't supposed to carry anything more than ten pounds with that arm. This morning he had carried the heaviest box, easily weighing more than ten pounds.

My phone rang. Anne Stetson reminded me of Marshfield's follow-up appointment from his illness in the morning. I agreed absentmindedly. What a waste of time, since Marshfield was doing so well. But I made a note in my datebook.

I put everything back in the box. I needed time to consider what I had learned. I decided to go to bed early and let everything percolate overnight and see what my brain came up with in the morning.

Seven hours later, at half-past four, I started downstairs with one thing on my mind. I'd forgotten about the third flash drive. I sat down at my computer and opened the file with ease now that I knew the password.

The first document I opened was dated April 22—a week before Sir Geoffrey's murder. My heart stopped beating for a second. He might supply the clues to his own murder in this file.

An hour later, I was certain he had. My phone rang, but I let it go to voice mail as I read the last few pages of the file. A few minutes later Georgina popped into the apartment. "Gran! Is something wrong?"

I felt guilty for making her worry.

"I think something may be right," I said.

"You figured something out."

I nodded. "Who do we have running the kitchen today? Can you get away for a couple of hours?"

She calculated beneath her breath.

"Kendra's coming in. She'll be super busy, but she's capable."

I agreed. "Marshfield needs to see the vet, and I'd like you to come along with me."

Of course Georgina understood there was more involved, but I felt safer if that's the reason she gave Kendra for her absence.

My granddaughter's eyes sparkled with questions she didn't ask. "What time should I be ready?"

"I think eight thirty should do it." I turned off the computer. "Now let's go bake something."

"Are you feeling up to it?"

"Of course I am. It's the least I can do since I'm taking you away." When we got to the kitchen, I studied the daily menu. Georgina and I discussed a few tweaks that would make it easier for Kendra to manage on her own. We removed one item and offered a special on the fresh fruit, yogurt, and granola platter with a muffin and all the coffee they wanted for free, a perennial favorite.

I also made half a dozen quiche pies that could be warmed and served fresh. It felt good to be back in the kitchen I had neglected for too long. I greeted the fishermen who came in at five, the travelers eager to get on the road at six, and before I had turned around, it was seven.

I finished washing the dishes and left the kitchen with reluctance. "I've got to feed Marshfield and take him for a walk before we leave."

"Go." Georgina pushed me out the door. "Thanks for your help. It should go as smooth as clockwork now."

I drove a short distance to the nearest open ocean space where Marshfield could run and bark without my having to worry about him bothering the neighbors. "We'll come back later," I promised him. "But first we have important business to finish. You want Sir Geoffrey's murderer to be caught, don't you?"

I stopped by the tea shoppe at the stroke of eight. Georgina climbed into the car holding a bag. "I thought I'd ask if Anne wants to sell some doggie treats on consignment."

Smiling, I shook my head at her unstoppable entrepreneurial spirit.

"So where are we really going?"

"To the vet, like I said."

She looked at me sideways. "Not that I mind, but why did you invite me along?"

"I think I know what happened to Geoffrey. I have another

theory to test out first though." Without further explanation, I stopped by the local hardware store. "I'll be right back," I said to Anne. "Stay in the car with Marshfield."

When I returned to the car, I showed Georgina my purchase and told her about my idea.

We drove to a deserted section of the beach, and Georgina and I got out of the car. I rubbed Marshfield's ears. "You stay here and wait for just a few minutes, Marshfield. You'll be safer in the car." I handed him a couple of Georgina's treats to keep him happy, rolled down the windows, and joined Georgina on the beach.

She held the six-foot-long fishing spear. "Now, let me get this straight. First you want me to see if I can thrust this just using one arm?"

"Yes," I said. I didn't know how much flexibility Freddy had in his injured arm, so it was best to go with the worst-case scenario for him.

She took the spear and bounced it down in her hand until she was holding it in the center, then lunged forward, holding it parallel to the ground. "That wasn't any trouble." She retrieved the spear. "Now you want me to throw it with my right hand and not use my left arm at all, right?"

"Yes," I said. "Pretend you can't even lift that arm. And you don't get to take any running steps either."

Georgina had been a javelin thrower in high school, so she knew what she was doing. She hefted the spear onto her right shoulder then reared back and threw it. Straight as an arrow.

Dr. Stetson gave Marshfield a thorough examination. "He's bristling with good health. You must be taking good care of him."

"We've made a connection." I rubbed the top of the dog's head, and his tongued lolled out of his mouth. "I have a favor to ask of you. I have a free bag of homemade dog treats as a bribe."

The vet arched his eyebrows. "I'll help if I can."

Five minutes later, Georgina and I were headed to the police station sans Marshfield. I had locked the files in the trunk to show to the police before I left the house.

"I'd better warn Kendra I'll be gone a little longer than we thought." Georgina made a quick call.

Our local stringer for the *Portland Herald* arrived at the police station at the same time we did. "What are you two doing here?" he asked as we walked up the steps.

I clutched my folder tighter and continued up the steps as he dashed ahead of me.

I glanced at Georgina. As one, we followed him as quickly as possible.

Freddy Guilfoyle blocked my view to whatever else was going on in the station when I reached the door. His eyes fell on me. "You."

He made me sound like the root of all his problems.

"I know the truth about the accident and your arm, Freddy," I said.

He stumbled back and his face crumpled.

I walked past him to the desk where Enos was sitting. "I need to speak with Tom."

"He's with the prisoner, Mrs. Holland. We don't appreciate your interference."

I drew myself to my full height and reminded myself to respect the law.

Georgina barged ahead. "She has information he needs to know. It's unlikely it came up in your investigation."

"I suppose you're going to tell me she's not guilty."

My granddaughter and I both nodded vigorously. "She's not," I said vehemently.

"What do you mean?" His curiosity got the better of him.

I opened my folder and pulled out Freddy's medical records. "These are the documents Sir Geoffrey kept regarding an accident that permanently injured his nephew thirty-five years ago."

Enos's shoulders went rigid. "You should have turned this over to the police."

"I am now. It's taken me time to go through Sir Geoffrey's things. I just figured out what happened this morning." I hesitated. "He also wrote something in his last journal entry—the week before his death—that has everything to do with motive."

Enos started to scold me again, but Georgina shushed him. "Give Gran a break, okay? You couldn't expect her to hand over the entire estate lock, stock, and barrel, especially after you released the crime scene."

"I knew that was a mistake," he said gloomily.

I looked at Georgina. She nodded, and I turned back to Enos. "Is it possible for us to sit down with Daisy and Freddy and I can present the evidence?"

Enos scratched his head.

Tom came out of the interrogation room. "You have no business here today, Ms. Holland. Why you don't you go home and brew some tea."

I felt Georgina's hackles rise.

Enos tapped his superior on the shoulder and whispered to him. In a louder voice, he added, "She's asking to see the prisoner, sir."

I held my breath while Tom studied me. At length, he said, "She keeps saying it was all a mistake."

"If it matters, I don't think it was premeditated."

Tom shrugged. "We need to hear what you've got, I suppose."

Daisy turned an incredulous look in my direction when Georgina, Freddy, and I followed Tom into the interrogation room. "What are they doing here?"

We all took a seat at the table. I put the folder down in front of me. "I asked to speak with you and Freddy, Daisy. You see—" I opened the folder. "I'm here on behalf of Sir Geoffrey. I wanted to let you know that he never forgave himself for what happened in that accident years ago."

His jaw tightened. "You can't know that."

"But I do, because he wrote about it. At the end, when he knew you were coming for a visit." I had reached the crucial point. "How long have you known your uncle caused the accident that left you permanently injured?" Sir Geoffrey's guilt had drenched that final file.

Freddy blinked. "He wrote me a month ago, telling me he was leaving me all of his holdings in Britain except for a lifetime stipend for. . .for someone else."

I took a very educated guess. "For a certain chauffeur and his family?"

Freddy ducked his head, looking stricken.

Tom stirred beside me. "What accident are you talking about, Mrs. Holland?"

I handed him all but one of the pages I'd printed from Sir Geoffrey's journal. "Thirty-five years ago, a drunken Sir Geoffrey caused an accident that disabled his infant nephew, Freddy Guilfoyle. The family blamed the accident on the chauffeur—whose word would never be taken over British royalty, no matter how far removed from the Crown." I pointed to the pages in his hand. "It's all there—Sir Geoffrey's confession and wish to make things right."

Tom frowned. "So are you saying that Mrs. Guilfoyle killed her brother-in-law to punish him for what he did to her son?"

I pulled the last printed page from the folder. "No. You've arrested the wrong Guilfoyle." I handed him the paper. "Sir Geoffrey received this email from Freddy just before he and Daisy left for the States."

Freddy lifted his head. With a weary sigh, he spoke in a low voice. "When Uncle Geoff wrote me and told me what really happened that night, I felt so betrayed and angry." He shrugged his left shoulder. "And it's not just because I have to live with this. My father died because I couldn't handle driving the car. That's Uncle Geoff's fault."

Tom held up the paper. "So you wrote him this letter, threatening to hurt him like he hurt you?"

Freddy dropped his head in his hands. "We argued all night. We were supposed to go spearfishing with Mr. Whitaker—that's why the gear was out."

Enos stopped taking notes and stared at him, his mouth open.

"I grabbed the spear, thinking I'd injure him, like he did me, but—it all happened so fast—he lunged to get the spear away from me, and I. . .I couldn't lower it in time." Freddy covered his face as his voice broke.

I had to know about Marshfield. "Did you have to poison your uncle's dog? He never did anything to you."

"Mother did that. She thought it might suggest someone else had snuck into the house."

The tape recorder in the center of the table whirred, recording every word. A part of me wanted to remind Freddy he didn't have to speak without a lawyer present. Surely he was aware of his basic rights.

Suddenly Freddy sat up straight. "I'll wait until my lawyer is present before I say any more."

Epilogue

Two hours later, Enos handed me a note from Georgina. Enos's wife has taken me home. You'll have to give me a blow-by-blow description of what happened.

I had seen her leave right after Freddy confessed. As I gathered my things, Enos stopped me at the door. "In case the chief didn't say anything, thank you, Ms. Holland."

I blew air through my bangs. "You're welcome, Enos. I'm just glad the questions are answered." A few minutes later, I was in the car, calling Paul. I explained what had happened. "Freddy asked for a lawyer. I didn't know if you could be his lawyer, or maybe your daughter?"

"I'll take care of it."

On the way home I found myself missing Marshfield. The way he had wormed his way into my heart in such a short time amazed me. I picked him up from the vet and headed for the tea shoppe.

All I wanted to do was head up to my apartment and cry. But that could wait. The people of Sea Side wouldn't be satisfied until they saw me in person.

As soon as I parked the car, Norman Dexter walked up. "You can't deny me an interview," he said reasonably. "It's in the public's best interest."

Of course I could refuse—if I wanted to read what his imagination put into print in place of the truth. "I'll make a statement today. Check with me tomorrow about a time for an interview."

He opened his mouth as if to protest then shrugged. "That'll do. I'll head by the police station to check their blotter." He wiggled his eyebrows suggestively.

"Come on." I put my arm through his. "Let's go face the lions."

Later—much, much later, as customers continued to pour in long past our usual closing time—Georgina locked the shop door and we headed upstairs. Marshfield had spent the rest of the day in the newly constructed kennel. He seemed relieved to see me and ready to settle down in his spot by the window.

A few minutes later, I took pizza slices out of the microwave and poured tall glasses of milk. I'd had enough tea, coffee, and soda pop to keep me afloat for a week.

"This is the way I like it," Georgina said. "Although I wish Mathew could have been here."

"Me too," I admitted. "He's due back sometime today." I pulled up a stool and rested my feet on it. "The Tea Shoppe sleuths can retire for good."

"Hear, hear," Georgina said.

In the distant future I heard someone laughing. I had a funny feeling our Tea Shoppe had not seen its last mystery.

PAUL HOLLYWOOD'S HOT CROSS BUNS

2¼ cups strong white bread flour, plus extra for dusting
2 teaspoons salt
⅓ cup sugar
2 teaspoons rapid-rise yeast
⅛ cup unsalted butter, softened
2 medium eggs, beaten
½ cup warm full-fat milk
½ cup cool water
5½ ounces sultanas
3 ounces chopped mixed peel (lemon & orange peel)
Finely grated zest of 2 oranges
1 dessert apple, cored and diced
2 teaspoons ground cinnamon

For the crosses:
⅓ cup flour
5 tablespoons water

For the glaze:
⅓ cups apricot jam

1. Put the flour into a large mixing bowl. Add the salt and sugar to one side of the bowl and the yeast to the other. Add the butter, eggs, milk, and half the water, and turn the mixture round with your fingers. Continue to add the water, a little at a time, until you've picked up all the flour from the sides of the bowl. You may not need to add all the water, or you may need to add a little more—you want dough that

is soft but not soggy. Use the mixture to clean the inside of the bowl, and keep going until the mixture forms a rough dough.

2. Tip the dough onto a lightly floured surface and begin to knead. Keep kneading for 5 to 10 minutes. Work through the initial wet stage until the dough starts to form a soft, smooth skin.

3. When your dough feels smooth and silky, put it into a lightly oiled large bowl. Cover with a tea towel and leave to rise until at least doubled in size—at least 1 hour, but it's fine to leave it for 2 or even 3 hours.

4. Tip the dough onto a lightly floured surface and scatter the sultanas, mixed peel, orange zest, apple, and cinnamon on top. Knead in until evenly incorporated. Cover and leave to rise for an hour.

5. Fold the dough inward repeatedly until all the air is knocked out. Divide into 12 pieces and roll into balls. Place, fairly close together, on 1 or 2 baking trays lined with baking parchment or silicone paper

6. Put each tray inside a clean plastic bag and leave to rest for 1 hour or until the dough is at least doubled in size and springs back quickly if you prod it lightly with your finger. Meanwhile, heat your oven to 425 degrees.

7. For the crosses, mix the flour and water into a paste. Using a piping bag fitted with a fine nozzle, pipe crosses on the buns. Bake for 20 minutes or until golden brown. Warm the apricot jam with a splash of water, sieve, and brush over the tops of the warm buns to glaze. Cool on a wire rack.

Bestselling author Darlene Franklin's greatest claim to fame is that she writes full-time from a nursing home. She lives in Oklahoma, near her son and his family, and continues her interests in playing the piano and singing, reading books, enjoying good fellowship, and watching reality TV in addition to writing. She is an active member of Oklahoma City Christian Fiction Writers, American Christian Fiction Writers, and the Christian Authors Network. She has written more than fifty books and 250 devotionals. Her historical fiction ranges from the French and Indian War to Vietnam, and from California to Maine.

SCONES TO DIE FOR

CYNTHIA HICKEY

Chapter 1

"Ashley Lawrence. Your attention, please." The professor's stern voice pulled me from the plot of the true crime show I'd watched the night before.

"Professor." I enjoyed taking the latest shows and comparing them to the lessons I learned in my summer session forensics class. Unfortunately, it left the instructor thinking me an addlebrained fool.

"Care to share with the class what I was talking about?"

"Uh, blood spatter?"

The class snickered. My face heated, even more so when I caught the amused glance of the handsome Brad Overson. Shrugging, I turned my attention back to Professor Lyons. "You were showing slides on how patterns can show a bullet's trajectory."

"Well, you were paying attention." He sneered. "Your semifinal will be a paper based on a real crime, how it was solved, and how you might have done things differently. Team up with someone. Papers are due one month from today." He shuffled the stack of papers on his desk. "Dismissed."

"Want to be my partner?" Brad leaned close from his desk a few feet away. "As much television as you watch, we're sure to get a good grade."

I laughed. There wasn't anyone I'd want to partner with more. "If you don't mind being paired up with someone the professor obviously dislikes."

"He doesn't dislike you," he said, hazel eyes twinkling as we left the classroom. "He expects great things from you."

"Because I'm an older student?" At twenty-five, I'd quit my receptionist job at Miller Inc., taken a part-time job as a delivery girl at Tea by the Sea, and enrolled in a forensics class as the first step toward fulfilling my dream.

"I'm older than you. Besides, age is just a number. I'd rather work with someone closer to my age than one of the kiddos." He held the outside door open. "When do you want to get together and plan our case?"

"I'm headed to work right now. Can I call you after I'm finished?" I didn't blame him for not wanting to pair with someone younger. The female students flocked around him like bees to a flower.

"Sure." He wrote his phone number on a sheet of paper and slipped it inside one of my books. "Talk to you later."

I had a skip in my step as I hurried to my car. I'd be working closely with the handsome Brad. Me, the dreamer. The assignment would be a piece of cake with us doing it together.

Fifteen minutes later, I entered Tea by the Sea to work the next five hours.

"We need you here tomorrow morning," Georgina, the owner's granddaughter said. "The other delivery girl has a doctor's appointment."

"I've got class at nine."

"Please?" She smiled.

I sighed. "Okay." The professor would have one more thing to be on my case about. Still, I couldn't go to school without money, and without a job, I wouldn't have any money. "I'll make it work." I flashed a grin and grabbed a bag of crumpets to deliver to the library.

After dropping the treats at the local book club meeting, I made my way to the front desk. "Are the books in?"

"I've got them right here." The librarian smiled. "You sure like blood and gore, don't you?"

"I like puzzles. Murder is a puzzle waiting to be put together." I carried the books to my car and returned to the tea shoppe.

The cute shop done in pink, green, and yellow never failed to calm me. I poured a cup of tea, grabbed a large cinnamon bun, and settled down to read until I had to make another delivery. The longer my classes went, the more the books made sense and filled me with purpose. I could see myself at a crime scene, taking notes and snapping photographs. I stared out the large front window, envisioning myself solving a difficult crime.

The bell over the door jangled on a regular basis as customers came and went. Some chose to sit and talk for a while.

"Delivery." Georgina set a striped bag on the counter.

"Got it." I left my books on the table, grabbed the bag, and noticing the delivery was for the local bookstore a few doors down, chose to walk. Who was the author doing the signing this time? It would be great if a true crime writer visited our town. I grinned. Maybe I could become that writer.

Professor Lyons had it right. My head was always in the clouds.

"Hey." Brad stepped from the drugstore.

"Hey, yourself." I grinned.

"You stepped in gum back there." He pointed at my shoe. "Dreaming again?"

"Yep." I glanced down and grimaced then scraped my shoe on a grate in the sidewalk. "Thinking of our assignment. I borrowed some books from the library. Want to come back to the shop with me and go through them?"

"Sure. Your boss won't mind?"

"Not as long as I make deliveries when needed. Be right back." I darted into the bookstore, dropped off the delivery, and then rejoined Brad. Since we'd run into each other, we could get a head start on our assignment. "Don't you have a job?"

"Yes, but Mondays are my day off. I work four tens at the construction yard."

Which would make it difficult to work together much except for the weekends. Still, I wouldn't want a different partner. We'd make it work.

Deliveries picked up the last half of my shift, and I left Brad digging through the books as I worked. The people of Sea Side, Maine, really liked their sweet treats.

On the way back from a delivery at a flower shop, I glanced at the double glass doors of Miller Inc. I usually had an order of scones to be delivered by now. Roy Miller served them, without fail, during the end-of-day meeting he usually had with clients. I pushed through the door before returning to Tea by the Sea.

"Good afternoon, Sue." I leaned on the reception desk, breathing through my mouth so as not to inhale too much of the woman's overpowering perfume. "Roy sick?"

"No, why?" Her fake eyelashes looked too heavy for her to fully open her eyes.

"I haven't seen an order for scones today."

She gasped, glancing at the clock. "I forgot to order them. Will you take care of it?"

"Sure, we all forget sometimes. How are you liking it here?"

"It's okay. It's a job." She leaned her elbows on the desk. "Roy's a bit of a hothead, isn't he?"

"I never saw that side of him." The man had always been a sweetheart. But then, I'd never forgotten to order his daily treats and always performed my job to his satisfaction. "I'll be back with the scones." I glanced at Roy's office door, hoping he'd look out so I could say hello. Maybe I'd see him later.

When I returned to Tea by the Sea, I placed the order for Roy. Since the shop was busy, I had time to sit with Brad. As long as the scones were delivered by four, Roy would be happy, and Sue out of trouble.

"Find anything interesting?" I pulled an unopened book toward me.

"Lots, but I'm hoping to find something unique, unusual, that maybe the other students won't stumble across." He rubbed his hands roughly down his face. "I'm going cross-eyed."

"Have a cup of tea, and I'll look for a while."

I'd barely gotten immersed in the pages before Georgina announced that Roy's order was ready. "I'll be back." I grabbed the order and practically ran down the street.

Sue wasn't behind her desk. No one answered my knock on Roy's door. I shrugged and headed for the conference room, where I placed the scones on the sideboard. "Hello?"

A door clicked shut down the hall. I peered from the conference room. "Roy?" Spiders skittered up my spine, and every B horror movie I'd ever seen ran through my mind. "Sue? I've brought the scones."

I checked the women's restroom and found no sign of Sue. I knocked on the men's room and received no reply. It seemed as if everyone had gone home early, but they wouldn't have left the front door unlocked, and I'd never known Roy to close up early. Millers Inc. was an insurance company for corporations, and he often stayed late.

I moved back to the reception area and stepped behind the desk.

Sue's scarlet purse sat underneath. Her cell phone, plugged into a charger, sat next to the desk phone. Where could she be?

Frowning, I headed to the supply room and found it locked. I felt a little foolish but knocked anyway. "Sue?"

A groan came from the other side.

"Where's the key?" I jiggled the handle again. "It's me, Ashley."

"Desk drawer."

I thundered down the hall and riffled through the skinny drawer under the computer until I found a key ring. A sparkling cat with pink rhinestones, one missing where the cat's eye should be, held several keys. I carried the ring back to the supply room and tried each key until I found the one that opened the door. I reached inside and flicked on the light.

Sue, face streaked with mascara and eye shadow, sat frozen on a folding chair. "Someone locked me in. It's not a very funny joke." She glared at me. "I hate the dark."

"Don't look at me. I just got here. Where's Roy?"

"He was in his office when I came to get the paper plates. He said his clients were going to be a little late, and that once I had the conference room set up, I could leave."

"I knocked on his door. He didn't answer." I stepped aside so she could move past me.

"Maybe he was on the phone."

True. I'd try again.

Sue returned to her desk. I knocked once more on Roy's door. Still no answer. The doorknob turned easily in my hand.

I opened the door to darkness. "Roy?" I reached over and turned on the light.

His office chair faced the wall behind the desk. I could see the top of his gray head. "Did you fall asleep?" I laughed. "It isn't like you not to be waiting on your scones."

When he didn't answer, I stepped around his desk. The first thing I noticed was the blood spatter on the landscape painting on the wall. The second thing was the gun in his hand.

I stumbled back, knocking over a desk lamp. "Sue! Call the police."

"What's wrong?" She entered the room, dropped her purse, and screamed.

Chapter 2

I whirled, gripped Sue by the shoulders, and gave her a shake. "Call the police," I said again. When she continued screaming, I shook her harder. "Now!"

As she dashed from the room, I squared my shoulders and studied the scene with a clinical detachment. I focused on what I had learned in my college class dealing with blood spatter. Yes, I might drift off to la-la land on a regular basis, but I could clearly see that Roy hadn't killed himself. He was left-handed for one, and the gun hung from his right hand. And the angle of the spatter was all wrong. It was even on the wrong wall. Someone had killed my former boss and tried to stage it to look like a suicide.

I removed my phone from my pocket and started snapping pictures, shoving aside my grief at Roy's death. I'd deal with that emotion later. Right now I needed to prove to myself I have what it takes to be a forensic scientist.

When sirens wailed to a stop outside the building, I slid my phone back into my pocket, took one last look at a good man, and then joined Sue by the front desk. I swallowed back tears and waited to be questioned.

Two police officers headed to Roy's office after I pointed, and another kept Sue in the reception area while telling me to find a different room and wait there. I went to the conference room and stared at the scones still sitting on the sideboard. I'd never deliver them here again.

"I'd like to ask you some questions, ma'am." A middle-aged officer, ROGEN, his badge said, took a seat across from me. "Name first."

"Ashley Lawrence. I work at Tea by the Sea."

"You found the body?"

I nodded. "I found it strange that Roy wasn't waiting for his scones." My gaze fell on the bag again. "I deliver them every day by four."

"How well did you know the deceased?" His pen scratched across the surface of his notepad.

"I used to be the receptionist here." I swallowed past the lump in my throat.

"Have you noticed anything different about Mr. Miller lately? Has he been depressed, out of sorts?"

"No, but I haven't worked here in several months. I only see him when I deliver his scones. Who wouldn't be happy knowing they were going to bite into one of those?"

"I wouldn't know." He sat back in his chair, spearing me with his glare.

After several seconds of silence, I blurted out, "He didn't kill himself."

"Who said he did?" Officer Rogen folded his hands on the tabletop. "What makes you sure it wasn't suicide?"

"The blood spatter, and he's left-handed."

"You're observant."

"I'm taking classes at the college."

"Let's assume you're right. Did Mr. Miller have any enemies?"

I shrugged. "Not that I know of. Sue said he had a meeting planned with some clients, but I don't know who they were."

"We'll get that information from her." He drummed his fingers on the table. "The receptionist said someone locked her in the storage room, and that you were the one to let her out. Were you the only one here?" He narrowed his eyes.

I frowned. "Are you insinuating I locked her up so I could kill Roy?" Seriously? Did I look like I could murder someone? "What would be my motive?"

"I'm not insinuating anything."

It appeared the questions had stopped, and the officer was just fishing for information. He couldn't really consider me a suspect, could he?

After several tense minutes, he stood and handed me a business card. "If you think of anything that will help our investigation, please call me. Don't leave town, Miss Lawrence."

I left the conference room. Sue was no longer at her desk, and crime scene tape fluttered in front of the building. It was then that I realized I'd left Brad almost two hours ago.

I darted back to the shop.

Brad met me at the door. "What happened? I started to go looking for you when I saw the police cars. Are you all right?"

"No." Tears poured down my cheeks. "Roy Miller has been murdered." I stepped into his open arms and sobbed.

"Come on. You need some tea." He patted my back, wiped my tears, and led me inside the shop. "Sit. I'll explain to your boss what's happened."

"Thank you." I folded my arms on top of the books and rested my head on them. Sadness over Roy's death couldn't quite mask the thought that the authorities listed me as a suspect.

"They always do," Brad said when I told him of the officer questioning me. "You found him, after all."

I turned my teacup around and around in my hands. Since I was now off the clock, I should focus on the professor's assignment. Instead, I couldn't stop thinking about blood spatter. Roy had been facing the back wall when I entered the room. The spatter had been on the wall he faced. "Someone turned him around. They didn't want his death to be noticed immediately when someone entered the room."

"Maybe he wanted time to get away." Brad shook his head and shrugged. "It doesn't make sense."

"Forget these books." I set down my cup. "Let's make solving Roy's murder our assignment."

"No way." He frowned. "That would be interfering with a police investigation, which is against the law."

"We'll just ask some questions, clear my name, that sort of thing." I grinned. "It'll be justice for Roy, and our assignment won't be like anyone else's." If we found Roy's killer, the professor would have to stop looking at me as if I were an empty-headed Barbie doll. "At least think about it."

"I don't need to. I say no."

"Time to close up," Georgina called. "Can you still work in the morning, Ashley? I'll understand if you can't."

"I'll be here." Asking questions and investigating on my own.

"You're going to do this anyway, aren't you?" Brad asked once we stepped outside.

"Yes." I peered up at him. "I have to."

"Why? You're going to get into trouble, or worse, end up like Roy Miller. I'm sure you aren't the only suspect. What about the receptionist?"

"Locked up, remember?" I arched a brow. "I need to find out who he was going to meet with and go from there."

"The building will be off-limits for a while."

"I'll contact Sue at home."

He crossed his arms. "Do you know where she lives?"

"No, but it shouldn't be too hard to find out." I headed for my car. "Let's meet back here tomorrow when you get off work."

"See you at six."

I could feel his gaze on my back, boring holes into me, as I climbed into the driver's seat of my car. While I really wanted him to work with me on finding out who killed Roy, I'd do it by myself if I had to. It would be double work, solving a real case and studying one from the past, plus my other classes and work. I sighed, seeing a lot of late nights in my future.

On my way home, I drove slowly past Miller Inc. My cell phone seemed to burn through my pocket. I'd wanted to show the photos to Brad, but since he didn't want to get involved, I'd held back. Besides, I needed to upload them onto my computer and print them out.

Half an hour later, I had several eight-and-a-half-by-eleven-inch photos spread across my kitchen table and a cup of coffee close at hand. Time to become detached again and find some clues. I pulled a notepad from my schoolbag and took notes: "Staged suicide. Chair turned to face the wall."

I tapped the pencil against my teeth. If Roy had a meeting scheduled, where were the people he was supposed to meet with? They should have arrived shortly after I did. I jotted down my question.

Then I searched for Sue's phone number online. No luck, but I did find her social media profile and left a private message there. Hopefully she wouldn't all of a sudden become close-lipped about today's events.

My computer dinged almost instantly.

THE POLICE SAID YOU MIGHT HAVE LOCKED ME UP AND KILLED ROY.

ARE YOU SERIOUS? HE WAS MY FRIEND. WHO WAS HE MEETING WITH?

WHY SHOULD I TELL YOU?

BECAUSE I WANT TO FIND OUT WHO KILLED HIM.

OH.

I stared at the blinking cursor for a few minutes.

HELLO?

I HAD TO LOOK IT UP IN MY BOOK.

YOU TOOK THE APPOINTMENT BOOK? *Good girl.*

OF COURSE. IT'S MINE. WHY WOULD THE POLICE WANT
SOMETHING BRIGHT PINK WITH YELLOW FLOWERS? ROY
WAS SUPPOSED TO MEET WITH A MR. LARRY JENKINS AND
A MR. JOE OLSON FROM SEA SIDE CONSTRUCTION.

THANKS!

I clicked off, hoping she didn't get in trouble once the authorities
realized she'd removed something that could be potential evidence
from the office.

Brad said he worked construction. I found his phone number in
the pages of my textbook and called.

"Hello?" From the grogginess in his voice, I could tell I'd awakened him.

I glanced at the clock. Midnight already? "I'm sorry. I'll talk to
you tomorrow."

"I'm awake now. What's up?"

"Are you familiar with Sea Side Construction?"

"Yes, I work for them. I'm supervisor of the day crew. Why?"

"Because Roy was supposed to meet with a Mr. Jenkins and a
Mr. Olson this afternoon, but they never showed."

"That's weird."

"Why?"

"Because they left this afternoon for an out-of-town meeting."

"Maybe they forgot they had one scheduled with Roy?" Or they locked Sue in the closet and killed her boss before leaving town. My unspoken thought hung in the air. I wanted to ask Brad to ask some questions around work, but his reluctance to help me put me in an uncomfortable position. I also couldn't very well go to Sea Side Construction and start asking random questions on my own. "Who are they?"

"Co-owners." He sighed. "You've been up half the night on this case, haven't you?"

"Yes. I took photos of the crime scene, and I've been studying them."

"You took photos before the police arrived?"

"I couldn't do it after they got there, now could I?"

"You're going to end up in jail, Ashley."

"I'll do my best to make sure that doesn't happen. I'm a suspect, Brad. You have no idea how that feels." I coughed to hide the fact that tears were gathering in my throat.

"Maybe they'll rule it a suicide."

"But it's clear it was murder. You should see the photos." I swiped my arm across my eyes. "I need your help, Brad. I'll bring them to the tea shoppe tomorrow."

"You can't flash them around in public." He sighed. "I'll come by your place instead. What's your address?"

I told him then hung up. Once he saw these pictures, he wouldn't be able not to help me. Not a good man like Brad Overson.

I left my notes and the photos on the table and carried my mug to the sink. Romeo, my tuxedo cat, decided to complain about the late hour by meowing at the top of his lungs. I scooped him up and carried him to the bedroom. "Sorry, buddy, Mama's been a little busy this evening." I'd be busy for many more to come.

I set the cat on the bed, changed into my pajamas, then climbed under a thin sheet. Summer evenings in Maine were still sometimes cool enough for a light covering. I lay in bed, the curtains at my window fluttering in a slight breeze, and closed my eyes, only to snap them open a few seconds later.

Sleep wasn't going to come easy with visions of Roy floating through my brain. The coffee hadn't helped either. *Lord, help me sleep. Oh, I should have asked You before racing ahead with this case. Sorry about that. Could You please save me from myself?*

I continued to pray for guidance, my gaze focused on the butterfly-shaped nightlight on my nightstand, until sleep overtook me.

CHAPTER 3

Brad showed up at my apartment at exactly 6:00 p.m. I opened the door and grinned. "Punctual."

"Always." He returned my smile. "The professor wasn't happy when you didn't answer roll call."

I shrugged. "He'll change his mind when I solve Roy's murder." I stepped aside to let him in. "Are you hungry? I made spaghetti."

"Starving." He glanced around my small apartment. "You're still determined to get involved?"

"Yes. Take a look at the photos on the table while I serve dinner." Fully convinced he'd change his mind about helping me, I pulled two plates from the cupboard and removed the garlic bread from the oven. "Clear a spot."

He moved the printed sheets to one side, and I set his plate in front of him. "Iced tea okay?"

"Perfect." He straightened in his chair. "Okay, you win. I'll help you if only to keep you from getting yourself hurt. These photos convince me. You've a good eye when taking photographs at a crime scene."

Answer to last night's prayer. "Thank you." I sat down across from him. "First step. . .find out about your bosses' trip."

He nodded. "I'll have to think of a subtle way to bring up the subject. I can't blurt out that they didn't show up to their appointment with Miller. They'd wonder how I knew that."

"I'm going to question Sue some more." I sprinkled a liberal amount of parmesan cheese over my pasta. You can never have too much cheese.

"Be careful, please. I'm still not crazy about us getting involved."
I wanted to clap. "We'll ace this assignment."

"If we don't get ourselves killed or arrested."

"Are you always gonna be a Debbie Downer?" Solving the crime would be way more fun if he got a little excited.

Brad tilted his head then laughed. "I promise to be more upbeat if you promise that if things get too dangerous, we back off."

"Agreed." I thrust my hand across the table.

After we ate and did the dishes, we bent over the photographs again. Brad studied one after the other more thoroughly than he had before we ate. "I agree Roy was murdered. I also agree someone turned his chair around. Remorse?"

"Maybe. Guilt could have taken over, and they didn't want his lifeless eyes watching them leave." I shuddered.

"Did you touch anything in his office?" Brad raised his eyebrows.

"I don't think so. It's been months since I worked there, so I doubt my fingerprints would still be on anything."

"Let's check the dumpster in back of the shop. Maybe we'll get lucky with a stupid killer. Garbage pickup isn't until tomorrow. The police probably already looked, but they might have missed something. Do you have gloves?"

I went to my linen closet and pulled out some rubber gloves I used for washing dishes and general cleaning. I handed him a pair. "These should fit you."

"Of course you'd have flowered gloves." He frowned. "These look like something housewives wore in the fifties."

"If a person is cleaning, they might as well look good doing it." I grabbed the yellow ones with ducks on them from the kitchen sink. "Fashion never goes out of style."

Brad drove and then parked half a block from where crime scene tape still hung in front of Miller Inc. The dumpster behind the building sat free of tape, which I thought strange. The setting sun cast the area in creepy shadows, and I shivered.

"Are you cold?" Brad asked.

"No, just spooked. Why isn't there tape back here like there is in front?"

"Maybe they actually did rule it a suicide." He clicked on a flashlight and handed me one.

If the police weren't going to treat Roy's death as a homicide, then that was one more reason for us to investigate. There wasn't a lot of crime in Sea Side, was there? At least not enough for them to rush an investigation.

I pressed the button on my flashlight and moved slowly around the alley. Asphalt didn't retain footprints. If there was a clue, it would have to jump out at me. "I don't see anything."

"You'll have to go diving."

"What?" My eyes widened. "Eew. Why don't you get in the dumpster?"

"Can you lift me?"

"Well, no. Can't you climb?"

"Why would I, when I can give you a boost? You probably don't weigh more than a hundred and fifteen pounds." His eyes twinkled in the light of the rising moon. "Scared?"

"No." I stepped into his cupped hands. "Don't throw me."

He didn't, but rather hefted and then tossed. I landed on a soft black bag, my hand in something squishy. The smell was enough to make me gag. "Hand me my light." I swallowed back nausea and breathed through my mouth.

"There's something dripping from your fingers."

"No doubt." I wrapped my gooey hand around the flashlight and aimed it around the inside of the full dumpster. If I wanted to find anything worth finding, I'd have to start digging, and I needed to use both hands. "You'll have to shine your light in, Brad."

I turned my light off and slid it into my pocket as Brad's light illuminated the dumpster. Thank goodness I wore gloves, because digging was gross. I tore through bags of soggy food, a couple of soiled diapers, and two bags containing papers. Those I tossed out of the dumpster to dig through later. "A couple of those have sheets with Miller Inc. on them."

"I'll set them aside."

"I'm ready to get out now." I held up my hands.

Brad gripped my hands and dragged me over the lip of the dumpster. I fell into his arms, breathless. Whether from the drag, or being pressed against him, I wasn't quite sure. I stared through the gloom into his eyes. "Uh, thanks for not dropping me," I whispered.

He chuckled. "My pleasure. Although you do emit a certain unpleasant odor, you feel good." His arms tightened around me.

I slapped his shoulder. Way for a guy to spoil the mood. But I could smell myself, and it definitely wasn't pleasant. I stepped away. "Do you want to take these bags back to my apartment or go through them here?"

A car stopped at the end of the alley and turned off its lights, its engine idling.

Brad grabbed a bag. "Apartment. We're too easily seen out here."

I grabbed the other bag and followed him between two buildings back to his car. The other vehicle pulled from the alley as we drove away. "Is that car following us?"

"Easy way to find out." Brad pulled into a drive-thru restaurant. "Want something to drink?"

"Yes, as long as I don't have to get out and have anyone see me smeared with who knows what. Diet Coke, please." I plucked my sticky shirt away from my body and desperately craved a shower.

The other car drove past. So much for paranoia.

Drinks in hand, we returned to my apartment. I made a beeline for the shower while Brad sorted through the garbage bags for anything of interest. A few minutes later, wet hair hanging down my back, I joined him feeling refreshed and odor-free.

"Find anything?" I pulled a stack of papers toward myself.

"Not yet, but I've been focusing on looking for something about Sea Side Construction. Maybe you could focus on something else." He lifted his drink to his mouth.

My gaze landed on his lips. What would it have felt like if he'd kissed me back there in the alley? I was an idiot for even considering such a thing when I'd stunk to high heaven, but I was a dreamer after all.

Brad stared at me. "What?"

"Nothing." My face heated, and I turned my attention to the printed papers in front of me. As I found names and mentions of meetings, I wrote them on the notepad next to me. By the time my eyes grew gritty, I had quite the list.

I straightened and blinked away the tiredness. "Find anything?"

"Not a thing. Is the receptionist sure my bosses had a meeting with hers?" Brad rubbed both hands down his face. "I'm done for the night. See you at class in the morning?"

I nodded. "Is Professor Lyons going to want to know which case our assignment is based on?"

"Most likely. Just pick something. We'll tell him we changed it once this is over. I don't think we should tell him what we're really working on. The fewer people who know, the better."

Professor Lyons glanced down at the day's assignment then back at me. "At least you were working while you were missing class. This case has been unsolved for twenty years. Do you really think you can solve it?"

I shrugged. "It's worth a shot. You didn't say we actually had to solve the case, just give our input on what could have been done differently. With today's achievements in forensic science and DNA—"

He waved a dismissive hand. "Okay."

If I were to look up *rude* in the dictionary, I felt certain I'd see his picture. Biting my tongue to prevent from saying what I thought, I returned to my seat. "He's impossible," I whispered to Brad.

"Only a few more weeks, and you'll be in another class." He reached over and patted my hand.

I tried to concentrate on the rest of the class, I really did, but all I wanted to do was start working my way down the list of names I'd made last night. I could make some calls after work, but that seemed so far away.

Instead, I forced myself to focus on today's lesson of finding out a perpetrator by fingerprints, hair samples, and skin flakes. I doubted I could use any of that in solving Roy's murder. I didn't have the tools. All I had was a nosiness and a drive for justice. Hopefully that would be enough.

After class I agreed to have Brad over again at six and rushed to work. The day filled with more than the usual deliveries, and I soon found myself running behind. I ducked into the corner drugstore to deliver pastries to the pharmacist then barged back outside, running smack into someone.

"Careful." Sue patted her teased-up hair. "You almost knocked me down."

"You're just the person I wanted to see." I grabbed her by the arm and pulled her to the side of the building. "Are you sure Roy was supposed to meet with Sea Side Construction? The owners left town yesterday afternoon."

She narrowed her eyes. "Of course I'm sure. I told you, it's in my book." She pulled the gaudy-colored appointment book from her purse and opened it. "See? I even wrote it in ink. It isn't like Roy announced his appointments on the street corner."

Sure enough. There it was. "Is that the only place you would have made note of it? Would Roy have jotted it down somewhere himself?"

She gave a one-shoulder shrug. "His desk calendar maybe, but that's taped off." Her narrowed eyes disappeared under the thick lashes she wore. "Why are you questioning me?"

"I told you, I want to find out who killed Roy. Have you spoken to the police again?"

"I'm headed there now, in fact. It occurred to them that I might have an appointment book." She slid it back into her purse. "They aren't as stupid as you think."

If they wanted the book, they weren't considering his death a suicide. That was good news.

She smirked at me. "Don't be surprised if they call you in for more questions, since you found him."

"You were the last to see him alive."

Tears sprang to her eyes. "You aren't a very nice person, Ashley." She lifted her nose in the air and marched off on four-inch heels the color of a pumpkin.

My phone rang on my way back to the shop. "Hello?"

"Ms. Lawrence, this is Officer Rogen. We'd like you to come to the precinct for more questions."

I closed my eyes. "When? Now? I'm working."

"As soon as possible." *Click.*

I sighed and went to tell Georgina I'd have to take the last hour of work off. Then I sent a text to Brad, telling him I might be late meeting him later and why.

CHIN UP, he replied. YOU'VE DONE NOTHING WRONG. LET ME KNOW WHEN YOU'RE FINISHED. I'LL BRING CHINESE.

I looked forward to another evening spent with Brad as I headed for the police station.

Chapter 4

After waiting in the reception area for the police to finish interrogating Sue, I was finally ushered into Officer Rogen's office. He motioned for me to take a seat, then steepled his fingers under his chin and narrowed his eyes.

I refused to squirm under his watchful stare, and arched a brow. "Am I here to endure the silent treatment, or do you actually have questions for me?"

He sneered. "Since the receptionist withheld information, I'm wondering if there's something you haven't told us."

Like digging through dumpsters? Wanting to solve the murder for justice and a good grade on an assignment? Taking photos of the crime scene? "No, not that I can think of." I put on my most innocent face, which, judging by the suspicious look in Rogen's eyes, wasn't very innocent.

He took a deep breath and released it slowly. "I do hope that your forensics class hasn't given you any ideas about meddling in my investigation."

"I'm a college student, not a forensic scientist." There. I could answer without lying. Not telling the truth to law enforcement could get me into a lot of trouble. Even a dreamer like me knew that.

"I don't want you discussing this with Sue Wilson either."

"We don't exactly run in the same social circles, Officer." Was he going to ask me any questions, or just tell me what to do?

"Tell me again every detail starting from when you entered Mr. Miller's office."

Ah, the change tactic routine. I told him everything except about taking photographs and noticing the chair turned around to face the wall. "Are you convinced now that it wasn't a suicide?"

"I cannot divulge that." He sat back in his chair. "You have a very observant eye, Ms. Lawrence. Are you sure you didn't see more?"

What was it he wanted or hadn't wanted me to see? "Finding my old boss and friend dead was traumatic. That's all I remember. Maybe when his death isn't as fresh, some facts may become clearer. It happens sometimes on TV."

"TV isn't real."

"I watch true crime shows on a regular basis." I had ever since high school.

"Spare me from wannabe law enforcement." He rolled his eyes. "We're done here. Remember. . .do not interfere."

Dismissed, I smiled and left the room, texting Brad that I was on my way home. I'd survived another encounter with the sour faced Officer Rogen and not told a single lie. Was omitting what I knew a lie? Maybe. I felt a twinge of regret, but I really, really wanted justice and to put my snide professor in his place at the same time. Add in the fact that Rogen seemed overly suspicious of me, and I felt I had plenty of reasons to get involved.

Once outside, I glanced around for Sue, wanting to know what questions she'd been grilled with. Not seeing her, I got in my car and drove home. I needed to study the photographs with a magnifying glass. There was definitely something in Roy's office I'd missed.

I sent Brad another text that the door was open and to come on in when he arrived. I poured two glasses of tea and settled down at the table with a magnifying glass I'd picked up at the drugstore on my way home.

"What are you doing?"

I jumped and screamed. "Sneaking up on me is not funny, Brad."

He laughed then sobered. "You shouldn't leave your door unlocked if you're this easy to sneak up on."

"Sea Side is a safe town, for the most part. Why should I be worried?"

"Because you're investigating a murder?" He raised his brows and set a bag of Chinese takeout on the table.

"No one but you knows that." My stomach rumbled at the delicious aroma of chow mein and kung pao chicken. "Officer Rogen seems to think I saw something in Roy's office that I'm either not saying or don't remember. I'm studying the photographs in more detail. He also told Sue to bring in the appointment book."

"Why should he care what you saw?" Brad handed me the box of kung pao chicken. "He's the police officer. He would have seen the same thing."

"Unless I saw something I shouldn't have seen." The thought sent a cold stab through my heart. "One, he's worried about my safety, or two, he's hoping I didn't see something he wants to keep hidden." I dropped the magnifying glass. "Do you think he could be a dirty cop?"

Brad shook his head. "You watch too much television."

Second time someone told me that today. "What if someone in the car we saw in the alley last night was actually watching us and not just passing by?" I unwrapped a set of chopsticks. "What if the person was there to do some searching of their own?" I tilted my head. "That same person could have said something to the authorities, and that's what has Rogen asking these questions."

Brad paused, an egg roll halfway to his mouth. "These types of what-ifs scare me."

"I could be onto something."

"Yes, you could." His brow furrowed. "That would mean the danger for us has already increased." He got up and locked the door. "Have you noticed anyone following you?" Moving to the front window, he peered through the curtains.

"No, but I haven't paid any attention." I dug into my food, refusing to be fazed about a possible follower without proof. Other than the possibility of the occupants of the car spying on us, no one could possibly know what we were up to except. . . "I think Sue might have said something to Rogen. I did mention to her that I wanted to find Roy's killer."

"What?" He stared at me, shock flickering across his face. "Why would you do that?"

"It's the only way I could get her to talk to me. She thought I killed Roy." I wonder what motive she and the police thought I could possibly have to commit murder?

Brad sat back down and continued eating. "That's it, then. Sue mentioned it to the police, and that prompted all the questions from Rogen." Some of the tension seemed to have left his shoulders. "I bet the car we saw last night was an officer patrolling the crime scene on his regular beat."

That would explain Rogen's suspicions that I withheld information. I'd have to be more careful with my snooping and what I mentioned to people.

"Do you want to study the photographs while I do some online searching of the names on my list?" I wiped my mouth with a paper napkin.

"I'll look at the photos then join you in looking up the names. Rogen wouldn't have mentioned you seeing something if there wasn't something to see. Since I wasn't at the crime scene, I might notice something you'd skim over." He smiled. "I'm surprised you haven't asked if I found out anything at work."

"Did you? I didn't think you'd have had time. Are your bosses back?"

"No, but our receptionist confirmed they were supposed to meet with Roy and had to cancel because something bigger came up." Satisfied with himself, he sat back. "They supposedly went to Portland."

"Oregon?"

"No." He laughed. "Maine."

"Did you confirm?"

"I couldn't, not without seeing an itinerary. I'll try to snoop during her lunch break tomorrow. If I can find out who they were to meet with, I can call and ask if they showed."

"If they didn't, that would mean they could have something to do with Roy's murder."

He frowned. "I don't see why they would kill him, but if we could eliminate them, we could focus our efforts somewhere else." He stood, gathered our garbage, and threw it in the trash before taking over studying the photographs.

I booted up my laptop and started googling names from my list. All were men from local and surrounding businesses. Not strange since Miller Inc. provided insurance for said businesses. Nothing fishy there. I appeared to be doing nothing more than finding dead ends.

"Do you have a Connor Shipping on your list of names?" Brad glanced up from the picture he studied.

"No, why?"

"Take a look at this." He handed me the magnifying glass. "Look at the desk calendar. Part of the word has been erased. Maybe you can tell what it said."

Hmm. It did look like Connor, but it could be something closer to Donley? I grabbed my list and set it next to the photograph.

"It could be Henry Shipping. Maybe."

"Never heard of them. Let me see your list." He circled a few names that could, at a stretch, be the erased company name. "You could try calling these tomorrow and see if they had a meeting with Roy. Figure out something you could ask them to follow up on."

I nodded and typed in corporations in Sea Side, Maine, in my search engine, adding a couple more names to my list. I compared my new list to my old list and wrote down the names of CEOs and managers next to each company. It gave me a very good starting point.

School and work didn't leave me with a lot of daytime hours to make calls, but I could do so in between deliveries. I really wanted to get back into Roy's office. "How much trouble does a person get into if they're caught entering a taped-off crime scene?"

"Arrest."

I could risk that, maybe, if it meant clearing my name. Sue would have a key to the building. I figured convincing her to help me would be harder than not getting caught.

"Don't do it, Ashley." Brad sighed.

"I'll be careful. I want to see what the desk calendar says before wasting a lot of time on calls. If I go in broad daylight, it won't look suspicious." I hoped the desk calendar hadn't been taken as evidence.

"What time?" Brad heaved another sigh. "You'll need a lookout."

"Let me get ahold of Sue." I sent her a text, asking for her help in retrieving something left behind in Roy's office. She agreed to meet me at noon.

"Right after class lets out," I said, grinning. "This is my chance to find out what Rogen thinks I saw."

"Great," Brad muttered. "I'm going to be late for work tomorrow."

CHAPTER 5

Having a substitute teach Professor Lyons's class the next day made the time pass faster and more pleasantly without his constant harassing of me. The former police detective told us to work on our semifinal projects and then basically ignored us the rest of the period.

Brad pulled our table and chairs to a far corner of the room. "We definitely don't want anyone to overhear what we're talking about." He reached over and closed the blinds against the bright summer sun. "Let's make a plan for getting in and out of Miller's office without getting caught."

I tapped my pencil against the tabletop until Brad put his hand over mine. "Sorry. I fidget when I'm thinking." His calloused hand cupped mine as if it were made to be there. "Sue has a key. I intend to go in, snap some more photos, and get out. Five minutes tops." Which, considering I had to be at work, was still pushing me getting to the tea shoppe on time.

"That sounds like a very good plan." He grinned and removed his hand. "I'll stand outside and make a bobwhite whistle if I see anyone. That means you hide."

"Where will you go if someone comes?"

"I'll shove my hands in my pockets and nonchalantly stroll away. No one knows we're working together, so they won't think anything if they see me."

Right. Good point. The police didn't seem to be looking at anyone but me. At least, if they did have another suspect, Rogen wasn't saying anything to me. Of course he didn't have to, but it definitely spurred me on to investigate in order to clear my name.

Brad and I were the first out the door when class dismissed. Since we both had separate places to go after I snuck into Millers, Inc., we drove separately. I parked in front of Tea by the Sea and walked to Millers after letting Georgina know I had an errand to run.

The sun hung high overhead. It was hot for a Maine summer and left me hoping the air conditioner was on in Miller's building. If cleaners hadn't been there yet, I'd be in for a nasty surprise as soon as I stepped into the office.

"I'm not going in," Sue said as she unlocked the door. No crime scene tape fluttered in front of the building. "I'm not taking the chance of encountering any ghosts."

I met Brad's amused glance over her head. "I'll be quick." Having Sue outside in plain sight wasn't ideal. If Rogen drove by, he'd definitely know something was up. I'm pretty sure he'd ordered her to stay away the same as he had me.

Ugh. No air-conditioning. The odor of death slapped me in the face.

Doing my best not to gag, I breathed through my mouth and entered Miller's dark office. I turned on the light, relieved to see his desk calendar in place. I snapped a photo of the current top page. Definitely looked like the name Connor had been partially erased.

I stepped back and studied the rest of the room. Could there be something else I missed?

I dropped to my knees, hoping a different perspective would reveal something. A wadded candy bar wrapper under the desk, a penny showing tails, and little else. The trash can had been emptied.

I stood behind the desk and stared at the door. Whose face had Roy seen last, friend or foe? From that vantage point, I snapped more photos. A red and green plaid throw pillow sat on the leather sofa against the far wall. I knew at one time there had been a matching set of pillows. Where was the other one, and was its absence a clue?

The picture above the sofa hung crooked. I pulled a tissue from a box on the desk and moved the landscape, revealing an unlocked safe. Had Roy been retrieving something when his killer arrived? I opened the safe the rest of the way and frowned. Empty.

I stepped back and continued my study. Come on, Roy. What was I supposed to see?

A bobwhite sounded from outside. Time was up.

A shadow moved past the office door. I ducked behind the sofa, my heart in my throat. A door toward the back of the building slammed. Whoever was in the building with me wasn't concerned about silence.

I moved slowly toward the door and peered out the large front window. No sign of Brad or Sue, but a squad car cruised slowly past. I'd have to go out the back. I stepped out of Roy's office and pulled the door closed as quietly as possible.

Staying low and close to the walls, I skirted past the storage room. The door hung open, light off, no sign of anyone inside. Same with the restrooms. Freedom loomed just past that.

The back door opened. I jumped into the women's room and hid behind the door, peering through the crack. Two people in white jumpsuits and masks and carrying cleaning supplies moved past me. I'd revisited the scene just in time. When they headed past the storage room, I darted out the back door. I stopped so suddenly my feet slid on loose gravel. Poking out from under the dumpster was the missing pillow.

Not seeing anyone lurking about, I grabbed the pillow then

sprinted around the building and headed for work. My heart beat so hard the front of my shirt moved with each pounding. I tossed the contraband into my trunk to evaluate later.

My cell phone vibrated with a text from Brad. SORRY. 2 POLICE CARS CAME, THEN CLEANING VAN. DID YOU MAKE IT OUT OK?"

I replied, ALL OK. AT WORK.

GOOD. I'LL BE BY YOUR PLACE AFTER WORK. STAY SAFE.

Georgina glanced up when I entered the shop. "Just in time to deliver to the police station."

I groaned. That was the last place I wanted to be. I grabbed the bag of goodies and two carafes sitting next to the bag. "They ordered the whole shebang."

"Yep. Officer Rogen said they're expecting a long night."

I set the delivery in the back seat of my car and drove carefully to the police station. With my hands full, carrying the ordered items from the car to the building, I struggled to open the door. The receptionist spotted my trouble and came to help.

"They'll want those in the conference room. Follow me." She led me into a nearby room, set the bag on the oval oak table, then left to answer a ringing telephone.

I gratefully set the two heavy carafes on the sideboard. As I turned to leave, I caught sight of the photo from my driver's license hanging on a whiteboard. "Wow. The case board," I whispered. I glanced around to make sure I was alone, then stood in front of the six-foot wall of clues.

Under my name was written, "No alibi" and "No motive." Next to Sue's was, "Locked in closet." No other photos of suspects hung on the board, but there were pictures of the crime scene. The ones I took were every bit as good as these, giving me a measure of pride in my abilities.

I moved down the board, reading the notes. The police didn't have much more than I did. It was quite obvious they needed whatever help I could give.

"Get away from there."

I squealed and whirled and found myself staring into the stern face of Rogen. "I brought your delivery."

"And started snooping." He narrowed his eyes. "See enough?"

"Roy Miller sold insurance to corporations in Sea Side and nearby cities. Maybe you should start asking questions of those he had meetings with." I flashed a grin at his expression of surprise and brushed past him. "If you don't want people seeing your case board, turn it toward the wall when you aren't in the room."

Score one for Ashley.

As I returned to the shop, I wondered who I could ask about someone named Connor. I sent a quick text to Sue, praying she wouldn't rat me out, but didn't receive an answer. I drove by Miller's Inc. and noticed the cleaning van was gone, but another one had taken its place. Very odd. Why would two cleaning services be needed for a one-room crime scene?

When Brad arrived at the house, I blurted, "What was the name on the cleaning van that showed up today?"

"Hello to you too." He grinned. "Cleaning Groupies. Why?"

"Because another one was there after that. The name on the side of the van was Keeping it Clean."

He frowned. "Why another one?"

I typed both names into my computer. "Only one is real: Keeping it Clean." I had a phone call to make. I dialed the number to the legitimate cleaning service.

"Hello, I was the receptionist at Miller Inc.," I told the woman who answered. "I'd like to thank you for your services today."

"You're welcome," she said, "but we didn't do much. The room was already cleaned."

"Oh, someone else must have called another company. I'm sure someone will be in touch with you regarding the mix-up." After saying goodbye, I hung up. "The fake cleaners took care of the scene."

"Removing all evidence before the real ones showed." Brad handed me a bag from a local burger joint. "I'm going to be as big as a house if we keep eating fast food and takeout."

"I'll cook again tomorrow." I sat at the table and sent the day's photos to my email to be printed. "Were you able to check around your job?"

He sighed. "No. The receptionist worked through lunch so she could leave early. By the time she left, I was out on a job. I'm not much help, am I?"

"You'll get an opportunity." I smiled to reassure him. "Thinking through with me what little we dig up is a tremendous help." Our assignment was due in three weeks. "We need to make copies of all this so you have a set to go over when the mood strikes you."

"That's a great idea." He glanced at my printer in the corner. "I'll do it before I leave tonight."

I bit into my burger. "Wow. Delicious."

"My favorite joint." Brad popped a french fry into his mouth. As if reading my mind, he said, "We should probably put what we do know, the events that have happened, into some sort of a report, adding to it as we go. Then, if the case is still open when our project is due, all we have to do is say what we would have done with more information."

I nodded. "See, you're always thinking." I tapped my temple, smearing ketchup on my face. I stared at my fingers. The resemblance to the blood on Roy's face almost made me lose my appetite.

I swiped at my fingers and then my temple with a napkin.

"Let me." Brad took the napkin and leaned close.

I breathed deep of a woodsy pine scent and sawdust as he dabbed away the ketchup. "Thanks." Face heated, I pulled back, our gazes locking.

He looked as if he wanted to say something, but smiled instead and returned to eating. "So, we need to find out who Connor is."

"A first name, maybe?" I arched a brow. "Although none of the names on my list have that for a first name or a last name."

"Personal friend of Miller's?"

I shrugged. "Must be." I wracked my brain to remember who his friends were. "We can ask around at the funeral this weekend. The killer will be there."

"How do you know?" He tilted his head.

"The killer always attends the funeral of his victim."

"Television again?"

I laughed. "This, I got from a book." I snapped my fingers. "The pillow." I rushed outside and grabbed it from the trunk. I picked up the day's paper on my way back to the apartment.

I tossed the pillow to Brad and explained why I'd taken it. "There's a hole," I said.

"From a bullet."

I nodded. "Someone used this pillow to muffle the gunshot. That's why Sue didn't hear anything when she was in the supply closet."

Brad locked gazes with me. "Why didn't we see it during our dumpster dive?"

"I imagine the cleaning crew had instructions to dispose of it."

I opened the newspaper to the obituaries. Poor Roy. It didn't say anything about leaving behind family.

CHAPTER 6

The sun shone bright on the morning of Roy's funeral. I wore a black pencil skirt and royal-blue blouse as I waited for Brad to pick me up. I never saw the reasoning behind not wearing some color to a funeral. I don't want any black at mine. Cheerful colors are what I want.

Grateful Brad agreed to go with me, I also hoped two sets of eyes and ears would be better than mine alone and that we'd hear something that would help us find out who Connor was.

I raced outside as Brad pulled up to the curb. I quickly slid into the passenger seat before he could get out.

He frowned. "I would have opened the door for you."

"I know." I clicked my seat belt into place. "I don't want to be late. We need good seats."

"It isn't a movie theater." He shook his head. "You act like you're excited."

"Aren't you?" I widened my eyes. "I mean, I'm sad that Roy is dead, but this could be our big break. It shouldn't be hard to find Connor, if he's there."

He pulled away from the curb and down the street. "You plan on just saying his name until someone answers?"

"Sort of." My whole plan sounded kind of callous when he said it out loud. "I'll try and be discreet, but time is ticking." I really wanted us to have a solution when we turned in our report. Solving Roy's murder wouldn't bring him back, but it would make sure justice was served and let me know whether I had what it took to work forensics. I realized I still sounded selfish. Perhaps it really was time to have a heart-to-heart talk with God and regain a proper perspective.

"You're a strange girl, Ashley Lawrence." The soft way he said it made it sound like a good thing.

Great. Rogen had beaten us to the funeral home and was standing guard duty by the double front doors. I refused to let that bother me. I had as much right to attend a friend's memorial service as anyone. I hiked up my chin, linked arms with Brad, and strolled past the officer.

"Ms. Lawrence," he growled.

"Officer Rogen," I said as sweetly as possible before entering the building.

Brad whispered in my ear, his breath tickling my neck. "I think I might be the only male in Sea Side who actually likes you."

I turned, bumping noses with him. "You like me?" Did he mean *like like* or just *like*, as in friends?

"Of course." He chuckled and tapped my nose. "You're cute and funny and never boring."

I sighed. As a friend, then. Very well, I'd keep my growing affection for him to myself.

The funeral home was packed, leaving Brad and me no choice but to sit in the back row. Sighing, I took my seat and watched as folks filed past the casket. I would not be going up. I'd seen enough of a dead Roy to last the rest of my life.

As if he read my mind, Brad took my hand. "I understand," he said softly.

I cut him a sideways glance. "About?"

"Not going up. When my grandfather died, I didn't want to remember him looking like a wax figure. In this case, though, a wax figure might be preferable than the image of your friend covered in blood." He gave my hand a squeeze.

"Good point." I got to my feet and joined the slow-moving line.

When I reached the casket, I closed my eyes then popped them open. The man inside didn't look as if he'd been murdered. Instead, Roy seemed asleep and at peace.

"I'll find out who did this," I whispered. "That's a promise." I glanced over my shoulder to see Rogen directly behind me. When had he cut in line? The look on his face told me he'd heard my promise. No matter. Short of arresting me, he couldn't stop me.

I joined some people in the other room where tea and cookies were being served. As if the man next to me was named Connor, I spoke the name out loud. By the time I approached the third group of people and called out, "Connor," most of those in attendance were staring at me as if I were nuts. But a man in the group, maybe ten years older than my twenty-five, jerked his head up and looked around. I tapped a woman on the shoulder. "Who is that?"

She dabbed her eyes with a napkin. "Roy's son, Connor."

"I didn't know he had a son." No mention of one in his obituary.

"They haven't spoken in years," she said, "but I heard they had recently connected." She tilted her head. "Why all the questions?"

"I used to work for Roy and wanted to give my condolences to his family." I smiled and waved to Brad where I was headed. Before I could question Connor, an attendant signaled it was time to take our seats in the chapel.

I quickly told Brad what I'd learned. "I think they were going to meet but canceled for some reason."

"A good assumption." He took my hand again, making me wonder if I was wrong about him liking me as just a friend. A dreamer like me could always hope for more, right?

The pastor spoke of how wonderful Roy was, how much he'd

be missed, and how he was survived by his only son, Connor, who would be taking over the business. That was a sure motive for murder in my opinion.

"Pretty suspicious that his son would show up, then Roy gets killed," I whispered to Brad.

He glanced around then lowered his head. "Most definitely. We still can't rule out my bosses though. The receptionist is taking a day off on Monday. I'll stay late and do some digging around." His head jerked up. "Speaking of."

I turned to see two men enter the room. With no seats left, they both waved at Brad then stood in the corner. Dressed in dark suits, all they lacked were the sunglasses to look like secret agents. I'd expected them to be older, but they looked as if they were in their early to midfifties.

"Stop staring." Brad gave my hand a tug. "Don't act suspicious."

Right. I refocused on the front of the room where Sue, fake lashes dripping tears, got up and gave her version of what a wonderful man Roy had been. Hadn't she thought him stern? Oh well. People tend to forget the bad things when someone dies.

After the talking was done, the pastor directed us to the adjoining room again to visit and enjoy the pastries and tea ordered from Tea by the Sea. I couldn't help but wonder who footed the bill. If they'd expected this kind of turnout, it wouldn't have been cheap.

Spotting Connor Miller receiving condolences from Sue, I rushed to join them, leaving Brad to get us a treat. "I'm so sorry for your loss." I thrust out my hand. "Ashley Lawrence. I used to work for your father."

"Thank you." Sorrow crossed his features. "It's been a bit of a shock."

"Had you gotten to meet with him since your return?"

"Now is not the time to investigate, Ashley." Sue shook her head then returned to fluttering her ridiculous lashes. "Can't you see poor Connor is grieving?"

"It's fine." The man looked like he wanted to be anywhere but here. "We were supposed to have lunch the day he died, but my father canceled. I'm actually surprised he left me the business."

"Why?" I held my breath. Here came the confession.

"I wasn't very nice to him when he divorced my mother." He shrugged. "Teenagers can be cruel."

"Is your mother here?"

"No, she passed away from cancer last year."

"Oh. I'm sorry." To lose them both within a year of each other, one to a horrible disease and the other to a violent act, had to be hard. "Do you know why your father canceled?"

"He said something came up." A muscle ticked in his jaw. "Excuse me." He strode away without a backward glance.

"That was very rude." Sue crossed her arms and glared. "You don't interrogate someone who just lost their father."

"What if Connor isn't grieving as much as he wants us to believe?" I raised my brows. "Estranged, now the owner of the business. Coincidence? Maybe." I searched the room for Brad. Seeing him with his bosses, his hands devoid of paper plates full of goodies, I headed for the table to fill a plate to share when he finished with the two men.

Georgina had provided some of everything. I gained ten pounds just looking at the delectable spread. I nibbled on a scone while I waited for Brad, hoping he'd come back with more information than I'd gathered.

Ugh. Officer Rogen marched toward me, a hard glint in his eyes. "Stop badgering the son of the deceased."

"I was merely offering my condolences." The scone dried up in my mouth. "Who said I was badgering?"

"Sue said you were asking questions about Connor's relationship with his father. I've warned you to stay out of this, Ms. Lawrence."

"I worked for Mr. Miller and didn't know he had a son. I asked questions out of mere curiosity. Really, the conversation took two minutes." I took another bite of my pastry, wishing Brad would come and save me. I gave an audible sigh when he did.

Officer Rogen met Brad's unabashed gaze then whirled and moved to the other side of the room. I gripped Brad's arm and pulled him to a secluded corner. "Thank you."

Brad looked back at the police officer. "Weird how he up and left when I arrived. Was he mistreating you?"

"Only warning me to stop asking questions. Did you find out anything?"

"They had a meeting, canceled because of out-of-town business, arrived back in town to find out Miller had been murdered."

"Do you believe them?"

"I'm not sure." His gaze drifted to where Jenkins and Olson stood. "They kept looking at each other before they'd answer my questions, as if they wanted to make sure their stories matched."

"Are you still going to snoop around the office?"

"Absolutely. Are you ready to leave? I don't think we'll learn much more here, and that officer is staring at us."

"He does that a lot." I tossed the plate in the garbage and strolled from the building as if I didn't have a care in the world.

The plaid shirt on a man getting into a truck reminded me of the pillow I'd found in the dumpster. I really should turn it over to Rogen. It was evidence, after all, and while I was actively looking into Roy's murder, I really didn't want to hinder an investigation.

Maybe I could turn it in anonymously? I shook my head. Nah. It would take Rogen about two seconds to link the pillow to me. I huffed in frustration, and Brad must have heard.

"Are you all right?" He put a hand on the small of my back.

"Thinking about the pillow and how to turn it in without getting into trouble."

"Just tell the truth. You were walking behind the building and found it and remembered it from when you worked there." He steered me toward his car.

"Why was I walking in the alley?"

"I guess that's what we have to figure out." He stopped walking. "What's that?"

A sheet of paper fluttered from under his windshield wiper. At first I thought it was a sales flyer, but no other cars sported one. I gently pulled the paper free and read, "Stay out of it or you'll end up like Miller."

CHAPTER 7

My knees gave way. Brad caught me before I crumpled to the ground. He opened the car door and helped me sit inside.

"Stay here. I'm getting that police officer." Before I could protest that the last person I wanted to speak with again that day was Rogen, he darted away.

I stared after him, the shock of the paper I held in my hand fading a little. Had someone at the funeral left the warning, or had they come and gone? Were they still here, watching from a parked car? I slammed the door closed and locked it, slouching in my seat.

The *beep beep* of the car's fob sent my heart into overdrive. I knew no one would have the fob except for Brad, but I still screamed when he opened the door.

Officer Rogen stared over Brad's shoulder. "You got a warning?"

I handed him the sheet of paper.

He read it. "I hope you will at least heed this warning, since you won't listen to me."

"Shouldn't you put that in an evidence bag or something?" I narrowed my eyes. He was handling it without gloves.

He stiffened. "Are you telling me how to do my job?"

"No, but. . ." I sighed and clamped my lips shut. In his defense, he probably didn't expect to find evidence at a funeral.

He folded the paper and slid it into an inside pocket of his suit jacket. "Go home, Ms. Lawrence." He whirled and marched away with military precision.

Brad's brows lowered. "You were right about the way he handled that paper."

Oh. I exited the car and raced after Rogen. I needed to tell him about the pillow.

He turned as I called his name. "What now?"

"Uh, I was walking. . .in the alley behind Miller's Inc. and, uh. . .found a pillow."

"A pillow?"

"Yeah. It belonged on Roy's office sofa. It has a bullet hole in it. I think it was used to muffle the gunshot. That's why Sue didn't hear anything when she was in the closet."

"Why were you in the alley?" He cocked his head.

"Walking."

"In the alley." He exhaled heavily. "Listen closely. You are entering dangerous waters. If you get in too deep, I won't be able to keep you safe."

"Do you want the pillow or not?" It sounded as if he was giving me a warning outside of his duty as a police officer. What was it about him that kept me from trusting him?

"Of course I want the pillow," he hissed through his teeth. "I'll follow you home." He turned again, this time to head for his car.

Back at Brad's car, I told him Rogen was coming for the pillow. "I didn't have a good excuse for being in the alley. Hopefully he'll chalk that up to my strange behavior."

"He didn't ask why you didn't bring the pillow straight to the station?"

"No." I tilted my head. "That is weird."

Brad was silent the rest of the way home. When we pulled up to the curb outside my apartment, he shoved open his door. "I'd planned on dropping you off and running some errands, but I'd rather you weren't alone with Rogen."

My blood chilled. "You think he'll harm me."

"I'm not sure what to think about him." Brad slid from the vehicle as Rogen pulled up behind us.

"I'll go get it," I called to Rogen.

"I'll come with you," he called back.

Brad followed me into the apartment. I froze. All our notes and photos were strewn across my table. "We need to hide this."

Behind me, Rogen cleared his throat.

I spun, stunned by the ferocious glint in his eyes. "It's a school project."

His gaze switched to Brad. "You're involved in this too?"

"Yes, sir. As she said, it's a project we're working on."

"You're meddling in my investigation for a class?" Rogen approached the table, studying the photographs. "This is worse than I thought," he mumbled. He took a deep breath. "I'm placing you both under arrest and confiscating all. . .this." He waved his arm over the table.

"You're arresting us on what grounds?" Brad crossed his arms. "It isn't against the law to keep up with an unsolved crime. You have no proof we're doing more than that."

Rogen narrowed his eyes. "Are you resisting?"

"Merely asking questions."

The fact Brad didn't back down from the officer's stare made him a hero in my eyes. "Please don't take our notes." I did my best to sound pathetic and pleading. "We've done so much work on this."

Rogen rolled his head on his shoulders. "I won't arrest you, but I am taking all this." He gathered up the photos and notes." Get me a bag."

I wanted to refuse but got him two grocery bags. One for the papers and one for the pillow. I kept a resigned expression on my face, hoping he wouldn't think we were smart enough to have copies.

He stopped in the doorway. "You're done here, Ms. Lawrence, Mr. Overson." He turned and stormed from the apartment.

"That was close." Brad fell onto my sofa. "I'll lose my job if I get arrested."

"But you didn't back down." I grinned and held up my hand for a high five.

Brad returned it and laughed. "Maybe you should lock your door in case he returns. It looks like any further collaborations will have to happen at my place."

I sat next to him, toed off my pumps, and crossed my ankles on top of the coffee table. "That's fine." Curiosity about his home came over me. I'd love to see where he lived. "Now?"

He shook his head. "We don't have anything else to go on until I have a chance to nose around the office after school tomorrow. Do me a favor and stay inside the rest of the day. Things are going to start heating up. We have four suspects now."

"I can only think of three. Your two bosses and Connor."

"My gut tells me we need to add Rogen to that list. Tell me again what you saw on the case board at the station."

I told him of the very little I'd seen. "I don't think I'm a suspect, since the board said I had no motive, but Rogen definitely believes I know more than I do."

"Which was proven when he came into your apartment. Do we know anything he doesn't?"

"If we did, he'll know what we know now." I bit the corner of my mouth as I thought. "He might not know about the safe or the two cleaning companies." Should we tell him? That would get me into deeper water with the officer. He'd know I hadn't stayed in the alley but had gone inside the building. That would most definitely result in my arrest.

"Okay, let's focus on those two things right now. What could have been in the safe?"

"Money? Important documents?" What could have been important enough to kill Roy?

"Could Roy have known something about someone and kept it in the safe?"

I gasped. "Roy sold insurance. Maybe he caught someone committing fraud?"

"Now you're thinking." Brad got up and paced my small living room.

"How would we find out who?" We had our short list of suspects, but Roy's company had stayed very busy with clients. If my assumption was correct, it could have been any of a long list of companies.

"We need to sit down with Sue. She'll know more than she thinks. As receptionist, she would have recorded all the appointments, made the calls, kept records."

I didn't want to involve Sue, but Brad had a good point. "I'll see if she'll meet us for dinner." I sent her a quick text, making a point of mentioning that Brad would be joining us. Sue struck me as a woman who liked men very much.

Sure enough, she replied yes. I told her to meet us at a diner I liked that had outdoor seating. Summertime or not, we'd be less likely to be overheard if we sat outside.

I went to my room and changed into a pair of jeans and a tank top. When I returned to the front room, Brad had changed into shorts and a T-shirt.

"I always keep an extra set of clothes in my car," he said, moving to the front window and peering outside.

"Expecting someone?"

"I'm not taking any chances. With Rogen knowing what we were up to, the questions we asked at the funeral home, the guilty party could be keeping a close eye on us now." He let the curtains fall back into place.

His extra caution filled me with dread. *Lord, please don't let me have gotten us into something we can't handle.* I thought it might be too late for that, so I added a quick prayer for safety and a quick capture of Roy's killer.

"Do you go to church?" I asked.

"Yes. You?"

I nodded. "My mind usually wanders, but I really do try and focus. I think we should have prayed before undertaking the task of finding a killer. I have a feeling we need divine intervention."

"It's not too late." He smiled, took my hands in his, and pulled me to my feet. His prayer went along the same lines as mine as he prayed for guidance and protection.

A few minutes later, we sipped on cold sodas and waited for Sue at a round iron table outside the diner. A few cars drove by, but none seemed overly interested in us. I didn't see a single squad car, so Rogen must be processing the confiscated evidence he'd taken off my kitchen table. A few other couples and a family occupied tables, but none sat close enough to hear our conversation.

"There she is." Brad nodded to where Sue got out of a brilliant red Mustang.

I had a sudden case of car envy. "Thanks for joining us, Sue," I said when she reached us.

"I know you have an ulterior motive," she said, taking her seat. "You're going to ask me more questions, but I didn't have anything else to do." She fluttered her lashes at Brad. "It's good to see you again."

"Likewise." He smiled. "And guilty as charged about wanting to ask questions."

We ordered our food—chicken fingers and fries for me—then I pulled a notebook from my purse. "Brad and I are thinking Roy might have some dirt on someone and that's what got him killed. Anyone come to mind?"

"Let me think." She tapped a pumpkin-orange sculpted nail against her teeth. "Roy had become more reclusive the last few weeks, staying in his office for longer periods of time. He was surly, almost rude on occasion. He no longer held all his meetings in the conference room either. He started taking more in his office."

"Anybody in particular?" I poised the pen over the paper. "I know Connor said their meeting was canceled, but did you ever see him at the office?"

"No, the funeral was the first time I laid eyes on him." She sat against the chair back and stared into the distance. Her eyes widened. "The last meeting he held in his office that I'm aware of was the guys from Sea Side Construction."

"I thought you said that meeting got canceled."

"The one the day he died was canceled. The one a few days earlier wasn't." She leaned her elbows on the table and lowered her voice. "There were a lot of loud voices coming from his office that day."

CHAPTER 8

I really wished I was snooping around Brad's work with him instead of delivering scones and pastries, but bills had to be paid. I glanced at the bag in my hand. It ought to have SCONES TO DIE FOR written across the front. Talk about promotion, if a bit macabre under the circumstances.

A lump formed in my throat. Roy hadn't gotten to eat his favorite pastry before someone had brutally killed him.

After making the delivery to the drugstore then making a much larger delivery to the bookstore for their weekly book club, I plopped onto a bench on Main Street. The deadline for our report loomed ever closer, and we were still a long way from solving Roy's murder. Maybe I could bribe Professor Lyons with some raspberry scones.

I smiled and lifted my face to the afternoon sun, closing my eyes and breathing deep of an ocean breeze. When was the last time I'd simply sat and enjoyed a beautiful summer day? Not since working and going to college. I needed to make time to relax a priority in my life. A time to sit, reflect, and pray. Maybe find a man to date.

Like Brad. Would he enjoy spending time with me if we weren't working on a project together? I really hoped so, because if he didn't ask me out when we finished with this, I'd ask him.

I stood and turned back toward Tea by the Sea. I looked both ways and stepped into the street.

A dark van sped up and stopped in front of me. The door opened, and a masked man reached out.

I reflexively punched him in the face and took off at a sprint in the opposite direction. Pounding footsteps alerted me to the fact he gave chase. Where were all the shoppers who usually strolled Main Street?

Snatching a half-empty water bottle from a trash can as I raced by, I chucked it over my shoulder and heard him curse. I darted into the tea shoppe.

"Call the police, Georgina. I was almost kidnapped." I sagged into a chair, both pleased with my quick thinking and shaking from my near capture.

"Here." She handed me a cup of tea after placing the call. "You need this."

Tea had been the go-to comfort drink for generations. "Thank you." I sat in silence, ignoring the coming and going patrons until Rogen marched in and took a seat across from me.

"What happened?"

I explained in great detail. "Look, my hands are shaking." I held up a trembling hand. "I'm not normally a nervous person."

He looked at me as if I'd sprouted a second nose. "Of course you're shaken up. Are you in shock? Do you need a doctor?" The hint of a smile teased his lips. "Where did you learn to fight like that?"

"Television." I shrugged one shoulder. "Say what you will, there's some helpful information on the tube."

He leaned across the table. "Do you see now why you need to stop sticking your nose in this?"

"But I have a project due."

"Seriously." He shook his head. "Pick a different topic. Anything besides an active murder investigation." He pushed to his feet.

"I was working, Officer. That's it. Not asking questions, not roaming down alleys, just working." Was that not safe anymore?

"Keep your wits about you, like you did today." He marched

from the shop, paused on the sidewalk for a second, then disappeared out of sight. It almost seemed as if he actually cared about my safety.

All my bravado disappeared when Brad arrived. Tears sprang to my eyes, and I launched myself into his arms.

"Whoa. What's wrong?" His arms tightened around me. He smelled like fabric softener and soap. He'd obviously taken the time to shower before meeting up with me.

He helped me into a chair and ordered two large sweet teas. "Tell me what's wrong."

I blubbered through an explanation of the attempted abduction. "It isn't safe for me to walk down the sidewalk anymore. Who knows about us investigating besides Rogen and Sue?"

"That's a very good question." He folded his hands on the tabletop. "One of them must have said something to someone they shouldn't have."

I nodded, wiping my eyes with a napkin. "Did you find out anything at work?"

He grinned. "Jenkins and Olson canceled their out-of-town appointment the same as they did with Roy."

"That's suspicious. How can we find out why?"

"We need to do some digging into their files. Care for a nighttime excursion to a construction office?" He wiggled his eyebrows. "Do you feel up to it?"

"You bet. The sooner we solve this, the sooner life gets back to normal. Besides, thinking about that will keep me from dwelling on how close I came to getting hurt today. Would you come with me for the rest of my deliveries?" I'd noticed the orders coming in and knew Georgina would do them herself if I didn't feel like I could. I didn't want that to happen. Delivering was my job.

Still, she protested as I loaded the deliveries into a box, only relenting when I informed her that Brad was going with me and working would take my mind off my ordeal. "I'll be fine."

Brad took the box from me. "People around here really like these pastries, don't they?"

"And the tea and coffee." I glanced up at him. "I think you need to mention to your bosses how wonderful this place is so I can deliver to them and gauge how they react to seeing me."

I'd be able to get a hint of. . .something if they intended me harm. My instincts were rarely wrong, except in regard to Rogen. That man confused me. I couldn't get over my suspicion that he was involved in some way outside of being the officer leading the investigation. But I couldn't for the life of me figure out how he could be. He didn't seem the type to be a dirty cop. Something weighed heavily on him, judging by how more rounded his shoulders seemed each time I saw him.

The rest of the deliveries went smoothly with no sight of a masked man or a dark van. "Right before the van blocked my way," I said, "I was thinking about how long it'd been since I've taken a day off to have fun."

"What do you like to do for fun?" Brad opened the passenger door of his car. "I thought you liked investigating."

"That was before someone tried to hurt me." I slid onto the seat. "I like walks along the shore, movies and popcorn, long drives in the country. . .those sorts of things."

After he got in the driver's side, he turned to me. "Do you want to stop this?"

"Nope." I flashed a grin. "We're in too deep now. Might as well see it through to completion. Do you have a key to the office?"

"Yes."

I raised my brows. "Did you steal it?"

He rolled his eyes. "No, I didn't steal it. I'm a supervisor, remember? We haven't done this before now because I had no reason to go in after hours. Now that we suspect Jenkins and Olson. . ."

I wasn't quite sure what I expected when Brad parked behind a trailer, but it wasn't a module that could be moved from construction site to construction site. Mounds of dirt lay off to one side of the building. I guess I'd thought we'd be going to a regular building, not a place where building was actually being done. I glanced down at my gym shoes, glad I hadn't worn my prettier flats that day for more than one reason. I wouldn't have been able to run from my potential abductor or snoop around a big hole in the ground. If we didn't find anything inside, I'd definitely want to look around outside. There had to be a clue here.

"What are they building?"

"Apartment complex."

Brad unlocked the door to the trailer and ushered me inside. "Don't turn on the lights." He handed me a flashlight. "Sometimes, the bosses drive by to check on things. There's a lot of equipment parked on the lot. It would be difficult to steal, but not unheard of."

I glanced around the one room. "Where would we hide if they came?"

"I'd have to come up with something real quick. Maybe I brought you here for a secret rendezvous." He shone the light on his face and winked.

A flush rose up my neck. "That wouldn't work if they killed Roy. They'd get rid of us just in case we were lying." I took a deep breath to still my heart and moved to a filing cabinet near the receptionist's desk. It was locked, but I found the key in the top desk drawer.

I flipped through file folders until I found one labeled INSURANCE. Sea Side Construction had a two-million-dollar policy through Miller Inc. Not unusual. What was unusual was that Connor Miller was listed as the agent. My stomach dropped. The address for Miller Inc. on the policy was not the same address for the building Roy owned. Had his son started taking clients away from Roy? Why would he, when he stood to be his father's only beneficiary, estranged or not? And did Roy know about this policy? "Brad? Look at this."

He joined me, reading the papers over my shoulder. "Clue number one." He laid another file on the desk. "Here's number two. They also had a policy under Roy."

My brow furrowed. "Why would they need two?"

"I'm thinking the one under Connor is suspicious. Maybe he stands to gain if something happens to Sea Side Construction."

I gasped. "That means something *will* happen, Brad. They wouldn't take out two policies without a plan of some sort."

He nodded, his mouth set in a grim line. "Fire or theft, most likely. Snap photos of these papers, and let's get out of here."

I pulled out my phone and took photos of each page before returning the files to the cabinet and the key to the desk drawer. When I clicked off my flashlight and opened the door, I saw headlights penetrating the darkness and headed our way. I pulled the door closed. "Brad, someone's coming."

He hurried us both outside, locked the door behind us, then pulled me behind the building, putting a finger to his lips. I crouched down and peered around the corner.

The automobile backed up to the large hole in the ground. A man got out and opened the trunk.

"Who is it?" I whispered.

"I can't tell, and I don't recognize the car."

Something landed with a muffled thud. The man slammed the trunk closed, got back in the vehicle, and spun gravel speeding away.

I needed to know what had happened. "Come on." I waved Brad forward. "He dumped something." I really hoped it was garbage.

Staying low, I approached where the car had stopped and stared at something in the hole about five feet long and wrapped in canvas.

"Did that just move?" I stared up at Brad.

"Yes." He slid down the embankment and turned on his flashlight. He peeled away the top corner of the canvas. "It's Sue."

Oh Lord, help us. "Is she dead?"

He felt for a pulse. "No."

"Why dump a live person in the hole? Check for blood."

He unwrapped her. "Other than a bump on the head, I don't see anything wrong. The bindings were too tight for her to get out of alone." His eyes widened in the beam of my flashlight. "Ashley, concrete is scheduled to be poured here first thing in the morning."

My blood chilled. Gagged and tied, Sue would have become part of the apartment complex foundation, never to be seen again.

"Can you get her up here?"

"Yes." He scooped the unconscious woman into his arms and struggled up to where I stood.

"I need to call the police," I said. "How will we explain what we were doing here?"

"Easy. You wanted to see where I worked, we observed something being dumped and went to investigate." He carried Sue to his car and placed her in the back seat. "Always stay as close to the truth as possible."

Right. Less chance of getting tripped up when talking to the police or the bad guys. As I stared down at Sue, it occurred to me that, if I'd been taken earlier, there could very well have been two canvas-wrapped bodies dumped in that hole.

CHAPTER 9

"Where's Rogen?" I peered around an officer I didn't recognize.

An ambulance pulled up behind him. Two paramedics got out and rushed to Sue's side.

"Gone." The officer's clipped tone left no room for questions, but I pressed on anyway.

"During an investigation? May I see your badge?" I wasn't trusting anyone at that point.

His badge told me his name was Officer Davis. "I'm well aware of who you are, Miss Lawrence, Mr. Overson. You've been the talk of the precinct ever since Rogen brought in your notes and photos. Even though I'm impressed with what the two of you discovered, I second Officer Rogen's opinion that you stay out of what is now my case."

I glanced at Brad, who shrugged. "The woman is Sue Moore from Miller Inc." He went on to tell Davis of us witnessing her being dumped as Brad showed me around the site.

"Why were you here in the dark?" Davis speared us both with a sharp gaze. "Wouldn't you be able to see more in the daylight?"

"We both work during the day," I said. "Besides. . ." I snuggled up to Brad, very much liking the way he felt. "This is way more romantic."

"Ma'am, it's a good thing you're taking forensics classes."

"Why's that?"

"Because it means that someday you'll be snooping into murder cases legally. I'd like the two of you to come into the station first thing in the morning to fill out reports. Go home now and let the police do their job." He turned and marched back to his car.

"Finally, an officer who realizes telling us to stay away is a losing battle." I glanced to where the paramedics loaded the still-unconscious Sue into the ambulance.

"Maybe it's more like he sees we can be an asset," Brad said. "I'd like to visit Sue tomorrow after we go to the station. Hopefully she'll be awake by the time our class is finished."

The next morning, irritable from lack of sleep, I stopped at Tea by the Sea and purchased scones for Professor Lyons. I plopped the bag on his desk and shuffled to my seat only to be called back to his desk before my rear hit the chair.

"Is this a bribe, Miss Lawrence?"

"Nope. I thought you might need sweetening up, that's all. If it is a bribe, it's to keep you from badgering me today."

He tilted his head, amusement crossing his face. "But you're so much fun to torment."

Slapping my hands flat on his desk, I leaned close. "Look. I was almost kidnapped trying to catch a killer in order to get a good grade on this assignment. I don't need grief from you." I gasped. "I'm sorry. I shouldn't have been disrespectful." Lack of sleep was no excuse for poor behavior.

"I do not expect you to put yourself in danger for a grade." He smiled. "I have a friend in the police department. I'm well aware of what you and Mr. Overson have been doing, and I also know that my friend, not to mention the new chief of police, is impressed with your work despite the headaches you give them. Please take your seat so I can attempt to teach you something else to help you as you hinder a police investigation."

I returned to my seat, wishing I could go home and catch up on lost sleep. I'd reluctantly taken the afternoon off work in order to go to the police station and then to the hospital. Davis would have to forgive me and Brad for not showing up first thing in the morning. I was paying for this course and wouldn't miss any more days unless it was an emergency. The money I'd been saving for years was for a down payment when the perfect house crossed my path.

Professor Lyons spoke on fingerprints and DNA until I wanted to pull out my hair and die. This was stuff we'd already gone over, which meant a test was coming up. I'd never felt so old, even though I was only twenty-five, until going back to school. I retained things I heard well, but digging into Roy's death left little time for actually studying a textbook.

When the bell rang, I practically raced from the room and out of the building. I leaned against the warmth of the redbrick wall and waited for Brad.

"You're out of sorts today," he said, joining me.

"You don't seem to be in a hurry to leave." I glared up at him. "We have things to do today. Things that most likely won't help us find Roy's killer."

"Come on, grouchy pants." He took my hand and led me to his car. "We'll come back for yours later. And, for the record, I'm hoping Sue is awake and able to talk to us. She might be another step forward."

"I'm sorry. Too many late nights and not enough fun."

"Here's an idea. This Saturday you sleep in, and I'll pick you up at noon for that walk on the beach."

"Really?" I turned in my seat. "What about our assignment?"

"We'll either have an ending for it or we won't. Your health is more important, and if you keep going this way, you'll make yourself sick." He patted my shoulder then drove us to the police station.

Officer Davis scowled when we stepped into his office. "I

thought I said first thing."

"We had class." I sat in a chair across from him. "I already took off work today to come in."

He sighed and handed each of us a form. "Fill these out to the best of your ability. The construction site is now a crime scene, Mr. Overson, so you for one won't need to worry about going there to work."

"No, sir, but I supervise other sites." Brad took his form and started writing. "My bosses, on the other hand, will not be pleased."

"You should look into them," I said to Officer Davis. "I won't tell you why, because it's pure speculation, but those two are fishy."

Brad nudged me with his knee.

"If the information you're withholding is part of this investigation," Davis said, "you're obligated to let me know."

"I'm not sure if it is at this point." I handed my form back to him. "I wouldn't want to cloud your judgment by telling you we suspect them of insurance fraud."

"I get it." He set the forms in a tray then folded his hands on top of his desk. "In time, you will, I guarantee it, especially if you keep getting into trouble and need to be bailed out. Oh, and the chief would like to speak to the both of you." He grinned. "Seems what I think best isn't the same as his thoughts on the matter."

Well, snickerdoodle. We'd finally crossed the line and were getting a talking to from the big guy.

I knocked and peered into a less sterile-looking office than Davis's had been. The chief seemed to warrant a wooden desk rather than a metal one, and an expensive leather chair. "Sir?"

"Please. Come in and close the door." The big man with his gray hair cut into a military style waved toward a couple of vinyl chairs. A brass plate on his desk said CHIEF WILEY. "Relax. You aren't in trouble. I have a proposition for you."

I exchanged a curious glance with Brad and sat down. "Sir?"

"As you know, we're a small police force here in Sea Side, and this murder is running us ragged. After speaking with Officer Davis and going over your impressive notes and photographs regarding Mr. Miller's murder, I would like to ask the two of you to work with us on a consulting basis. Well, more than that actually. I'd like your help in solving this case."

"You mean we won't be interfering in an investigation?" I asked.

He shook his head. "You'd be in a legal capacity to snoop."

I glanced at Brad, who looked as shocked as I felt. "I'm—we're—honored. Will we be getting paid?"

"Not on a full-time basis, but there will be compensation."

Thank you, God. I should know better than to worry about money. God had always looked out for me in the past.

"What about safety?" Brad spoke up. "Someone attempted to kidnap Ashley yesterday, and Sue Moore was abducted and dumped last night."

"Do you intend to stop your investigation, Mr. Overson?" The chief leaned back in his chair. "Because if the answer is no, what difference does it make if you work for me or go out on your own? Doing so in an illegal capacity could result in your arrest. This is for your protection against prosecution."

Brad stood and thrust out his hand. "We accept."

"That was weird," I said once we stepped outside. "Is this type of thing normal?"

"With Rogen disappearing, I don't think the department has much to go on other than what we found. He could have hidden any evidence if it pointed back to him." Brad opened the passenger door for me. "They're desperate."

"Obviously, since we're just average citizens." I slid into the car and buckled my seat belt. While danger still hovered on the horizon, we could at least investigate now without the threat of arrest. "Where do you think Rogen is?"

"I believe your thinking of him being a dirty cop had him fleeing for fear that we'd figure him out."

I exhaled heavily through my nose. "Something about him says there's more to him than just being a bad cop."

"Maybe. Let's go see if we can talk to Sue."

Luckily, she was awake and allowed visitors. I hardly recognized her without the heavy makeup and teased hair. The Sue in the hospital bed was a lot more attractive, in my opinion.

"How are you feeling?" I sat in the chair on one side of the bed, and Brad pulled a chair from the unoccupied other half of the room.

"I've got a headache. Concussion, the doctor said."

"Can you tell us what happened?" Concern crossed Brad's face.

She closed her eyes and took a deep breath, then opened them again. "I came out of the bookstore, my arms full of books. A van stopped in front of me. A man in a mask dragged me inside, and that's all I remember until I woke up here."

"Nothing about being wrapped in a sheet of canvas and tossed in a hole?" I glanced up at Brad. The look on his face told me he didn't think I should have said anything about that.

"No!" Sue's eyes widened. "I could have died."

"But you didn't." Brad patted her hand. "Ashley and I were there to get help. Can you remember anything about your captors?"

"There were two. One driving the van and one that grabbed me and put a pillowcase over my head. Then he hit me." She glanced from Brad to me and back to Brad. "That's all. They never said a word."

"You know something that has them worried, Sue. The same people tried to take me yesterday." I took her hand. "I understand you've been attacked and are scared. Help us find who did this."

"Except for the loud voices I heard coming from Roy's office, I don't know anything." She groaned and lay back on the pillows.

"Were you aware that Connor Miller was also selling insurance and that Sea Side Construction had a policy under him and one under Roy?"

Her brow wrinkled. "I told you I'd never seen Connor before the funeral." Her eyes widened. "Do you think he killed his own father?"

"We don't know," Brad said. "We suspect Jenkins and Olson were in on it with him to commit fraud."

"And Roy found out." She did the glancing back and forth thing again. "You will find his killer, right? Before he strikes again?"

"We're doing our best." Brad got to his feet. "You rest and be careful." In the hall, he turned to me. "We need to ask the chief to put an officer outside her room."

CHAPTER 10

Saturday morning I slept until nine and stretched like a very satisfied feline before getting out of bed. Not only had I slept well, but I would be spending the day with Brad, not investigating. A day of fun!

I lounged around until time to get dressed and then put on shorts and a flowered top. Casual, but with my hair bouncing around my shoulders in a ponytail, I felt pretty. Brad had said he would bring a picnic lunch. My contribution was dessert—strawberry scones.

When his car pulled up outside, I locked my door behind me and skipped to the curb. "Good morning."

He laughed as he opened the passenger door. "I guess you really were looking forward to a day off."

"Oh yeah." I kept my window open as we headed for the coast, closing my eyes and letting the ocean breeze rejuvenate me. Nothing better than sun and surf to raise a girl's spirits.

When Brad pulled off the road and parked the car, I saw a set of stone steps leading down to a small beach. Not far away, a red and white lighthouse rose against an azure-blue sky. Waves crashed against rocks as seagulls dove for their food, filling the air with their cries.

After retrieving a cooler and blanket from the trunk of his car, Brad led me down the steps. "How's this?"

"Gorgeous." I glanced around in surprise. "There's no one else here."

"Nope. I know the lighthouse keeper. This isn't a public beach." He grinned and set the cooler on the ground before unfolding the blanket. "You wanted peace, you got it."

What a guy. I removed my phone from my pocket and sat on the blanket, stretched my legs out in front of me, and leaned back on my arms. I could stay there all day watching the waves kiss the sand.

Brad stretched out beside me. "Sleep well?"

"Yes. You?"

"Surprisingly so after the events of the last two days. I called the hospital to check on Sue. Officer Davis will be escorting her home today."

"You must be the most thoughtful person I've ever met."

He turned on his side. "It isn't hard to be nice."

"Sometimes it is." The ease with which he thought of others filled me with remorse. "Take Rogen, for instance. That man rubbed me wrong from the moment we met."

"He was a bit abrasive." He opened the cooler and handed me a bottle of tea and a sandwich. "Ham and swiss okay?"

"Perfect." I continued to watch the water as I ate, the events from the moment I found Roy dead snaking through my mind like an unfurled ribbon. Sea Side Construction was behind his death. Whether Connor was involved in more than fraud was left to be figured out.

"You're supposed to be taking a break," Brad said. "I can see thoughts about the case written all over your face."

"I can't help it. Until we solve this, I can't stop thinking of the what-ifs and the empty holes. We suspect fraud. How do we prove it?"

"You told Davis. Let's see what he does with the information." Brad got to his feet and held out his hand. "Walk with me. I can't think of anything better than a stroll on the beach with a pretty girl."

"There you go, being all nice again." I smiled and slipped my hand in his, allowing him to pull me to my feet. I didn't think I'd ever tire of him calling me pretty. I slipped off my shoes, eager to feel the water and sand on my toes.

We entwined our fingers and strolled slowly along the shore. Despite the summer heat, the cold water took a few minutes to get used to, then felt delicious.

"I think the fact the chief has allowed us to investigate is promising for our future in forensics," I said, stopping to watch a gull swoop to the water's surface.

"Maybe we'll get hired on together in Sea Side." He gave my hand a little squeeze.

"Who's the dreamer now?" I glanced up and smiled.

"Maybe you're rubbing off on me."

"Hmm." It would be nice to continue working with him, unless I went through with asking him on a date and he refused. Wait. "Are we on a date?" I blurted. I clamped a hand over my mouth.

"I call it a date." His smile warmed my heart. "I like you, Ashley. I hope we have more dates in the future."

Wow. I lost my breath for a second. "I like you too."

He cupped my cheek and lowered his head. He was going to kiss me!

I yelped and jumped back as sand stung my leg. "Ouch." I glanced down as more sand was kicked up.

Brad tackled me to the ground. "Someone is shooting at us. Get to those rocks."

I scrambled for the safety of the huge boulders a few yards away. Once there, I ran my hands up and down my calves, feeling for blood or bullet holes. When I didn't find any, I sagged with relief.

"You hurt?" Brad asked, joining me.

"No. Thank God the shooter has bad aim."

"Using a silencer at a distance isn't easy." He wrapped an arm around me and pulled me close. With his other hand, he fished his cell phone from his pocket and called 911. After being assured that someone was on their way, he pressed another button that set off a screaming alarm.

That was bound to attract anyone within hearing distance and scare away the shooter. "That's brilliant."

"You should download the app. It's louder than any car alarm."

I made a vow to myself to download it ASAP. Unfortunately, my phone lay on the blanket by the cooler at the moment. "Do forensic scientists run into these situations on a regular basis?"

"No idea. I've never been one. I think we'd work more behind the scenes."

I sure hoped so. When no more shots came, I crawled a few feet and peered out at the beach. No sign of anyone. I glanced upward and spotted someone near the lighthouse. I prayed it was Brad's friend and not the shooter. "Do we stay or make a run for it?"

"I suggest we stay until we hear actual sirens." Brad pulled me back to his side. "We can cuddle to take our mind off the bad guy." He arched a brow.

I leaned closer and our gazes locked. I closed my eyes only to hear police sirens rise above the wailing of Brad's phone. I sighed and pulled away as he shut off the reverberating noise.

We stepped from our protected place to see Davis, weapon pulled, sprinting in our direction. "I didn't see anyone. You both all right?"

I nodded. "A little shook up, but we aren't harmed." A bit disappointed that our first kiss kept getting interrupted.

"I'll escort you back to your car." Davis turned and led the way to our blanket.

So much for a relaxing day. I glanced at my half-eaten sandwich then around the area we'd sat. "Where's my phone and the scones?"

After searching for several minutes and gathering the rest of our things, it became obvious my phone was gone and the thief had a taste for pastries. "Why would the shooter take my phone?"

"The photographs and photos of the files," Brad said. "That means they now know we know about the second policy."

Yikes. The danger had escalated tenfold.

"Report the phone stolen and see if the phone company can keep anyone from accessing it." Davis's features hardened. "I assume you have it password protected."

I nodded. "Won't be hard for someone to figure out if they think hard enough."

"Please tell me you didn't use your birthday." He narrowed his eyes.

I shrugged, having done exactly that. I had a tendency to forget passwords, so kept them simple. "Brad, may I use your phone?"

He handed it to me, and I placed the call to the company, changing the password to something harder and asking that the phone be shut off immediately. Hopefully I'd done it in time to keep the photos from being accessed.

As we headed back to town, Brad reached over and patted my arm. "Our day isn't over. How about some ice cream?"

"That sounds wonderful." I'd take what I could get. Obviously, a day of fun in the sun wouldn't happen until this case was solved. "What do you think about asking Jenkins and Olson point blank about the insurance policies? Or the receptionist? She has to know about the two policies even if she didn't put the pieces together."

"I'd rather ask her first. The less my bosses know we're onto them, the better."

"What about Connor? We should also talk to him."

"I agree. Someone is bound to say something to incriminate someone else."

Rather than sit outside on a nice day, as I would have preferred, we chose to sit inside the ice cream parlor for our protection. I ordered a strawberry sundae while Brad chose chocolate. Some of the brightness of the day had dimmed, despite Brad's attempt at keeping my day off enjoyable. Being shot at did that to a person.

"What are you thinking?"

"That I don't want this career if it means someone will always be trying to kill me."

"They won't. You'll only be searching through what evidence is found to help out the detectives."

I nodded. "I guess you're right. The trouble came when I stepped where I didn't belong." Without praying for guidance beforehand. I sighed, something I felt I did a lot of lately. I dug into my sundae.

"Cheer up. This will end at some point, and we'll get a good grade on our report because Lyons and Davis are friends." Brad grinned. "What do you want to do next?"

"Go back to my place and watch a movie and eat popcorn?"

"As long as it isn't a sappy chick flick."

I laughed. "I don't think we need an action movie. I feel as if we're living in one."

"You're right. Let's find a comedy."

We headed to my place and rented a movie online. A romantic comedy between two detectives. Just what I needed as we laughed our way through the next two hours and shared a bowl of popcorn. Our hands brushed when we reached into the bowl at the same time, and I really did feel as if we were dating. I wasn't quite sure how to act after I realized Brad actually did like me. Being a dreamer who often lived in the clouds, I didn't have many boyfriends growing up. Books had been my friends more often than not.

Brad brushed my hair back from my face. "You look sad."

"Feeling a little insecure is all." I reached for the empty popcorn bowl.

"Don't be. Everything will work out. You're a strong, smart woman." He took the bowl from me and cupped my face. "I think I'm going to give you that kiss I've been trying to give you all day."

He lowered his head, his lips landing on mine with all the sweetness of sugar and a touch of salt from the popcorn. When I leaned into him, the kiss deepened. Brad was right. Everything would be just fine.

CHAPTER 11

"With the trailer office being a crime scene," Brad said as he pulled in front of a small cottage-style house, "Brenda is on paid time off."

"Will she talk to us?" I sure hoped so, since we'd both decided against going to our class that morning.

"Oh yeah. The woman loves to talk." He grinned and shut off the engine. "I should have spoken to her a lot sooner but didn't feel we had enough information. I guarantee that once we let her in on our suspicions, she'll start digging around too. I didn't want her looking for the wrong thing."

I shoved open my car door and joined Brad on the sidewalk. "Let's hope today gets us a lot closer to the end of all this."

Brad took my hand, led me to the front door, then pressed the doorbell. A woman in her fifties, pleasantly plump with a friendly smile on her face, opened the door. "Brad. What a welcome surprise. Come in."

"Brenda, this is my friend Ashley. We're hoping you can help us with something."

"Let me fetch tea and cookies, and I'll be glad to help. Have a seat."

We sat on a brown tweed sofa. The crocheted afghans and homemade decor set me right at ease.

A few minutes later, Brenda set a tray with cups of tea and cookies that I could tell would be on the dry side just by looking at them. Still, I wouldn't be rude. I took one. Gingersnap. Yum.

She sat across from us and crossed her ankles. "What can I help you with?"

Brad explained Roy's murder, the canceled appointments, and the two insurance policies. "Did you know about any of this?"

She wrinkled her brow. "I did know of the policies, but not about the canceled appointments. Mr. Jenkins said they didn't want to take a chance of losing everything, thus the need for the second policy. I don't question their decisions. I just do what I'm told. It isn't my place to ask questions."

"What do you know about Connor Miller?" I took a sip of tea. I bet she asked a lot of questions to herself. Unless I was wrong, not much got past Brenda.

"He's been around a lot lately. Well, until we were told not to go to the office for a while. Seems friendly enough, but I can't draw that young man into a conversation to save my life. Close-lipped that one. In fact, whenever he came by, Jenkins and Olson would leave the building with him. There isn't a lot of privacy in a one-room trailer. I figured it was none of my business."

Brad smiled. "But you suspect something, don't you?"

"Of course I do. I'm observant." She leaned forward. "Mr. Jenkins has a gambling problem. Mr. Olson pays out of the nose for alimony to his ex-wife. Those two are hard up for money, which is another reason two expensive policies didn't sit right with me. Where did they get the money to pay the monthly premiums?"

I didn't know how to answer, and since she was looking at me, I shrugged. "A loan?"

"Exactly! But from whom?"

I jumped at her loud exclamation. "From Connor Miller."

"Good thinking." Brad sent an appreciative glance my way, then turned back to Brenda. "Do you have Connor's contact information?"

"Silly boy." She got to her feet and opened a drawer in a side table. "I know everything about anything that has to do with Sea Side Construction." She pulled out a bright green folder and handed it to him. "I have no idea how you'll get him to talk."

"Did you ever see an Officer Rogen at the site?" I asked. "He seems to have disappeared."

"If I saw him, he wasn't in uniform, but yes, Connor wasn't the only regular visitor. Would the officer have been a man around my age, in good shape, handsome but sullen?"

"That's him."

Brenda got a mischievous look in her eye. "Some folks are saying that that tea shoppe you work for is cursed. Too many bad things have been associated with that place. Seems every season a new cloud of mystery hangs over it."

"We stay quite busy with customers, so I don't see how this has to do with that," I said in defense. "Tea by the Sea has nothing to do with the evil of others."

"No need to get your feelings hurt. Just a lot of mysteries lately."

"Roy Miller didn't die from eating scones. I discovered his body while delivering them." I hated insinuations that cast a bad light on one of Sea Side's favorite businesses. One more reason to solve Roy's murder—get the focus off Tea by the Sea except for the treats it had to offer.

Brad put a settling hand on me. "We're getting off the subject. The shop has nothing to do with our investigation."

"Oh, but it does," Brenda said. "That officer—Rogen, did you say?—always brought your pastries when he came."

That was news to me. Our four suspects were definitely tied together. Now to find out who was guilty and who was simply hanging out with the wrong people.

"Do you think Sea Side Construction is guilty of fraud?" Brad asked.

"With everything you've told me, yes." Brenda nodded. "I guess I should probably start looking for a new job."

Brad stood and held out his hand to pull me to my feet. "You've been a big help, Brenda. You wouldn't happen to have proof for any of this, would you?"

"Just what I've seen and not heard." She chuckled. "You go talk to Connor. Maybe you can scare him into saying something."

Hopefully. I followed Brad back to the car. "We learned that Rogen is definitely involved, but not much else." I also feared the officer might be dead.

"I'd hoped for more." Brad opened the passenger door for me then hurried to the driver's side.

It didn't take long to arrive at the apartment complex where Connor lived. If he wasn't home, we'd have to come back, wasting more time. Time we didn't have. In one week our assignment was due, and we didn't have a solution. I hated leaving anything undone.

"How do you want to handle this?" I asked.

"Let's be straightforward and try to gain information from what he says as well as what he doesn't." Brad knocked on the door of apartment 212 several times before a sleepy-eyed but fully dressed Connor answered the door.

I glanced at my watch. Past ten.

"Good morning," I said with a smile. "Remember us from your father's funeral?"

He rubbed his eyes. "Yes. What do you need? Wait a minute. How did you know where I live?"

"Actually, we thought you were only here to settle your father's affairs. May we come in?"

His eyes narrowed. "Since I now own Miller Inc., I thought it best I settle down in Sea Side." He reluctantly stepped aside. "I've got a meeting later but can spare a few minutes."

His apartment was a direct contrast from Brenda's. Where hers had been warm and welcoming, Connor's was modern and cold. He didn't offer us a seat, so Brad and I took up a position near the open door. It didn't bother me. We'd have a quick getaway if things turned ugly.

"Well?" Connor crossed his arms.

"I work at Sea Side Construction," Brad began, "and I ran across some documents that confused me. Two insurance policies from Miller Inc., one in your name, dated before your father died. I thought you and your father were estranged."

"So? I still stood to inherit should anything happen to him."

"How could you sell a policy from a company you didn't own yet and you weren't a part of?" I tilted my head. "Unless you knew your father would die soon."

"Are you accusing me of murdering my father?" His face darkened. "Since the two of you know so much, you'll also know I wasn't in town when he was killed. I haven't been here for years. I'm sure you've asked around."

"We have." I mimicked his stance by crossing my arms. "We know you've been at the construction office a lot since you arrived in town. Maybe you laid low for a while and have been here longer than people think. Where is Rogen?"

"Who?"

"Officer Rogen. He's been seen visiting there a lot too, and now he's gone."

"I think you should leave." Connor pointed at the door. "Adios."

Brad took my arm and steered me out of the apartment. "We'll be around, Mr. Miller, acting on official business with the permission of Sea Side Police Department." He marched me down the stairs and back to the car.

Rather than drive away, he said, "Let's wait. He's obviously getting ready to go somewhere. I think we should follow. Scrunch down in your seat so he doesn't see us."

I slouched, a much easier task for me than for the over-six-foot-tall Brad. He squirmed, trying to find a comfortable position. "You think he's going to warn Jenkins and Olson?" I asked.

"That's what I'm hoping."

We didn't have to wait long. Ten minutes later, Connor hurried to a dark blue sedan in the parking lot and sped away.

Brad kept a car between him and us, slowing as Connor pulled up to a coffee shop. I guess Rogen was the only one of the suspects who frequented Tea by the Sea.

As he drove slowly past the coffee shop, Brad asked me to try and see where Connor sat. "With the high booths the place has, we might be able to sneak in and listen to their conversation without them spotting us."

"It looks like he headed toward the back."

Brad circled around and parked across the street. We entered the shop and stealthily took the booth directly in front of the one Connor was at. He was facing our booth, and we ducked low and sat in the seat with our backs to him. We couldn't see who he was meeting with, and he couldn't see us. Hopefully we wouldn't be run out for not purchasing anything. Brad set his phone on the table and pressed the RECORD button.

"I'm telling you they know too much. They must have gotten some of their information from your receptionist," Connor said. "How else would they know about the two policies?"

"By snooping."

Jenkins, Brad mouthed.

"They told me they're working with the police. We need to end this before we end up in jail. I didn't come here to spend time behind bars."

"Stop whining. The death of your old man makes it worth it to you. Jenkins did a poor job of making it look like a suicide." That had to be Olson. "We'll send Overson on out-of-town business. While he's gone, we can arrange an unfortunate incident. Same with the nosy girl. The receptionist won't be a problem either."

"We would have got away with it if not for that girl."

"The police would have figured it out, imbecile."

My blood chilled at how easily they spoke of killing. I'd be a sitting duck with Brad gone, and I couldn't watch his back either. We needed to let Davis listen to the recording ASAP and get protection for Brenda. It proved these three were up to no good.

"They asked about Rogen."

"If he hadn't started having second thoughts about his involvement, he'd still be here. Slipping poison in those scones he loves so much was brilliant."

I widened my eyes. They had killed Rogen. Was his body lying in the same pit Sue had been dropped into?

"We need to find those papers your father had," Olson said. "He was always jotting something down during our meetings. We need to make sure there wasn't anything incriminating. The safe was empty. Where would he have hidden them?"

"I don't know. I haven't had time to search the building thoroughly. They've only recently removed the crime scene tape to allow me access. Don't worry. If they're in the building, I'll take care of it." Connor's voice carried a sharp edge.

"We need that money," Jenkins said, his voice cold. "We aren't going to jeopardize our business without you doing the same with yours."

Chapter 12

With only an hour to spare before I had to go to work, Brad and I snuck out of the coffee shop and sped toward the police station. I waved as we dashed past the open-mouthed woman at the front desk.

Davis frowned when we barged into his office. "I'm busy." He motioned for the other officer he was meeting with to leave. "You two have a lot of nerve. This conversation might have been a private one."

"Sorry. You'll want to hear this." Brad set his phone on the desk and pushed Play.

Davis rubbed both hands roughly over his face then picked up his desk phone. "Get some men over to the construction site and start digging. We may have a body out there." He hung up and turned to us. "I don't even want to know how you got this."

"It's enough to bring those men in, right?" I asked. "Was Rogen married? Did he strike you as the type of man to get involved with crooks? Was he in a financial bind? Do you know where Roy Miller lived? He moved recently, I heard. Did he have a safe-deposit box?"

"Whoa." Davis held up a hand. "Slow down." He suddenly looked very exhausted. "Yes, we'll bring the men in for questioning. Keep your wits about you. It won't be hard to figure out you're the ones who gave us this info. Yes, Rogen is married. His wife suffered a stroke and is in an assisted living facility—"

"Blackmail." I glanced at Brad. "They could have threatened him with his wife's safety to get him to help them. She's vulnerable in the nursing facility."

"Possibly," Davis said. He grabbed a sticky note and wrote down an address. "This is Roy Miller's house. We've just released it from being a crime scene. We've gone over it and found nothing. I'll call the bank and see about the box. If he had one, I'll let the manager know to let you have access."

"Thank you." I really didn't expect him to be so accommodating. "Can we get protection for Brenda?"

"We'll do our best, Ms. Lawrence, but we're running on a skeleton crew as it is. That's why we allowed you to help us." He straightened in his chair. "Be careful, and don't go anywhere alone. Either of you."

"I can bunk on Ashley's sofa for a few nights," Brad said. "We'll keep you posted." He took my hand and led me from the building. "Since you have to go to work, do you want me to head to Miller's alone?"

"No, I'll let Georgina know I'll be late today. I told her we were helping with the investigation. She may call in someone to take over my shift for today." I hated to let her down, but things were coming to a head in Roy's murder, and I didn't want to lose our momentum.

Georgina assured me things were fine at the shop. "I have to get a new phone," I told Brad. "We need to be able to reach each other if we get separated."

"Agreed, but we'd better make sure we stay together." He squeezed my hand. "I don't want anything to happen to you, and these men play dirty."

"I don't want anything to happen to you either." My throat clogged. "The phone is just a precaution. I plan on staying right by your side."

By the time we'd replaced my phone, Davis had texted Brad to let him know that Miller had a safe-deposit box and that the bank manager was expecting us. We grinned at each other like goons and raced down the sidewalk to the bank. Confident we'd find the information we needed to bring Roy's killer to justice, optimism bubbled in me like sea-foam.

The manager frowned as he met us at the door. "This is unorthodox, but since the chief of police approved it, I suppose you can have access to the box." He handed us rubber gloves. "Officer's orders in case you find something."

I appreciated Davis's professionalism and willingness to work with us. I pulled the gloves over my hands as the manager led us to a vault of safe-deposit boxes.

He pulled one out and set it on a table. "I'll be outside when you're finished. Do not take anything with you. If you find something, I'm to have it sent to the department."

I was already reaching for the box. Inside lay a stack of papers with Sea Side Construction's logo on them and an envelope with one sheet folded inside. Bingo!

I removed the pages and spread them on the table. "He's been taking notes on your bosses for quite a while." I tapped the page from the envelope. "Look. He suspected Connor. Right here, he wrote that his son was wanting the business, or at least a large sum of money. Oh wow. He left his house to the city. It doesn't belong to Connor at all."

"Daddy refused and son found a way." Brad leaned over my shoulder.

I don't think a man ever smelled as good as he did. No cologne today, just the fresh scent of soap.

As if he knew what I was thinking, he chuckled and pulled back. "Let's tell the manager to get these to the chief immediately, and then we'll head over to Roy's place."

Face heated, I nodded and put the papers back in the box. I hated to leave them in someone else's hands, but having them in our possession would be too dangerous.

After we arrived at Roy's home, I knew why he hadn't willed the house to his son. The historical house was a Victorian work of art. Something to be cherished and cared for. This was the type of house I'd like to own someday. "How will we get in?"

"Let's try the back door and windows."

I followed Brad to the rear of the house and into a yard that reminded me of photos I'd seen of English gardens. Yep, I was in love with the place.

My prayers were answered. A small kitchen window sat open a few inches, enough for Brad to get a hold of and push up.

"I'll have to hoist you. There's no way I'll fit." He cupped his hands.

I stepped into his hands, and he lifted me up and through the window. Once inside, I took a moment to appreciate the charming but up-to-date kitchen before opening the back door. Since I still wore the gloves the bank manager had given me, I wasn't worried about leaving fingerprints in case the department decided to make another run through the house.

"Let's take it one room at a time," Brad suggested, "although I doubt we'll find anything more than what we've already discovered."

I agreed. We already had enough to put the three men behind bars. Still, I wouldn't miss a chance of exploring my dream home.

I heard sirens wailing and glanced out the front window to see smoke rising in the distance. After saying a quick prayer for the safety of all those involved, I headed up the winding staircase to the second floor.

Roy had taken great care of the historical house. Updating, but keeping the old charm. I wondered whether the city would sell me the place if I agreed to take the same care. Oh, who was I kidding? I'd never be able to afford the place. But there was always a maybe, and I'd be a forensic scientist soon. I'd hold on to hope.

I wandered through bedrooms, looking in drawers and under beds, in closets, and running my hands over the walls in search of hidden passageways. In a room lined with bookshelves and large leather furniture, something clicked when I touched a cherub on the fireplace mantel.

"Brad!"

Footsteps thundered as he raced up the stairs to join me. "A hidden passage." A grin spread across his face. "Isn't this place wonderful?"

"Like a dream." I stepped into the passage and reached up to pull a chain illuminating the tunnel with light. "What do you think it was used for?"

"Smuggling, most likely. This house has to be over a hundred years old."

"Do you think Connor knows about the tunnel?"

"No way to know."

We followed the tunnel to a room carved into the hillside. Someone had definitely been there before us, because Rogen sat propped up against the wall, very much dead. Strawberry scones, covered with mold, lay scattered around him. I put a hand over my nose to stifle the smell of death and swallowed past the nausea.

"I think they know about the tunnel. Do you think they planned on coming back for him before the site was off-limits?" I asked.

"Maybe." Brad glanced at his phone. "Oh no. Miller Inc. is on fire."

"That's what the sirens were for." Connor's way of "taking care of things" was to burn the evidence. I prayed the papers at the bank had been delivered safely into Davis's hands.

"Do you smell smoke?" Brad turned toward the entrance.

"The house!" I pushed past him into the library and down the stairs. The beautiful front door was ablaze, flames reaching long fingers under the door and licking at the curtains on the windows. "Help me, Brad."

"We have to get out of here." He wrapped his hands around my waist and tried to pull me toward the kitchen.

I slapped his hands. "I can't let my house burn."

"Your house?"

"Someday. Maybe." I slipped from his grip and yanked a curtain from the window, then another and another, until the windows were free of flammable fabric. "Get a bucket or something."

Shaking his head, Brad mumbled something about getting ourselves killed and sprinted for the kitchen. He returned a moment later with a bucket of water. He tossed the water on the door. "Not enough. I'll have to go find a hose or something. Call the fire department."

I quickly called 911 and resumed a mad dash back and forth from the kitchen to the front room, dousing everything I could. Repairing warped floorboards would be easier than rebuilding a one-of-a-kind house.

I heard the sound of water spraying against the door and windows and knew Brad had found a hose. We might not be able to put out the fire, but maybe we could prevent it from doing too much damage before the fire department arrived.

"Hey!" Brad shouted.

I glanced out the window to see Connor approaching the

porch, a shovel raised over his head. Choosing Brad over the house, I grabbed a fire poker and rushed out the back door to his rescue. By the time I got around to the front, the two men were throwing punches and rolling on the ground. I raised the poker and stood over them.

"Stop it, Connor, or I'll lay this across your head. Not only for Rogen, but because you tried to destroy my house."

The man's eyes widened as a fire truck stopped in the driveway. Behind them, Officer Davis jumped out of his patrol car, a look of fury on his face. Within seconds, Connor's hands were cuffed behind his back and the fire was put out.

"Good job, you two. Anyone hurt?" Davis glanced back and forth between us.

"No. Rogen's body is in a secret passage of the house," Brad said, sagging against a railing of the porch, trying to catch his breath. "He's dead."

"I'll take you to him." I led Davis to the room, confident Brad was all right, although he'd be sporting a black eye by morning. "Did you find Jenkins and Olson?"

"Seems the two have skipped town. Miller's business is a loss. Connor must have gone there first."

"At least the house isn't a pile of rubble."

Davis nodded toward the moldy scones. "Guess Tea by the Sea really does have scones to die for."

"Not funny."

"Trying to lighten things up." His expression sobered. "Be careful, Miss Lawrence. Jenkins and Olson will surface, and they will come after you."

Of that I had no doubt.

CHAPTER 13

We didn't believe it was safe to stay at either of our houses, so we rented two motel rooms connected by a bathroom. Brad ordered me to prop a chair under the doorknob of my outer door. Sleep didn't come easy, and I again awoke gritty-eyed and less than charitable.

I shuffled sleepily into class the next morning, ignoring Lyon's curious gaze, and took my seat. It wasn't until the tests were passed out that I groaned and laid my head down. Today had to be the worse day for a semifinal, and I hadn't studied a bit.

"Relax," Brad said. "You've got this. You've been living these questions."

True. I picked up my pencil and got to work. Once I'd finished, the professor said I was free to go. Go where? Brad was still taking the test, and I'd been warned not to leave him. Sitting outside wouldn't be safe, so I headed for the college cafeteria. I sent Brad a text of where I'd wait for him.

While I waited at one of the round tables, nursing a soda, I pondered our next move. We didn't have one. We'd solved the case. I grinned, mentally writing the final paper that would earn me my degree.

All that was left was for Jenkins and Olson to join Connor in prison. "We did it," I whispered. Justice was being served.

Footsteps behind me caused me to smile. "About time you finished the test."

"Get up real slow." Something poked me in the back. "You wouldn't want one of these innocent students to die now, would you?"

I tossed my soda hard over my shoulder and ran, expecting a bullet in my back any second. "Call the police," I shouted at the cafeteria staff.

Curses followed as whoever threatened me gave chase. I wasn't going to slow down long enough to see whether it was Jenkins or Olson.

I bypassed the bathrooms, not wanting to be cornered, and took a left, barging out a side door of the building. I turned the corner and ran smack dab into Jenkins and his gun.

"Smart little thing, aren't you?" He motioned the gun toward the parking lot.

Olson joined us, soda still dripping from his hair. "Shoot her now."

"No. We need to get out of here before the police arrive. I know just the place for her."

The two men ushered me to the same van that stopped me the day I was almost abducted. Tied up inside, rope around his mouth and one eye quickly bruising, was Brad. Jenkins must have grabbed him while Olson went after me.

"Where are you taking us?" I glanced back as I climbed into the van.

"Somewhere your bodies won't be found." Olson slammed the back door and opened the passenger door. "A place needing a foundation poured."

"Shouldn't we tie her up?" Jenkins asked.

"She ain't going anywhere."

"Still. . ."

The door opened again, and Olson zip-tied my hands behind my back.

I glanced at Brad. "Are you badly hurt?"

He shook his head. "No."

I slumped down next to him. "We can't stay tied up," I whispered.

"I know how to get out of these. I've watched plenty of videos. Besides, there's a loose screw in the panel behind me. I've got it unscrewed enough I can use it to help me with these ties."

"I never thought they'd be brazen enough to take us from school."

"Neither did I. By the way, I saw your score when I turned in my test. You aced it." He grinned.

Small consolation when I was about to die. I wouldn't take dying easily. I might be small, and a girl, but I'd fight as long as I could. I glanced to where a mesh curtain separated us from Jenkins and Olson, wanting to strangle them.

"Shut up back there," Olson growled over his shoulder, "No amount of whispering is going to get you freed."

I scooted around the dim back of the van as quietly as possible in search of a chain or a strap. Anything I could use to get the numbers down to two on our side and one on theirs. Since Jenkins drove, Olson would be my target.

"What are you doing?" Brad hissed.

"I'm going to choke Olson once you get us freed."

"For crying out loud." Brad started sawing his hands behind his back. "You're going to get us shot if we don't crash first."

"Shhh." A crash was what I counted on. My fingers grasped a roll of thin cording. Hopefully it would be strong enough.

Once his hands were free, Brad took the cord from me then cut the ties around my wrist with a piece of metal he'd found. "You be ready to reach around Jenkins and grab the wheel. The minute the van stops, fling the door open and run. I'll be right behind you."

I nodded and quietly got into position. Jenkins chose that

moment to glance in the rearview mirror. "Hey!"

Brad lunged, shoving aside the mesh curtain, and wrapped the cord around Olson's neck.

I leaned over Jenkins and fought for the wheel. His elbow caught me in the nose, bringing tears to my eyes. The van swerved across the freeway and across oncoming traffic.

A tree loomed in front of us. Slamming Jenkins against the door, I jerked the wheel away from the tree, taking the van through a stand of saplings instead. When the van stopped, I bumped Jenkins hard enough to bang his head against the window then rushed for the door.

I jumped out, Brad right behind me, and made a mad dash for a nearby cliff. I'd take my chances with the sea given my other option. I glanced over the edge, glad not to see any jagged rocks or a beach directly below.

Brad grabbed my hand, and we jumped as a shot rang out.

The icy waters of the Atlantic closed over my head. I lost Brad's hand as I struggled to break the water's surface. Summer or not, the water was cold. Once I emerged, I took a gulp of air and glanced around me. Waves moved me to and fro but steadily closer to a large group of rocks.

Fighting the current, I eventually made my way to shallower water and lay on the beach gasping for air like a stranded fish. I turned my head as Brad crawled to my side.

"Come on. We aren't out of trouble yet." He pointed to where a gun-wielding Jenkins was making his way down to the beach.

"Did you kill Olson?" I got to my feet.

"No. The second he passed out, I followed you. Bad guy or not, I don't want to be the one who kills him." He grabbed my hand again, and we sprinted away from Jenkins.

With our phones wet from seawater, we couldn't call for help. "Make for the lighthouse," Brad said. "Locking ourselves inside is our only chance of surviving this day."

Fear propelled me faster. My body could complain later. My lungs burned from the exertion. My feet kicked up sand, and still we ran.

When a shot rang out, Brad swerved closer to the cliff rising above us. "Stay as much in the shadows as you can."

I wouldn't argue with that reasoning, but we'd have to stop sooner or later. I didn't have much more to go on. *Please, God, give our feet wings.*

Seagrass made our running more difficult the farther we got from the beach and the closer we got to the abandoned lighthouse. I tripped and fell. "I've got nothing left, Brad."

"If you don't get up, you'll die." He yanked me to my feet and spurred me on.

The lighthouse didn't have a door. Tears sprang to my eyes. Whether from exhaustion, fear, or disappointment, I couldn't tell.

"Up the stairs." Brad gave me a shove.

"We can't lock him out."

"There'll be another door at the top." He reached down and grabbed a stick of driftwood. "Find a weapon."

I found a long piece of wood about the circumference of my wrist, took a deep breath, and forced myself to climb. I focused on putting one foot in front of the other, ignoring the weakness in my legs. Stopping wasn't an option. Giving up meant not only my death, but Brad's. I focused on the benefits of living, like more dates and kisses with him. A new career. That beautiful house I would find a way to own.

Thank you, God. A solid door waited at the top of the stairs, and it wasn't locked.

We rushed inside and slammed it behind us. The lock had rusted away.

I glanced around the tower for something to place against the door but found only a shattered chair of no use to us. I removed my shoes and jammed them under the door. Not a surefire method, but it would slow Jenkins down.

Brad smiled and arched a brow.

"Television," I said. I folded to the dust-covered floor. Regardless of the dirt, I lay flat on my back and stared at the glass above me. Some panes were missing, but all in all, the lighthouse was still a thing of beauty.

The sound of feet climbing the iron staircase jerked me back to a sitting position.

"Can he shoot us through the door?"

"Not easily. It's pretty thick," Brad said, raising his wooden cudgel. "If he opens the door, I'll break his hand before he can shoot."

"Aim for the head." I was over his bosses.

Grabbing my piece of wood from where I'd dropped it when I'd fallen to the floor, I took up a position next to Brad. Fight together or die together.

"It doesn't have to be this way," Jenkins said from the other side. "I can make this fast."

"You're delusional," I said. "Why not come and get us?"

"You have nowhere to go. You got out of the house, but if I set fire here, you won't be as lucky."

"Stone and iron won't burn fast."

"Then you'll die of smoke inhalation!"

I could tell I was really getting under the man's skin. I met Brad's amused gaze and shrugged. "Frustrated people make mistakes."

"TV again?"

"Yep."

The door inched open.

Brad slammed his body against it.

Jenkins cursed. "When Olson catches up, you don't stand a chance."

I glanced out the window. Olson had just started making his way to the beach. We had a while. "Why don't you go get him? He doesn't seem to be doing very well. I think his throat is bruised."

"Why don't you just leave town?" Brad suggested. "The police know you're guilty. It's only a matter of time before they find us."

"Because I don't leave loose ends behind. The two of you ruined my plans. Do you know what loan sharks do to people who can't pay?"

"They'll still be after you, even if you kill us," I said.

"But I'll feel better." He rammed the door again.

His gun hand slipped through.

Brad brought the wood down on his wrist.

The man cursed and withdrew. "You broke my arm!"

"I told him to aim for your head," I said. "I'm getting hungry and thirsty. I'm not a nice person when I'm either of those. Add in lack of sleep, and I could probably take you down myself." This entire situation was getting old.

"Open the door, Brad," I said softly. "I'll stand where he can barely see me. You stand behind the door and bash him when he comes in."

"Too risky. He can get a shot off at you."

"Not with a broken wrist."

"We'll keep stalling until Davis finds us. Someone will have seen the van and called it in."

Ever the voice of reason, Brad Overson. I sighed and leaned

against the window, knowing we were too high for anyone to shoot us from the ground.

"How did you do on your test?" I asked.

"Good. A few points lower than you." Brad chuckled. "I guess I should watch more true-crime shows like you do."

"It's going to get dark. We could be stuck up here for a long time. I don't like the dark, Brad."

"That surprises me. You don't seem frightened of much."

"When I was a kid, we lived in the country. The nights were really dark, and we lost electricity frequently. Once it happened when I was home alone. The coyotes howling sounded like they were right outside the door. When my parents finally got home, I was a basket case. I haven't been a fan since."

"I'm here, Ashley. You won't be alone, and the only coyotes you have to worry about are the two-legged ones outside. We can handle them."

I really hoped so.

Chapter 14

"Davis is coming, and he's brought another officer." I jumped to my feet and started waving my arms. *Look up!*

"There's nowhere else for us to hide," Brad said. "He'll come here."

"He needs to know that Jenkins and Olson will be waiting to ambush him." I looked around for something to throw.

I grabbed a leg from the broken chair and tossed it through one of windows that was missing a pane. It landed in the bushes next to the path.

Davis glanced up.

I pointed then waved my arms in a "don't go there" gesture, hoping he'd get the message that the two men waited for him.

Davis ran at a crouch toward the lighthouse, the other officer following suit. Within seconds, they'd dashed out of sight. All we could do now was wait.

I moved over and put a hand on Brad's arm. "Will you go out with me?" My voice shook.

A slow smile spread across his face. "A date? We had one. An exciting one at that."

"I want one where people aren't trying to kill us."

He leaned over and gave me a quick kiss. "I'm looking forward to it. How about a nice restaurant and a moonlight walk on the beach?"

"Sounds like a dream." My smile faded as I heard Olson yell something at Jenkins.

They pushed against the door.

Brad and I pushed back. If they got in before Davis made his way to us, we'd be dead.

"Get whatever pieces of that chair we can jam under the door," Brad said.

"They're all too big. Besides, you can't hold them off by yourself." I leaned my back against the door and braced my feet in front of me.

Shouts echoed from the other side of the door.

Shots rang out.

The gunfight had started. I prayed the good guys would win and that one of the bullets wouldn't pierce the door.

Night had fully fallen, casting us in semi-darkness, broken only by the moon and stars. Ocean waves pounded the rocks below us. What could have been a beautiful place felt more like a prison as my stomach complained and my mouth filled with cotton. I closed my eyes and kept holding the door with what little strength I had left.

God hadn't forsaken us. He'd given us this tower to live or to die according to His will. I really hoped it was to live.

Something hit the other side of the door with a thud. Someone cried out. The shots ceased.

"Is it over?" I glanced up at Brad.

"I think so. Now we need to know who won."

"Open up. It's Davis. It's safe to come out."

"Thank you, God." I stepped back and let Brad open the door.

I impulsively threw my arms around Davis. "You're an angel in blue."

"Uh, okay." He unwound my arms and handed me to Brad. "Olson is dead, Jenkins wounded. They won't be bothering you again."

I nodded as tears filled my eyes.

Brad took me in his arms. "We're going to be fine. Let's go home."

Three months later, I stood on a stage in my graduation gown and received a diploma. I was to start my new job as a forensic scientist, along with Brad, on Monday. This afternoon I'd sign papers to purchase Roy's house. God had blessed me in immeasurable ways.

Impressed with our report and help in solving Roy's murder, the chief had said he couldn't imagine hiring anyone but the two of us to help fight crime in Sea Side. I'd miss my job at Tea by the Sea, but the future filled me with hope.

Diploma in hand, I joined my fellow graduates and gazed into Brad's face. "Ready for dinner?"

"Our real date, at last. No classes, no homework to get in the way. Now that school is over, I plan on spoiling you on a regular basis." He crooked his arm.

Brad took me to an upscale Italian restaurant with white starched tablecloths, staff wearing ties, and low lighting for ambiance. I'd never been to such a romantic place or had a handsomer date.

"Did you ever think we'd be here, diplomas in hand, having brought down three murderers?" I peered at him over my leatherbound menu.

"Of course. I knew you'd be my girl the first day you arrived late for class, your head in the clouds." He reached across the table and placed his hand over mine. "I was a little nervous about going to school at my age, but I thank God every day that I didn't give in to that fear. What I didn't count on was my life in danger. But it's all good now."

My face warmed at the look in his eyes. "The chief promised we could stay safely in the lab from now on."

He winked. "Boring but safe."

"Boring?" I arched a brow. "I'd rather study blood spatter patterns than be shot at. I like puzzles. This job will be one puzzle after another. I don't see anything boring about that. Plus, we get to work together every day. Maybe that's what you think will be boring."

"Sweetheart, time with you will never be boring." He laughed and returned to his menu. "With work and helping you repair the damaged front of your house, I won't have time to be bored."

I'd do everything in my power to make sure that was true. I smiled at him and ordered lasagna, looking forward to my promising—and hopefully not boring—future.

Cynthia Hickey grew up in a family of storytellers and moved around the country a lot as an army brat. Her desire is to write about real but flawed characters in a wholesome way that her seven children and nine grandchildren can all be proud of. She and her husband live in Arizona where Cynthia is a full time writer.

CRUMPETS TO DIE FOR

LINDA BATEN JOHNSON

CHAPTER 1

I didn't expect Grandpa John to pick me up and twirl me around like he did when I was a girl. After all, I'm a professional woman, a CPA, and I now stand five feet seven and weigh—more than I should. I did expect a huge smile and bear hug, because he'd invited me to Sea Side, Maine, from my home in Dallas, Texas. Grandpa asked me, not my parents, aunt, uncle, or cousins, to help him transition from his rambling two-story Victorian home to a retirement apartment. But instead of greeting me, he huddled in the back of the group.

"Grandpa, is this a welcoming committee?" I motioned to the two African American women, a dapper gentleman, and a woman clad in black who brandished a sign with my name, LADESSA NO-LAN, printed on it.

The middle-aged lady with blunt-cut blond bangs and straight shoulder-length hair inserted herself between me and my grandfather. "We're from the Happy Days Retirement Village. I'm Betty Boyd, the activities director. When John wanted to meet your flight, I asked if anyone else wanted to go for an outing, and here we are. What color is your luggage?"

"Burgundy, with green ribbons."

Betty nodded to the other man in my welcoming entourage. "Trent Sharp will get your bags."

I wriggled past the black-clad woman and grasped Grandpa John in a fierce embrace. He was a head taller than I, still bald, with the same round face, chocolate-brown eyes, and a small scar on his right cheek, but he appeared deflated, diminished.

He placed his lips by my ear. "Ladessa, I need help. Don't leave before we talk."

"I won't. May I sleep in the front bedroom?"

Grandpa led me toward the double doors. "I don't live at home. I'm in a Happy Days apartment."

"Well, why? Uh, when?" I stuttered, wondering why he asked me here if he'd already moved.

"Sold the house. You'll live in the apartment over the garage. House is rented until year's end to Logan Hernandez, a newspaper reporter. Have you heard of him?"

I shook my head. "You sold the house?"

"I did."

"What about your things? Your furniture?"

"In the garage. That's mine until the end of the year."

"Your things are in the garage?" These announcements perplexed me.

"Had space because I sold the car."

"You sold the car?" I sounded like an echo, repeating each of Grandpa's surprising statements. "I guess I'll rent a car."

"No need. Saved you a bike. You love riding bikes."

The incongruous idea mystified me. Grandpa wanted me to ride a bike? In Maine? In October? I struggled to comprehend these revelations.

Trent Sharp, a well-groomed man who resembled movie star Pierce Brosnan—the older version with the silvery hair and nice tan—returned with my bags. Betty resumed her role as Mother Hen.

"Thank you, Trent." I detected frostiness in her tone when she acknowledged Sharp. She patted her oversized tote. "Does anyone need anything before we go? Tissue? Band-Aid? Lozenge? Hand sanitizer? If not, load up."

Grandpa John and I waited as Mr. Sharp used his nasal spray for two loud snorts before heaving my bags into the van.

Mr. Sharp moved beside me and placed his hand on the small of my back. "Lots of luggage. Didn't realize you were moving here, my love. Thought this was a visit."

I flinched at his familiar touch. "Fall weather in New England zigzags from warm to freezing cold, so I prepared."

He flashed me a white, toothy smile and moved closer. "Ladessa, we have shops in Sea Side, or I could take you on a shopping spree. Shall we set a time?"

Before I responded, Betty shoved Sharp toward the passenger seat. "Keep me company up front and stop annoying the young woman."

Grateful for Betty's intervention, I slid into the back with Grandpa and the two other women. "Betty didn't introduce us. I'm Ladessa Nolan."

"My daughter and I both know you. You attended our church when you stayed with your grandparents. I'm Mary Rollins."

"Mrs. Rollins, of course." I squeezed her hand. "We called you Mary *Christmas*, because you told us you were born on Christmas Day."

"That's me. Mary Christmas is an easy name for children to remember. Please, Ladessa, call me Mary. My husband served the congregation as associate minister for eighteen years. He's gone to his heavenly reward. Our daughter was supposed to be a December baby. Noelle means Christmas gift, but this contrary girl stayed put until January."

"Noelle?" I peered at the elegant woman who offered a conspiratorial wink.

I remembered Noelle, my partner in crime when we skipped

church and used our offering to buy doughnuts at the corner store. Noelle hadn't eaten many sweets lately. Her svelte form reminded me of a runway model or a yoga instructor. I bet she could manage tree pose and sun salutations, and place her palms on the floor without bending her knees. I sat straighter, hoping to look a few pounds thinner.

"Do you live at Happy Days, Noelle?"

Noelle's rich laughter made me smile. "No, seniors only, no youngsters allowed. Mom does hair and nails for the residents and plays piano for special events, so she gets a break on the rent."

Mary patted my hand. "It's a nice place for your grandfather, Ladessa. He won't have to worry about keeping up with house maintenance or remembering to pay his bills."

I filed that information with tonight's other bewildering events. Was Grandpa having memory problems?

The van's sharp turn caused me to bump into Noelle. "Ladessa, I'm here to beg you to work at Tea by the Sea. Our manager, Georgina, extended our breakfast hours, and we're shorthanded. Georgina is Evie's granddaughter. I'm sure you remember Evie. She was the original owner of the shop. When your Grandpa heard about the business needing another waitress, he suggested you."

"I did waitress there once, but. . ."

Grandpa squeezed my shoulder. "Big festival in October, and my friend needs help. Working will keep you busy."

"You think I should wait tables again?"

"Georgina would appreciate it, and the change might be good for you."

Bewildered by Grandpa's encouragement for me to waitress, I turned to Noelle. "Do you work at Tea by the Sea?"

"Yep. I'm a baker."

"So, I'm working at the tea shoppe?"

Noelle nodded. "We open at seven, and early-rising New Englanders will be waiting by the door."

"I took three months off to help Grandpa move and to record his memories for the family. I don't need an interim job." I twisted my body toward Grandpa, but he rested, eyes closed, with his head against the seat's back.

Mary stroked my hand, which I'd balled into a fist. "Your grandfather has suffered several upheavals. Major changes can overwhelm us, can't they?"

This rhetorical question required no answer, so I didn't give one. I struggled to quell my resentment that these people knew more about what was going on in my grandfather's life than I did. And why would my grandfather arrange a job for me? I'd waitressed as a physically fit teenager. But how would my thirty-year-old body respond to standing all day, carrying trays, cleaning tables, and biking to and from work?

Noelle chatted about my future in Sea Side. "All businesses gear up for pumpkin month, and Tea by the Sea expects record sales. Crumpets are my signature offering." She lowered her voice. "Now, weren't you the one who dragged me from church to indulge in decadent pastries when we were kids?"

Noelle's companionship provided a bright spot in my evening. I'd dreaded returning to Sea Side, where my heart had been broken ten years ago, because I still bore the scars. But when Grandpa called me, I reconstructed the Norman Rockwell–style community from my childhood memories, not the college years when I'd suffered the roller-coaster, heart-squeezing pangs of love freely given but not returned.

Soon Betty maneuvered the van into a parking spot and issued a command to disembark.

I linked my arm through Grandpa John's. "Want to show me your new place?"

"Not now, sweetie. I'm tired. Why don't you bike out here tomorrow?"

"Okay. You're not going to check to see if I have a nickel behind my ear?" I tilted my head so he could perform his magic ritual.

He appeared confused then recalled the ceremonial habit. "Uh-oh. I'm fresh out of nickels, Ladessa. Noelle offered to drive you to town." He entered the doors labeled HAPPY DAYS without turning to wave goodbye.

Noelle sensed my mood and drove in silence until she reached the beautiful Victorian that had been my grandparents' home.

"Thanks for the ride. I guess I'll see you tomorrow. Are there uniforms for the waitresses?" Maybe I could delay my start date until properly attired.

"Wear jeans. And don't fret. Diana, the other waitress, will help you," Noelle said. "On the wardrobe front, we're getting October shirts promoting Punkin'-Chunkin' Month tomorrow."

"I'm afraid to ask what that means. See you in the morning, and thanks again for the ride."

After I unloaded my bags, Noelle beeped the horn and drove away.

My first hours in Sea Side dumbfounded me. I'd be living in a garage apartment, not in the Nolan family home where I'd spent summers from my birth until my college years. I had a job as a waitress. My grandfather lacked the clarity he'd always possessed. And some reporter lived in the home I loved.

Scenes shared with my sister in the beautiful house reeled

through my mind. We readied fishing gear on the porch, watched seagulls dip and soar, baked brownies, and sang show tunes with Grandma. We flew kites with our cousins, decorated bikes for the Fourth of July, primped for church, and then returned for the week's best meal, Sunday dinner.

Tears snaked down my cheeks. Could Grandpa John's change be a delayed reaction to Grandma's death? He'd whispered for me not to leave him until we talked, and then he'd sent me away. Grandpa wasn't the robust, cheerful man I'd idolized in my childhood. His eyes didn't twinkle.

I wrestled my suitcases up the outside garage steps and wondered what other surprises awaited me. Then the stairs creaked, and someone shone a light into my eyes. The brightness blinded me.

"Who goes there?" Chuckles followed the question, but the brilliant light remained unwavering.

"I've always wanted to say that," said a second voice.

I sheltered my eyes. "It's been said. Now would you please lower the light? I have permission to live in this garage apartment."

"We've been expecting you. My pal, Will Tomlinson, is a Sea Side short-timer, and I'm Logan Hernandez, featured reporter for Maine's finest newspaper. Have you heard of me?"

"No, I haven't." The speaker's cockiness stoked my annoyance after his spotlighting joke. "I'm Ladessa Nolan, a doggone good CPA for Mullins and Hancock. Have you heard of me?"

"Ignore Logan and come join us for a slice of pizza. Delivered minutes before you arrived." That voice, warmer and more personable, must belong to Will Tomlinson.

Curiosity about the state of my grandparents' home trumped my good sense. Anyway, this was Sea Side, and perhaps the obnoxious reporter could explain why he inhabited my grandfather's beautiful house while I bunked in the garage apartment.

"I am hungry, and pizza sounds great. I'll be down after I stow my bags." I flipped the switch, and when the lights blazed, I offered a prayer of thanks for working electricity. I rolled my luggage to the bedroom, brushed my teeth, checked to make sure my eyes weren't red from crying, and headed to the house I loved.

The aroma of cheese, pepperoni, sausage, and onions elicited a rumbling from my stomach. I accepted a large slice and noted familiar family furniture in unfamiliar spots. The navy-and-white striped sofa where I'd read *Number the Stars* and *Dear Mr. Henshaw* sat against the far wall. In place of the game table where Grandpa and I clashed in chess, Battleship, and Monopoly stood a card table with a computer. A metal bookcase replaced my grandma's glider, and pictures of our clan on the beach, at cookouts, sailing, and hiking were nonexistent.

The renowned reporter led the way to the kitchen's familiar oak trestle table. "Ladessa Nolan, doggone good CPA, what brings you to the little town of Sea Side?"

"If you're a good investigator, I'm sure you know." I regretted my snarky comment when I bit into the pizza and the cheese burned my mouth. The pain served me right for being mean-spirited. "Sorry."

Logan's dancing brown eyes betrayed amusement, not chagrin, and an alertness that told me he might be good at his job.

Will Tomlinson's taller, lanky frame reminded me of a scarecrow dancing in the wind, but his nice cheekbones and friendly openness invited trust. His preppy attire of slacks and collared shirt contrasted with Logan's tight jeans and fitted T-shirt that showed off hard-earned muscles.

I allowed the pizza to cool. "I should ask you two that question.

Logan, Will, what brings you to a coastal town in autumn?"

Logan, not the style of reporter who listened more than he talked, answered. "Will is jumpstarting a business development, bringing bigger stores and maybe some cottage industries to Sea Side. He's lining up backers and fighting city hall to get permits. I'm here to cover local fall festivals in Maine, and I'm chasing a big story on a topic I'm not at liberty to disclose." He offered a devilish grin.

"Too important to share with peons?" I instantly lamented my comment and muttered another apology. If I spent much more time around Logan Hernandez, I'd have to put a rubber band on my wrist to pluck each time he annoyed me. I maintained my best behavior through two more slices and chitchat with the interlopers inhabiting my grandfather's house.

When Logan offered more pizza, I demurred. "I need sleep. I'm waitressing at Tea by the Sea tomorrow."

Demonstrating his good manners, Will rose before I stood. "Logan and I will see you there. Tomorrow is the punkin'-chunkin' demonstration, and Sea Side will be elbow to elbow with tourists and inquisitive townsfolk."

I groaned, dreading my first day as a waitress after ten years. On the bright side though, I wouldn't have time to worry about my grandfather's mental state or grieve over the changes in the home where I'd spent happy childhood days.

CHAPTER 2

I did a double take when I checked the clock. I'd only waitressed an hour, but my calves ached and my biceps burned from carrying trays laden with enticing goodies to customers and then dirty dishes to the kitchen. Willing the minute hand to move faster, I retreated to the bakery area where Noelle reigned.

"You made it through the early bird group." Noelle kneaded dough on a flour-covered island. "The next wave will arrive about nine."

"I hope they're as patient as the first group. I served scones instead of crumpets to three tables by mistake."

Noelle gasped. "No! When you can't remember the order, serve my scrumptious crumpets."

"Thanks for the tip." I pushed the swinging door with my backside while carefully balancing the order for table six. The mix-and-match tables and chairs painted in cheerful yellow, green, pink, and white created an ambiance of shabby chic and happiness. The atmosphere, combined with aromas of baking breads and sweets, elicited smiles from most who entered Tea by the Sea.

The warmth in the shop came from companionship as much as the ovens in the back. Minutes became hours as customers chitchatted across tables about neighbors, families, and travel plans. The talk reminded me of the sheltering love I'd felt during my Sea Side summers from elementary school until my sophomore year in college—when my sister showed up. I knew I couldn't allow my sis to shoulder all the blame for stealing my ideal man. I later made my own mistakes in the relationship department. I'd chosen poorly four times. Maybe five, not three, would be the charm.

This year I'd acted on my New Year resolution to change my loner habits. I joined the singles group at church and took a class about coaching your life to success. Last night I shared pizza with Logan Hernandez and Will Tomlinson, a baby step in independent socializing. Maybe this visit to Sea Side would prove beneficial. The door banging interrupted my musings.

Cool salty ocean air accompanied a striking red-haired woman who waved an orange T-shirt in her right hand while holding a box tucked against her left side. She stopped at each table to talk, her rapid-fire speech sounding like a jackhammer's *rat-a-tat-tat* as she worked her way around the room. The pink sweater flattered her fiery short hair, freckles, and green eyes. When she offered me an orange shirt, I realized how short she was, even with her three-inch heels.

"I'm Jane Mills. I work with the Chamber of Commerce, and I know you're Ladessa Nolan, John's granddaughter. We're delighted you'll be helping with the fall festival."

Chalk up another surprise for me.

Jane continued, hardly taking a breath. "We're gearing up for October events. You may know about Damariscotta, Maine. They do pumpkin smashing and a regatta where contestants paddle pumpkin boats. We hope our town's experience will rival theirs."

I'd never heard of Damariscotta's festival, but if anyone could organize a bigger and better event, I'd bet my money on this tiny, enthusiastic redhead. I gestured to new customers entering the shop, and she took the hint.

"Just pull your October shirt over what you're wearing."

Orange is a horrible color for me. I envisioned myself looking sallow and washed out for the whole month, attired in the ghastly shade that promoted Sea Side's Punkin'-Chunkin' and other fall festival events.

Jane addressed the customers. "Folks, the punkin'-chunkin' demonstration is at three today, right in front of Tea by the Sea. Remind your friends to come watch. We're also having a pumpkin derby race. You'll love the events we have planned."

The woman's vitality infected both patrons and employees. When she finally took a breath, employees hustled from the kitchen to claim shirts.

Jane rummaged through the box. "Georgina purchased two shirts for each of you. I'll snap a picture of the employees under the Tea by the Sea sign. The shop could use some good publicity to counter the negative press. Come outside. Line up."

I stood next to Noelle. "What did Jane mean about negative press?"

"Gossips have tried to connect murder and death to Tea by the Sea. The shop struggled, but the longtime residents support the business. And then, of course, there's Harlan Gramford."

"Who is Harlan Gramford?"

Jane admonished us to smile as she photographed the group, then promised Georgina a poster for the window with our picture and a listing of October's events.

Noelle led the way inside. "You asked about Harlan Gramford. He owns Happy Days, where my mom and your grandfather live. I think he champions the shop because he loves baked goods. Harlan reminds me of the Pillsbury Doughboy. Short, pale, and puffy. Anyway, he schedules the van to bring the seniors for tea each week. Tea by the Sea is a fixture in the village. The locals want it to survive."

"Is that why we're working here?" This made more sense than Grandpa's suggestion that I needed spending money or something to do.

Noelle shrugged. "Might be. My mother nudged me to work here, just like your grandfather encouraged you. Think working will keep us out of trouble?"

"I'm a changed woman, Noelle. I go to church voluntarily." I glanced at the front door where several people pressed inside, including Grandpa John.

"The Happy Days crowd has arrived." Noelle mouthed, *Crumpets*, as she retreated.

I recognized Betty, the activities director, and Mary, Noelle's mom. I guessed the pudgy, fair-skinned man with Grandpa would be Harlan Gramford. His black-rimmed glasses perched too far forward on his nose, and his double chin attested to too many sweets and too little time in a gym.

I went over to Grandpa John's table and kissed his cheek, pleased that his eyes looked brighter today.

"Ladessa, say hello to Harlan Gramford. He owns Happy Days. He makes certain we have stimulating opportunities. The facility has current event sessions, book clubs, exercise classes, and games. Sometimes we play Clue, Monopoly, or Battleship. Remember the hours we spent playing games?"

Harlan extended his hand. "We have the best residents in the world. John loves living in our place, although Sharp and I had to persuade him he should move."

I massaged Grandpa John's shoulders. "My grandfather isn't easily convinced to do anything. We grandkids had to present facts and reasons for any request. Begging, whining, and whimpering never worked."

Harlan said, "I think my four-legged pals, Sunrise and Sunset, convinced your grandfather."

"His dogs," Grandpa explained. "They're powder puff dogs—don't bother people with allergies."

"Bichons. The residents like the dogs more than they like me," Harlan said. "My mother suffered from allergies, among other things."

"Nice to meet you, Mr. Gramford." I suggested the crumpets and got several takers.

The place buzzed with talk about upcoming events and the shirts worn by the staff. I even sold four ugly orange shirts to senior citizens, who were pleased the purchase would support the tea shoppe and Sea Side.

Grandpa waved me to his table. "Ladessa, come to Happy Days about six, have dinner with me and see the apartment."

"I'll be there." I wanted to see the furniture, pictures, and mementos he chose to keep.

My shift ended at three, which meant I could watch the punkin'-chunkin' event, if I didn't collapse. I alternated standing on one foot and flexing the other, then bent my knees to alleviate their aching. Another of my resolutions was to drop fifteen pounds, but I'd never established an exercise regimen. Maybe waitressing and riding a bike would remove the unwanted weight.

I'd just wolfed down a petit four—not a healthy choice—when Logan and Will arrived. As I grabbed menus, I noticed they were not alone. Logan's arm encircled Jane's waist, and Will followed Trent Sharp. They took table four in the back corner.

When I arrived with menus, Logan whispered in Jane's ear while she beamed. Will's face looked like a storm cloud ready to burst, and Sharp offered me a sunshiny smile.

"Ladessa, my offer for a shopping trip still stands. Just name the time." Sharp placed his nasal spray on the table.

"I think my wardrobe is set. We employees just received these nifty work shirts." I glanced toward Jane for a reaction, but Logan held her attention.

"Uncle Trent, consider your age." Will glared at the older man.

"Just being polite." Sharp turned to me. "I can't have anything with peanuts."

"Everyone knows you can't have peanuts," Will said.

The handsome senior tapped the menu. "What do you recommend, Ladessa?"

I suggested the spiced orange or the pumpkin crumpets, and Sharp ordered a combination platter for the group. I placed the order, bussed tables, and took my time rolling silver in napkins to avoid going back to table four. Logan and Jane continued their short-distanced conversation while Sharp and Will were nose to nose in what appeared to be an argument.

When their order arrived, I deftly managed trays of food as I dispensed mugs of steaming tea. "Enjoy. These crumpets are to die for."

"Bad joke, Ladessa." Sharp selected a spiced orange crumpet. "Since you're new here, you probably don't know that death's shadow looms over this wonderful eating establishment."

I yearned to hear the story, but ear-splitting sirens broke the calm.

Jane jumped to her feet. "Come on! It's time for the punkin'-chunkin' demonstration." She herded the employees from the back and diners in the front toward the street.

I marveled as the catapult contraption mounted in the bed of a pickup was lowered to the grassy area facing the ocean. Three giant pumpkins, which I gauged with an uneducated eye to be at least fifty pounds each, waited on the green grass for their transport into space. The viewing numbers swelled as a high school band with a drum line played rousing music, preparing the excited crowd for flying pumpkins.

Georgina flipped the sign to CLOSED and asked if I would watch the shop entrance. I leaned against the door, happy to relax.

"Anyone want to use the facilities before the big show?" Betty led some people past me and inside the shop while the rest of the crew from Happy Days staked out a prime viewing location. When Betty's group left the shop, she rummaged through her giant bag and dispensed hand sanitizer squirts.

So much for my vigilance in guarding the premises. But I couldn't deny a senior citizen the right to use the restroom.

Jane manned the public address system and directed a countdown for the release of each missile. The folks cheered when the catapult chunked the pumpkins through the air.

After the last pumpkin flew into space, I scooted inside, eager to end my shift before the onslaught of customers. All tables were empty except table four.

"Mr. Sharp?"

When Trent Sharp didn't raise his head, I jostled his shoulder. His posture wasn't normal.

I felt his hand. Cold.

I checked for a pulse. None.

I placed fingertips on the artery in his neck. Nothing.

I turned his head and lifted an eyelid.

Dead. The man was dead.

I locked the front door and punched 911 on my cell phone.

CHAPTER 3

Despite entreaties and some threats, I kept the front door locked, ignored the persistent phone, and waited for the police to arrive. My TV binge-watching included detective shows like *Elementary*, *Inspector Morse*, *Law and Order*, and the initialed ones like *NCIS*, *CSI*, and *FBI*, so I knew to keep the area surrounding a dead body sacrosanct. Surely Sharp died of natural causes, but I honored my screen knowledge of an investigator's code, just in case. My heart hammered as I paced and maintained my vigil. I glanced toward the inert body and stifled a nervous giggle. Instead of finding a tip at table four, I'd found a corpse.

Who would laugh at a time like this? Maybe I should request a doctor's appointment for myself, not my grandpa.

The screaming sirens grew louder as a patrol car and an ambulance slowed for the punkin'-chunkin' crowds to clear a path. The two vehicles screeched to a stop, using half the sidewalk as parking spaces, and two policemen, followed by a medical duo, hurried toward the tea shoppe. One officer brandished a yellow crime scene tape bracelet around his wrist, and the medical team carried a gurney.

Gawking onlookers formed a gauntlet for their entrance, and my stomach churned as I recalled Noelle's comment about Tea by the Sea fighting negative publicity. A dead body might kill the business. I tittered nervously as I unlocked the door and stared into the angular features and steady blue eyes that had altered the course of my life a decade ago.

"You the one who found the body?" His badge identified him as Detective Hardy.

I swallowed and nodded toward the table in the back.

"You touch anything?"

"Him. I shook him then checked for a pulse."

The detective placed fingers on Sharp's carotid artery then motioned for the gurney. When he actually looked at me, he harrumphed. "Well, if it isn't my brother's Brillo-headed beauty. What are you doing here?"

An unsophisticated whimper emerged. "Discovering a dead body?"

"Don't try to be cute."

"I wasn't." Seeing the uncanny likeness I'd spent ten years trying to forget unnerved me.

"Sit down. I've got questions."

I chose a chair painted sunshiny yellow, hoping it might ward off the chills.

"I'm Devin. Doubt you remember me. You were all wrapped up in my big brother, until he fell for your sister."

My cheeks burned as my mind flew back to those tender and terrible days. The detective's face transported me to that vulnerable summer of my first love followed by rejection.

Devin Hardy asked questions, and I mumbled answers. Two men bearing the draped body stopped by the table.

The younger one spoke. "Might have a murder on your hands, Detective. I'm not a doctor, but something's not right." He talked in a low, slow voice. "Nobody keels over in a tea shoppe. I suspect foul play."

I gasped. "Couldn't it have been natural causes?"

The detective shook his head. "Autopsy will tell us. Man was not popular. I can name several people who wanted Trent Sharp six feet under."

The man's callousness upset me. Maybe he'd seen dead bodies before, but this was new to me.

"I can't imagine anyone killing another person." I hoped Devin Hardy would reassure me, but he didn't.

The detective stood and hooked his thumbs in his belt loops. "Don't let that medical tech spook you. And don't leave town. You've kept your curls. Always liked them."

My fingers went to my short brown curls. I'd reverted to my natural curly hairstyle only this past spring. Now I wanted an appointment for hair straightening. When Hardy walked out, Sea Side residents surged inside to see what details they might garnish from the new waitress who'd discovered a dead body.

Logan Hernandez bulldozed his way toward me and covered my shoulders with his leather jacket. "I'm taking you to your apartment and then to your grandpa's. He's worried about you."

Logan's orders caused my shoulders to relax, even though I knew his reporter's nose for a story probably motivated his actions. I yearned for a shower and clean clothes but doubted I could bike home as shaky as I felt.

After threading his car through the clogged streets, Logan helped me up the porch steps and into what I considered my grandparents' home. He reheated leftover pizza and offered coffee from the Keurig, which I gratefully accepted. The chills, which started during my conversation with Detective Hardy, morphed into the shaking kind. Logan's jacket proved ineffectual against my shivers. He grabbed a quilt from the couch and placed it around my shoulders.

"Thanks." I tugged the coverlet tighter with my left hand and used my right to manage the pizza and coffee in turn.

"You're in shock," Logan said.

My shaking continued. "The medical guy thinks Sharp was murdered."

He patted my back with the universally accepted gesture of consolation. "What else did he say?"

"Nothing, but the detective wasn't happy. Guess a murder requires more paperwork than a routine traffic stop."

"Ladessa Nolan, are you making a joke?"

"Not a very good one."

"What questions did the detective ask?"

I tried to remember. "Normal things like, when did Mr. Sharp come in? Who sat with him? What did he order? How was his mood? Did anyone come visit the table? Did I see him use a phone?" I shook my head. "Since this was my first day, I concentrated on doing my tasks and getting my orders to the right tables. I wasn't helpful."

"We're all more observant than we realize. Maybe a week from now you'll remember more details."

"Finding Mr. Sharp's body panicked me. Then seeing Detective Hardy shocked me."

"Devin Hardy presents himself as the law's stern face, but women don't consider him shocking." Logan chuckled.

"He looks like someone I knew, someone. . ."

"That sounds like an intriguing story," he said quietly.

"Old story." I brushed my lips with a napkin.

"I'm a good listener. I grew up the only boy in a Puerto Rican family. My three older sisters spoiled me, and my three younger sisters idolized me, but they all taught me to listen—and not judge."

"Did you like growing up with all sisters?" I turned toward him.

Logan slid onto the barstool next to me. "Loved it, and our neighborhood was Puerto Rican, so you had a parent in every doorway watching out for you. I had the family circle, neighborhood circle, and then our church circle. How about you?"

"One sister, four years older. She neither spoiled nor idolized me."

"Are you friends as adults?" Logan asked.

"Not yet. My fault, not hers. I've allowed past hurts to define me. I'm journaling about the sister relationship."

"Writing is good. I make my living at it."

I appreciated that he didn't push me for more information. "I'm better with numbers than words."

"Most CPAs are better with numbers. I might have a job for you." He raised his eyebrows, waiting for me to ask him what he meant.

"I don't want another job. I'm a vacationing CPA. My grandfather roped me into the waitress gig."

"And your first day was a heart-stopper!" He placed his hand on mine. "Did my bad joke top yours?"

"Yes." I removed the quilt from my shoulders. "I'm finally warm. If your offer to take me to my grandfather's is still good, I'll shower and change."

"Take your time. I'll call Jane and Will, see if they noticed anything."

"Were Sharp and Will arguing?"

Logan shook his head. "Nothing serious. They were bickering, not arguing."

"Jane's very attractive." I pictured Logan and Jane's flirtatious behavior at the tea shoppe as I folded the quilt.

"She is." Logan pulled his phone from his jeans.

"And interesting," I added.

"She is. I think all women are interesting." His killer smile caused his dark eyes to sparkle.

When I turned to place the quilt on the counter, my foot caught on the barstool, and he arrived with Spiderman speed, cupping my elbow in his hand. I held up my palm to indicate I was fine and exited with all the grace I could muster.

Hay bales topped with pumpkins lined the Happy Days driveway, and the front columns wore spiraling gold, burgundy, russet, and green leaves. The apartment complex in daytime looked substantial, well maintained, and inviting. The cheerful facade allayed fears that my grandfather had made a bad decision. If Grandpa John's apartment looked as good as the building's exterior, I would be reassured about his new living quarters. However, I needed a long conversation with him, and perhaps the staff, to convince me that my grandfather's mental and emotional health remained stable.

Logan and I autographed the sign-in register, stating our arrival time and the person we wished to see, and indicating that we would be sharing an evening meal. The receptionist suggested we wait in the reading room until Grandpa arrived. The blended fragrance of chicken, rosemary, apple, and cinnamon forecast a delicious dinner.

My grandfather entered before I could examine any book titles on the library shelves.

"Ladessa, how awful that you discovered Sharp's body." He wrapped his arms around me. "Were you scared? You're a grown-up now, but I see you as the tentative toddler who loved building sandcastles and collecting shells."

"Grown-ups can be scared too." I turned so Grandpa could

acknowledge Logan. "You remember Logan Hernandez. He's renting your house."

"Sir." Logan shook Grandpa's hand while pressing his other hand against my waist.

When Trent Sharp placed his hand in the same place at the airport, I cringed. I hadn't liked the dead man's possessive, teasing attitude, but I couldn't imagine anger, hurt, or rage powerful enough to consider ending a person's life. Wanting someone dead was as intriguing a thought as it was repulsive. Maybe I'd quiz the tenants about their former neighbor, the handsome and debonair Mr. Sharp.

A chime sounded for the first dinner seating. The tables, topped with white cloths, had autumnal centerpieces with a battery-operated candle amid the leaves and nuts. Grandpa led Logan and me to a table near the back where Harlan Gramford and Mary Rollins waited.

"I invited people you know to sit at our table," Mary said. "I asked Betty Boyd, but I'm not sure she'll have dinner. She's upset about Trent Sharp's death."

"Were Betty and Sharp close friends?" Logan, the reporter, asked *my* question.

I'd discovered the body, and I wanted to play amateur sleuth and prove to Detective Devin Hardy that I wasn't a starry-eyed kid.

Mary answered Logan's question. "Betty worked for Sharp's company before she came to Happy Days. You know, women tell hairdressers as many secrets as they tell their pastors, something I've learned over the years cutting and styling."

I turned to Mary. "Betty spoke harshly to him at the airport. Did she dislike him?"

"Try these freshly baked rolls." Harlan Gramford cut off the conversation between Mary and me.

"Mr. Gramford, did you know that Sharp and Betty had worked together previously?" Logan asked.

I admired my escort's efforts in steering the conversation back to why someone would want Sharp dead. I could learn from Logan Hernandez, and from Harlan Gramford, who ignored the question by lifting a dog for us to admire.

"Did you meet my dogs today? I visit the tables with Sunrise and Sunset after each meal. The residents love them. Oh, here's Betty." Gramford stood.

Logan held a chair for the heavyset woman, whose face looked splotched and puffy as if she'd been crying.

Mary squeezed Betty's hand. "I'm sorry about Trent."

Betty blinked rapidly and fingered her pearls. "Thanks, Mary. I loved him once."

"It must have been hard to love him after he targeted you for embezzlement," Logan said. "I reported that case. Sharp appeared to be the guilty one, but you went to prison."

My brain registered two important facts. Betty had a criminal record. She loved Trent Sharp. In the past or now? After Sharp tried to make a date with me, Betty ordered him to join her in the van's front seat. That could have been jealousy at work.

Mary put a hand on her heart. "Betty, love can last a lifetime. I miss my husband every day, and Noelle still grieves for her father. I prayed to forgive Trent Sharp, and God answered. But Noelle still harbors bad feelings toward the man."

Surprise, surprise. This dinner was harvesting a bouquet of clues. I couldn't imagine Mary *Christmas* Rollins feeling animosity toward anyone.

My grandfather peered at Mary over his coffee cup. "I didn't like the man either."

Mary nodded. "John, you and I aren't the only ones Mr. Sharp caused to suffer."

I concentrated on eating, with my ears open. Maybe a good hairdresser or a good amateur sleuth's secret was simple—be quiet and listen.

CHAPTER 4

Logan visited with Betty, Mary, and other residents while Grandpa showed me his apartment. The considerate and handsome Puerto Rican reporter might have aroused my romantic interest if I hadn't seen him with Jane.

Grandpa's place was smaller than I expected. Chairs, a sofa, and side tables, which belonged in a larger venue, competed for space and lost. Seeing his apartment prompted the recollection of how I felt when I saw him at the airport. He'd appeared diminished, and his apartment surroundings elicited the same cramped, restrictive feel.

"Grandpa, where are your drawings, your awards, your precious mementos?" He'd worked as a researcher at the Woods Hole Oceanographic Institution for decades and earned accolades galore. He also invested in marine biology first edition books and drawings, but they weren't evident.

Grandpa scanned the room, bewildered. "Could they be in the garage? I moved so quickly. I didn't go through all my things."

"What was the rush? You knew I planned to help." Grandpa's baffled expression tugged at my heart.

"Mr. Sharp had a renter for a furnished house. The movers gave me three boxes and told me to pick things I needed. They crated the rest and stored them in the garage." Tears filled Grandpa's eyes.

The process he described bordered on cruelty. How could anyone say a quick goodbye to a lifetime of memories? How can one earmark what to pack in a day?

"We'll sort through each box in the garage." I glanced at the petite bookcases, not generous enough to house the books on marine biology, model shipbuilding, and regional recipes he'd collected over the years.

"I saved some personal things." He motioned to photos on the top shelf. In decorative frames, Grandma tossed bread into the air for seagulls, I worked on a sandcastle in my Minnie Mouse swimsuit, my cousin Martin waved a diploma, and in the last, my sister kissed her groom. My throat caught when I saw the couple's sunshiny faces with my squall-like countenance on their right and Devin Hardy, sporting an impish grin, on their left.

Grandpa sighed. "Ladessa, what happened between you and your sister?"

I pointed to the groom. "He happened. I thought he cared for me. Then Aletha showed up, and they became engaged within months."

Grandpa's face betrayed astonishment. "He was my colleague. I can't imagine him acting inappropriately."

I shrugged, shocked at the naked pain etched on my face in their wedding photo. "I was young and naive. When Devin Hardy showed up in the tea shoppe today, I tumbled back in time. He looks exactly like his brother."

Grandpa smiled at the photo of the couple. "They complement each other. They have a good marriage. You should be happy for them."

Grandpa showed no befuddlement now, so I asked the question nagging me. "Grandpa, why did you invite me here?"

"You're my favorite grandchild." Grandpa touched my nose. "But I really need your intuition, practicality, and puzzle skills. Remember that Shakespeare quote about something not being right in the state of Denmark? Well, something isn't right in Maine, specifically Sea Side, and you're the one to figure it out. My mind tricks me. Sometimes I see things clearly. Sometimes I don't."

His admission offered an entry for my concern. "Let's visit your family doctor. Maybe your meds need adjustment."

"I don't see my old doctor. The Happy Days medical staff cares for us."

A persistent tapping on the door stayed my response.

Logan jangled his keys. "Sorry to interrupt, but Detective Hardy asked Will to claim his uncle Trent's body, and Will asked me to go with him."

Grandpa motioned for me to leave. "Run along, Ladessa. Detective Hardy is a stickler for the rules. His brother was a colleague of mine. Did you know him?"

My heart constricted. Grandpa had conversed so lucidly just moments earlier. "Yes, Grandpa. That brother married my sister." I slung my pocketbook over my shoulder. "Can you come to town with the Happy Days group tomorrow? We'll go to the garage apartment, unpack a few boxes, and see what we find. I'll cook dinner."

"Why don't I cook?" He searched the bookcase. "Where are my cookbooks?"

"We'll look for them tomorrow. Don't forget." I kissed his cheek.

Logan shook Grandpa's hand. "I'll see she gets home safely, sir."

Before Logan eased the car from the parking space, he began interrogating me. "What is your grandfather looking for?"

"Cookbooks and other things." I faced him. "What did you learn?"

We sparred for information until Logan said, "I'm interested in your grandfather's relationship with Trent Sharp."

I reciprocated. "Sharp insisted on a sudden sale and property transfer. The man serves as one piece in my grandfather's upheaval. My puzzle-solving skills impressed Grandpa when I was a kid, and he wants me to employ them again."

Logan stopped by Will's car. "I'm a puzzle master. We should work together."

"Sure you wouldn't take all the credit?"

Logan rubbed his chin and asked in a playful tone, "If I do the majority of the work, shouldn't I take the majority of the credit?"

"Then I think I'll work alone," I answered in an out-of-practice flirtatious manner.

When we arrived, Will and Noelle descended the steps from Grandpa's wraparound porch. I cringed, mentally correcting myself. The beautiful blue two-story trimmed in white served as Logan's rental house, not Grandpa's home.

"Sorry to disturb your evening, Logan, Ladessa." Will chewed on his lip. "I don't want to go to the morgue alone. Noelle offered, but no lady should see a dead body."

"And you had no trouble asking me?" Logan teased.

"You're the strong, manly type. I knew going to a morgue wouldn't bother you." Will's kidding didn't fool me or anyone else. He was anxious, uncomfortable, and scared.

"Do you have an appointment?" Logan asked.

"Eight thirty," Will said.

Noelle grasped Will's hand. "Ladessa and I will go with you. We'll wait in the car. We can get coffee after." Noelle turned to me for confirmation.

I nodded, happy she suggested waiting in the car. I'd been in the same room with Sharp's corpse longer than I'd wanted.

Our wait in the car for Will's official identification took less time than the drive to the morgue. Both men showed somber faces as they walked across the parking area.

Logan spoke. "The doctor says the death was anaphylactic shock, a horrible way to die, but fairly quick. He wouldn't have been able to breathe. It happened while we watched the punkin'-chunkin' exhibition." Logan's words trailed off as he fastened his seat belt. "Is the pancake place on Fir Trail okay for coffee?"

Will blew out a long breath. "My uncle always carried an Epi-Pen because of his peanut allergy. Why didn't he use it? My grandparents are arranging the cremation and memorial service. Glad they're doing it, because I wouldn't know where to start."

Noelle touched Will's shoulder. "When Dad died last year, I went through the grief stages of denial, anger, and depression while Mom handled the funeral and estate details. I was useless when she needed me. I returned to Sea Side to make up for failing her during that time."

"I don't know much about your uncle. Would you like to talk about him?" I felt it was a lame suggestion, but Will responded.

"Uncle Trent was my mom's only sibling, and they weren't close. My grandparents give. . ." Will paused. "I should say they *gave* Uncle Trent an allowance every month, and he was over fifty years old. The man had plenty of money from all his endeavors, yet they gave him a monthly stipend, which he banked."

"Did your grandparents give your mom an equivalent allowance?"

"She refused it. My parents have plenty, and Mom wasn't close to her little brother. Trent flitted from school to school growing up. My grandparents would arrange admittance, but he'd mess up, and they'd find somewhere else. They stopped educating him and created jobs for him in their philanthropic endeavors. He reveled in the galas and the big events, but routine administration bored him. He always had a get-rich-quick scheme going, which usually worked."

Logan edged his RAV4 into a front-row parking spot. "Not too many people eating pancakes tonight, no nosy eavesdroppers."

After our drinks arrived, Will circled his spoon in his coffee until the dark liquid sloshed out on the saucer. "My parents think I'm like my uncle. Maybe I am. It's hard to measure up in a type A family that socked away millions. My mother resented her brother mooching off their parents, so she and Dad adopted a tough-love policy for me. I'm to receive none of the family money until I'm forty. Forty! They want me to earn my own way. In one way, I am like my uncle Trent, I guess. I never met family expectations."

Noelle stopped him. "Don't sell yourself short. You handled this land development deal by yourself."

I listened without contributing. I remembered Mary's comment earlier about how talkative people could be, and I was learning a lot about Trent Sharp. My fingers itched for pen and paper to jot down salient points.

"Will has faced a setback, Noelle," Logan said.

"More than one," Will added. "Jane Mills has it in for me. She blocks my every suggestion with the city council. I can't get the permits or zoning changes. At breakfast Uncle Trent told me my building requests had been bumped again, but he knew whose palms needed to be greased."

"Will, you wouldn't do anything illegal." Noelle gazed at Will, who squirmed.

"Noelle, small gifts or favors are considered business expenses."

"Can you get the project funded without giving gifts? Greasing palms sounds like bribery," Noelle said.

"Uncle Trent promised seed money for the project." Will gave us a wry smile. "Actually, my uncle may contribute a sizable invest-ment. I expect to be his beneficiary. He has no one else. The family can't withhold proceeds from a death."

"Whoa!" The exclamation escaped my lips before I realized I'd said the word aloud.

Noelle and Will hadn't heard me, but Logan mouthed, *Whoa*, which made me snicker, and I spilled my coffee.

Will's comment whooshed me to the tea shoppe and the medi-cal man's comment that Sharp's death didn't feel right. Would Will resort to murder to fund his pet project and to gain access to the family money he considered his birthright?

CHAPTER 5

Logan agreed to go with Will to Boston for Trent Sharp's memorial service. I wasn't surprised, because he'd shared stories about his own family's closeness and proved himself observant, kind, and considerate. I didn't link the adjectives *kind* and *considerate* with investigative reporters, but I decided Logan might be the exception. And his absence permitted me to continue sleuthing.

As a waitress, I overheard many conversations about the recently deceased. People ignored my presence just as they did the squawking seagulls and the roaring ocean. I jotted notes on my phone between taking and delivering orders and perused them at day's end.

After four days, I surmised Sharp enjoyed the ladies—of all ages. He fawned over established Sea Side women, aka women over sixty. He sought companionship with eligible Sea Side women, aka women from eighteen to sixty. He teased younger girls, aka any female under eighteen.

I also discovered he liked himself as much as the ladies. He had standing appointments for manicures, massages, tanning, and hairstyling—not haircutting. A beautician at table three explained the distinction between cutting and styling to her companion and confided that Sharp didn't tip well, expecting his charm to suffice.

"Ladessa." Noelle spoke loudly.

I poked my phone back in my pocket. "What? Do I have an order up?"

"No. I asked you twice if you wanted to join my yoga class and our church choir, but you were in another world."

"When do they meet? I'm going through boxes with Grandpa on Tuesdays and Thursdays. He's answering questions so I can document his memories for the family."

Noelle nodded. "Perfect. Both are at the church from six thirty to seven thirty. Yoga is on Mondays, choir on Wednesdays. Don't bother saying you can't sing. You hum old show tunes all the time. Want me to pick you up for yoga tonight?"

"No, I'll walk or ride the bike. I'm not getting on a scale until November, but if I'm not losing weight, I'm getting fitter. A CPA does more sitting than walking, and I'm discovering muscles I never knew I had."

"You'll love yoga. Uh-oh. Our friendly law enforcement officer is here. I'll get his favorite crumpet, and Ladessa, he prefers the house blend tea with cream."

Before Detective Hardy settled into his chair, I served his tea and crumpet.

"I've got more questions for you. Come by the station after you get off work." He didn't say please or ask if the time was convenient. He acknowledged my agreement before continuing. "I wanted Mr. Sharp's death to be accidental, but you don't always get what you wish for, do you?"

Did his offhand remark refer to Sharp's death being a murder, or to the whirlwind marriage of my sister to his brother, which broke my heart? I scurried off to serve other customers. My previous investigating involved determining the dead man's character, a morbid curiosity about someone I barely knew. Now the detective implied Sharp's death was murder.

One thought led to another. Was I a suspect?

At the police station, Detective Hardy placed me in what my TV crime shows called the interrogation room. I tried to relax, knowing the mirror allowed others to view the suspect from the hallway.

After a suitable wait time, Devin Hardy strode in and threw a file on the table. "Ladessa, you found the body, secured the scene, and called 911?"

I muffled a nervous giggle. "Yes."

"Describe exactly what you did, and don't leave out anything." Detective Hardy leaned back as if getting comfortable for a lengthy stay.

I repeated what I'd reported to him when he first arrived at the tea shoppe.

"Did you check Sharp's pockets?"

"No," I said. "Why would I?"

"I don't know. Maybe you felt he owed you a tip. He was not a generous tipper. Or maybe you removed the peanut-tainted scone from the table."

"He didn't have scones. He had crumpets."

"Don't joke about a police investigation." Detective Hardy scowled.

"I wasn't joking. I thought you were trying to trip me up."

"Why would I?" He leaned across the table, his face now inches from mine.

"I don't know. Maybe you don't have any suspects, so you're focusing on the person who found the body, me."

"We have a long list of suspects, including you. Isn't it strange that Sharp drops dead at your table the day after you arrive in Sea Side?"

"But I had no motive. I only met him once."

The detective crossed his arms. "You love your grandfather, don't you?"

"Yes. Do you love your grandfather, Devin?" I bit my tongue. I shouldn't throw out sarcastic comments, especially in an interrogation room.

"My grandfather is not a suspect, Ladessa. Yours is."

"You can't be serious! My grandfather would never hurt anyone."

Hardy stood and looked down at me. "Don't leave town. We'll talk again."

"Is that it?"

"For now." The detective held the door.

My mandatory interrogation was a ruse. Detective Hardy brought me in to gauge my responses. Despite the law officer's hokey bluster, my rubbery knees barely supported me as I left the building. I walked the bike to the apartment. I didn't trust my balance.

∞

When I arrived for yoga class, several women sat cross-legged, chatting. Noelle waved a magenta mat in my direction. Even in loose-fitting pants, she exuded grace and composure. If this class earned me Noelle's carriage and presence, I'd endure the aches and pains.

Noelle instructed us in mindful quieting, urged us to listen to our bodies and ignore our classmates. I couldn't obey. I peeked at ladies in front, who did not suffer the wobbles. Jane Mills, the petite redheaded dynamo, did downward-facing dog and tree poses like a master. Betty Boyd, Mary Rollins, and I might have been mistaken for the Three Stooges, but then no one gawked at the exercisers except me.

At the end, Noelle praised us for making time to care for our bodies and lowered the lights. Then she guided us through corpse pose, a deep relaxation technique. Within minutes, Betty Boyd's sonorous snoring echoed off the basement walls.

Subdued talk emanated after class, and Noelle invited Jane, Betty, and me to her apartment for cucumbers, hummus, and protein shakes to celebrate Jane's birthday. Her offer sounded great—except for the cucumbers, hummus, and protein shakes.

While pretending to sip my thick green drink, I zeroed in on Jane Mills. She'd sat at the table with Sharp on the day he died, which garnered her top billing on my suspect list.

"Jane, how did you end up in Sea Side?" I hoped her relocation did not involve handsome reporter Logan Hernandez.

"Trent Sharp," Jane said. "I wanted to get to know him."

Betty, sitting on the sofa, leaned forward to stick her nose in the conversation of the floor-sitters. "But you didn't like Trent, Jane."

"I didn't. My mother worked for him in Boston, but when she became pregnant with me, Sharp dismissed her." Jane dipped a cucumber slice in the hummus.

"But that's illegal," I sputtered.

"I know. My mother was not the confrontational type. Sharp liked attractive secretaries, not waddling pregnant ones, so he ousted her. Mom managed—she was tough. Breast cancer took her two years ago, and the medical expenses gobbled up her savings and mine."

I remembered Betty had been Sharp's office manager and

glanced her way, but she appeared to have lost interest in our conversation.

"I'm sorry about your mom, Jane. Is your dad still alive?" This was turning out like a college all-nighter with facts flowing, only we drank protein shakes, not alcohol.

"I never knew my dad. Mom said he left when he found out she was pregnant."

"How heartbreaking. Your mom lost her job, and your father ducked out on her?"

Jane bobbed her head. "Noelle, this dip is amazing. Ladessa, don't feel sorry for me. I had a super childhood. Mom showered me with love."

My mind leapfrogged from one topic to another. Jane Mills had a motive for bumping off Sharp—her mother's unjust treatment at his hands. "Did your mom get her job back after you were born?"

"No. I was a sickly baby and needed constant care. I also needed operations to fix my eyes. Mom begged Sharp for her job, but he refused. She told me that he feigned sympathy and presented her with a termination settlement, which didn't come from him but from a trust account. It was the Sharp family who offered a lump sum. My mom accepted, and my eyes were fixed."

I bumped Betty's leg with my shoulder, looking up at where she sat on the couch. "Betty, could you have known Jane's mom?"

"No, how could I? Jane and I are close to the same age." Betty kept her eyes closed, head resting on the sofa's back.

I raised my eyebrows and looked at the others, who fought to stifle laughter. Betty had to be at least twenty-five years older than Jane.

Noelle did a few neck rolls then turned to Jane. "Your story explains why you might not like Sharp, but why don't you like Will?"

"Same family, same values," Jane said.

My yoga instructor reminded me of a cat ready to pounce. "That's unfair. Are you creating stumbling blocks for Will's development because of his family?"

"Noelle, I'm against Will's development because I believe such an enterprise would destroy Sea Side's charm. Tourists flock here to experience rustic and rural magic. That project would decrease, not accelerate, this town's growth." Jane crossed her arms.

Noelle stood. "Then we have differing opinions."

"About the development, we do. About yoga, we're aligned. I should go." Jane rose from sitting on the floor to standing in one clean motion.

"Me too." I struggled to get up, steadying myself with one hand on the small table and the other on the couch. "We'll have those crumpet-hungry New Englanders waiting for us before the birds start singing."

"Thanks for the reminder," Noelle said. "Mom, are you and Betty ready to go back to Happy Days?"

I gleaned information this evening and survived yoga and a protein shake. Life was good.

My days melted into a cycle including work, yoga, Grandpa, and choir. I loved the little church with the stone facade and bright red door. The worn wooden floor and pews testified to generations worshipping in the same sanctuary. Some kneeling benches had needlepoint covers, each with a unique design and the stitcher's name. All the handiwork was impeccable.

It had been years since I sang in a choir, and harmonizing with others awakened a joy I didn't realize I'd missed. Reviewing hymns and practicing special music for Sunday service each week in this two-hundred-year-old church fostered both contentment and a yearning for a closer walk with God.

Life in Sea Side took on a special rhythm as time passed and the temperatures dipped lower. My yoga friends hailed me in the grocery store or Tea by the Sea. Choir members encouraged me to join a weekly Bible study on Sunday afternoons, which I did. Time with Grandpa provided many fascinating stories about his life before he met my grandmother and then snippets of their courtship and early years.

We developed a system. I opened a box in the garage, tucked all I could in the bike's basket, and pedaled off to Grandpa's. I listened to memories about the items then journeyed back to the apartment and documented the stories. This worked until I opened the box labeled CHURCH and discovered why Detective Hardy believed my beloved grandpa wanted Trent Sharp dead.

Chapter 6

I called Grandpa and canceled our evening in order to explore my own inquiry. I created a computer file and labeled it MONEY TRAIL. Why were three years of church financial books in Grandpa's possession? Could this be a second set? Mary might know. If Grandpa served as treasurer, he should have transferred the ledgers to the succeeding officer. I started at the beginning. Engrossed in checking each credit and debit, I jumped when the phone rang. Logan's name popped up, and I swiped to answer.

"Logan, how are things in Boston?" My neck and shoulders ached from hunching over financial books, so I massaged my tight muscles with one hand while listening to Logan's report about Sharp's memorial service.

"Will and I are staying in Boston another week."

"And missing the fun activities in Sea Side? Pumpkin carving is scheduled this weekend, with prizes by age category."

"If I don't enter, then some other adults will have a chance," Logan said.

I pictured his teasing expression. "Competition scare you? I carve a mean jack-o'-lantern."

"I make friendly ones." He paused. "Ladessa. . ."

"What can I do?" If he wanted a favor, he could've called Jane. When I saw either Jane or Logan, a mental image of their flirting ballooned in my head.

His tone became all business. "Will expected to be Sharp's beneficiary, but he's not."

"Oh no. He needs funds to keep his dream afloat."

Logan sighed. "The project fails without start-up money, and his parents and grandparents refuse to back his venture."

"Do you think they should?" I waited for his answer, knowing his response would color my opinion of his character.

"No. In profile stories I've researched, people who have to fight and struggle to attain their dreams are happier and more successful."

I remembered the Bible verse about the love of money being the root of all evil. I grabbed a pen and jotted Will's name with "Fortune expectation," followed by a question mark. "Did Mr. Sharp change his will recently?"

"The third week in September, and he died on October 2. The lawyers, yes plural, are tracking down designees. The prior document named Will as recipient. If Sharp's death had occurred two weeks earlier, Will would be wealthy."

Not sure how to respond, I changed the subject. "Since your return will be delayed, should I water your plants, feed the cat?" I teased.

"Don't have either, but I could use your help. Also, if you need to get in the house, the key is under the decorative urn next to the porch swing."

"Happy to help." I muffled my excitement, thrilled to have Logan's blessing to enter Grandpa's house. Maybe I'd find more financial records connecting Grandpa and the Sea Side church.

"I've unearthed new leads for my blockbuster story about a scheme called 'lifetime investment living' complexes. I may need your help following a money trail."

"What?" I inhaled too quickly and suffered a coughing fit. "What money?" I finally squeaked.

"I don't want to get it wrong, because most retirement homes serve older people with love and care. Unfortunately, I've discovered some strange statistics for seniors who select an assisted living complex with a lifetime investment model. Their life span is less than average, and their investment is greater than average. My fear is that older citizens may be in mortal danger in these facilities because of the greedy owners. I can't print anything until I have a larger sampling to support my premise of money obtained unethically by this scheme. Will you help?"

"Sure," I agreed. "I have a nose for numbers."

His money investigation had nothing to do with the church financial irregularities, so I breathed easier. The conversation waned. I praised the glorious leaf colors, a visual treat for me since I'd lived in Dallas for the past eight years. Logan reminded me to enjoy lobster rolls, baked beans, and clam chowder. He didn't ask about the investigation into Sharp's death, and I didn't bring it up.

My spirits soared after a weekend of zaniness in Sea Side. The town selected a pumpkin princess, opened the pumpkin maze, and fielded a contest for Sea Side's original pumpkin song. I loved Maine in autumn. Fall is the best time in a fiscal year for a CPA to take a vacation, and this respite proved delightful—except for discovering a dead man.

Grandpa and I developed a sweet rapport as I recorded his memories. We visited the Happy Days physician, who assured me Grandpa was fine, but his officious words didn't convince me.

Not content with that doctor's evaluation, I sought out Noelle the following Monday at work.

"Will your mom be at yoga tonight? I'd like to ask her opinion about my grandfather's mental health—and mine."

Noelle lifted her hand. "I can help you on the second item. You're crazy, lady."

"I'd prefer a kinder, gentler consultation."

"She'll be there." Noelle pointed to the dough she was mixing and motioned for me to leave. "Go sell crumpets, Ladessa."

When yoga class ended, I fidgeted while waiting for my one-on-one visit with Mary. I was mentally planning my speech when Jane's comment to someone else snagged my interest.

"Those DNA kits are a popular item for Christmas. I received one for my birthday, but I'm wary of delving into the past."

"I'd do it in a minute," I said. "I know my parents and grandparents, but I'd like to find a dashing pirate or a member of some royal court in my family line."

Jane turned. "What about children who find out they are adopted, or twins who were separated? I think there's more sadness than joy in chasing down DNA roots."

"So you're not going to do it?" I asked. "You said your dad left before you were born. Would you want to meet him? You might have another family."

"My mom loved and cared for me every day. Trying to find a dad who abandoned me would be disloyal to her memory. Why open Pandora's Box?" Jane tucked her rolled yoga mat under her arm and headed for the exit.

I knew that if I were in Jane's shoes, I'd search for my biological father. I'd confront him about leaving. I'd want him to see me as a healthy, happy, successful adult and to regret abandoning me. Those thoughts circled back to my own reluctance to repair the damage with my sister, a consideration I discarded when Mary signaled me.

"I'm looking for wisdom," I told her.

"Ladessa, your heart often knows the answers you seek." Mary patted a metal folding chair.

"It's about my grandfather. The Happy Days doctor says he's fine, but what do you think? You see him every day. Should I encourage him to get a second opinion?"

"What are you looking for, Doctor Ladessa?"

I interlocked my fingers and thought. "Well, some days he's forgetful. I worry that he has dementia or the beginning of Alzheimer's."

"He's been through a lot."

"Mary, you said the same thing when I arrived. Help me understand."

"Perhaps his mind is on past events that can't be changed." Mary had a faraway look in her eyes as if she meant the statement for herself, not me.

"Maybe it's my accounting background, but I like concrete explanations."

Mary took my hand. "Even if the facts can't be erased or altered?"

"I want to help him."

"You are, Ladessa. Your grandpa looks forward to those sessions when he shares stories about the items in the boxes. All grandparents should be granted time with a grandchild. He's pleased you came. I'd love for Noelle to marry and give me a couple of grandkids to spoil."

I debated about bringing up topic two but barreled ahead. "Mary, among Grandpa John's boxes, I discovered three church ledgers. Why would he have them?"

Mary dabbed at her eyes with the hem of her yoga top. "Your

grandfather is an honorable and loving man, just as my late husband was. The two tried to salvage an unfortunate situation and couldn't."

"Could you explain it to me?"

Mary's eyes suddenly gleamed with anger, and she erupted with vehemence. "Trent Sharp killed my husband. He might as well have plunged a knife into that sweet man's heart. Sharp presented a 'foolproof' investment for church funds, which failed. In addition, he blamed my husband, who was dismissed in disgrace from the pastorate he'd served eighteen years. Don't go there, Ladessa. Nothing good can come of it."

Despite Mary's wise words, I knew I wouldn't leave the mystery alone.

CHAPTER 7

"Grandpa, what are these?" I held the church ledgers that I'd been through line by line.

He traced the letters on the first cover. "You know what they are, Ladessa."

"Why do you have them?" I didn't enjoy grilling my grandfather, but Mary's response made me want to clear the names of two innocent men, Grandpa and Mary's husband.

"These are duplicates. The church has the originals—the updated originals," Grandpa said.

"For the same period?"

Grandpa stared at the ocean and squinted at the glare of the evening sun reflecting off the water.

I tried again. "Most businesses keep all their records in one place."

"Some errors cropped up. They were fixed," Grandpa said softly.

"Did you fix them?"

"I helped. Mary's husband, the associate minister, tried to be a good steward. We invested the capital campaign monies in a sure investment and lost the money. I put personal funds into the same venture, bet my house on it. Shows how confident I was."

"So you both lost money?"

"Pastor Rollins and I scratched up enough cash to reimburse the church fund, but news leaked out about our bad decision. The church board requested that Rollins resign. Leaving the church broke his heart. I think it killed him. I don't think Mary knows the whole story."

I decided not to mention what Mary told me and brought up Noelle's opinion. "Noelle blames Trent Sharp for discrediting her dad. Do you?" I asked.

"Sharp fed the town gossips news about the imprudent investment."

"But wasn't Sharp on the committee?"

"Yes. He portrayed himself as an innocent and didn't contribute a nickel in reimbursement to the church. Sharp blustered about the incompetence Rollins and I displayed in not analyzing potential investments. He insisted the church stewards, meaning me and Rollins, bear the blame and make restitution."

"So you lost the house and then forfeited your savings to reimburse church funds. Is everything gone?"

"Everything. Don't tell your parents, your aunt, uncle, or anyone. I hoped you could help me with this huge mess, but I'm sure it's too late."

Grandpa's calling it a "huge mess" understated the problem.

"Where did you invest the money? I wasn't able to tell from the disbursements."

"Trent Sharp had connections with a venture capital company backing senior apartment complexes like Happy Days. He showed us all the figures. Pastor Rollins and I believed the investment would multiply the money, like the talents in the Bible." Grandpa's retelling seemed to shrink him.

"Then the venture failed?"

"Company moved its headquarters to the Bahamas and disappeared, along with our church's money and my personal investment."

"And you created two sets of financial records—one that showed the specifics of the disbursements to the bogus company and another that only showed the withdrawals and the reimbursements. The result is the same, Grandpa, whether the funds disappear because of a bad investment or embezzlement."

"Not the way I see it. Embezzlement is willful. We placed our trust in the wrong person. The fiasco bankrupted both Rollins and me. I have my pension, but the church revoked Pastor's retirement allowance. So Mary does hair and nails, plays the piano, anything to bring in a buck, and I don't have any money to help her."

"Does Noelle know what happened?"

"She knows Sharp fueled the rumors about her father's lack of integrity. She blames him for the loss of her father's position and his self-respect. She doesn't know that Trent was the one who suggested the investment then left her father and me to make up the shortfall in the church coffers."

"Oh Grandpa." I held out my arms, and he allowed me to hold and comfort him.

"That's not the end. When I sold my house to replenish the church funds, Trent bought it, turned it into a rental, and shuttled me off to Happy Days. I stay here until my death, with room, board, and medical provided."

My smart grandfather didn't make foolish decisions. I couldn't imagine him investing money in any stock or company without examining it thoroughly.

He continued. "I signed so many papers, I was dizzy. Felt like I'd been bilked, but I was too ashamed to call my daughter or son and admit my foolishness. Then I remembered you're a CPA. My situation is beyond help, but if you can figure out what happened, maybe my misfortune can warn other seniors."

I didn't want to disappoint Grandpa. But was his current situation the result of a conspiracy to fleece elders or just the culmination of bad decisions?

Somehow, waiting tables increased my self-esteem and made me believe I could help my grandfather. I felt better about myself today than I had two months ago when I labored in a prestigious firm. I wore an orange Punkin'-Chunkin' shirt and running shoes, not a tailored suit and heels. My clients were friendly regulars or tourists rather than stressed-out company executives. I offered happiness with crumpets and tea, which wouldn't work with accounting clients organizing detailed records.

That's what I needed: records—Sharp's records. Grandfather said Sharp presented this certain-to-make-money investment. If I connected Sharp to the scheme, then I'd have. . .

Then I'd have a motive for Grandpa or Mary to commit murder.

At Wednesday's choir practice, I saw Mary and Noelle seated on the front pew. Even from the back, I could tell the mother-daughter exchange was confrontational. Their rigid body postures warned me not to interfere. Of course I did.

"Evening, Mary, Noelle. Is it cold in here, or is the frosty atmosphere coming from the vibes you two are giving off?"

Both murmured hellos, and Noelle answered, "Mom's being stubborn. I want her to leave, to shake Sea Side's dust off her feet. She can live with me in Boston. I left a thriving business there, and they've requested I come back. It would be a clean start for Mom. She can put the past behind her."

When Mary turned to me, I felt like a judge, with the Rollins women each pleading her case. I hoped I wouldn't have to render a verdict.

Mary spoke as if Noelle wasn't an arm's-length away. "Noelle knows her father is buried in the church graveyard and that I place flowers on his stone every week. She should understand why I don't want to leave."

"And my mother should understand why I do want her to leave. Visiting Daddy's grave every week is admirable, but it prevents her from starting a new life."

I learned things by keeping quiet, so I endeavored to keep my face neutral and my mouth closed.

Mary turned to me again. "Noelle needs to give up this campaign to get me to leave. She can go back to Boston. I'm happy here, just as I am."

This three-way tête-à-tête was becoming weirder and weirder.

Noelle took her turn. "Ladessa, Mom knows I don't want to abandon her. She knows a location change will be in her best interest."

"Noelle needs to forget about me going to Boston, a big city I don't know. A young woman needs her space, and so does an old one. Ladessa, you agree with me, don't you?"

Both waited for my astute conclusion. I had nothing. "Maybe this is a no-win argument."

Noelle and Mary grumbled their agreement, and arriving choir members thwarted any extended analysis. We vocalized before practicing Sunday's congregational hymns and the choir's special music. I loved singing in a group. How could anyone be angry with another when all worked together to create harmony?

The music convinced me not to tell Mary or Noelle what I learned studying the ledgers. I recalled a verse from Ephesians Mary had us memorize as children. "Be ye kind one to another." In kindness I would say nothing until I had facts I could prove about Sharp's role in the disgrace of a beloved husband and father.

We stopped in the tea shoppe after choir practice, where my fellow waitress, an orange-clad Diana, offered us sweets and tea. We chose tea.

"Will is returning next week," Noelle said. "He's coming for the vote on his development center, but he's not optimistic. He didn't mention Logan."

"Logan called. I collect his mail and keep an eye on the house." I added honey to my tea and stirred.

"You two make a nice-looking couple," Mary said.

"I like Logan. He's friendly and flirtatious when we're together, but he behaves the same way with Jane. Could he be interested in me? I'm not sure what to think. My Texas church friends say I push people away because I'm afraid of relationships. What do you think?"

"Good grief, Ladessa." Mary slammed her teacup down so forcefully the amber liquid spilled on the saucer. "Just follow the Golden Rule, and you'll be fine."

"I agree with Mom." Noelle shrugged into her jacket. "Ready to go, Mom?"

I'd accomplished one thing. I'd reunited Mary and Noelle, even if their forged truce was at the expense of *my* lame approach to relationships.

Walking home, a police car pulled alongside, and Detective Hardy lowered the window. "Want a ride?"

"In the front or the back?" I gestured to the barrier between the seats.

"Front, for now."

"I planned to call you tomorrow." I got in and fastened my seat belt. "I remembered something about the day I discovered the body. Sharp's nasal spray was on the café table the day he died. I noticed because he'd used it at the airport and made loud, obnoxious snorts. I remember hoping he wouldn't do that in the tea shoppe."

"Your point?" Detective Hardy kept his eyes on the road.

"When I found him, or rather his dead body, it wasn't there. So I wanted to ask you if the nasal spray was in his pocket."

"I can't tell you." He stopped at my apartment. "Don't meddle in police business."

His attitude annoyed me. "When Will officially identified the body, the coroner gave him his uncle's belongings, and there was no nasal spray."

"I'll be making an arrest this week. But your little tidbit proved helpful. I'm confident I have the killer. Good night."

As I tackled the steps to the apartment without using the handrail, I realized my legs were stronger than when I arrived. Inside, I tugged another blanket from the trunk, resisting the urge to turn up the heat. I brushed my teeth, cleaned my face, and snuggled under the covers.

The sheep I counted to put me to sleep mutated into suspects until I got up, grabbed my computer, studied names and motives, and tried to organize my thoughts. For a man who appeared to be so charming, Trent Sharp had a full house in the enemy department.

Chapter 8

My focus flitted from discovering a murderer to recording family stories for posterity. Bundled in a heavy jacket and wearing a ski hat and gloves, I biked to Happy Days, computer in my backpack, to hear tales from other apartment residents. The sessions Grandpa and I held had stimulated a desire for residents to share their personal histories.

Betty commandeered the craft room for the evening, and coffee and tea urns dispersed enticing scents. I counted eighteen people in line. The staff distributed sliced pumpkin rolls with cream cheese filling, so I wasn't sure whether these people waited for me or for the delicious dessert.

Dressed in her usual black attire, Betty passed out the suggested story starters I emailed in advance. I wondered if her closet held any color except black. Betty ferried the residents to Tea by the Sea weekly, and her spirits seemed more cheerful each time we met.

I set up individual files with the residents' names and standard questions. We aimed to create a comfortable atmosphere by eliciting innocuous responses, such as birthdates, information on living family members and past residences, and how they'd selected Happy Days. Betty recommended timing each person's answers, warning me that some residents might dominate the discussion. She also provided a disclosure agreement. Perhaps Betty wanted favorable comments to use in future marketing.

All our participants were widows or widowers. Either Trent Sharp or Betty Boyd had contacted them within a year of their spouse's death and offered a free week in the complex's guest apartment. They all raved about the facility, the director, Harlan Gram-ford, and his dogs. Another similarity in the backgrounds concerned family proximity. None had relatives in town, and most close relatives lived at least three hours away. The residents claimed this as a plus, explaining that Sea Side was close enough for family to visit but not too near for them to be a bother to their grown children. I considered Mary and Noelle. They fit the pattern until Noelle took a leave from her job to be with her mother. And Grandpa lived in isolation until I showed up from Texas.

I capped the evening by promising more interesting meetings in the future. For the next time, I challenged them to recount the best day in their life and list three things that made them happy. Betty hoped these sessions would foster new and deeper friendships. The chatter as guests left the area made me believe she was right.

I pedaled toward my temporary home, thrilled with the new program Betty and I had initiated. In my apartment, I switched on the lights and shrieked at the sight of a man in my rocking chair.

"Surprise." Logan acted pleased with himself.

"How did you get in here?"

"Not the welcome I expected. I thought you'd be glad to see me." He rose and dangled a key. "As the house's tenant, I have a key to the garage apartment."

"Hand it over." I held out my hand, palm up.

Logan deposited the key. "Aren't you glad to see me?"

"I might be happy to see you tomorrow, when I can breathe again." I pointed toward the door. "Is this the only extra key?"

"Yes. I'm sorry. I thought it would be funny." He looked contrite.

"Your being here in the dark wasn't funny. Your having a key to my place is definitely not funny." My heart still raced, and my hands felt clammy. I scanned the room for items out of place. "Did you snoop through my things?"

"No. I entered, sat, and waited."

"In. The. Dark?" I emphasized each word to show my anger.

"If I'd turned on a light, you'd have called the police, wouldn't you?"

"Yes. But you could've waited in the house, not my apartment. You could've turned on lights in every room, and I would've known you were back. Leave." I pointed toward the door again, as he'd made no progress in departing.

"I wanted to talk to you. I uncovered some shocking information related to my big story." Logan's earnest brown eyes tugged at my heartstrings.

I ignored the temptation to weaken, jerked the door open, and pointed toward the darkness. "Get out. Your shocking information can wait."

With my back leaning against the door, I listened to Logan's fading steps on the creaky stairs. Then I put the kettle on for tea and surveyed my apartment. Nothing appeared to be disturbed. I paced until the whistle sounded, indicating the water was ready. Tea connoisseurs claim chamomile tea lowers stress. I used it frequently in Texas, but tonight marked my first cup in Sea Side.

Soothed by the calming brew, I relaxed. Then my mind went into overdrive. What shocking news brought Logan to my apartment? Should I go ask? No. I needed to stick to my guns.

I slept soundly until the alarm jarred me awake for another day at Tea by the Sea.

I flipped the lever on the coffee brewer and lifted a blind slat to look at the driveway. No car meant no Logan. Where was he at five thirty in the morning? The coffee machine beeped. At this point, I desperately wanted to hear the shocking findings he considered paramount to his investigation. But I couldn't chase him down. I showered, dressed, and reported for work as usual.

Before nine, the Happy Days troop descended upon Tea by the Sea, even though it was Wednesday, not one of their regular days. Betty practically glowed with her makeup carefully applied, her nails manicured, and the ubiquitous black dress livened by a brilliant aqua scarf.

"What's the occasion? You're Thursday people." I handed out the daily special sheets once they found their accustomed spots.

After a few weeks, I knew the tables favored by regulars. I preferred the same pew in church, the same seat at the lunch shop close to my CPA firm, the same seat in the conference room. Did Trent Sharp sit at *his* spot on that ill-fated morning? He entered with three others that day. Was table four his choice? Jane's? Logan's? Will's? Did it matter?

Betty helped me deliver tea and treats to her group despite my protests. She said, "The residents shared stories after you left. I'm glad we'll have this as a regular event."

"You have a diverse and interesting group." I remembered the dissimilar vocations and previous home locations mentioned.

"You inspired me, Ladessa. I busy myself taking them places, when what they need is people, friendships. That's my new mission."

Brisk business kept me moving. Despite the full shop, Betty and her group lingered.

"May I get you anything else?"

Betty's face clouded, and I thought she might start crying. "I must apologize for what happened to your grandfather."

"What? We can talk later." I patted Betty's arm and pointed to people waiting. "Maybe you should shepherd your flock to the ceramic shop. They're excited about making Thanksgiving decorations for their apartment doors."

"Your grandfather's problems rest on my shoulders too." Betty turned, tapped her cup, and announced the Pottery Toss as their next stop.

I wanted to run after Betty and beg her to explain her mysterious comment, but new customers swarmed toward the emptied tables, and Diana had called in sick today.

Detective Hardy tipped his hat to me and joined the mayor and Jane Mills. I heard the three discuss logistics and security for the pumpkin toss—a variation on the raw egg toss, but with larger and untidier results. Jane must have known what people liked, because October profits at local hotels, bed and breakfasts, restaurants, and shops surpassed all previous years.

Jane, who might or might not be Logan's primary love interest, touched my arm. "Ladessa, what do you think about a pumpkin paddle event, where contestants row across the inlet inside hollowed-out giant pumpkins?"

"I think they'd capsize."

"Me too." Jane clapped her hands. "Our volunteer firemen promised to man rescue boats. It's a first, so we have no idea how many in the pumpkin armada will reach the far shore."

"You're the master, Jane. Now, what can I get for you today?" I readied my pen and pad.

Detective Hardy spoke up. "We'll all have the special and the house blend tea. Jane takes cream with hers."

When I served the order, Detective Hardy asked when my break was. He wanted to talk. Being short-staffed on a chaotic day left no time for speculation about anything people wanted to share. Logan wanted to talk to me. Betty wanted to talk to me. Detective Hardy wanted to talk to me. And I already yearned to go home, steep in a hot tub, and listen to the ocean's rhythmic cadence.

I joined Detective Hardy at a back table during my break, glad to sit, if only for a few minutes.

He leaned forward. "I'm making an arrest today. I thought you should know since you provided crucial evidence."

My exhaustion vanished. "Who did it?"

"Betty Boyd. She and Trent worked and *played* together, if you get my meaning."

I did.

"Betty went to prison for their crimes, and charges against Sharp were dropped."

"That's old news. Even I, as a newcomer, know that."

The detective continued, "When released, Betty couldn't get work, then Sharp offered her a position at Happy Days. My thinking is that Betty assumed they'd continue their romantic involvement as well as business, but Sharp rejected her."

"My dear detective, if all scorned women committed murder, there would be a lot of dead men."

"Including my brother?" Detective Hardy raised his eyebrows.

"Getting over him took time. Grandpa has a picture of their wedding. I'm beside Aletha, a woebegone look on my face. You're next to your brother, looking quite chipper."

"At the time, I hoped I might have a chance with you."

His comment stunned me. Was he flirting with me? I directed the conversation back to the pending arrest. "So Betty had motive. How about means and opportunity?"

Thanks to my detective binge-watching, I could talk the talk about murder investigations.

His countenance changed. "First, she knew the seriousness of Sharp's peanut allergy, and she had two—count 'em, two—EpiPens in her giant bag the day he died. I believe she took his so he didn't have one when he needed it. And you told me his nasal spray was missing from the table. Betty had nasal spray in her bag that day too."

"Betty doesn't seem like a killer, and she kept everything the residents might need on an outing in her giant tote. That doesn't mean the nasal spray in her bag was the murder weapon."

"She'll confess. Criminals prefer a clean conscience." Detective Hardy winked. "I always liked your Brillo-pad curls."

I ignored that remark. Had Betty wanted to confess to me before leaving earlier that day? She mentioned sharing blame for Grandpa's problems. Why didn't I listen?

"Detective, could I go with you to see Betty?"

"Absolutely not. I don't want you interfering." He pulled a ten from his pocket.

"The mayor paid," I said.

"Can't have that, wouldn't be ethical. I'll stop by his office before I make the arrest. My town will rest easier when the killer is in custody."

CHAPTER 9

"Ladessa, come get me. Come now!" Grandpa's panicked voice scared me.

"Where are you?"

"Happy Days. Hurry." He hung up without explaining his emergency, which left me in a quandary about what to say to cut my shift short.

"I need to check on my grandpa." My face must have betrayed my anxiety, because Georgina shooed me toward the back and Noelle tossed me her car keys.

I drove faster than the posted speed limit and slammed on the brakes to park behind the van idling under the covered drive. Residents milled in the foyer and whispered behind cupped hands.

I inventoried the people before shouting. "John Nolan? Has anyone seen him? Has anyone seen my grandfather?"

Residents shook their heads and kept their eyes lowered. I stalked toward the administrative offices but glimpsed Grandpa on the second floor crosswalk holding a finger to his lips. He pointed to the dining room exit.

Honoring his signal to avoid making a scene, I pulled out my phone and exclaimed, "Oh, false alarm. Grandpa's meeting me on the walking path. Sorry."

My speech fell on disinterested ears as everyone concentrated on the resident director's office. I scooted around back and wondered if one of Mr. Gramford's precious bichons had passed away. What were their names? Sunrise and Sunset? If only one died, I'd put my money on Sunset, just because of his name.

Grandpa threw his arms around my neck. "Ladessa, I need to get out!"

I shivered as his cold hands brushed my cheek when he released his grasp. "I borrowed Noelle's car. I'll take you to my apartment where you can get warm and tell me what's going on."

"I don't want anyone to see me leave. I'll meet you where the driveway meets the road." He hurried out the back exit.

I raced to the front, threw the car in REVERSE, then stopped. Two men in Happy Days staff uniforms carried a sheet-shrouded gurney through onlookers toward a van.

I left the area at a respectable speed and spotted Grandpa.

He slipped into the passenger seat. "Ladessa, can you afford a hotel room? They'll look for me at your apartment."

"Who are *they*? What's going on? Was that a body? Did one of your friends die?"

"Betty. Betty's dead."

"No!" Had she known that Detective Hardy planned to arrest her? Had she committed suicide to avoid going back to prison?

"And I might be next." Grandpa sounded completely coherent.

"We'll find a hotel, and you can explain." Was harboring my grandfather the best course of action? Was he paranoid, or in real danger?

"Drive, Ladessa. Go to the Extended Stay Motel in Upton. The institution used to book long-term researchers there."

I programmed my phone then remembered this was not my car. I needed a rental. "Grandpa, can you drive?"

"Of course I can drive." His words were tart and sharp. "I was driving long before you were born."

November weather predictions provided a reason to switch my mode of transportation from a bike to a car. Was I thinking like a criminal, trying to hide my tracks?

Maybe. I rented a small SUV for two months, then Grandpa followed me in Noelle's car back to Tea by the Sea.

I calculated we'd be halfway to Upton in the rental before Noelle's shift ended. Was I obstructing justice, harboring a fugitive, abetting a felon? Like Scarlett O'Hara, I vowed to think about those things tomorrow.

On our route, we stopped at a Walmart for basic foodstuff, some clothes, and toiletries for Grandpa. I tossed in laundry soap and dryer sheets in case he ended up with an extended stay at the aptly named motel.

In the room with a fully furnished kitchen, I heated water and mixed up mugs of hot chocolate, sliced some pound cake, and set our snack on the small table.

I did a deep cleansing yoga breath before asking, "Now, what's going on?"

Grandpa wrapped his hands around his mug. "I sat with Betty on the ride back to Happy Days. She usually drives, but today Mr. Gramford did. We'd finished making the door decorations early, so we—"

"What happened, Grandpa? Why did you call me with the urgent message to rescue you?"

"As I said, Betty and I sat next to each other in the van." Grandpa returned to his original thought pattern, and I willed myself to be patient. "Betty told me she had an unexpected call from a lawyer who asked to meet her this afternoon."

"Did she say why?" I prompted.

Grandpa shook his head. "I saw him arrive. He wore a black topcoat, a fedora, and leather gloves."

"Did he drive a car or come in a taxi?" This lawyer might have been the last one to see Betty alive, or he might have ended her life. Grandpa thought. "He drove a black car."

I asked other leading questions to decipher make or model but knew that was futile. My grandfather, who could name and describe every fish in the ocean, couldn't tell one car from another. He purchased only silver sedans and then wedged a red ball between the dashboard and the passenger windshield so he could recognize his own car.

Grandpa continued. "Betty said the lawyer needed to verify her identity for an inheritance. She wanted me to hear her good news, so I waited for her meeting to end."

"What did the lawyer tell her?" I laced my fingers around the warm mug.

"I don't know. The lawyer came out. Betty didn't. After a while, Harlan Gramford and his dogs went into Betty's office, but they didn't stay long."

"You didn't knock on her door?"

"No. Some friends needed a fourth for bridge, and we played several games in the foyer book nook. I could see her office from where I sat. I thought she forgot about me. After the staff doctor went in, I knocked and asked if Betty was okay. The doctor said she died. Ladessa, the lawyer must have killed her, and I saw him."

"Did you recognize him?"

"No. His hat was tilted forward." Grandpa hadn't drunk any of his hot chocolate.

"You can't identify the car or the man?" I asked.

"No, but what if he can identify me?"

"Did he see you?" Concern for Grandpa's safety escalated when he responded with a nod.

"He touched his hat brim in a salute when he left. He knew I was there."

"Did you tell Harlan Gramford or the staff doctor?"

"No. I called you. I'm afraid to stay at Happy Days. The killer knows where I live." Grandfather assessed his surroundings. "I can hide out here, but I'd like some sudoku and crossword books, and my e-reader."

"We can get the books, but we shouldn't go back to Happy Days for your reading device. We should eat. We'll get the puzzle books when we get take-out. How about Chinese?" I prayed I could figure out what was going on so I didn't have to leave my grandfather here by himself for very long.

After sharing dinner, we hugged good night, and I returned to Sea Side, to normalcy. Was normalcy possible for an amateur sleuth with more questions than answers? I called Happy Days and informed a yawning receptionist that my family invited Grandpa to join them for a long weekend. She assured me she'd log the information.

Tea by the Sea buzzed about the town's second death in October. When Noelle asked about Grandpa's urgency the day before, I laughed it off and said my family swooped him away for a short visit. That little fudging of the truth went over rather well, if I do say so myself. I asked Noelle for scuttlebutt about Betty's death.

"Mom said Betty had a heart attack," Noelle said.

"Did she have a history of heart problems?"

"Mom wouldn't speak ill of anyone, but she said Betty suffered with high blood pressure, was borderline diabetic, and weighed more than she should. If you add those factors to her stressful environment, you have a recipe for a heart attack."

Contrary to Noelle's opinion, Mary had spoken ill of Trent Sharp, but today I needed to focus on Betty.

"When is the service? The viewing?" I remembered the aqua scarf livening Betty's black attire on her final day. The residents would miss her, and so would the people of Sea Side.

"No viewing. She was cremated," Noelle said. "Memorial is at five on Saturday at Happy Days. Harlan gave Mom the songs Betty wanted played at the service."

"Cremation? No autopsy?" I asked.

"No autopsy. Ladessa, do you have a will? I don't."

"No, we should do that. Two unexpected deaths makes you think." I found the scenario of dual deaths in October too buttoned up, too pat.

"Mom says all residents are required to have wills, powers of attorney, medical directives, and instructions for final services." Noelle rubbed her arms as if warding off the cold. "That gives me the chills. It's practical but creepy."

"Who files the documents?"

"I don't know. Happy Days probably has a lawyer who does those things." Noelle nodded toward my waiting customers.

As I went to their table, my mind lingered on the unexpected lawyer visit, a sudden heart attack, and a hasty cremation.

During my break, I called Harlan Gramford and offered to guide a special memoir session that afternoon focused on writing tributes to Betty. I mentioned that some residents might wish to read their pieces at Betty's memorial, and Gramford complimented me on my thoughtfulness.

What he considered my concern was in actuality cunning, because I planned to sneak into Betty's office and search for clues.

As it turned out, I didn't have to sneak. Gramford opened Betty's office so I could look for memoir session materials, which I knew weren't there. I grabbed several sheets of plain paper from the copier and searched for anything indicating foul play. Nothing. The writing session produced glowing homages about Betty, and we voted to determine which tribute should be shared at the memorial service.

I returned home and opened another of Grandpa's boxes. Surely a clue would miraculously appear.

"Anyone home?" Logan stood on the threshold, balancing a large pot of golden mums atop a pizza box. "Trying to make amends. May I come in?"

"Yes, since you come bearing pizza. I was just wondering what I could rustle up for dinner." I placed the mums on a table near the window.

"Plates or paper towels?" He opened the pizza box then removed soda cans from his jacket pockets.

"Both. How about a salad?" I handed him paper towels, plates, and glasses.

"Salad sounds good, and I have dessert in the car. Thought I might need to offer dinner, flowers, and a box of chocolates to get back in your good graces."

"Time heals, and so does chocolate. Get the candy while I chop our salad."

In a few minutes, he returned, waving a Russell Stover's box.

I dished up the salads and sat. "Mind if we say a prayer before we eat?"

In lieu of an answer, he held out both hands and bowed his head.

Sharing a meal with him felt cozy and natural. I embellished the wild events Jane Mills organized for Sea Side during his absence, and he told me about his forays around New England, checking other festivals and researching senior living facilities.

"Senior living facilities? Happy Days? Does your research involve info you uncovered before you waited in the dark in my apartment?"

"I'll explain when I have more facts."

I wanted to know more about his investigation, but I cut him some slack since he provided chocolate, flowers, and dinner.

After the meal, Logan helped me tidy the kitchen. "Will came back with me. He's going to push one more time to get the development approved, but the project seems doomed. He has no money and no backers, and the city officials are leaning toward rejection."

"How is he?" I remembered how animated Will had been when we first met.

"He runs hot and cold. Seeing Noelle will be good for him. The lawyer told Will that Sharp's conscience caused him to change his will."

"Who's getting the money?"

"Sharp made bequests to several people he'd wronged, but the majority goes to a love child. This hasn't been announced, because eager claimants would be crawling out of every bog in New England."

Was it a coincidence Jane Mills worked in Sea Side? Did Logan know Jane's story?

Chapter 10

Despite a dizzying day with Grandpa and my late night with Logan, I felt energized as I began work. Noelle, on the other hand, looked exhausted and burned her first batch of crumpets, which resulted in a run on scones. She snapped at my cheeriness and ignored my attempts to lift her dark mood.

When a disheveled Will Tomlinson arrived, demanding coffee at a tea shoppe, I surmised the reason for Noelle's distraction. I served Will a black brew without sugar or cream and offered a spirited welcome back to the community. He grunted a response, leaned his elbows on the table, and stared at the coffee.

The best and worst thing about a small town is that you know everyone and their business. Word about Trent's bequests and Will's exclusion circulated in whispered conversations before his return to Sea Side, though how people possessed that knowledge remained a conundrum. His appearance this morning brought a crescendo of whispers.

The phone in my pocket rang. Grandpa. "Hi, are you okay?"

"I guess so. I ate some leftover Chinese for breakfast, and I have a little heartburn. I could use some antacids. And I'm going to need a more difficult sudoku book."

"Are you okay?" I repeated the question, hoping to get to the reason for his call as I noticed two orders waiting for pickup.

"Yes. You said to call if I needed anything. I need antacids and a sudoku book." He sounded indignant.

"Why don't you call me after three when I get off work? You might think of more items you'd like."

He clicked off without comment.

I began to question my judgment. I'd spirited him away from Happy Days to keep him safe. Was that the wrong decision? Did he need full-time care? I'd raced around yesterday trying to protect my grandfather. Perhaps I exposed him to harm instead. Was he in peril at Happy Days, or did the senior living facility shield him?

As I placed the plates on a tray, Noelle told me the crumpets were ready and slid me a small plate with a couple fresh from the oven. "Take these to Will and tell him to eat."

Will's coffee level hadn't changed when I set the plate on the green table. "Will, Noelle sent these for you. You should eat something."

He looked up with heavy-lidded eyes. "Uncle Trent lied. He didn't leave me a penny. I expected his entire estate and got nothing."

"I'm sorry." Those words seemed inadequate.

"Meeting with the city council this morning, to make one last pitch. If it doesn't work, I don't know what I'll do." Will idly picked at a crumpet. "This is all Trent's fault. He told me all I had to do was show up, shake a few hands, and earn a huge commission."

"Will, don't you want to look your best for the presentation? You know the expression about it not being over until it's over." I hoped he would take the hint and go shower and shave.

"Right, I'll dazzle them with my charm." He stumbled out without finishing his coffee or crumpets.

I didn't know whether to pity Will or be angry with him, but I had too many customers to think about either action. My dedicated grandpa phone buzzed again.

Grandpa whispered, "Ladessa, someone just knocked on the door. What should I do?"

"Ask who it is. I'll stay on the line." I waited.

"The lady said she's with housekeeping. What do you think?"

"Grandpa, tell her you won't need housekeeping this week. Tell her you'll take care of things yourself." I heard Grandpa repeat my words and the maid's agreement.

"But what if I need soap or paper towels?" Grandpa fretted.

"Make a list. We'll go get things when I'm free. See you soon." I slipped the phone back in my pocket. I needed a different plan for him.

Bouncy, cheerful Jane Mills, dressed in bright purple and green, entered with Logan. Her high heels clicked across the shop and straight to table four. People began using what I considered the *death table* without hesitation the day after the murder. Apparently murder didn't faze stoic New Englanders.

"Morning!" I offered menus and a bright smile.

Jane ignored the menu. "I'll have the special. Oh, the big event in Sea Side this week is pumpkin poems. You should enter the contest. Make up some words about pumpkins or autumn leaves or spooky nights and write them in rhymed verse." She paused to appraise me. "Ladessa, I think you're losing weight. How many pounds have you dropped?"

I felt my face burning.

"Make that a double on the specials, please." Logan held up two fingers.

I practically ran from their table. I did not want to chat about pumpkin poetry or my weight with Logan sitting there. Jane Mills exhausted me. The woman had obviously received a double dose of gusto at birth.

I sneaked back into the kitchen to see Noelle. "I suggested Will shower and change before his appointment."

Noelle offered a wan smile and glanced at the clock. "His appointment is at eleven. I made him promise to stop by after the meeting."

"What will he do if this doesn't work out?"

"Work for his parents, I guess." Noelle shrugged. "This land development job is the only thing he's done on his own, and they hired him based on his uncle's connections."

I grinned. "It isn't easy being rich."

She didn't return the smile. "It isn't easy being poor if you've always been rich." Noelle nodded to the front. "Your detective is here."

"He's not *my* detective, but please pass me his favorite crumpet. He never looks at the menu. He's boringly predictable."

Detective Hardy nodded his appreciation when I placed the crumpet and the house-blend tea with cream on the table. "Thanks, Ladessa," he said. "I can relax now. A murder solved and a murderer no longer with us. With Betty Boyd's death, Sea Side's investigation into Trent Sharp's demise can be sealed."

"You never explained your proof. Betty was a good person. She'd never murder another human being."

"I guess she fooled Sea Side's amateur detective."

Should I gloss over the insult he'd just served me? "Why don't you tell me what I missed, Detective."

"Well, on the day of the murder, Betty had nasal spray and an EpiPen in her bag."

"That doesn't make her guilty. It makes her perceptive and prepared. I bet she also had bandages, alcohol swabs, lozenges, and tissues."

Detective Hardy motioned for me to stop my defense. "The

spray thing, the nasal spray, was Trent Sharp's. What do you think of that?"

"She worked with him daily. They had a connection. That doesn't surprise me."

"It had been doctored with peanut oil. When Sharp inhaled, he experienced a severe allergic reaction. The medical examiner said death occurred within five minutes. First the airways constrict, which limits the breathing, and then the circulation shuts down. Sharp did not have an EpiPen on him, and he always carried one." Detective Hardy raised his eyebrows, as if asking for a compliment.

I tapped my pen on the order pad. "And Betty's sudden and unexpected heart attack solved everything."

He rubbed his hands together. "Yep. Report's been filed, and I can get back to catching out-of-town speeders and policing Jane's zany events."

The phone in my pocket buzzed again. Grandpa. I excused myself. These frequent calls meant he felt lonely and scared. After acknowledging we would buy Raisin Bran on the next grocery run, I called Logan and invited him for an early dinner. I needed to trust someone, and why not the hunky reporter?

Now that I had a car, I was able to shop for more than four things. Toting groceries on a bike was not easy. I gassed up the rental, made a pharmacy stop, and lingered in the grocery. I hadn't eaten, and every aisle offered delectable possibilities. I planned to wow Logan's taste buds with a black olive lasagna then propose my idea before heading to Grandpa's extended stay. If everything fell into place, I could be with my grandfather before seven.

Both Logan's SUV and Noelle's car occupied spots near the

house. Could Logan, Noelle, and Will be celebrating the success of Will's land development proposal? My gut told me no, so I fussed with storing away purchases and put together the lasagna, which delayed my visit.

The silence when Logan answered the door told me my instinct was correct. He shook his head. "City turned down Will's proposal, and when he informed the development company, they terminated his employment, effective immediately."

"Sorry, Will." My lame condolences added an additional layer to the already glum atmosphere. "I brought snacks and lasagna. Mind if I pop it into your oven, Logan?"

He set the temperature and eyed the contents of the snack bag—a cheddar wheel, apples, crackers, walnuts, and yogurt-coated pretzels. "I see you shopped when ravenous. We can help you eat some of this."

"Want the cider hot or cold?" My comment elicited no response, so I filled four cups and placed two in the microwave.

Will finally spoke. "I don't want to rely on my parents or grandparents, but I don't have a work history. I've just been fired from the only job I've held outside the family circle."

Noelle handed him the cold cider. "We'll work something out. You're smart, you're hardworking, and"—she poked him gently in the chest—"you're a good-looking guy with great presence."

I emptied the walnuts onto the platter. "Noelle's right. Take a month or two, decide what you really want to do."

Will lifted his cup in salute. "To a new and improved Will Tomlinson, whoever that may be."

I answered with the first "Hear, hear," but somewhere in my mind lurked the niggling belief that Will's depression might be hiding something more nefarious than a job loss.

I didn't believe Detective Hardy's premise that Betty had committed the murder. Could Will have done it?

The timer buzzed, and my phone rang. I checked the time, only five. After taking the call, I motioned for Logan to join me in the living room. I prayed he would be amenable to hiding my grandfather in the house where he'd lived for fifty years.

CHAPTER 11

Rain and overcast skies dampened the yoga participants' spirits, but after Noelle led us through the poses, we relaxed and remained on our mats, chatting.

Jane's popular ventures to promote Sea Side's tourism produced fruitful results, with local businesses showing substantial increases over the previous year. She blathered on about November and December plans. Even though she'd mentioned my weight in Logan's presence, which ticked me off, I found her effervescent attitude irresistible. Both her employment and mine would terminate before Christmas, and I'd miss her.

My customers reported that the malaise at Happy Days continued as residents mourned the loss of Betty and her efficiency and direction.

"Noelle, why don't you apply for Betty's position? You're organized, caring, and you like telling people what to do." I winked to assure her the last part was a joke.

Mary reached for her daughter's arm. "Honey, that's a wonderful idea. You wouldn't have to go back to Boston, and Ladessa is right. You'd be perfect."

Noelle gave a slight nod. "I might. Will is meeting with Harlan about Sharp's position. He could handle publicity and presentations to attract new residents for Happy Days."

"Does anyone think it's unusual for Betty to be cremated so quickly?" My new topic didn't stimulate much interest.

Jane shook her head. "I think cremations are done quickly because you don't embalm the body. At least that's what I've heard.

I haven't made funeral plans, but I'll either donate my body to a medical school or request cremation."

"I could never do that," Mary said.

"Since breast cancer took my mother, perhaps my body holds information that would help researchers." Jane rolled up her mat. "I had an interesting call today from the DNA website where I submitted my sample. They're asking for a more detailed test. They've found a possible match for a close male relative. I wonder if the man could be my father."

"Would you meet him?" I asked.

Jane inhaled. "I don't know. I'm curious, but I still feel connecting with him would be disloyal to my mother. I haven't even decided whether or not to do the test they requested."

I recalled Logan's comment about Trent's love child named as the estate's recipient. Could that child be Jane? One glance at Noelle told me our thoughts ran parallel.

Noelle turned to Mary. "Mom, we need to call it a night. I have to return the key to the church office before eight."

"When you take me home, Noelle, ask for the activities director's application," Mary said.

I held the basement door, and Noelle switched off the lights. "I agree with your mom," I said. "You should apply."

"I will," Noelle said. "It seems Trent Sharp is trying to ruin another person's life from beyond the grave. His crazy disbursements ruined Will's life. What if Jane is the heir? If she gets the money Will thought would come to him. . . Well, I don't know how he'd react."

Logan flashed the porch lights when I parked. I appreciated him allowing Grandpa to stay in the house. The two men had developed a compatible relationship, and Grandpa no longer called me at work. I hurried across the path with my laptop and tapped on the door.

"Come on in." Logan's rich voice sounded as good as the chocolate aroma permeating the house smelled. He lifted a bowl with vanilla ice cream peeking over the rim. "Double chocolate brownies fresh from the oven. Help yourself."

"No. I just finished a yoga class."

Logan waved a full spoon toward me. "One bite?"

I scarfed it up before he could change his mind. "Delicious."

"Your grandpa made them. He adds cinnamon and walnuts. And, before you ask, he's fine."

Grandpa looked up. "Have you seen this Ken Burns special on country music?"

"I haven't. Is it good?" I placed my hand on Grandpa's shoulder. "Want me to take your empty bowl to the kitchen?"

Grandpa nodded. "Have you seen this show on country music?"

"No, I haven't." Was my grandfather aware he'd repeated himself? I took his bowl to the kitchen then squeezed into the space between the two men on the sofa.

Logan leaned and whispered in my ear. "I think you should have his medications analyzed. I have a friend in a Boston laboratory who can do it."

I grimaced. "I'm still searching for Grandpa's medical records. I'd like to compare the meds he received before he moved to Happy Days with the ones he's getting now. His scripts are currently filled by the on-site pharmacy." I stole a glance at Grandpa. "I think getting those checked is a good idea. Let me know what it costs."

"I can put it on my expense account. The prescription thing might be a sidebar for my story."

"When are you going to tell me about your hot story research?" I admired Logan's physique, which distracted my concentration. Even his winter sweaters fit snugly, showing off his muscular upper body.

"When you tell me about your murder investigation."

"Murders, plural. I think someone killed Betty too. I'm putting together my suspects and motives."

"Are you working with Detective Hardy?"

"No. He's convinced Betty killed Sharp and then suffered a heart attack. Two deaths tied up with a pretty ribbon."

"I thought the detective might want to keep the case open so he could consult you."

"Consult me? What are you talking about?" I scooted farther from Logan and bumped Grandpa, disrupting his TV watching.

"Gossip travels fast in a small town. I hear he's a tea shoppe regular, but I'm not insecure. The lawman is a handsome guy, but not as good-looking as I am." Logan's banter was light and funny. He didn't exude braggadocio, but spoke the truth. Logan Hernandez was one fine-looking man, and I felt as if he had some heavy-duty magnet pulling me toward him.

"The detective is practically family. His brother married my sister." I pointed to my laptop.

"Oooh." Logan drew out the sound. "I'll clean up the kitchen and let you work."

With Grandpa zoned in on the story about country music's legendary Carter family, I opened a spreadsheet on my laptop labeled MURDER SUSPECTS. I deleted the word MURDER then deleted the word SUSPECTS and retitled the column SEA SIDE FRIENDS. Unfortunately, all the murder suspects were friends. I listed the deceased Betty Boyd first. Technically, she ranked as a candidate for Sharp's murder. My headings also included RELATIONSHIP TO SHARP, MOTIVE FOR MURDER, OPPORTUNITY, and MEANS. Then I set up a page for Betty's murder with the same headings. Were there two villains or one?

Engrossed in my list, I didn't notice Logan until he sniffed ostentatiously.

"Your hair smells great. Is that a hint of pear? What product do you use?"

"Really? You're asking about hair products? You're spying, trying to look at my suspect page."

Logan feigned hurt. "I told you about my six sisters. I was their judge for shampoos, lotions, and perfumes. The same soaps or body wash smelled different on each one. I have a good nose."

"You also bragged about your nose for news. Is that why you peeped at my spreadsheet?"

"Ladessa, we should work together."

"We're working on two different things. You're researching Maine fall festivals and senior living facilities. I want to find Trent's and Betty's murderers."

I slanted the laptop's cover, curious if Logan noticed his name on the list.

"I'm a suspect? If you plan to strap me down and grill me, you should do it soon. I have another lead to chase." He gave me that melt-your-heart grin. "Do you think your grandfather can manage while you're working?"

"I guess we'll find out. Thanks for letting him stay here."

My grandfather's rapt attention to the screen seemed to make him oblivious to the discussion between Logan and me.

"Perhaps he should go back to Happy Days," Logan said. "You could ask Noelle's mom to keep an eye on him."

Logan's practical solution made sense, but the idea raised the hairs on the back of my neck.

"When do you leave?"

He ran his fingers up and down my arm. "Thursday. I need to go, but I wanted to give you a heads-up."

His consideration earned him more points on the likability meter. I hoped he wouldn't break my heart. My past assessment of men and their motives was less than stellar. My first love dropped me for my sister. My next romantic disaster involved a man I met at college who charmed me until I discovered he lied about attending college, where he lived, his age, and his recreational hobbies. The following calamity involved a CPA I met on a company retreat then found out he already had a wife. My last love, a church friend, chose seminary over our relationship. Should I trust my feelings for Logan?

I placed my hands over his. Logan might be a deceiver, a liar, a married man, or committed to his career, but right now I needed the kindness and practical advice he offered. "You're right. I'll talk to Gramford tomorrow."

Logan cradled my head in his hands and then bent to kiss my forehead. Surely this gentle and considerate person wasn't a murderer.

The country music credits ran, and Grandpa turned to me. "Great show. I love those Ken Burns specials. Ladessa, did you see the one about baseball?"

"I think I missed it."

"Honey, if you want me to go back to Happy Days, I will." Grandpa had heard our conversation.

"You said you didn't feel safe there. What changed your mind?"

"I don't want you to worry about me. Adults worry about their children and grandchildren, not the other way around."

Logan patted Grandpa's shoulder. "No need to rush, Mr. Nolan. I'm not leaving for a few days. I've enjoyed getting to know you and hearing stories about Ladessa."

I wondered what stories Logan had heard about me but instead addressed Grandpa's return to Happy Days. "Grandpa, your group visits the tea shoppe tomorrow. I'll tell Harlan to expect you."

Grandpa looked from Logan to me. "I'm like a body being spirited away from the crime scene, except I'm still alive."

I didn't like that image, and I prayed this decision was the right one.

After saying good night, I went to my apartment, reopened my spreadsheet, and studied the suspects for Sharp's murder. Betty Boyd, Noelle Rollins, Mary Rollins, Jane Mills, Logan Hernandez, Grandpa John, Will Tomlinson, and Harlan Gramford. Only Logan lacked a motive—that I knew about. All the others had a motive, an opportunity, and the means to kill him. Sharp's peanut allergy was common knowledge. Any person could have tampered with the spray. Then Sharp administered the fatal dose to himself when he sniffed to clear his allergies.

I closed my eyes and went back to the horrific day I discovered the body. What was I missing?

Chapter 12

October screamed toward November with a rolling thunderstorm and a drenching rain, which transformed into sleet. We had no Halloween trick-or-treaters, so Grandpa watched another television special while Logan and I compiled his medical history. I selected samples of prescriptions my grandfather used and bagged them for analysis.

I'd confirmed his return with Harlan, who asked no questions about Grandpa's vacation with family. That was a relief as I'm not good at lies, and Grandpa might not remember.

"I'll see you tomorrow." I tried to sound cheerful.

"I'll walk you across the lawn and up your stairs. The steps might be icy." Logan buttoned my coat, tightened the hood around my face, and kissed my nose.

I liked his sheltering arm around my shoulder as we plodded toward the garage, our faces turned down, avoiding the pelting ice. He waited until I produced a flashlight, in case the power went out.

"You could sleep in the house," Logan said. "It's a miserable night." He stood on the small entry rug, jacket dripping.

"No, I don't want to go back out in the weather, and my alarm rings at five thirty, which might be too early for you."

"I'll call you with the drug results." Logan didn't open the door.

"Knowing the truth about that will give me peace. I prefer to blame Grandpa's forgetfulness on something other than aging." I returned to where Logan stood, touched his cheek, and lifted my face in invitation.

When his lips touched mine, lightning followed by a thunderous boom caused us both to jump.

I giggled. "Wow! That was some kiss."

"Should we see if it happens again?" Logan kissed me a second time, a lingering, tender kiss, unaccompanied by bright light or noise.

Despite the icy designs on the window the next morning, I felt like warm sunshine surrounded me. We were now in November, which meant no more October Punkin'-Chunkin' shirts. I pulled on a yellow polo, much better suited to my coloring. The festivities Jane had arranged for the past month brought cash into the local businesses and tourists to Sea Side, as well as fostering goodwill in the community, but I happily dispensed with October's ugly orange uniform.

I shucked off my heavy coat and headed to the kitchen, which smelled of pastries and a symphony of flavored teas.

Noelle handed me a steaming mug. "Coffee, don't tell."

"Umm. Thanks. Are your crumpets ready yet?" We had eight minutes to chat before the hour.

"I've mastered the timing. They'll be ready when the front door opens."

"Grandpa's returning to Happy Days tonight." I swilled down a big gulp to ensure I didn't add details.

"Mom missed him. She says the residents are in different grief stages." Noelle leaned against the counter. "I didn't know either Sharp or Betty very well, but even I'm sad. Maybe it's Sea Side's small-town atmosphere, where everyone bonds."

I eyed the clock. "Did Will apply for Sharp's position at Happy Days?"

"He did, and I have an interview for Betty's position this afternoon. Will and I think it's a bit creepy that we're both applying for dead people's jobs."

Incessant knocking indicated someone wanted inside before the big hand pointed straight up.

I peered around the corner. "It's Jane. I'll let her in."

When I turned the key, Jane squeezed inside with four stacked boxes.

"I have new shirts for the employees." Jane reminded me of a birthday cake candle as her fiery red hair topped an all blue outfit.

When she lifted the lid, my heart sank. No beautiful russet, dark green, burgundy, or apple-red Thanksgiving shirt colors. These were the same horrid orange as October's shirts. The front lettering said Thankful to be in Sea Side, Maine, and the shop's name and logo showed on the back. Surely December would be red, green, or white.

Jane, bubblier than usual, passed shirts to employees. "Oh Ladessa, I have the most amazing news. Remember the DNA place that wanted additional testing? They confirmed a match, but the man is dead. I'm going to be wealthy!"

Noelle emerged from the kitchen. "Don't forget your friends."

Jane's enthusiasm waned as she spied Noelle. "Oh, you may not be happy, Noelle. Trent Sharp was my biological father. It's his estate I'm receiving."

"Really?" Noelle couldn't mask the sarcasm in her voice.

"The estate lawyer said Trent specified amounts for people he'd wronged, and I get the rest."

"Do you know if Will, his only nephew, got anything?" Noelle's crossed arms told me she fought to curb her temper.

"Why should he? Will's family has money, so he'll be fine. My mother deserved this windfall. I'm sorry she can't enjoy it, but I'll take every penny that scoundrel bequeathed." Jane's exuberance and happiness seemed to devastate Noelle.

I moved between the two women. "Jane, you despised Trent Sharp because he treated your mother unfairly, yet you're willing to accept the money."

Jane bobbed her head, accenting her wavy red hair. "I am. This is Sharp's guilt money, and I'll delight in spending every penny."

"Jane, did you know Trent Sharp was your father before hearing the results of the test?" I asked.

"The thought crossed my mind," Jane admitted.

That comment moved Jane up to my number one suspect slot. "Did you know Sharp planned in his will to right the wrongs he'd done?" I persisted.

"Rumors aren't facts. You're a CPA. You should know that." Jane did a finger-roll wave and headed for the front door. "I have a whole new life ahead."

Noelle's face looked as turbulent as last night's thunderstorm. "How can she be happy about snatching Will's inheritance? Will needed that money. He counted on it."

I kept my mouth shut. I feared anything I said would feed Noelle's rage and resentment. I slipped the orange November shirt over my head and offered one to Noelle.

"I'm not wearing that thing!" She flung the shirt on the counter and stalked to the kitchen.

After work I picked up Grandpa and we went to The Old Mill Inn, a restaurant Logan recommended. A harpist serenaded us as we enjoyed a lobster dinner in a room with a cheerful fire. As we concluded our meal with lemon sorbet and coffee, I decided to address the return to his apartment.

"Grandpa, will you be okay at Happy Days?"

"Yes. I've been concerned about Mary. I need to keep a watchful eye on things."

"What things?" Tonight his conversation had been lucid, and I wanted to understand his comment.

"Gramford, Sharp, and Betty ran Happy Days, and only Gramford's left."

"Yes." Where would this conversation lead?

"Mary Rollins should run Happy Days." Grandpa added more sugar to his coffee.

"Is that what she wants?" I asked.

"She knows the people better than Sharp or Betty ever did." He patted his lips with a napkin. "We must tell Logan about this restaurant."

I rephrased the question he hadn't answered. "Does Mary want to be in charge?"

"She should. Sharp received a big salary."

I tried again. "Have you and Mary discussed her assuming the administrator's position?"

Grandpa pushed away his sorbet glass. "I'm ready to go."

His comment made me uneasy. He saw Mary as the natural replacement for Trent and Betty. I knew this revelation would keep me awake tonight long after the coffee's caffeine wore off. Could my grandfather. . . ? No. Impossible.

We pulled into the circular drive before nine, and Harlan Gramford and his two bichons waited near the front desk. He shifted the dog he held to the crook of his arm so he could shake hands with Grandpa.

"John Nolan, glad to have you back. Sunset has missed you." He moved the dog a little closer, and Grandpa scratched the dog's ears.

"I'll grab his suitcases and help him get settled. We had a great dinner on the way back from Boston." I noticed Grandpa's puzzled expression and grabbed his arm. "Grandpa, help me with your luggage."

I remembered the old saying about loose lips sinking ships. Had I made a critical mistake by mentioning a fictitious trip to Boston?

Chapter 13

I couldn't sleep, so I pulled out my laptop and looked at my suspect list. I started with the dead woman, Betty Boyd. Detective Hardy believed she killed Sharp, and closed the case. Yes, Betty had a previous relationship with Sharp and worked with him in a company that failed. After Sharp implicated her in wrongdoing, she served prison time. Then she ended up with Sharp at Happy Days. Did she suspect he might fleece the facility and use her as the scapegoat again? Maybe the detective was right, but doubt pricked the assumptions.

After Betty, I stared at Will Tomlinson's name. He believed he was Trent Sharp's heir, and he needed money to get his project off the ground. I'd witnessed an argument between Will and his uncle Trent the morning of the murder, and Sharp's last will and testament devastated the young man.

Next, Noelle Rollins. She loved Will and wanted him to succeed. She also believed Sharp led the movement to remove her father from his job, which caused his despondency and despair. But Noelle? I wanted to mark her off the list, but there she was, my childhood friend, the woman who worked with me, who taught me yoga, and a prime murder suspect.

Mary's out-of-character outburst in our private conversation moved her up on the list. I'd discounted her because she was a God-fearing woman who taught me Bible lessons. But she'd lambasted Sharp for organizing the church funds' theft and placing the blame on her husband. She said she'd forgiven Sharp, but I knew from personal experience that sometimes we humans like to take back our forgiveness. We chew on our anger again and savor the deliciousness of being wronged. Could her bottled-up rage spur her to commit murder?

I deliberated about Harlan Gramford. His partnership with Sharp might have been on shaky ground. He seemed invested in the facility, but was the program on the up-and-up? Logan's investigation, the one he wouldn't explain to me, centered on senior living facilities in the New England area.

Logan? I added his name. He rented my grandfather's house from Sharp. He bragged about his reputation for finding a scoop, for getting the story, doing research pieces. Nothing criminal about that. He sat at the table with Sharp that morning, but I couldn't come up with a solid motive to put with Logan, or maybe I didn't want to look.

My fingers flew over the keys. Jane Mills also sat with Sharp that fateful morning. She was Sharp's love child, but he'd rejected Jane and her mother. The Sharp family trust paid off her mother, and Jane admitted she had an inkling that she was Sharp's daughter. She also hinted she knew about Trent's changing his will.

I had to list my grandfather as a suspect too. The man I loved in my childhood could never commit murder, but he was different now. He had a motive. Make that plural. Trent Sharp had tricked him into the bad church investment and orchestrated Grandpa's losing his home and self-respect. Sharp continued to live lavishly while Grandpa and his friend's widow and daughter, Mary and Noelle, struggled. Motives piled up on the debit side for him.

I slammed down the laptop's cover. I should make it easy for myself and go with Detective Hardy's findings that Betty murdered

Sharp and that her death was a heart attack. Shouldn't I?

When Detective Hardy arrived for his morning crumpet, I asked to stop by his office after work. If Trent Sharp had changed his cheating ways, as the country-western song lyrics said, the detective might offer an unbiased opinion.

After the shift, I perched on a stool near Noelle's work station and removed my green, yellow, and pink striped apron.

"What a day." I exhaled an exaggerated sigh.

Noelle groaned an agreement. "When you're busy out front, we're twice as busy back here. We do your orders and also outside deliveries. I'm off to see Will."

I'd biked to work, so rather than go to my garage apartment and then back downtown, I elected to head straight to Detective Hardy's office.

His secretary gestured to the office on the left. "He's expecting you."

I knew the police receptionist. She was a scone and strawberry jam regular at the tea shoppe, whose two daughters lived locally. The older one was at loggerheads with her teenage son, and her younger girl's marriage was going through a rocky patch. Information a waitress could glean astonished me. I knocked on the door bearing Hardy's name.

"Come in. You smell like Tea by the Sea's bake shop, my favorite fragrance."

"I came straight from work. I have a question about Trent Sharp."

"Why?" His abruptness startled me.

"Curiosity. I hear things at work. Some folks mentioned Sharp had changed recently. I thought you'd know." Would a compliment encourage him to share information?

"Sharp began attending the men's Bible breakfasts at my church each week. I think his original intent was to promote vacation home leases. But then he started listening to God's Word." He pointed to the chair opposite the desk. "Why are you asking? You're not still nosing around, are you?"

I reverted to the childish habit of crossing my fingers before I answered. "No."

"Good. Don't stir up mischief." He checked his watch.

"I'm interested because people seemed to love Sharp or hate him, which I find unusual."

"Ladessa, the case is over. I served as Sharp's prayer partner, and he told me he intended to make restitution to those he'd wronged, beginning with Betty Boyd."

"Did Betty know she'd get money if Sharp died?" I tilted my head and gave him my best innocent look.

"I don't know." The detective glanced at his watch again. "Sharp repented a couple weeks after school started. I remember because my daughter began kindergarten this year. And it's time for me to pick her up. Anything else?"

I followed him from the office. What a fool I'd been! Detective Hardy had kids, at least one, which meant he probably had a wife. How could I be so wrong? I obviously couldn't tell the difference between flirting and being polite. I said goodbye to the secretary, the scones and strawberry jam lady, zipped my jacket, and tugged on my gloves before biking home.

Detective Hardy was married. Some sleuth I was. And what about Logan? Was he being kind, or did he like me?

I'd neglected to share two critical remembrances with the

detective. The Happy Days folks had returned to the tea shoppe to use the restroom before the punkin'-chunkin' demonstration, and I'd only locked the front door for the event. Restaurant workers or regulars could have slipped in or out the back entrance before the police arrived. I'd seen Trent Sharp's nasal spray on the table when I served their order, but the vial was gone when I discovered his body. Unfortunately, anyone could have removed the murderous nasal spray and planted it in Betty's tote bag.

I spied Logan's car when I turned the corner toward home. I should ask him flat out if he was married and if he had a kid in kindergarten. I didn't want to be mistaken about him. As my list of suspects waxed, my possible love interests waned.

I raced up the steps and turned on the shower, waiting until the steam coated my tiny bathroom mirror before stepping under the soothing spray. I was dressed, but my hair was still towel turbaned when I heard four knocks, a pause, and then two more.

I slipped my feet into fuzzy cat slippers and opened the door to gorgeous, good kisser Logan Hernandez.

"Logan, are you married?"

"What?" He took a step backward then shook his head. "Uh, no. I'm not married."

"Good to know. Come in." I pulled the door a full ninety degrees and allowed him to pass.

"Should I come back later? Do you need to do something with your hair?" He studied the purple towel wrapped around my head.

"I wish I could. My hair decides how it will behave. Give me a minute." I probably scared him by asking about his marital status, but now I knew, and knowing was important.

Logan still stood on the entry rug when I returned. "Something to drink?"

"No. I have the results on your grandfather's pills from my pharmacist friend." He retrieved a paper from his jeans' back pocket.

"Sit, please sit." I plopped on the sofa and patted the cushion next to me.

He eased down and thrust the paper toward me. "Your grandfather is getting sedatives mixed in with his blood pressure, thyroid, and cholesterol pills. The lab person said those meds usually come in tablets, but your grandpa's samples were capsules that contained what he needed and more."

"That explains his exhaustion and sleepiness. Could the sedatives account for his disorientation, his forgetfulness?"

"Possibly. My friend suggests purchasing his prescriptions from a different pharmacy."

"Why would a doctor do that? What reason would he or she have?"

"Might cut down on office calls," Logan said. "I'd like to interview your grandfather. I know the facility provides meals, but would he agree to share dinner with us in his apartment? I can pick up Chinese food or take-out burgers. If my theory is right, I can connect Happy Days to other senior living facilities I've researched."

"For the story that's going to win you a Pulitzer?"

He offered a winsome smile. "I might've daydreamed about that possibility, but my findings will shake up an industry."

I punched in Grandpa's number and offered him dinner, which he accepted. He requested the local deli's soup and sandwich combo. Unmarried Logan Hernandez and I picked up the food and drove to Happy Days.

Over the meal served on the small table in Grandpa's cramped apartment, I broached the idea of Grandpa seeing another doctor, one not affiliated with Happy Days.

"Why? The doctor here is included. We all use him," Grandpa protested.

"I'd pay for the doctor's visit. After all, it's for my peace of mind," I urged.

Grandpa put the soup spoon down with a heavy click. "Ladessa, I won't have you spending your money on me. My arrangements are settled. I'm fine."

"Women!" Logan slapped his forehead. "The ladies like to fuss. Don't they, Mr. Nolan? I have six sisters, which means I have seven women trying to tell me what to do."

Grandpa sighed. "I pity you, son."

Logan gave an eye roll in Grandpa's direction. "My mother thinks she'd like senior living, complains about cleaning our big house. Tell me about your arrangements at Happy Days. I'd like to give her some advice for a change."

Grandpa pointed to the plates and bowls. "Well, she wouldn't have to do the dishes, clean, or cook at Happy Days. And we have washing machines and dryers too. I do my own laundry, but they'll do it for you if you ask. Her only decision would be what activities she wanted to do."

"My mother isn't rich. I doubt she could afford such a swank place. When I ate here, I enjoyed a fantastic meal." Logan stacked the dishes and placed them on the counter.

I admired Logan's interviewing technique.

"Happy Days has a system. You sign over your house. They told me mine was worth five hundred thousand dollars, which entitled me to live rent-free for the rest of my life with three meals a day and health care. No property taxes, no repair bills, no yard maintenance, and you're not dependent on children or grandchildren." Grandpa glanced my way then continued. "You live at Happy Days until your death, whether you stay one day or forty years."

Logan nodded. "What if someone gives them a cool half million then dies the next week?"

"They told me the numbers balance out. Some live a short time, others a long time. I'll probably be one who lives a long time. Right, Ladessa?"

I threw my arms around his neck and kissed his cheek. "I hope you'll live a very long time."

"Some people leave their children problems galore. The heirs have to sell the house, the contents, figure out all the financial holdings. This makes it simple. When I die, my family won't have to worry about a thing, even a funeral. Cremation is included."

"Like Betty?" I asked.

"Yes, like Betty. The family can have a memorial service at a convenient time, instead of that week, and there's no concern about selecting a casket or transportation to a burial plot. I know how many details must be considered for a funeral."

"You've said 'they' explained the procedure, the benefits. Who presented this option to you?" Logan asked.

"Trent Sharp and Harlan," Grandpa said. "And Sharp owned a real estate and rental company. Logan, mind if I ask what type of rent you're paying for my house?"

Logan shook his head. "You don't want to know. The rent is high, and the minimum lease is six months."

Grandpa looked alarmed. "Ladessa, did I do the right thing?"

"Are you happy at Happy Days?" I countered.

"I guess. I miss the house. When I picture my family, I see them in the big kitchen or playing games in the family room or sitting on the porch." He gazed into the distance as if viewing past family gatherings.

"You should get some sleep," I said.

"I'll walk you to the front door, give these old legs some exercise."

Harlan sat behind the front desk and greeted us. "Our receptionist needed a break, so I offered to man the desk. You're the last visitors. I'll lock up after you leave."

"I hope we didn't inconvenience you." My grandfather patted Harlan's dogs.

"Not at all." Harlan followed Logan and me to the front door and waved goodbye, or was it good riddance?

Logan spoke as soon as I scooted into the front seat. "Did you hear what your grandfather said about some residents living a short time while others live longer? He said they told him it all balances out."

"Yes?"

"Well, the death rate in the facilities I investigated is much higher than in the general population."

"You must have it wrong," I said.

"I don't." The set of Logan's jaw accentuated his declaration.

If Logan's premise proved correct, I'd just left Grandpa in a dangerous situation.

CHAPTER 14

Back at the house, Logan showed me his files on various senior centers and his interviews with staff and residents. I compiled a spreadsheet for his data. The profitability spiked upward every time a resident died. I searched for a correlation between the money a resident contributed to the center and the years or months they lived after moving to the facility.

By midnight my head throbbed. "I should go. I have to be up at five thirty for work."

"You could call in sick," Logan said.

"I wouldn't. I know what it's like to work shorthanded. Maybe some new idea will come to me while I'm serving tea." I grabbed my jacket, refused his offer to escort me, and trudged home.

Even with all of Logan's information, the spreadsheet didn't offer the conclusive proof he needed for his award-winning piece of journalism. And I wanted sufficient evidence to gain my grandfather's release from his Happy Days contract and a proportional return of his half-a-million-dollar investment.

In the morning, the blustery wind with accompanying temperatures in the high thirties blasted me as I made my way from my car and into work. I scurried through the kitchen, stored my things, and donned my orange shirt, which, as had been the case for over a month now, clashed with my pastel-striped apron.

"Noelle, can we talk about Happy Days?"

Her face brightened. "You remembered! My interview went well. The main responsibility is organizing activities, which would be simple. I'll add yoga, line dancing, watercolor painting, and origami to their regular classes. The director also schedules field trips and drives the van. Gramford said I'd need a special license for the bigger vehicle."

"Did he make you an offer?" I checked the clock—three minutes until customers flooded through the door.

Noelle wrinkled her nose. "No. I told him Will and I would be a package deal. Gramford said he doubted Will could do Sharp's job, but he didn't say no to the idea. He promised a decision by next week. The job would boost Will's ego."

I gave Noelle a thumbs-up and opened the door for business. The cold rushed in with the customers, and soon the tea shoppe hummed with chatter.

An older woman at table three whispered, "An ambulance passed my house before dawn, probably going to Happy Days. I wouldn't be caught dead in that senior living place. People die there."

Her table mate waved her hand back and forth. "Good grief! Those people are old. You don't go there to die. You go there to live before you die. If you ask me, they have a good time out there."

I turned in my orders and told Noelle the prattle I overheard. "If you get a break, could you call your mom? I'd like to know she and my grandpa are safe."

"On it." Noelle pulled her phone from her pocket. "That's your order for table one."

I filled a tray and tucked menus for other customers under my arm. The locals were hungering for sweets and tea today, and earlier than usual.

When I retrieved the beverages for my latest customers, Noelle gave me the okay sign. I sighed with relief but hurried to the kitchen during the next lull.

"Was the ambulance for Happy Days?" I asked.

Noelle nodded. "Mrs. Hodges died in her sleep. Mom did her hair and nails yesterday. The woman moved in six months ago and raved about her Happy Days experiences."

"Six months?" I recalled Logan's assertion that life spans in facilities he investigated were shorter than average. I wondered how much money Mrs. Hodges had contributed. Did each person contribute a half million, or was there a sliding fee?

"You're not listening," Noelle said.

"Sorry, my mind was elsewhere. What did you say?"

Noelle said, "I've scheduled a yoga class at Happy Days tonight. I asked if you'd help. You're pretty good at the poses. You should ask your grandpa to attend. Men need flexibility too."

"Great idea. I'll grab a quick nap this afternoon. Logan and I stayed up late talking."

My friend wagged a finger. "I think you like him."

"Noelle, did you know Detective Hardy is married?"

"You changed the subject, and yes, the local law officer is married. His wife teaches at the high school," Noelle said. "They have two darling girls. You know them. They sit on the fourth pew on the right in church. Detective Hardy ushers, so he stays in the back."

"I didn't know he was married. I mistook his friendliness for flirtation."

"He's nice to everyone, even when he gives tickets. Be warned, Ladessa, I plan to grill you about Logan on the drive to Happy Days. Oh, the class will only be thirty minutes, a teaser, something to get the residents interested."

"Got it." Maybe the ruse Logan used on my grandfather would work on Gramford. I'd inquire about the Happy Days admission policies by pretending a Texas friend expressed interest.

Without an activities director's encouragement, only eight people showed for the yoga class. Betty's death definitely changed the ambiance of Happy Days. Harlan Gramford should hire a replacement immediately, someone like Noelle Rollins.

Noelle gave instructions for the poses, and I attempted to do them. My final postures didn't look as polished as Noelle's, but she wanted students to know that the effort, not the final result, mattered.

Noelle challenged the attendees to embrace yoga for improved strength and flexibility. In between stances, my mathematical brain churned numbers. If the deceased woman forked over a cool half million, and expenses were five thousand per month, the facility would hit the break-even mark for her residency around eight years. With her death occurring after six months, Happy Days pocketed about four hundred seventy thousand dollars.

After Noelle closed the session with corpse mode, which I hoped wasn't an omen, Harlan Gramford appeared, dogs in tow.

"Ladessa, I need a word." Harlan walked toward his office, expecting me to follow.

Had he heard me asking about the latest death? Maybe it was Noelle's application. I knew she listed me as a reference. Or was it about Grandpa's fake visit with my family?

He held the door and his dogs until I sat in the wingback maroon leather chair. When he released Sunrise and Sunset, they rushed to me for petting.

"What's up?" I acted casual.

"Ladessa, let me explain what's happening to your loved one."

In tones and vocabulary suitable for a child, Harlan warned me that my grandfather might need more care than Happy Days could offer.

"What kind of care?" I jiggled my feet, trying to hint to Harlan's dogs that I didn't like their weaving around my ankles.

Harlan snapped his fingers to call Sunrise and Sunset. "Our doctor says John is slipping both physically and mentally. Our medical expert believes your grandfather may have lost the will to live. I'm not sure Happy Days is the best place for him."

"Wait. He told me Happy Days was his final stop—so to speak. Are you trying to kick him out?" I never expected this.

"Happy Days is like the family the residents don't have. Since you arrived, your grandfather has changed. He's no longer happy here. He left for a 'vacation' after Betty's death. Everyone shared their grief and worked through the feelings about her death together. Everyone except your grandfather, because he wasn't here, was he?"

"No."

"Do you want him to live with you? You're a young woman. Do you want the responsibility of an elderly man who has health and mental challenges?"

"Mr. Gramford, I appreciate your diplomacy, but what are you trying to say?"

"Ladessa, it's a simple question. Are you going to care for your grandfather, or do you prefer our professional team to administer his care? I'd like your decision within the week." He stood, indicating my dismissal.

Noelle waited with her mom and my grandfather in the open area. "What was that about?" Noelle asked.

"Some suggestions he wanted me to consider." I gently punched Grandpa's shoulder. "How's my favorite Grandpa today?"

"Sad. That lady who died was my Thursday night dinner partner. Betty came up with the idea. We rotated tables so we'd get to know each other. She was my Thursday partner. I'll miss her."

Mary spoke. "We'll all miss her, John."

"What was her name?" Grandpa asked.

Mary smiled. "Her name was Alice. Pretty blue eyes, always wore pearls to dinner."

"Alice." Grandpa turned toward me. "Alice was her name. She had pretty blue eyes and always wore pearls."

I kissed his forehead. "Grandpa, I'll see you tomorrow. You can tell me more stories."

"I don't tell stories!" Grandpa glared at me. "And I'm sick of picking through boxes."

"I meant family memories, not stories, and I thought you enjoyed going through the mementos in those boxes."

"Well, I don't." Grandpa walked away without allowing me to give him a hug.

∽

Noelle loaded her yoga mats into the trunk and slid behind the wheel. "You want to talk about Logan?"

"No."

"How about what Harlan really said?"

"No."

"Why you asked me if I knew Detective Hardy was married?" Noelle persisted.

"No."

"Then you must want to listen to my problems," Noelle said.

"Yes, let me listen to your problems, for once."

"It's Will. We had a huge fight. I said I blamed Trent Sharp for destroying my father's reputation and for the sadness that caused him to end his life."

I turned as far as the seat belt allowed. "Didn't he know that?"

"Apparently not. He blew up. His uncle treated him terribly, but when I said something negative about the man, Will turned Sharp into a saint."

"He'll realize his mistake," I said.

"I don't know. Telling him I'd asked Harlan to accept us as a package was like throwing oil on flames."

"He'll calm down." I didn't know Will Tomlinson well enough to know whether he would or wouldn't. "You'll win either way. If he decides to be mean, you'll be lucky for him to be gone. If he decides to grow up, you'll be lucky to have him in your life."

"So I'm going to be lucky," Noelle said.

"Absolutely." I believed that about Noelle, but I wondered what my Grandpa's future held. Would he be lucky?

CHAPTER 15

Sleep eluded me. Noelle knew about Sharp's peanut allergy, and she could have sneaked into the shop via the back door to nab the doctored nasal spray, but so could a dozen other people. I'd positioned myself by the front door for the demonstration and after I discovered the body. More possibilities to keep me awake.

I also fretted over the conversation with Harlan Gramford. His demand for my decision fit with the pattern Logan described about other facilities. They isolated the residents who relied on their new home for social interaction, food, shelter, and medical care. Isolate, the key element. Harlan wanted Grandpa under facility control, or out, a simple decision. Before my arrival, no one questioned Grandpa's new doctor, one employed by Happy Days, or the prescriptions he wrote. Because of my presence, Grandpa was no longer isolated, and Harlan did not want that.

Grandpa's future depended on his permanent escape. I didn't want him to be another Alice Hodges, dying and leaving Happy Days a tidy bundle. Grandpa's tenure at Happy Days measured the same as the recently deceased. I needed to act, now. Happy Days locked their doors at eleven. Locked? That sounded like a prison. My phone showed ten. I could get there before they shut the place down.

When I arrived I tapped the front desk bell, and Harlan appeared. He invited me into his office for the second time that evening.

"Ladessa, this is a surprise. Have you reached a decision so quickly?"

"Yes. I want my grandfather free from your clutches, now. I know what you're doing."

Harlan's eyes narrowed. "What do you mean?"

"I had Grandpa's meds analyzed, and I know you're sedating him. Your medications create his confusion."

"You had his prescriptions evaluated? Why would you do that?" Harlan leaned back in his chair.

"Just a hunch. Grandpa's not the man I knew." I didn't mention Logan's investigation into similar complexes as money-making machines.

"He wouldn't be the man you knew. Even a year can alter an older person's cognitive and physical abilities, and you haven't visited him for. . .how long?"

His point hurt. Holiday cards and the occasional phone call didn't make up for personal visits.

"I'm here now." My lame protest sounded hollow.

"How do you plan to care for him? Where will you take him?" Harlan stroked one dog, then the other.

"Texas. He could live with me."

Harlan pushed his black-rimmed glasses up on his nose. "Has your grandfather ever lived in Texas? Would he have any friends? Who would care for him while you work? We've created a complete support system for older individuals. You're an impetuous young woman."

"I'm a CPA, which means I'm not impetuous. I'm practical, organized, and efficient. Grandpa's medication analysis compels me to act. He'll be different off your laced prescriptions."

"I know nothing about 'laced' prescriptions, but I do know that aging affects abilities."

"I'm not leaving without him." I lifted my chin.

"Ladessa, Happy Days exists and grows based on contented, active residents. Having someone ranting about doctored prescriptions would be damaging." He slapped his thighs. "My dogs haven't had their evening constitutional. Would you mind?" He riffled through a drawer and held up his find. "Treats and bags. We'll go out front. There's a nice area over to the side for the dogs."

I buttoned my coat against the cold.

Harlan affixed the leashes on the dogs and hit the door buzzer.

I attempted to explain my position calmly. "The drugs I had analyzed were supposed to be for blood pressure, thyroid, and cholesterol. They were those medications, with a sedative added to each."

"Was the authority you hired a friend or professional? Go Sunrise, Sunset." Harlan shooed his dogs away, their leashes trailing behind them. "They like that spot under the trees." He focused the flashlight's small beam to a dark area outside the facility's wreath of lights.

"Mr. Gramford—"

"Harlan. We're informal."

"Harlan, I want to remove my grandfather from Happy Days, and I think the life fee he deposited should be reimbursed."

"Have you consulted other family members?" Harlan watched as the bigger dog scratched in the dirt.

"No, no. I intend to handle the paperwork for Grandpa's move, and then I'll explain the situation to my dad, aunt, cousins, all the family."

"So you haven't told anyone about the pills or your absurd rescue or, should I say, kidnapping plan?"

"I haven't, but you can't hold him here like a prisoner."

"I created a home, a sanctuary for the elderly. My childhood was not idyllic, Ladessa. My macho plumber father ridiculed me for not being able to catch, throw, or kick balls, depending on the season. I was short, overweight, and near-sighted, a natural target for bullies. Because my mother was unwell, I spent most of my adult years caring for her. Now I provide a haven for people like my mother. Our residents need their Happy Days family."

"My grandfather doesn't."

Harlan made clicking noises with his tongue. "Where was his loving family when he lost all his money? Where were they when he needed a place to live? Trent Sharp offered him an option. Your grandfather received a medical evaluation and was certified as competent."

"By the same doctor who now prescribes his meds?" I pushed.

"Your grandfather needs medications."

"This is a circular argument. I demand you produce the papers for me to sign to remove my grandfather, legally and immediately."

The moon hid its face behind a lonely cloud, leaving the sky an inky black.

"Ladessa, perhaps you're the one agitating your grandfather."

"Mr. Gramford, I mean Harlan, I did not add sedatives to his meds. I didn't create a scheme to have senior citizens forfeit their life savings for room and board."

"But I didn't do that," Harlan protested.

"If not you, then who? Was Trent Sharp responsible? Was he the kingpin in the swindle?"

Harlan gasped. "Did that man use my facility for personal gain? Did Betty? Were they defrauding my residents? My friends?" His voice quivered. "I trusted them with recruitment of clients and the day-to-day operations."

"You honestly didn't know that prescriptions were being altered?"

"No! Do you think I'm a monster?" Harlan's earnest denial reverberated in the stillness.

Perhaps Detective Hardy nailed it. He pegged Betty as Trent's killer and her subsequent death as a natural heart attack. I sought a conspiracy theory when the simple truth made more sense. Harlan deserved an apology.

"I don't think you're a monster. But I'd still like to move my grandfather."

"Terminating the agreement is complicated. We offer sanctuary to those in their sunset years using the facility's lifetime investment model."

Lifetime investment model? I gulped. Harlan's use of the term set off flashing red lights in my brain. "You did partner with Trent Sharp in this fraud, but then Sharp gave his life to God. He must've threatened to end the scam and make amends to those wronged."

"My dear, you should be a fantasy writer instead of a CPA."

Everything fell into place. Sharp's charm lured the residents to Happy Days. Betty's computer skills checked the prospect's background and net worth. Harlan's facility provided the setting. Stir in a doctor willing to write bogus scripts, and the arrangement hemorrhaged money to participants who didn't concern themselves with larceny or the occasional death. Happy Days was not an isolated facility operating under nefarious guidelines, but one of many.

Harlan sidled next to me. "Figure it out?"

I nodded, as the horror of being in a secluded area with a murderer washed over me. Harlan Gramford was a small man, one who loved dogs, an innocuous-looking fellow who generated trust. "Sharp threatened to expose you?"

"He did." Harlan moved closer.

"Why kill Betty?" If he bragged about his accomplishment, I

might buy some time to come up with an escape plan.

"When Sharp's lawyer told her she would get a sizable distribution from his estate, she announced she was through with our lucrative enterprise. I couldn't allow her to destroy what I'd built. We had tea, hers with a powerful sedative. Then, when she slept, I injected a high dose of insulin in her ear. No medical examiner looks there. Betty was prediabetic and had high blood pressure. The doctor never questioned the heart attack."

"You can't keep killing people. What about Mrs. Hodges?"

"She died peacefully. Isn't that what everyone wants? She was happier here than she'd been in years." Harlan laughed. "Actually, the food Mrs. Hodges ate was intended for your dear grandfather. He gallantly switched places with Alice because she complained of a draft before the poisoned food arrived."

Despite the dark, I saw the rock when he raised his hand. I ducked before he could crash it into my skull. He shoved me against a tree with a strength that shocked me.

"Help! Help!" I yelled.

"No one can hear you." Harlan's left arm pinned me as he prepared to strike again.

I swiped with my foot and cut his legs out from under him. He toppled to the ground, and Sunrise and Sunset raced to their master, weaving their leashes around his arms while covering his face with wet doggy kisses. I unclipped the leashes and tied Harlan's legs and arms behind him. Then I wriggled my phone from my back pocket and called 911.

Ignoring Harlan's entreaties to release him, I relived my powerful swipe kick that dropped him to the ground. If I'd faced this danger two months ago, I might have died. In only a month and a half, my biking, walking miles as a waitress, and performing yoga poses had transformed my body from chubby couch potato to a lean fighting machine. That might be an exaggeration, but I survived to tell the story. And I could tell that story any way I wished.

I welcomed the blaring siren and waved my phone's flashlight beam to guide the car to our location.

Harlan started yelling before Detective Hardy stopped the car. "Detective, over here. This woman is mad. She attacked me. She's as crazy as her grandfather, and you know we have to keep him locked up."

Detective Hardy extended a hand to me, then Harlan.

I voiced my own accusations. "That is not true, Detective. He tried to kill me."

"In the car. Both of you," Detective Hardy commanded.

"My dogs," Harlan wailed. "I can't leave my dogs."

"We'll take care of them."

Harlan clicked his tongue. "Well, I can tell you what happened, but who can explain a broken mind like hers? Like her grandfather's?"

"I do not have a broken mind. That man is a serial killer. He killed Trent, Betty, and Mrs. Hodges, and he almost killed me."

Detective Hardy instructed his junior officer to cordon off the site with crime scene tape, photograph the area, and round up the two fluffy bichons.

CHAPTER 16

Instead of receiving praise for catching a killer, I sat in a closed room with a metal table, waiting for my turn to convince Detective Hardy that my version was the truth. I demanded my phone call. From watching *Law and Order* reruns, I knew arrested people received a one-call option. I punched in Logan's number and got his voice mail.

Exhausted from my long day that began at five thirty this morning and ended in a battle for my life, I rested my head on the table. I must have drifted off, because when the door opened, the clock showed midnight.

Logan slipped past Detective Hardy and grasped my hands. "Ladessa, how are you?"

I was so happy to see him that I didn't mention the absurdity of his question. "Scared, tired, hungry, and relieved."

The concern, and perhaps affection, in his dark brown eyes erased my shock and trepidation. Logan's investigation supported my story about the shady goings-on at Happy Days. Together Logan and I would present the facts to Detective Hardy. Then the lawman would release me and place Harlan Gramford behind bars, permanently.

Detective Hardy started with the caution: "You have the right—"

"What? Gramford tried to kill me!" I jumped up with as much indignation as I could muster.

Logan and Detective Hardy bumped fists.

"Got you." Detective Hardy grinned.

"Not funny!" I glared at the detective, the one I thought flirted with me, but who was actually happily married. "Did you charge Gramford? Is he locked up?"

"He's in a jail cell. He'll transfer out to await trial. We're not equipped for long-term care."

Hardy's droll comment made Logan chuckle. Their repartee amused the two of them but not me.

"I'd like to leave. I need a hot shower and some sleep."

"I'll take her home," Logan said. "After all, you had to rescue her."

"He did not rescue me. I saved myself, and I caught the killer." I flung open the door and stalked out.

Logan hurried past me and held the heavy oak exterior door. Outside, he wrapped his arms around me, enveloping me in a tight embrace, a scene I'd often envisioned. At that moment, however, my anger made me incapable of response. He released me and led me to his black RAV4.

In the car, I began to shiver, and Logan cranked the heat up to high. Soon the blower's force felt like a blazing hot desert wind. I couldn't wait to get home.

Home?

When had Sea Side become home?

Muscle memory aided me the next day as I bustled about work duties. I expected chatter about Gramford's arrest but heard none.

Noelle waved and held a fist to her ear, indicating I had a call. "It's your grandfather."

I took the tea shoppe phone.

"Ladessa, he's here again," Grandpa whispered.

"Who?"

"That man, and he's wearing the same hat and coat, and he

arrived in a dark car." Grandpa's voice had risen slightly, which made him easier to hear. "The man who was here the night Betty Boyd died. He's back. I spotted him on my way to play pinochle."

"Where is he?"

"In the lobby. I'm hiding behind the big decorative vase. I heard him ask the receptionist to page Mary Rollins. Do you think he's planning to kill her? What should I do?"

This captivated my attention. "Grab as many friends as you can and stay with Mary. He won't harm her if she's with a dozen people. I'm on my way, and I'll call Detective Hardy."

Overhearing my comment about someone harming her mother, Noelle had her coat zipped before I removed my apron.

In Noelle's car, I dialed Detective Hardy after fastening my seat belt—which I needed—because Noelle's driving resembled that of a high-speed stunt man. We arrived within five minutes and bounded from the car, ready to save Mary Rollins.

No chaos.

The scene looked like a photographer's pose. Mary, Grandpa, and a gentleman in a tailored suit occupied the sofa, with a dozen residents curved in a horseshoe behind them. Smiles bloomed on all faces.

"Grandpa, Mary, what's going on?"

Screaming sirens drowned all responses. Members of the tableau broke their pose, and giggling and talking generated a spirited cacophony as Detective Hardy sprang from his police car followed by three armed patrolmen.

The detective whistled, and quiet reigned.

I asked my question again. "What's going on?"

The distinguished gentleman rose. "I'm the executor of Trent Sharp's estate. He came to me two weeks before his death, a contrite man who wished to make amends to those he'd wronged. He requested that fixed monetary amounts go to some individuals and percentages of the remainder to specific recipients. Betty Boyd ranked first on the list. But the woman died of a heart attack the same day I informed her of her impending windfall."

"I'm not so sure about that, are you?" I gave Detective Hardy a conspiratorial glance.

He nodded to the lawyer. "Let's hear what this man has to say."

"Betty hadn't signed the official papers, so her allocation reverted to the estate, which meant all the figures changed. I came here today to impart good news and money to Mary Rollins and to John Nolan." The lawyer smiled.

Mary raised her hands above her head. "Praise God. Trent Sharp admitted in writing that he was behind the scheme to siphon off the church funds—not my husband, and not John Nolan."

The lawyer continued. "Mr. Sharp also requested his confession be read aloud in a service and mailed to the entire church membership. He wanted to clear the name of a good man and reimburse Mr. Rollins's widow for the personal funds her husband gave to replenish the church coffers, an act that ruined the Rollins family financially. He also has a bequest for John Nolan for the amount of money he used to correct the shortfall in the budget."

"I knew about Trent Sharp's conversion," Detective Hardy said. "God worked on that man's heart. Men in the Bible study group share their pain and joy openly and honestly. Sharp realized his actions generated suffering for many. He asked for forgiveness and vowed to make amends to those he wronged."

"But one person didn't want Sharp to change. Isn't that right, Detective?" I mentally patted myself on the back for giving the local lawman the acclaim for my findings as an amateur sleuth.

Detective Hardy leaned back and hooked his thumbs under his belt. "I know this will be a shock to you here at Happy Days, but I've arrested Harlan Gramford for the murders of Sharp, Betty Boyd, and Alice Hodges."

Exclamations, questions, and cries of outrage and denial buzzed. The police officer held up both hands, palms facing the residents.

Logan sidled up behind me. "Nice of you to give law enforcement the credit."

"What can I say? I'm a generous gal." I didn't know how Logan happened to be there, but I didn't care. I leaned back against his broad chest, feeling secure, safe, and something else I wasn't ready to acknowledge.

The church named the Sunday after Thanksgiving *Rollins Day*. Noelle, Will, Logan, and I sat in a reserved spot on the second row so we could see a beaming Mary seated next to the pastor. Packed pews meant many people flanked the sanctuary's perimeter as the minister invited Detective Devin Hardy to speak.

"Trent Sharp came to our breakfast prayer group as a skeptic but became a believer," the detective began. He recounted Sharp's spiritual journey and his quest for righting the wrongs he'd committed. He told the congregation that one heavy burden on Sharp's conscience was his trespass against Pastor Rollins.

After Hardy's testimony, the minister read Sharp's confession and invited congregational members, past and present, to place personal recollections of Pastor Rollins in a basket in the foyer. Then the minister escorted Mary out of the sanctuary, where the two greeted the departing worshippers.

I nudged Noelle. "You should stand with your mom."

"No, it's her day, hers and my dad's. Can you believe how many people came? She'll read and reread every one of those notes." Noelle dabbed her eyes. "Nice gesture on the part of the minister, don't you think?"

Logan leaned around my shoulder. "Will, Noelle, can you come to my place this afternoon about four? Ladessa and I have some news."

Noelle's eyes opened wide.

I felt heat rush up my neck and over my face. "No, not what you're thinking."

"Do we have to wait until four?" Will asked.

Logan chuckled. "No, come anytime, and bring Mary."

Will, Noelle, and Mary arrived at four, the last of the guests.

"Come in, take a seat, or grab something to drink and then take a seat. Oh, let me introduce you to all these people." Logan's nervous, disjointed chatter showed a side of his personality I'd never seen.

"I'll take your coats." I hung jackets on the coat tree in the foyer.

Logan stood in front of the fireplace and paced like a lecturing professor. "I've been working on a newspaper feature for months and never dreamed where it would lead. One story led to another, but this one introduced me to real friends. It also gave me an opportunity to expose a ring of criminals with the skill of my sleuthing CPA buddy, Ladessa Nolan."

That was my cue to speak. "Logan's research into several senior living facilities confirmed what we witnessed happening at Happy Days. In my memoir course, I heard about the older residents being tricked, bilked, cheated, and cajoled—whatever term you want to use—out of their homes in exchange for a carefree life in a senior living complex. The skimming and windfall profits generated were divided by four insiders at each facility."

Will waved his hand, and Logan held up a finger. Logan said, "The plan is quite ingenious, but they had to have stockholders. I tracked down many of the principal shareholders, and they had no knowledge of the fraudulent schemes. They own shares, which produce reasonable and fair returns on investments. One of the investors agreed to come here today."

The silver-haired lady sitting in the animal-print chair indicated Logan should continue.

"The investors want to continue their support of the apartments for seniors, but each facility will need a new staff. The investors found two exemplary resumes on file at Happy Days. Will, they'd like you to assume Gramford's position as executive manager. Noelle, they're offering you the activities director's position."

I watched Will squeeze Noelle's hand, and I knew what their answers would be.

Will turned to the woman identified by Logan as representing the investors. "We accept the offer. We'll make sure the residents enjoy *happy days* and carefree nights."

Their decision delighted me. Will and Noelle would make Sea Side their home. I thought of other friends from the tea shoppe, from Happy Days, from the church choir, and knew I'd made the right decision.

"While we're all together, I have some personal news to share," I said.

"Does it have to do with a wedding?" Noelle asked.

"No, it has to do with returning home. I'm buying my grandfather's house. I plan to move to Sea Side and set up a CPA practice with my office right here. I'll operate as a bed and breakfast on weekends until I establish my business. Jane Mills created a dynamic marketing plan for me before she left, so it may not take that long." I clapped a hand over my mouth. "I didn't mean to mention Jane. I'm sorry."

Will rolled his eyes. "No problem, Ladessa. I know Jane received the bulk of Uncle Trent's estate as his biological daughter. Jane admitted she sabotaged my land development deal because of how Uncle Trent and my family treated her mother. I wasn't even alive when that happened, but Jane blamed the whole family."

"Jane booked a round-the-world cruise with part of her inheritance." Noelle turned to Will. "Does that bother you?"

"Not at all. My world is right here." He kissed her nose. "Mary, may I have permission to marry your daughter?"

"Yes, but I should forewarn you that she's quite opinionated." Mary's comment elicited smiles and laughter.

"Mom said yes, Will. We need to start planning a wedding." Noelle inched closer to Will.

"The sooner the better. Our guests can use Ladessa's new bed and breakfast," Will said.

"Then your wedding will have to wait until February." Logan draped an arm around my shoulder. "My family is booking Ladessa's bed and breakfast for all the January weekends. I want my six sisters, their families, and all my extended family members to meet Ladessa."

"You do?"

"I do." Logan's eyes danced.

Those two words sounded sweeter than birds singing in the spring. I hoped I'd get to hear him say them again, soon.

Linda Baten Johnson grew up in White Deer, Texas, where she won blue ribbons for storytelling. She still loves telling tales. A tornado destroyed the town when Linda lived there, and watching faith-based actions in rebuilding lives and homes after the tragedy influences her writing. Her historical fiction books for young readers, cozy mysteries, and squeaky-clean romances are available in print and e-book and on audio.

Introducing the Doors to the Past Series

The Lady in Residence

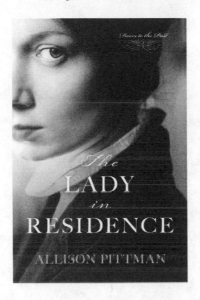

A new series of dual-time period novels takes readers to famous landmarks and opens in San Antonio, Texas. Hedda Krause checks into the Menger Hotel but never checks out, and one hundred years later her presence is still felt. Will tour guide Dini Blackstone be open to hearing a new version of the eccentric old woman's story?

Paperback / 978-1-64352-748-2 / $12.99